"Do you believe me now, Nikki?"

She glanced up and, like a magnet, her gaze automatically latched on to Jonas's mouth. Seeing the shape of his damp lips made her lick her own when she remembered why his were wet. Yes, she believed him. After the way he had devoured her mouth, she had no choice. And the thought that he had enjoyed the kiss as much as she had sent her head spinning. He was fire, and if she thought she could play with him without getting burned, then she was only fooling herself. And her mother hadn't raised a fool. To keep her sanity, she needed to distance herself from him as soon as possible.

"You got the kiss, so now you can leave." In reality, he'd gotten a lot more than that. He'd snatched her common sense right from her, which was why she needed to hurry him out the door.

"Okay, I'll go, Nikki. But if you change your mind about coming on board for the Fulton project, let me know within the week."

She stared at him. Did he honestly think she could work with him now? Whenever she saw him, she wouldn't think of work; she would think of kisses.

HER SECRET SEDUCTION

NEW YORK TIMES BESTSELLING AUTHOR

Brenda Jackson

AND

Reese Ryan

Previously published as *Private Arrangements*
and *Savannah's Secrets*

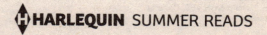

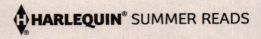 **HARLEQUIN**® SUMMER READS

Recycling programs
for this product may
not exist in your area.

ISBN-13: 978-1-335-17994-4

Her Secret Seduction
Copyright © 2020 by Harlequin Books S.A.

Private Arrangements
First published in 2012. This edition published in 2020.
Copyright © 2012 by Brenda Streater Jackson

Savannah's Secrets
First published in 2018. This edition published in 2020.
Copyright © 2018 by Roxanne Ravenel

This is a work of fiction. Names, characters, places and incidents
are either the product of the author's imagination or are used fictitiously.
Any resemblance to actual persons, living or dead, businesses,
companies, events or locales is entirely coincidental.

This edition published by arrangement with Harlequin Books S.A.

For questions and comments about the quality of this book,
please contact us at CustomerService@Harlequin.com.

Harlequin Enterprises ULC
22 Adelaide St. West, 40th Floor
Toronto, Ontario M5H 4E3, Canada
www.Harlequin.com

Printed in U.S.A.

CONTENTS

Brenda Jackson is a *New York Times* bestselling author of more than one hundred romance titles. Brenda lives in Jacksonville, Florida, and divides her time between family, writing and traveling.

Email Brenda at authorbrendajackson@gmail.com or visit her on her website at brendajackson.net.

Books by Brenda Jackson

Harlequin Desire

The Westmorelands

The Real Thing
The Secret Affair
Breaking Bailey's Rules
Bane

The Westmoreland Legacy

The Rancher Returns
His Secret Son
An Honorable Seduction
His to Claim
Duty or Desire

Visit the Author Profile page at Harlequin.com for more titles.

PRIVATE ARRANGEMENTS

Brenda Jackson

To the man who is my first, my last, my everything, Gerald Jackson, Sr.

To my fellow author, Adrienne Byrd, the Queen of Plots. Thanks for letting me borrow Quentin Hinton and his Doll House for a spell.

You do not have because you do not ask.
—James 4:2

Prologue

"So, Jonas, what do you think?" Nicole Cartwright asked as she handed the man standing in front of her desk another photograph she'd taken a few days before.

She watched as Jonas Steele studied the photograph and then his green eyes found hers. The smile that touched his lips made her heart pound like crazy in her chest. His company, Ideas of Steele, was on the upward move, getting a lot of attention, and she felt fortunate to be a freelance photographer working with him on this particular project.

"These are great, Nikki, and just the shots I wanted," he said, handing the stack of photographs back to her. "I'm glad you agreed to help me out on such short notice. Three weeks wasn't a lot of time," he added.

"Thanks, and like I told you, I work better under pressure."

He opened his mouth to say something, but at that moment his cell phone rang.

She inhaled deeply as he shifted his gaze from her to focus on his telephone call. She wondered why on earth she was drawn to him so much. She certainly wasn't his type. Just last Sunday his face was plastered across the gossip pages; his name was linked to some former fashion model. And the week before, the papers had connected him to some senator's daughter. It was obvious he much preferred the Barbie-doll type—sleek and sophisticated, without a strand of hair out of place.

She pushed an errant curl back from her face and thought that certainly wasn't her. And there definitely wasn't anything sleek and sophisticated about her. Jeesh. She couldn't recall the last time she'd worn a dress.

She tried not to listen but couldn't help overhearing his conversation. He was confirming a date for tonight. She tried to not let it bother her that the man she'd had a secret crush on for close to a year was making plans to spend his evening with someone else. Story of her life.

For the past twenty-seven years she had been living in a dreamworld and it was time for her to wake up and realize she'd been living a friggin' fantasy. As much as she wanted to believe otherwise, she didn't have a soul mate out there after all. There was no knight in shining armor who would come charging in and whisk her away to a place where the two of them would live happily ever after. It was time for her to accept that marriages like her parents' and grandparents' happened just once—maybe twice—in a lifetime. They weren't the norm.

And, she thought as she glanced over at Jonas, a

leopard couldn't change his spots. So why had she fallen for a man who didn't know the meaning of an exclusive affair with a woman? She looked down at her computer keyboard, trying to ignore the pain that sliced through her chest.

"Oh yeah, now where were we, Nikki?"

She glanced up, tempted to say, *Nowhere.* Instead she said, "I believe you needed me to print out more photos."

"Yes, that's right," he said, smiling.

She wondered if his smile was for the photos or the phone call he'd just ended. Deciding it wasn't any of her business, she stood and crossed the room to the printer. Her office was small but efficient. The one huge window had a beautiful view of Camelback Mountain.

At that moment he took another call and she figured it was probably another woman. But when he let out a loud whoop, she glanced over at him and saw the huge smile on his face.

When he hung up the phone, he was smiling from ear to ear. "That was my secretary. Gilbert Young's assistant called. We got the Thompson account! They were impressed with those brochures we gave them last week and don't need to see any more!"

She clapped her hands while grinning, not able to contain her own excitement. "That's wonderful, Jonas."

"Wonderful? That's fantastic. Simply amazing. Do you know how many other marketing outfits wanted that account?" he asked, crossing the room to her.

Before she knew what he was about to do, he reached out and pulled her into his arms for a hug. "And I owe it all to you, Nikki."

It was meant to be just a hug. She didn't know what

happened, but the next thing she knew Jonas Steele was lowering his head and slanting his mouth over hers in one hell of a kiss.

Chapter 1

Eighteen months later

Jonas Steele felt an argument coming on.

"I hear you, Mom, but I just don't feel what you're saying," he spoke into his iPhone.

His lips tightened to a frown as he alighted from the shiny black BMW two-seater Roadster and glanced around while sliding his aviator-style sunglasses into the pocket of his jacket. *Whoa! But I'd love to feel all over on those*, he quickly thought when his gaze landed on the legs of a woman who was getting out of her car. And they were definitely a gorgeous pair. Long, smooth and shapely.

"You and I need to do lunch to discuss this further, Jonas."

His attention was immediately pulled back to the

conversation with his mother. He rolled his eyes heavenward. "I'd love to, Mom. Anytime. Any place. You are my number-one girl. But certain topics are off-limits."

He glanced back to where he'd seen the pair of sexy legs just seconds earlier only to find the owner gone. *Crap!* Frustration seeped into his pores. He would have loved seeing the rest of her; certainly he would not have been disappointed.

His frown deepened when his mother said, "That's utter nonsense, Jonas. You can't restrict me from certain topics. I'm your mother."

He shook his head as he made his way across the parking lot. He loved his mother to death, but lately, talking to the beautiful Eden Steele, former international fashion model and the woman who had captured his father's heart close to forty years ago, was draining on his senses. "True. However, you leave me no choice. With Galen and Eli married off, now you want to give your remaining four single sons grief, but we won't let you."

"You won't?"

"No. Although I can't speak for the others, I can speak for myself, and like I've told you numerous times before, I intend to be a bachelor for life."

Her soft chuckle flitted across the phone. "You sound so confident about that. Do I need to remind you that Galen and Eli used to tell me the same thing? And quite often, I might add. Now look what happened to them. Both got married in the last year."

Jonas didn't want to look. In fact, he didn't want to spend a single moment analyzing what could have possibly made two intelligent, fun-loving, die-hard womanizers like his brothers Galen and Eli fall in love. Galen had gotten married ten months ago, and Eli had tied the knot on Christmas Day. Granted, Jonas would be the first to admit they had married gorgeous women, but still, look how many women they'd given up to be committed for the rest of their lives to just one. It made no sense. Bottom line, Galen and Eli were whipped and the sad thing about it was it didn't seem to bother them.

And he was sure his mother had heard by now that another bachelor friend of theirs by the name of York Ellis, who lived in New York, was taking the plunge this weekend in time for Valentine's Day. Again, Jonas was convinced that like Galen and Eli, York needed to have his head examined for giving up his bachelor status.

"You will be here for dinner Thursday night, right?"

Her words intruded on his thoughts. "Do I have a choice?"

"There are always choices, Jonas."

Just like there are always consequences, he thought, remembering what had happened to his brother Mercury when he'd decided to skip one of their mother's weekly Thursday-night dinners. Before Mercury could get out of bed the next morning, Eden Steele had arrived on his doorstep. She had informed her AWOL son that since he had missed such an important family function, she was duty-bound to spend the entire day with him. And then she had the nerve to invite the woman Mercury had spent the night with to tag along. Their mother had deliberately overlooked Mercury's bed-them-but-never-wed-them policy when it came to women.

Since then, none of Eden's sons had been brave

enough to miss a Thursday night chow-down. The last thing any of them needed was an unexpected drop-in from Mommy Dearest.

"I'll be there, Mom," he said, deciding he needed to get her off the phone.

"I'll hold you to that, and you're welcome to bring a lady friend."

He caught himself. He was about to tell her he didn't have lady friends, just bed partners. "Thanks, but no thanks. As usual I'll come alone."

Then an idea popped into his head. "Since Galen and Brittany will mark their one-year anniversary in a couple of months, you might consider convincing them that you need a grandbaby or two. Heck, they might hit the jackpot and luck out with triplets like Cheyenne," he said of his cousin living in Charlotte.

"Hmm, triplets. You might have something there," his mother said thoughtfully.

He hoped so. Then maybe she could turn her attention away from him, Tyson, Mercury and Gannon. His brothers would owe him big-time if he could get her to do that. He smiled, deciding to go for the gusto and said, "You might not want to scare them with the multiple-births idea though. Just push for the single birth for now. Come to think of it, I'd love to have a little niece or nephew, and I know you and Dad would make the best grandparents any child could possibly have."

He inwardly chuckled as he moved toward the revolving doors. He'd just laid it on rather thick and if word got back to Galen of the seed he'd planted inside their mother's head, his oldest brother just might kill him. But then drastic times called for drastic measures.

"Personally, I would prefer a niece," he added. "I can

see her now, cute as a button dressed in lacey pink."
In all actuality, he couldn't see a damn thing, but his
mother didn't have to know that.

"Yes, I can see her as well," Eden replied in a voice
filled with excitement. Apparently the idea was growing on her and fast.

Jonas breathed out a deep sigh of relief. "Good."

"But I'm envisioning her dressed in lacey lavender
instead of pink."

Whatever. He glanced around hoping that he would
run into the owner of the legs he'd spotted a while ago.
Although he didn't have a clue how the woman looked,
with legs like hers she shouldn't be hard to spot.

"Well, I'm at the hotel for my business meeting
and—"

"Hotel? Business meeting? Really, Jonas, I think
you can do better than that. I wasn't born yesterday."

He fought back a smile. It was pretty damn sad when
your own mother didn't trust your motives. "What I
should have said is that I'm meeting someone for dinner
at Timothy's." He was well aware that Timothy's, the
restaurant inside the five-star Royal Blue Hotel, was
one of his parents' favorite places in Phoenix.

"Oh. Nice choice. Are you still celebrating?"

He smiled. "Kind of."

Had it been a week ago already since he'd gotten
word that his company had been chosen to spearhead
a marketing campaign of a lifetime? Over the years,
his marketing group, Ideas of Steele, had made pretty
decent profits, but with this new project there was no
doubt in his mind that he was about to pull in the big
bucks. Eighteen months ago the Thompson account

had helped to get his company's name out there, and now the Fulton account would blast it off the charts.

"Well, don't celebrate too much tonight. I don't want you to get sick. You know you can't hold liquor well."

He breathed out a deep sigh. "Thanks for reminding me. Now, I really have to go."

"I'll see you Thursday night."

"Okay. Goodbye, Mom." He clicked off the phone, both amused and curious, wondering which one of his brothers she would be calling to harass next.

He felt confident that whoever her next victim was, his single brothers would be able to keep Eden out of their business. Like him, when it came to the women they were involved with, they didn't think any further ahead than the present.

He glanced around the luxurious, immense lobby of the Royal Blue Hotel, taking in the polished marble floors, high ceiling and rich mahogany crown moldings. He could remember the first time he'd come here as a boy of ten. It was to attend a fashion show raising money for charity, and his mother had been one of the models. On that day he'd realized Eden Steele might be just "Mom" at home, but to the rest of the world, she was Eden, a renowned international fashion model whose face graced the covers of such magazines as *Vogue, Cosmo* and *Elle.*

Jonas's gaze shifted to the massive windows on one side of the lobby to take in the panoramic view of crimson-hued mountaintops. It had reached a high of seventy today, a beautiful day in February, which accounted for the picturesque sunset he was now seeing.

He checked his watch and saw that he was a good ten minutes early. He could use that extra time to get a drink at the bar, but he knew his mother was right. His system had very low tolerance for alcohol, and too much of the stuff made him sick. So to play it safe he kept within his limits and would usually end up being the designated driver.

Deciding against the drink, he slid his hands into his pockets and crossed the lobby to the restaurant. There was another reason he wished he could take that drink. Nikki Cartwright. The thought of meeting with her had him feeling tense. For any woman to have a Steele feeling that way was unheard of. But he knew the reason.

The kiss they had shared a year and a half ago.

He'd kissed plenty of women, but none had ever left any lingering effects like the one he'd shared with Nikki. And none had managed to haunt him like a drug even after all this time. It had been an innocent kiss, one neither of them had meant to happen, one that had caught her off guard as much as it had him.

He could clearly recall that day in her office. He had been so excited when he'd heard he'd gotten the Thompson account that he had pulled her into his arms to hug her, and the next thing he knew they were locking mouths. And it had been a kiss that had nearly knocked him off his feet. It had made him feel emotions he hadn't known he was capable of feeling. And it had scared the shit out of him.

Jonas would be honest enough to admit he'd been attracted to her from the start and could vividly recall the day they'd met.

It had been raining all week and that particular day was the worst. She had burst into his office soaked to the skin with her blouse and jeans plastered to her in a way that should have been outlawed. He doubted he would ever forget how her jeans had hugged that tight and round bottom of hers.

He had rushed to get her a towel, but not before taking in everything about her, even the way her short curly hair had gotten plastered to her head. And he hadn't missed how her nipples had shown through her wet blouse, or what a curvy body she had.

She had looked a total mess, but at the same time he thought she'd also looked simply gorgeous. He'd also fallen over backward when he'd gazed into her eyes. They were so dark they almost appeared navy blue. And her lips…with their seductive curve had tempted him to taste them on more than one occasion.

His attraction had been stronger than anything he'd ever encountered, and during the three weeks they had worked together it hadn't diminished one iota. And the thought that any woman could have that kind of hold on him unsettled him immensely.

He hadn't understood why the attraction was so intense. And at the time he definitely hadn't wanted it and had done a good job of fighting it until that day. He doubted that she knew what he'd gone through those three weeks. Nikki Cartwright was a looker, no doubt about that. But then all the women he dated were. However, none had provoked the kind of strong reaction from him that she had with that kiss.

In all his thirty-three years, no woman had dared to invade his dreams or made him envision sexual positions he'd like trying out just with her. His taste in women often varied, but he usually was drawn to the slim and sleek. But it was just the opposite with Nikki. She had curves. The jeans she always wore showed off a perfectly proportioned body. A body that had been plastered against his while he'd drowned in the sweetness of her mouth.

The kiss had nearly knocked him to his knees, which was the reason, when he'd finally released her mouth, he had quickly left her office and intentionally put distance between them for eighteen months.

Then why was he now seeking out the very woman he had tried staying away from? The one whose single kiss had him longing for more.

Shivers ran down his spine, and for an instant, he thought about turning around and canceling the meeting. But there was no way he could do that. For this new marketing campaign he needed the best photographer in the business and as far as he was concerned, Nikki was it.

He would just have to steel his senses and hold his own against her. He had hoped with the passing of time his desire for her would lessen, but he found that wasn't the case. When he'd seen her on Christmas day at his brother's wedding, he had been drawn to her even more, which was why he'd left the reception early.

When Jonas reached the top step that led to the restaurant, he could feel lust beginning to stir his insides and anticipation invading his senses. It was happening again and it seemed he couldn't do anything about it. No woman was supposed to have this sort of effect on him. Not Jonas Steele. The master of one-night stands. The man who had a revolving door in his bedroom and who was enjoying the single life and didn't mind the reputation he and his brothers had acquired over the years.

He loved the opposite sex—all shapes, sizes and

styles. Race, creed or color didn't mean a damn thing to him, nor did religious affiliation.

He was the fourth-oldest of Drew Steele's sons. Drew had been run out of Charlotte while in his twenties when his reputation as a womanizer had gotten the best of him. Fathers were threatening him with shotguns, and mothers were keeping their daughters locked behind closed doors. Jonas had heard the stories from family members many times over.

Luckily, Drew had finally met the woman he'd wanted, fallen in love, gotten married and had kept his wife pregnant for seven straight years, which accounted for he and his brothers being born within a year of one another.

Jonas didn't know of a better-suited couple than his parents. Or a more loving one. But then, happily married or not, unfortunately, his father had passed his testosterone-driven genes on to his six sons.

He quickened his steps, thinking testosterone be damned, he was determined to stay in control. He was the womanizer the society tabloids pegged him to be and was making no apologies. He had a reputation and was proud of it and felt he was living a good life. And to top things off, last week he had been awarded the marketing deal of a lifetime and he didn't intend to screw things up.

When he entered the restaurant he glanced around and saw Nikki sitting at a table across the room. She smiled when she saw him and he felt his stomach do a somersault. And as if on cue, his pulse began hammering away and air felt as if it were slowly being sucked out of his lungs. *Holy hell.*

He drew in a deep breath and tried purging the

deep, unwanted attraction for her out of his system. He moved across the room toward her, thinking that no matter what, he was in full control. And this time he would make sure things stayed that way.

Nikki Cartwright watched the man approaching her table with a stroll that was so sexy it bordered on sinful. She tightened her grip on the glass of water while trying to downplay the sensations rolling around in her belly.

Her instinctive response to Jonas Steele was something she should have gotten out of her system by now. There was no reason why a warm rush of desire was invading her insides, almost making it difficult for her to breathe.

Then she quickly decided that yes, there was a reason. Walking toward her had to be one of the most gorgeous men she'd ever seen. Tall, powerfully built, with dark wavy hair flowing around his shoulders, he was pure masculine sex on two legs.

A quick glance around the room indicated she wasn't the only female who thought so. There was nothing quite like a group of women taking the time to appreciate a good-looking man, and Jonas was definitely a looker. Eye candy of the most scrumptious kind.

She'd known working with him on that brochure wouldn't be easy. After all, he and his brothers were the hottest bachelors in Phoenix. They weren't known as the "Bad News" Steeles for nothing, and their reputations for being die-hard players were legendary. There was a joke around town that a woman hadn't been bedded unless she'd been bedded by a Steele. From what

Nikki had heard, their skills in the bedroom were off the charts.

The air seemed to shiver the closer he got with a stride that emitted the masculine power that all Steele men seemed to possess. Like his brothers, he had inherited his mother's green eyes. Smokey Robinson eyes, she called them, as they were the same color of those of the legendary R & B soul singer. And then there were the rest of his prominent features—medium brown skin, strong chiseled jaw and one luscious looking pair of lips.

She'd heard that of all the Steele brothers, Jonas was the one everyone considered a rebel. He wore his hair longer than the others and owned a Harley. She understood he had several colorful tattoos on certain parts of his body. She definitely knew about the ones on both shoulders since she'd seen him a couple of times wearing muscle shirts.

Nikki wished she could look right past all six feet three inches of him, see beyond the well-toned muscles beneath the designer business suit that symbolized the growing success of his marketing company.

And more than anything, she wished she could look at his lips and not remember the kiss they'd shared that day.

Had it been a year and half ago when they had last worked together? When she'd constantly fought to control her attraction to him? An attraction that definitely had been one-sided.

Still, he had kissed her that day—she hadn't imagined it. They'd both been caught off guard; however, when he should have ended it, he'd kept right on kissing her, even deepening the kiss. And of course, she'd let him. When he'd finally come to his senses and let her go, he had mumbled something about being late for an appointment and had hightailed it out the door without once looking back.

The memory of that day sent a warm rush of sensations flowing through her, and she sighed. The man was not husband material. He didn't even believe in having a steady girl. She'd heard about his one-and-done policy. It had come as a surprise, a real shocker, when two of those "Bad News" Steeles had fallen in love and gotten married. In fact, Jonas's older brother Galen had married her best friend Brittany.

That left four brothers still single and swearing up and down Bell Road that they'd never fall in love. And she had no reason not to believe them. And as if to make that point solid, she'd heard the four had stepped up their game and were chasing skirts more so than ever these days, especially Jonas.

To break eye contact she glanced around the room again and saw every single female eye was still on him. And then, as if of its own accord, her gaze returned to slide over him. She appreciated what she was seeing. *Oh, mercy.*

With the eye of a photographer, she thought Jonas's features were picture perfect. She tried not to be one of those women who judged a man on looks, but his looks were so sharp, so compelling, so pinch-a-sister-in-the-butt gorgeous, it took everything she had not to start drooling.

"Hello, Nikki. Thanks for agreeing to meet with me."

She jumped at the deep baritone of his voice, which sounded like Barry White reincarnated. She had been so deep into her "Jonas" thoughts that she hadn't been aware he'd gotten close.

"Sorry if I scared you just now," he said.

"You didn't," she replied simply, forcing a smile to her lips. "I'd gotten lost in a few thoughts, that's all."

"I see."

Pulling herself together, Nikki watched as his body slid easily in the chair across from her. Sensations stirred in her tummy again. Unknowingly, he was playing havoc with her senses. Deciding there was no reason for her senses to suffer any more abuse, she spoke up. "When you called you said that you wanted to discuss something with me. A business proposition." Like there could be any other reason for him calling and asking to meet with her. In a way she was surprised that he wanted to use her services again, considering how they'd parted eighteen months ago.

Nikki crossed her legs, hoping the action would tamp down the tingling vibrations she felt between them. The man emitted testosterone that was attacking her big-time.

"We'll talk business later," he said, smiling.

Later? She lifted her brow, a little surprised by his comment. If they didn't talk business then what else were they supposed to talk about? Surely, he didn't intend to bring up that kiss.

"We haven't worked together in months. How have you been?" he asked her.

She stared at him. Evidently he had forgotten they had just seen each other at his brother's wedding on Christmas day. If he'd really wanted to catch up on her life he could have inquired about her well-being then. Instead he'd been too busy checking out the single ladies, friends of the bride from Memphis. He had done the courteous thing and spoken to her, but that was about all. It was as if he'd been careful to avoid any lengthy contact with her.

"I've been doing well."

He nodded. "That's good. I saw Eli and Stacey's wedding photos. As usual you did a great job."

"Thank you."

He was about to say something, but paused when the waiter approached with menus. Seriously, why all the small talk? she wondered. Why did he feel the need to lay on that lethal Steele charm in such a high dosage? Sharing a table with him had her nerves on edge. There was that usual degree of desire she always felt whenever she was near him, making a rush of heat flow through her body. She shifted in her chair.

"And what about you, Jonas? What are you up to these days?" she asked, like she didn't know. Like she didn't read those society tabloids.

"I've been staying busy. Just got back from a business trip to South Africa a few weeks ago. Enjoyed the trip."

"That's good," she said, deciding to study the menu that had been handed to her. He did the same, and she couldn't help taking a peek over the top of hers to do a close-up study of him.

Why was he smiling so much?

As if he read the inquiry in her gaze, he looked up and said, "Last week I received a very important call from Wesley Fulton."

She nodded, very much aware of who Wesley Fulton was. Who wasn't? The man was a self-made billionaire who was building a global financial empire.

"And I have reason to celebrate."

His words cut through her thoughts. She could hear the excitement in his voice. "Do you?"

"Yes. You might have read in the papers that Fulton Enterprises expanded into the airline industry by introducing what they're calling a luxury airship."

She nodded. "Yes, I did hear something about that."

There was no way she couldn't have since it had dominated the media lately. Fulton had hired the best technological minds and engineers to build what everyone was saying was the largest airliner in the world. In fact she'd heard it was so large it made the Airbus A380 look small in comparison. She had seen photographs and it appeared to be an airplane and zeppelin rolled into one, with such amenities as individual sleeping quarters, a nightclub, a movie theater, a casino and a restaurant.

"Ideas of Steele was selected to head up marketing for this venture."

Now Nikki understood why he was in such a cheerful mood. That was certainly good news for his firm. To be selected by Fulton was a feather in any business owner's cap. "That's wonderful, Jonas. Congratulations."

"Thank you." He features turned serious when he met her gaze. "And the reason I wanted to meet with you, Nikki, is because I'll need a good photographer and I want you as part of my team."

Her chest tightened. To know he wanted to include her as part of his high-profile marketing project was almost overwhelming. Especially considering how their relationship had somehow crossed the line the last time they'd worked together. Being a part of something as significant as the project he was talking about could make her career. And it definitely needed a boost right now, especially financially. The economy had taken a toll on just about everybody and freelance photography assignments weren't coming in as steadily as before. Lately she'd had to resort to doing weddings, anniversary parties and private photo shoots.

"I don't know what to say, Jonas."

He chuckled. "Say you'll hear me out over dinner while I tell you about the project. Hopefully, I'll be able to convince you to come on board."

She drew in a deep breath. "Of course I want to hear about it," she said. But then a voice out of nowhere whispered, *Go ahead and hear him out, but you might also want to consider turning him down. Think about it. Will you be able to endure being around him constantly? How will you handle that intense and mind-boggling attraction that eradicated your common sense the last time? Do you honestly want to go through that sort of torture again?*

Nikki inwardly sighed, thinking that no, she really didn't. But she would be crazy to turn down his offer. She had bills to pay, a roof to keep over her head and a body that needed to be fed on occasion. But then, it was that body she wasn't sure about when certain parts of it were so attuned to him. He could charm the panties off a woman without blinking, and that's what bothered her more than anything. When it came to Jonas Steele she needed to keep her panties on. She had a weakness for him and it was quite obvious the kiss they'd shared that day in her office had meant more to her than it had to him.

His voice broke into her thoughts. "I hope my timing isn't bad and you're not involved in a project that I can't pull you away from."

She thought about the job offer she had received a few days ago. It was election year, and one of the candidates wanted her as part of his team. Following around a politician as his personal photographer for six months was something she'd prefer not doing. But she didn't want to hang around Jonas and constantly drool, either.

She drew in a deep breath and said, "I do have a job offer that came in a few days ago, but I haven't accepted it yet."

"Oh, with whom?"

"Senator Waylon Joseph's election campaign."

He stared at her. "Whatever amount they've offered you as a salary, I'll double it."

She blinked, not believing what he'd just said. "You will?"

"Yes. My business has been doing well, but what Fulton is offering is a chance of a lifetime. It'll take us to a whole other level and I want the best people on board to work with. And I consider you as one of the best. Your photography speaks for itself."

She was definitely flattered. The Joseph campaign had offered her a decent salary and to think Jonas was willing to double it had thrown her in shock. She forced herself to regroup. She needed to weigh her options and think things through with a level head.

"I'll cover the strategy plan I've come up with over dinner. I think you'll like it."

There was no doubt in her mind that she would like it. When it came to marketing strategies, Jonas was brilliant. His company was successful because he was picky about those he did business with. In the world of marketing, a stellar reputation was everything. And unlike some CEOs, who liked to delegate duties and play golf whenever they could, Jonas was very much hands-on.

She knew what coming on board as his photographer meant in the early stages of any project. They would work closely together again, just like that time before—sometimes way into the wee hours of the nights and on weekends. He would come in Monday through Friday dressed in his designer business suits, and then on the weekends, he would wear his T-shirts and jeans and ride around on his Harley. It was as if he were two different men, yet both were sexy as sin.

She would drool during the day and have salacious dreams of him at night. It had gotten harder and harder not to react to him when he was around. Hard to keep her nipples from pressing against her blouse and to keep her panties from getting wet each and every time he opened his mouth to release that deep, sexy baritone voice of his.

He kept looking at her now and she knew he was waiting for her response, so she said, "All right, Jonas, I'm curious to hear your plan."

He smiled, winked and went back to studying his menu. Nikki drew in a deep breath as she turned her attention to her own. But she couldn't ignore the play of emotions that spread through her. As usual, he was having that sort of effect on her and there was nothing she could do about it but sit there and suffer through it.

She wished there was a way after hearing him out that she could just thank him for considering her for the project and then graciously turn him down. But whether she wanted to admit it or not, she wanted the job.

She needed the job.

But what she needed even more was the use of her common sense when it came to Jonas. And she wasn't sure that was possible.

Chapter 2

Being around Nikki was doing a number on him, Jonas thought, taking another sip of his wine. Wasn't it just a short while ago he'd given himself a pep talk, confident that he would be the one in control during this meeting? But that was before he'd had to sit across from her for the past half hour or so. More than once he had to bite down on his tongue to keep from telling her how good she looked or how sweet she smelled. And her hair, that riotous mass of curls that she tossed about, made her features even more attractive.

Crap. When would this intense attraction for her end? And why was he feeling as if he was about to come out of his skin? And to make matters worse, he had a hard-on that was about to burst his zipper. Why was the thought of doing intimate things to Nikki so much in the forefront of his mind? Why hadn't time away from her eradicated her from his thoughts? And why did he remember that kiss as if it were just yesterday?

He shifted in his seat again, feeling edgy. Horny. Lusty. Those were physical states he usually never found himself in. Never had a reason to. As a rule, he got laid whenever he wanted, which was usually all the time. But at the moment, he felt sexually deprived. Overheated.

Where was a Tootsie Pop when he needed one? Sucking on one of those usually took his mind off his problems. Eight years ago when he'd quit smoking, his brothers had given him a huge bag of the lollipops as a joke. They had told him to lick one every time he got the urge to smoke, and pretend he was licking a woman's breast instead. It worked.

Now if he wouldn't feel so friggin' hot…

If there was any way he could remove his shirt and just sit there bare-chested, he would. His attraction to Nikki was overpowering his senses and he didn't like it at all. No woman was supposed to have this sort of effect on him. But he knew no way to stop it. He took another drink and felt a bit queasy. Why was he drinking the stuff? He knew why, and the main reason was sitting across from him.

He glanced at Nikki again. She wasn't what he would consider drop-dead gorgeous, but her beauty seemed to emit some sort of hypnotic appeal. Her eyes were dark, her nose the perfect size and shape for her face, and her lips were sensually full…and tasty, he remembered. Combined, the features on her medium-brown face were arresting, striking and expressive. For him a total turn-on.

He just didn't know what there was about her that tempted him to clear the table and spread her out on it and take her for the entrée as well as for dessert. Then he would proceed to lick and lap a body he had yet to see or touch underneath those jeans and shirt she normally wore. But he had a feeling she was hiding a body that was ultra sexy. Her curves hinted as much. What color bra was she wearing? What color panties? Bikini cut, hip huggers or thong? He had a thing for sexy underwear on a woman.

He shifted in his chair, thinking he needed a Tootsie Pop and bad.

He put down his wineglass to cut into his steak. But each and every time he would glance up and stare at her lips, he would remember that kiss. And the memories were filling his head with more foolish thoughts…as well as questions he didn't have any answers to.

One question that stood out in the forefront was that if he'd been so attracted to her when they'd first met, why hadn't he hit on her long before that kiss? It wouldn't have been the first time he'd broken his strictly business rule by making a professional relationship personal. Hell, he was one who believed in taking advantage of any opportunity, business or personal. Then why hadn't he placed her on his "to-do" list long before their kiss that day?

He knew the answer without thinking hard about it. From the first, there had been something about his desire for Nikki Cartwright that wasn't normal. He'd sensed it. Felt it. And it had scared him. He had never reacted so viscerally to a woman before. She had a seductive air about her that had come across as effortless as breathing, and he was sure it was something she wasn't even aware she possessed.

Thoughts of her had begun taking up too much of his time, and he couldn't shake them off like he did with other women. It was as if they occupied the deep recesses of his mind and intended to stay forever. And Jonas Steele didn't do forever with any woman.

And there was also the fact that around her his active imagination was worse than ever. Some were so downright erotic they had startled even him. That much desire made him feel vulnerable, and it was a vulnerability he could and would not tolerate.

Things had gotten worse after the kiss. He had started comparing every single kiss after that with hers, and so far none could compare. And then at night, he would wake up in a sweat, alone in his bed, after dreaming of making love to her in positions that were probably outlawed in the United States and their territories.

At one time he'd thought the best thing to do was just to work her out of his system by sleeping with her. He figured that one good night of sex ought to do the trick. But then there was this inner fear that an all-nighter might not do anything but make him want some more. Then he would start begging.

And the thought of a Steele begging was unheard of. Totally out of the question. A damn mortal sin. Definitely something that wouldn't be happening anytime soon. Never.

Then why was he freaking out about a kiss that happened eighteen months ago?

He figured one of the main reasons was that he had tasted something in that kiss he'd never tasted before—the type of passion that could ultimately be his downfall, his final hold on the world that he wanted for himself. The only world he could live in. A world filled with women, women and more women. He refused to let his body's reaction to one particular woman end what he considered the good life.

He needed a Tootsie Pop.

"So what's your marketing strategy for this project, Jonas?"

Her voice was low and seductive. He knew it wasn't intentional. That's the way it was. He glanced over at her. Was she wearing makeup? He couldn't tell. She had what most women would call natural beauty. And this wasn't the first time he'd noticed just how long her eyelashes were. Most women wore the fake ones to get that length, but he knew hers were the real deal.

His fingers tightened around the glass, and he took another sip before saying, "Fulton wants me to capitalize on the fact there hasn't been an airship of this kind since the Hindenburg…while at the same time minimizing the similarities." He breathed in her scent again, liking it even more, and getting more and more aroused by it.

Nikki nodded. She understood the reason Mr. Fulton would want that. It had been decades since the luxury airship exploded while attempting to dock. Of the ninety-seven passengers and crew on board, thirty-five people had lost their lives. If Fulton had built a similar airship, the last thing he would want people to remember was the fate of the original one.

"That tragedy was seventy-five years ago," she said. "I'm surprised no one has attempted to build another luxury airship of that kind before now."

"People have long memories," he said, pushing his plate aside and leaning back in his chair since he'd finished his meal. "Fortunately, the ones who do remember are no longer around to tell the story of that fateful day in May 1937."

He paused a moment and then added, "I remember reading about it in school. I had a history teacher who ranked the Hindenburg explosion right up there with the sinking of the Titanic."

Nikki could believe that. Both had been major catastrophes. She had studied the Hindenburg in school as well, and was well aware that the disaster had effectively destroyed the public's confidence in any type of giant, passenger-carrying air transportation of its kind, abruptly ending the era of the airship. But at the time they didn't have the technological advances of today. She'd heard the airship that Fulton had built was in a class all by itself, definitely a breakthrough in the world of air travel.

"My ultimate plan is to rebuild people's confidence in this type of air travel." Jonas interrupted her thoughts. "After the Titanic, people were leery of cruise ships, but now they don't give a thought to what happened with the Titanic years ago. I want the same mind-set in getting the public back interested in luxury air travel. Especially on the airship *Velocity.*"

She arched her brows. *"Velocity?"*

"Yes, that's the name of Fulton's airship, and when you think of the meaning I believe it will fit."

He leaned back in his chair. "*Velocity* is being billed as the wave of the future in air travel, and is capable of moving at four times the speed of sound and uses biofuel made from seaweed with minimum emissions."

"Seaweed?"

He chuckled. "Yes. Amazing, isn't it? Fulton will bring a hypersonic zeppelin-design aircraft into the present age. It guarantees a smooth flight and will trim the time getting from one place to another by fifty percent. Ideas of Steele's job is to tie everything together and present a package the public would want to buy into. When the *Velocity* is ready for its first series of air voyages in April, we want a sold-out airship. Fulton's designers have created a beauty that will be unveiled at a red-carpeted launch party in a few weeks."

Jonas paused a moment when the waiter returned to clear their table and give them a dessert menu. Jonas looked over at her and said, "Fulton is well aware the only people who will be passengers on his supersonic airship are the well-to-do, since a ticket won't be cheap. My job is to pique everyone's interest, restore their confidence in the safety of hypersonic travel and make sure those who can afford a ticket buy one. I will emphasize all the *Velocity* has to offer as a fun and exciting party airship."

He paused a moment, then continued, "I'll need photographs for the brochures, website, all the social networks I'll be using, as well as the mass media. The launch party will be held in Las Vegas. Then the next day the *Velocity* will take a trial flight, leaving Los Angeles, traveling to China, Australia, Dubai and Paris on a fourteen-day excursion. That's four continents. Fulton has invited certain members of the media, and a few celebrities. You will need to be on board for that too, to take as many marketing photos as you can."

Jonas met her gaze. "As my photographer I'd like you to attend all events as well as travel with me. We'll want to highlight the airship to its full advantage, to give it the best exposure."

Nikki breathed in deeply in an attempt to downplay the racing of her heart at the thought of all the time they would spend together. Here he was, sitting across from her, all business. She drew in a deep breath. Evidently he had put the kiss they'd shared out of his mind and was not still dwelling on it like she was. Had she really thought he would?

Get real, girl. Do you honestly think that kiss had any sort of lasting effect on him like it had on you? You're talking about a man who's kissed countless women. In his book, one is probably just as good as another. No big deal. So why are you letting it be a big deal for you? If he can feel total indifference then why can't you?

She knew the answer to that without much thought. As much as she boasted about no longer believing in fairy tales of love and forever-after, and as much as she told herself that she could play with the big boys, she knew she could not compete with the likes of Jonas Steele. Nor did she want to.

She had deep apprehensions when it came to him and they were apprehensions she couldn't shake off. What if her attraction to him intensified? What if it moved to another level, one that could cause her heartbreak in the end? Could she handle being a Jonas Steele castoff?

"Um, this dessert menu looks delicious. What would you like?" he asked.

What would I like? Having him wasn't such a bad idea. Deep, dark chocolate. The kind of delectable sweetness that you could wrap around your tongue, feast on for hours and still hunger for more. She wondered about those tattoos she'd heard he had. Where were they? How did they look? How would they taste under her tongue?

Suddenly she felt breathless and her heart was thumping like crazy in her chest. She should feel outright ashamed at the path her thoughts were taking. She needed to get a grip.

She took another sip of wine thinking any time spent around Jonas would drive her over the edge. Already she was imagining things she shouldn't. Like how his lower lip would taste being sucked into her mouth. She shifted in her seat and forced the thoughts away. And he thought they could work closely together again. Boy, he was wrong.

At that moment, considering everything, she knew what her answer regarding his job offer would be. She would be giving up a golden opportunity, one any photographer would love to have. But she had to think about her sanity.

"Nikki?"

She met his gaze. "Yes?"

"Dessert?"

It was hard to keep her mind on anything but Jonas, and that wasn't good. "Yes, the apple pie sounds delicious, but the slice is huge. That's more than I can eat."

He closed his menu. "No problem. We can share it."

She swallowed deeply. He wanted to share a slice of pie with her? To him that might be no big deal, but to her that was the beginning of trouble. It was so sad that he didn't see anything wrong with it.

"Nikki?"

If she kept skipping out on their conversations he

would begin questioning her attention span. "Okay, we can share it," she said and regretted the words the moment they left her lips. Sharing a slice of pie seemed too personal, and this was a business meeting. Wasn't doing something like that considered unprofessional? Evidently he didn't think so.

The waiter returned to take their dessert order. After he left, Jonas said, "I need to be up front with you. If you do take the job it will require long workdays, but I don't see it as being as exhausting as the last project we worked on together."

In a way Nikki wished that it would be. Then she would be too tired to do anything but collapse in bed each night. Too tired to replay over in her mind every nuance of feelings she'd encountered around him. And too tired to remember that one darn kiss that he'd already forgotten.

Jonas made it through dinner—barely. His gut had tightened each and every time he'd glanced up to see her mouth work while chewing her food. He imagined that same mouth working on him.

And sharing that slice of apple pie with her hadn't helped matters. They'd had their own utensils, but more than once he had been tempted to feed her from his fork, hoping that she licked it so he could cop her taste again.

He'd meant what he said about doubling whatever salary Joseph's campaign was offering her. One thing she didn't know was that Jonas had kept up with her over the past few months. He knew no big accounts had been knocking on her door.

Like he'd told her more than once, she was the best

and could handle a camera like nobody's business. And from the way she was acting she probably didn't even remember that kiss. She hadn't even brought it up. In fact she was acting like it had never happened. He didn't know whether he should be relieved or insulted. He wasn't conceited, but to think one of his kisses hadn't left a lasting effect on any woman was pretty damn annoying.

His thoughts drifted to what he'd told her about the job and the time they would spend together. She'd nodded and asked a few questions. Otherwise, she'd mainly listened while he had explained the marketing strategy to her. It was something he knew she could handle.

He only hoped and prayed he could handle it as well. That he would be able to keep his libido in check and his hands to himself. He had a voracious sexual appetite, and considering the fact he was already strongly attracted to Nikki, that meant he had to do whatever was necessary to stay in control at all times.

Control suddenly took a backseat when he looked at her chest. He really liked the shape of her breasts, which were pressing against her blouse. The tips of her nipples seemed like little hardened buds, as if she was aroused. That couldn't be the case when she was sitting over there eating the last of her pie and not paying him any attention.

His stomach tightened when she finished it off by licking the fork. He again imagined all the things he'd like her to do with that tongue. And since he already knew how it tasted, he could feel sensations stirring in his gut.

Knowing he had to stop thinking such racy thoughts, he cleared his throat. "So, now that you know what the project will entail, do you have an answer for me now or do you need to sleep on it?" *And how about sleeping with me in the process?* He had to tighten his lips to keep from adding such a suggestion.

Before she could respond, the waiter came again to remove the last of their dishes and to leave him with the check.

It was then that she said, "Thanks for your consideration of me for the job, and I appreciate the offer. But I won't be able to take it, Jonas."

He blinked. Had he heard her right? Had she just turned him down? Shocked, he fought to keep the frown off his face. No woman had ever turned him down for anything. Business or pleasure.

There was a long pause and he knew she was waiting for him to say something, so he did. "Uh, all right. Would you like to order another cup of coffee?"

Hell, what else was he going to say? Tell her that it wasn't all right?

"No, I'll pass on the coffee. One cup was plenty for me. And thanks for being understanding about me not taking the job," she said.

Was he being understanding? He doubted it but decided to let her think whatever she wanted. Shouldn't he at least ask her why she had refused his offer? He quickly figured it wouldn't matter. There was nothing left for him to do but to move to the number-two person on the list, George Keller. George was a good photographer but could get on his last nerve at times. The thought of spending two weeks with the man had his teeth grinding.

"Well, thanks for dinner. I need to leave now."

And now on top of everything else, she was running

out on him. Automatically, he stood as well. "You're welcome. If not this time, then maybe we can work together again on another project in the future."

She shrugged. "Possibly."

Possibly? Was she for real? Just what was with this *possibly* crap? His lips curved into a forced smile. "I'm glad you're willing to keep your options open," he said, trying to keep the sarcasm from his voice.

At that moment she moved around the table getting ready to leave, and he felt a sucker punch deep in his gut. Nikki Cartwright was wearing something other than jeans. She had on a very short dress that showed all of her curves and legs he was seeing for the very first time. Long, gorgeous legs.

His gaze ran up and down her body and his breath caught in his throat when he realized that she was the same woman whose legs he'd seen in the parking lot earlier. Damn. Holy, hot damn.

Before he could stop himself, he looked up, met her gaze and said in an incredulous voice, "You're wearing a dress."

There was something about the look in Jonas's eyes that gave Nikki pause. Was that heated lust in the dark depths staring at her like she was a slice of strawberry cheesecake with a scoop of French vanilla ice cream on top? He had never looked at her like this before. Not even after the time they'd kissed. She was more than certain that she would have remembered if he had.

She was definitely confused. Did seeing her in a dress finally make him aware that she was a woman in a way that kiss hadn't? She would have worn a dress around him a long time ago if she'd known it would grab this much attention.

She drew in a deep breath, feeling sexy and seductive for the first time in years. "Yes, I usually wear jeans or slacks because they're more comfortable for the work I do. But I decided to wear a dress tonight since I'm going to spend some time upstairs."

He lifted his brow. "Upstairs?"

"Yes, at Mavericks. Tonight is jazz night."

Jonas nodded. Mavericks was an upscale nightclub on the thirty-fifth floor that had a rooftop bar and a wraparound terrace that provided a panoramic view of the mountains and Phoenix's skyline.

He stared at her and her outfit for a moment, wondering if perhaps she had a date. Of course if she did it was none of his business. But still, for some reason, he wanted to know.

"Sorry, I hope I didn't detain you unnecessarily. I wouldn't want you to be late for your date," he heard himself saying.

She smiled. "I don't have a date. I like jazz and thought I'd spend my evening doing something other than watching television."

He lifted a brow. "You aren't meeting anyone?"

She frowned. "No. I don't need someone to take me out if I want to enjoy good music."

He was well aware of that. However, a woman who was alone and looked like her would be inviting male attention whether she wanted it or not. There was no way he wouldn't hit on her if he saw her sitting alone. Men made plays for attractive women with only one thing in mind. It was the way of life. He of all people should know.

Imagining her sitting alone in a club while listening to jazz didn't sit well with him. He met her gaze. "I don't have anything else to do tonight and I love jazz as well. Mind if I join you?"

Chapter 3

Nikki struggled to retain an expressionless face as she walked into Mavericks with Jonas by her side. She was determined that nothing would make her come unglued, even the feel of his hand in the center of her back as he led her toward an empty table.

"I think this is a good spot," he said, pulling out her chair.

She had to hand it to him and his brothers when it came to manners. They were on top of their game, and she knew their mother could be thanked for that. Eden Steele had raised her sons to be gentlemen. Becoming notorious playboys was their own doing.

"There's a nice crowd here tonight."

She had noticed that as well. She had found out about the lounge's jazz night from a woman in her aerobics class this morning. Like she'd told Jonas, she enjoyed jazz, mainly because her parents were huge fans and she and her brother had grown up listening to it.

"Would you like anything to drink?" he asked when a waiter materialized at their table.

Remembering what he'd told her over dessert about having to limit his drinks, she smiled and said, "Just a glass of water with lemon."

Jonas gave her order to the waiter. "And I'll have the same."

He glanced toward the stage. The musicians were still setting things up. "Looks like we made it before the start of the show."

"Yes, it looks that way."

She had turned her head to look around the lounge, but Jonas got the distinct impression she'd done so to avoid eye contact with him. Did he make her uncomfortable? Nervous?

Then again, she could be avoiding his eyes because she was upset that he had invited himself to join her. The waiter returned with their waters and he watched as she took her lemon and gently squeezed it into the water before lifting the glass up to her lips and taking a sip. He sat there, transfixed and aroused, as he watched her part her lips.

She caught him staring, tilted her head and asked, "Is anything wrong?"

If only you knew, he thought when he shifted his gaze from her lips to her eyes. Her short, curly dark brown hair crowned her face like a cap and emphasized the darkness of her eyes and her high cheekbones.

Her question didn't give him pause. His brothers claimed he could BS his way out of any question so he said, "No, nothing is wrong. I was thinking about your lemon."

She lifted a brow. "My lemon?"

"Yes. Did you know there aren't any in India? They use lime instead. I was disappointed when I visited there a few years ago and couldn't get any lemonade."

She smiled grimly and he figured she was probably thinking, *Whatever.*

"So what's your favorite jazz group?" he asked her as he squeezed his own lemon into his water, still picking up on her nervousness.

She shrugged. "I basically love all of them, but I grew up on music by the Diz. My parents were huge Dizzy Gillespie fans. I also like Branford Marsalis."

He nodded and smiled. "Same here. My parents enjoy listening to jazz as well, and my brothers and I grew up on the music. But nothing dominated our house like the Motown Sound."

He chuckled and then added, "My parents are actually members of Motown Is Forever Association, which is a group of die-hard Motown fans who meet once a year to get their old-school, back-in-the-day groove on."

Selecting another lemon off the tray he squeezed it into his drink. She had gotten quiet on him again. The conversations at the tables around them were low and steady, which made the quietness at their table all the more noticeable. He took a sip of his water and wondered what the heck he was doing here. Why was he determined not to let their time together end at Mavericks just yet?

He knew the answer. It was simple. He needed to know why the kiss they'd shared had done him in.

* * *

By the time the first artist hit the stage, Nikki's brain cells were almost fried. She was certain Jonas was generating just that much heat. She could actually feel it all over her body, in some places more so than others, which was why she tightened her legs together.

What was his secret when it came to women? Not only did he have the looks but he also had the gift of gab. Although she had very little to say, it seemed he was determined to keep the conversation going. She had discovered there were no lemons in India, that Walt Disney's body had not been put in cryonic storage and he was convinced a bar of soap between the bedsheets prevented your legs from cramping. She figured if anyone would know about the latter it would be him, considering the amount of time he probably spent in bed with women.

She tried shifting her focus off Jonas and onto the performer. He was killing his saxophone, emitting sensuous sound waves that floated in the room. She recognized the piece and always thought she liked it better with the words, but the sax player was giving her thought. Without the words of undying love, the music still had a message of its own. And the message was stroking her senses, stirring across her skin and caressing certain parts of her body.

"I don't understand why you'd come here alone, Nikki."

She glanced over at Jonas and saw he had tilted his head while studying her as if she was a complex object of some sort. Was she that hard to figure out? Evidently he was a man who thought a woman wasn't complete without a man. She would be the first to admit she assumed a man and woman complemented each other, but only when they were on the same accord. When they wanted the same things in life and when there were no misunderstandings about their relationship.

"Why wouldn't I come here alone?" she asked.

"Why would you feel the need to?" he countered.

At that moment she felt that she could respond to his questions several different ways since he evidently didn't understand that some women preferred peace to drama, solitude to unnecessary commotion. But more importantly, a loving relationship to a purely sexual one.

She left his question hanging for a few moments before finally saying, "I don't date much by choice. At the moment I don't have time for the games men like to play."

He met her gaze, held it while he took a sip of his water. "So you're one of *those* women."

He'd said it like "those" women were a dying breed. Probably were if he had anything to do with it. Since she knew exactly what he meant, she said proudly, "Not really. I stopped believing in forever-after a while ago. I don't mind having a good time myself. But on my own time."

Nikki was convinced when he curved his lips into a challenging smile that her already wet panties got even more soaked. "Your own time? An interesting concept. One you'd toss to the wind with the right man," he said, as if he knew that for certain.

She knew his words were both a challenge and an invitation. He was one of those Steeles, those "Bad News" Steeles, so he would think that way. He was of the mind-set that everything would begin and end in the bedroom. And the end result would be hot, sweaty, sexually satisfied bodies.

Nikki noticed the sudden darkening of his eyes and flaring of his nostrils. If she didn't know better she would think that the pure animal male in him had picked up an arousing element in her scent. She'd heard some men had the ability to do that. Men who were acutely in tune with a woman.

And she wished Jonas wouldn't look at her the way he was doing now, like he could see more than normal people could with those green eyes of his. It was as if he could see right through her blouse, past her bra, directly to her nipples, which were responding to everything male about him. Certain things a woman couldn't evade, and her response to a gorgeous man was one of them, no matter how wickedly sinful the man was. And he was wickedly sinful. From the crown of his wavy hair to the soles of the Salvatore Ferragamo shoes he was wearing.

Thinking too much quiet time had passed between them, she decided to address what he'd said. "By the 'right man,' you're talking about a man like you, I presume."

That sinfully sexy smile widened. "And what kind of man am I, Nikki?"

Why did he have to say her name with such passion, such sensuality? And why was he intent on engaging in what she considered wasteful conversation? He knew the kind of man he was; he certainly didn't need her to spell it out for him. But if he wanted to hear it directly from her lips then...

"You're a man who loves women. Not just one or two, but plenty. You'll never settle down with just one, nor do you want to. Life is about women and sex, but mostly sex and more sex. You play safe. You play fair. But you play. And you will always play."

Jonas shrugged. Yes, that pretty much sized him up and he had no shame. There would never be a single woman to capture his heart like they'd done to Galen and Eli. There would never be a woman to make him feel anything other than a tightening in his groin. And that's what was so hard for his mother to understand and accept. But eventually she would. She had no choice.

Instead of responding to what Nikki had said, since her words really needed no response, he settled back in his chair to continue listening to the music. And to think some more about the woman sitting across from him. She might not want the hot sheets, sex and more sex, but something about being here with him was getting to her. He was a hunter and could pick up the scent of an aroused woman a mile off. And some part of his presence, and their conversation, had turned her on. He was certain of it.

He had no doubt she wanted to believe everything she'd said. Although she hadn't admitted such, he had a feeling that deep down she did believe in that nonsense about forever-after. He'd bet at one time she'd been wrapped up in the notion of a house with the white picket fence, babies and the words of undying love from a man's lips.

Who was the real Nikki Cartwright? his mind demanded to know. She'd peeled off a layer tonight by wearing a dress instead of jeans, and he liked what he saw. Who would have thought she had legs that looked like that? Legs that could probably wrap around a man real tight, grip him pretty damn good while they had nitty-gritty, between-the-sheets sex.

He took a sip of his water and appreciated how the cold liquid flowed down his throat to cool his insides. He knew the score with her and conceded he needed to leave her alone. Her turning down his job offer was probably a smart move. And to be quite honest, he really didn't have any reason to be sitting here with her, sharing her table, and listening to jazz.

He had tried not to notice her at Eli's wedding when she'd moved around the room snapping photographs. She had looked cute then…and busy. To keep his attention off her he had pretended interest in a couple of single women who'd flown in to attend. He'd eventually left the wedding reception with one of them.

And talk about leaving… Jonas knew he should go, tell her it was nice seeing her again and that he regretted they wouldn't be working together again and that he understood. His jaw tightened knowing that was one lie he could not tell because he did not understand it. Why was she walking away from an opportunity that could ultimately boost her career?

"That was beautiful," she said when the saxophonist ended the song. Like others, she stood to applaud, and Jonas's gaze automatically lowered to her legs. What a pretty-damn-stunning pair of legs they were. He had never considered himself the leg man in the family—everyone knew that was Eli. His favorite part of a woman's body usually was the middle. Specifically, what lay at the juncture of her legs. All the others parts—the legs, the breasts, the thighs, hips and backside—just whet his appetite. And as he continued to stare at Nikki's legs he could feel not only his appetite being whet but also himself becoming fully aroused in one hell of a way.

"Wasn't that just great?" she asked him, sitting back down.

"Totally tantalizing," was his response. He knew she was talking about the jazz instrumental that had just been played. He was talking about her legs and her curves in that short dress.

When the waiter came and refilled their water glasses and brought more lemons, he settled farther into his seat. He would stay, enjoy the rest of the show and at the same time enjoy the woman…at least enjoy the company of the woman. He'd learned his lesson with women who thought they could change their thinking that a wedding came before the bedding. Nikki might think she had it down pat, but deep down she would still look for wedding bells. There were really no sure converts when it came to that sort of thing. Just the pretenders.

He'd run into several of those in his lifetime. And the last thing he wanted to do was get mixed up with another. He glanced at his watch, thinking it was time to bring this evening to an end. But for some reason, he couldn't. At least, not yet.

Nikki ran her fingers through her hair as she walked beside Jonas to her car. It was close to midnight and he had hung with her longer than she'd thought he would. She had figured he would leave at some point during the evening but surprisingly, he hadn't. In fact he genuinely seemed to have enjoyed the music as much as she had.

But she wasn't fooled into thinking that he hadn't

been trying to size her up, figure her out. More than once during the course of the evening, she had glanced across the table in the semi-darkened room to find those green eyes leveled on her. It had been during those times, when her heart would beat like crazy in her chest, that she wished she had something stronger to drink than just water.

She was convinced there weren't too many men like Jonas Steele, then quickly remembered there were six of them, four still single. But each was different in his own way, although when it came to women there were definite similarities.

When he led her straight to her car, she glanced up at him. "How did you know this car was mine? I didn't tell you what I was driving, and it's different from the last one I had when we worked together before."

He smiled. "I knew it was yours was because I saw you when you got out of it, although I didn't know it was you at the time. I recognized the legs later."

She stared at him, saw he was dead serious and couldn't help but laugh.

"What's so funny? "

If he didn't know… "Nothing," she said, shaking her head. She pulled the key from her purse. "Well, I'll be seeing you."

"I'll follow you."

She lifted a brow. "Why?"

"To make sure you get home okay."

She looked at him like he had a visible dent in his brain. "You don't have to do that. It's not like we've been out on a date or anything."

"It doesn't matter. We've spent the evening together

and it's late. There's no way I'll not make sure you get home. I wasn't raised that way."

She let out an exaggerated breath. "What if I get your number and just text you to let you know that I made it home?"

"Unless you deleted it, you already have my number from the last time we worked together. But texting me won't work. I removed that feature from my phone."

"You did? Why?"

He shrugged. "I was getting too many unnecessary messages."

"Yeah, I bet." She brushed a curl back from her face. "Look, Jonas, your wanting to make sure I get home safe and sound is thoughtful but truly not necessary."

"Your opinion, not mine. Ready to go?"

When she saw there was no use standing in the middle of the hotel's parking lot arguing with him, she opened her car door to get in. She then watched in her rearview mirror as he crossed the lot to his car. As she turned on the ignition, she shook her head. He had recognized her legs. Of all things.

She pulled out of the parking lot and another glance in the rearview mirror showed he was right on her tail. *Right on her tail.* That same heat she'd been battling between her legs all evening returned at the thought. Okay, she was an intelligent and sensible woman, but that didn't mean she couldn't get tempted every once in a while. Just as long as she didn't ever yield to such temptation, she was safe.

Still in the mood for jazz, she turned on the CD player in her car and the sound of Miles Davis flowed through, bringing back the mood that had been set earlier. Good music and the presence of a handsome man sitting at her table. It hadn't been a date, she reminded herself, although it had appeared as such.

It took twenty minutes to get home and she tried not to think of the man following her. Every time she would look in her rearview mirror he seemed to be staring back right at her. And when she pulled into her driveway she was surprised when he pulled right in behind her. It would have been fine if he had parked on the street.

Her throat tightened when he joined her on the walkway. "You don't have to walk me to the door, Jonas."

His lips curved into a wide grin. "Yes, I do."

She eyed him, one brow arching. Did he have an ulterior motive for wanting to walk her to the door? Was he hoping she would invite him in? Did she want to?

She wondered what kind of game he was playing with her now, and more importantly, why she was letting him. She'd given him her answer regarding working with him again—a decision she figured she would regret in the morning.

In a way she was already regretting it. But her sanity and peace of mind were more important and she was certain working with him again would rob her of both.

"Your key, please."

She blinked when his request jerked her back to the here and now. She looked up at him. They were at her front door. "My key?"

"Yes."

"Why would you want my key?"

"To see you properly inside."

Yeah. Right. He wouldn't be the first man who tried testing her, and she knew he wouldn't be the last. But then she also knew that this was Jonas Steele, a man who'd probably perfected his game. And for some reason he intended to try his game on her. Did she have something plastered on her forehead that said, Try me?

"Thanks, but I don't need you to see me inside, properly or otherwise," she said, using the key to unlock the door herself. "This is where we part ways."

"Do you really want to do that?" he asked, easing closer to her, too close for her comfort. His cologne was getting to her. His very presence was getting to her.

"Why wouldn't I? Besides, we both know I'm not your type."

He chuckled. "And what is my type?"

She blew out a breath, feeling herself getting annoyed. "Someone who enjoys playing your kind of games." She'd thought that she would, had convinced herself she could handle a man like him if she began thinking like he did, but she saw that wasn't working.

He inched closer. "And you don't enjoy playing my sort of games, Nikki?"

That answer was easy. "No, I'll pass."

"You're really not going to invite me in?"

He actually looked crushed, but she knew it was a put-on, just one of the many faces of Jonas Steele. He played whichever one worked at the time. "No. Sorry. Usually a woman invites a man inside when she offers him coffee, tea or something else to drink. I'm plum out of everything. I didn't make it to the grocery store this week."

He leaned against her door front. "We do pretty good on just water."

"I don't have any lemons," she said quickly

"We'll find our own pucker power," he said, easing a little closer to her. He had taken off his suit jacket and tie and was standing there, under her porch light, looking laid-back, cool and calm. And it didn't help matters when his gaze roamed over her. He was up to something and she felt she deserved to know what.

"Okay, Jonas, what's going on?"

"What makes you think something is going on? And what kinds of games do you think I like playing?"

Another simple answer. "Musical beds, for starters."

He nodded slowly. Then a smile touched his lips. "Are you worried about your fair share of my time in the bedroom?"

The man was impossible. Now she saw she'd done the right thing in turning down his offer for that job. "I wouldn't have been the one who needed to worry," she said snappily and regretted her words the moment they'd left her lips. Of course he would see it as a challenge. The notion was written all over his face.

"Umm, that would be interesting."

"Not if you can't even remember a kiss," she muttered under her breath and then wished she hadn't when he stared at her, letting her know he'd heard her.

"Oh, I definitely remember it, Nikki."

She waved off his words. "Whatever."

"Um, maybe we need to go inside and talk about that kiss."

She shook her head. "No, we don't. We can say our good-nights right here."

"Not until we talk. Evidently we aren't on the same page."

"Doesn't matter to me," she lied.

"It does to me. It won't take more than five minutes to clear this up."

There really was nothing to clear up, but she figured

she would be wasting her time trying to convince him of that. Besides, deep down she was curious about what he had to say. Men could talk their way in or out of anything. But what concerned her now more than anything was why he was coming on to her after all this time.

"I'm going to ask you again, Jonas. What's going on? Why are you trying to do me?" A girl couldn't ask any plainer than that.

He inched even closer. "Because the thought of doing you has been on my mind ever since that kiss."

She stared at him. Did he honestly think she would believe that? There was no way he could convince her that that kiss had meant anything to him. It wasn't like they lived in separate towns and it wasn't as if she was hard to find. Her best friend was married to his oldest brother, for heaven's sake.

Besides, if a Steele wanted a woman he strategized things to his advantage and went after her with no time wasted. Eighteen months had gone by and he hadn't made a move. They had run into each other at several functions and he'd deliberately gone out of his way to avoid her. She wasn't stupid.

She must have worn the look of disbelief well because he then said, "You don't believe me."

She shook her head. "No, I don't believe you. Good night."

He stuck out his hand to block her entrance inside. "What about another kiss? One for the road."

Nikki drew in a deep breath because deep down, she wanted another kiss. No joke. All she had to do was look at his mouth and remember the taste of it. Good Lord, how could she think of such things and especially with this man? The man who had a player's card with no expiration date.

"What would another kiss do, Jonas?"

"Prove you wrong."

Could it? She doubted it. But…

She studied his features. There was a look in his eyes that was more intense than the way he'd been staring at her in Mavericks. She let out a frustrating sigh. That's another reason she thought she wasn't cut out to be in the fast lane. A woman could get gray hairs trying to figure a man out. "A kiss and then you'll go away?" she asked softly, feeling her resistance to him slipping away.

"Yes. Scout's honor."

She stared at him for a moment and then said, "I'm taking you at your word." She opened the door and moved inside with him following quickly on her heels as if he thought she would change her mind.

Jonas closed the door behind him as both desire and tension stirred deep in the pit of his stomach. He glanced around. She had left a light burning on a table in the foyer, and he figured chances were she wouldn't invite him in to see the rest of the house, which was fine with him. All he needed was the area where they were standing.

She was in front of him, looking agitated and annoyed, ready for him to kiss her and get it over with. His jaw twitched as irritation filled him. First she turned down his job offer, and now she was trying to rush him off like he was a bother. And she even had the gall to tap her foot.

She tilted her head back and looked up at him. "Well?"

"Well?" he countered, moving a little closer to her.

"What are you waiting for?" she asked, lifting her chin.

"For you to get your mind in check."

Sighing, Nikki doubted that would happen. Her mind would never be fully in check when it came to Jonas. She really didn't understand what the big deal was. Why was he taking so long to kiss her? He was the one who suggested they do it again. She would have been perfectly satisfied with her memories.

"You have beautiful eyes, Nikki."

She blinked and her heart began beating a little harder when she noticed he had eased even closer to her. When had he done that? "Thank you. You have beautiful eyes yourself."

His lips curved into a smile as he took a step closer. Instinctively, she took a step back. He reached out and gently grabbed her around the waist. "Where do you think you're going?"

"Nowhere."

He towered over her, but his face was close, almost right in hers. His breath smelled of lemons and she recalled what he'd said about pucker power. "Why are you taking so long?"

"Nikki," he said in what sounded like an exasperated tone. "Some things you can't rush. Be patient. Besides, I'm thinking about a few things."

She cocked a brow. "What things?"

"Like how much I enjoyed kissing you the last time. How your taste remained on my tongue for days, months, and how no degree of brushing could get it off."

She looked stunned. "That's impossible. You left, almost knocking over my trash can in your rush to leave."

He reached out and lifted her chin. "It was either that or I stripped off your clothes and took you right there where you stood."

He spoke the words low and all but breathed them against her lips, making her pulse quicken and her heart rate increase. "I don't believe you," she whispered as a shiver of desire ran all through her.

"Then maybe I need to make a believer out of you."

He advanced. Instinctively she backed up again until she noticed the wall at her spine. She also noticed something else. He had braced his hands on the walls on both sides of her head, caging her in. When he shifted positions the lower part of him rubbed against her middle. He was hard. Extremely hard. Diabolically hard.

"Why is your heart beating so fast, Nikki?" he asked, moving his lips even closer.

"It's not."

"Yes, it is. I hear it. I can feel it."

She swallowed, thinking he probably could. When she'd decided to go ahead with the kiss she'd figured it would be an even exchange. It was something they both wanted. But now she had a feeling she would be paying a bigger price than he would.

She stared into his gaze and he stared back, but there was something in his look that gave her pause, made her heart, which was already beating like crazy, thump even faster. And was the floor actually moving beneath her feet?

"Place your hands on my shoulders. Both of them."

His words were whispered across her lips, and automatically she lifted her arms to comply. The air between them was electrified, charged. She didn't just place her hands on his shoulders; instinctively her fingertips dug into his shoulder blades. If he was bothered by it, he didn't let on. Instead his gaze moved from her eyes to her mouth and she watched as he gave her a soft smile.

She focused her attention on the shape of his lips and wondered about their texture. Their taste. And then before she could take her next breath, his mouth lowered to hers.

Chapter 4

Jonas felt as if he'd come back to a place he should never have left. Never had kissing a woman made him feel that way before. The memories he had of their last kiss hadn't done it justice. His lips felt like a magnet, fused to her in the most intimate way. The heat that had blazed to life the moment his mouth touched hers had his body quivering inside.

He was taking her mouth with a hunger that he felt all the way down to the soles of his feet. This was no mere kiss. This wasn't even about reacquainting their mouths. This was the forging of fires in the broadest sense of the word. He didn't want just to play on her senses, he wanted to dominate them. His mouth was relentless, untiring and filled with a hunger that had him devouring her as his tongue mated fiercely with hers.

A man with his experience could pick up on the

fact that moisture was gathering between her legs. The scent was being absorbed in his nostrils. He wanted to touch her there. Taste her there, like he was tasting her mouth. Mate with her there, the way his tongue was mating with hers. He was consumed by an urgency, an insatiable hunger.

His hands moved from the wall to grip her hips, then behind her to cup her backside. The soft material of her dress was no barrier against the hard erection he pressed against her. Her fingertips were pressing hard into his shoulders, eliciting pain and pleasure at the same time.

For him, kissing had always been a prelude to the next phase of sex. It was foreplay that he enjoyed, but he knew the prize was when he penetrated a woman, going deep and riding her hard. But with Nikki he had a totally different mind-set. His taste for her was relentless. Never had he craved kissing a woman so.

And to think she had assumed he hadn't enjoyed this the first time around. If only she knew the reason he'd left that day had had nothing to do with not enjoying the kiss but everything to do with enjoying it too much.

And now his insides felt as if they'd burst into flames and the only way to put them out was to take her to the nearest bed and lose himself. With that thought in mind he lifted her into his arms.

The feel of being swept off her feet caused Nikki's senses to return in full force. She pushed against Jonas's chest before easing out of this arms. There was no need to ask where he thought he was about to take her. He'd been headed in the direction of her bedroom.

And there was no need to ask how he knew just

where the room was located when he'd never set foot in her house before. Men like Jonas had built-in radar when it came to a woman's bedroom. She pulled in a deep breath, thinking that had been some kiss, definitively hotter than the last.

"Do you believe me now, Nikki?"

She glanced up, and like a magnet her gaze automatically latched to Jonas's mouth. Seeing the shape of his damp lips made her lick her own when she remembered why his were wet. Yes, she believed him. After the way he had devoured her mouth, she had no choice but to do so. And the thought that he had enjoyed the kiss as much as she had sent her into a head spin. He was fire and if she thought she could play with him without getting burned then she was only fooling herself. And her mother hadn't raised a fool. To keep her sanity, she needed to distance herself from him as soon as possible.

"You got the kiss so now you can leave." In reality he'd gotten a lot more than that. He'd snatched her common sense right from her, which was why she needed to hurry him out the door.

"Okay, I'll go, Nikki. But if you change your mind about coming on board for the Fulton project, let me know within the week."

She stared at him. Did he honestly think she could work with him now? Whenever she saw him she wouldn't think of work; she would think of kisses.

"There's no way I can work with you even if I had a change of heart, Jonas."

He took a step back and placed his hands in his pockets. "Why not? You're a big girl. I'm sure you can handle a one-night stand."

She frowned. There was no way she would consider such a thing. "That's not the point."

"Isn't it? You said you knew about my type so now let me tell you what I perceive as yours. Although you claim you no longer believe in that fairy-tale nonsense of everlasting love, you're still holding out for it. You want to believe that somehow your lucky number will get pulled and you'll meet a guy who wants to put a ring on your finger, marry you and give you babies. But my question to you, Nikki, is this. Are you willing to live your life and hold out waiting for a possibility? What if it doesn't happen? We both know the statistics. Chances are it won't."

He paused a second and to give her more food for thought, he added, "Just think of all the time you waste waiting for Mr. Right who just might not come at all."

She glared at him. "How can you be so cynical when your parents have been happily married close to forty years, and two of your brothers—who use to be die-hard bachelors—are now married?"

A crooked smile touched his lips. "Easily. I consider my parents' marriage one in a million, which means they beat the odds. And as for my brothers... the jury is still out as to whether their marriages will last. Don't get me wrong, I believe they love the women they married and the women they married love them. But a marriage is built on more than just love, so I'll wait and see if either of them will celebrate any five-year anniversaries."

She could only stare at him, not believing he said such a thing. She didn't know Eli and Stacey that well, but anyone who hung around Galen and Brittany long enough knew they were destined to share their lives together forever. How could he not see it? She knew the answer immediately. He didn't want to see it. He simply refused to do so.

"So there's no reason why you shouldn't enjoy yourself, Nikki. Have fun. If not with me then definitely someone else. But at the moment I'm thinking only of myself and the fun the two of us can have together. Why let life slip you by? You're nearly thirty, right?"

Now that was a low blow, Nikki thought. A man never brought up a woman's age. And before she could take him to task for doing so, he went on to add, "Don't get me wrong. You look good for your age. But time isn't on your side. Neither is it on mine. It happens. Life happens. So we might as well enjoy it while we can."

She crossed her arms over her chest and lifted her chin. She wondered if this was the game he ran on his women who eventually gave in to him. "Is that all?"

"No, but I figured that, along with the kiss, is enough for you to think about for now. However, if after all your reflections you still decide affairs aren't your thing, I still would like to work with you again. I'll even keep my hands and lips to myself and retain a strictly business relationship with you. Like I said at dinner, you're the best photographer around and I need the best for this project."

A smile curved his lips. "Good night and I hope to see you around."

Nikki blinked when the door closed behind Jonas. She then drew in a deep breath, wondering if she had imagined the whole thing. Had she and Jonas actually kissed again?

She touched her lips with her fingertips. They felt

sore and she knew why. This kiss had been more powerful than the last one. Jonas hadn't just kissed her, he had devoured her mouth. And she hated to admit that she had enjoyed it. Immensely. Slowly drawing air into her lungs, she could still taste him on her tongue. Her body was in shock mode with tingling sensations rushing through it. Every muscle was quivering, and she was overheated with want and need that had her insides sizzling.

She moved away from the wall thinking Jonas had read her loud and clear. She wanted to be a bad girl with a good-girl mentality. She even had Brittany convinced that she was a woman with no hang-ups about engaging in casual affairs. The lie had sounded so true that she had begun believing it herself. But Jonas had shown her she was way out of her league.

Okay, he'd told her he was attracted to her, and the kiss somewhat proved that he was. What he hadn't told her was why he had kept his distance for eighteen months.

She rubbed her forehead, feeling a humongous headache coming on, but she knew what she had to do. Tomorrow she would call Senator Joseph's campaign headquarters and accept the offer they'd made. The sooner she got busy with her life, the sooner she could put thoughts of Jonas out of it.

Jacketless, shirtless and horny as hell, Jonas let himself into his house. On the drive home he kept calling himself all kinds of fool for kissing Nikki again. Why was he a glutton for punishment? At least he didn't have to wonder why he was so drawn to her.

There was something about her taste that even now

was causing an ache in his lower extremities. When had a kiss been so overpowering? So downright delicious that his entire body was revving up with thoughts of another one? And then another…

Besides that, there was something different about their date—and whether he wanted to admit it or not, what started out as a business meeting had ended up as a date. He had enjoyed her company more than any other woman's. Mainly because in addition to being a great conversationalist, she had a sense of humor. She had shared with him some of her and Brittany's escapades as teens growing up together in Florida.

What he needed to do was clear his mind and he knew the best way to do it. A way that worked each and every time. Taking the stairs two at a time he entered his bedroom and changed into a pair of jeans and a T-shirt, the perfect outfit for a late-night ride on his Harley.

A short while later he was in his garage, putting a band on his hair to hold the strands together before placing a helmet on his head. He straddled his bike, ready to hit the open road. Adrenaline flowed through every part of his body when he fired up the engine and took off like the devil himself was chasing after him.

He knew the route he was traveling. Could follow it with his eyes closed since it was the same one he always took whenever he rode his bike late at night. This was his favorite time for riding with a big beautiful dark sky overhead and stars sprinkled about. Usually he felt at peace, but on this particular night his mind was in turmoil. He definitely needed this ride.

He settled in his seat, drew in a deep breath and let the adrenaline flow. The sound of the thrumming engine had a calming effect, one he felt all the way down to his bones.

Now if he could only get Nikki out of his mind. A frown appeared between his eyebrows. Why even now, when he was out on the open road in the middle of the night, could he still inhale her scent? And why couldn't he get out of his mind just how she'd looked tonight in that outfit?

His frown deepened. How she looked tonight had nothing on her taste, which was something else he couldn't seem to get over. But he would. No matter what it took. Damn, hadn't he made that same resolution eighteen months ago?

The only reason he'd kissed her tonight was because he'd undergone a moment of temporary insanity. He was convinced that had to be it. And he was equally convinced that by this time tomorrow he would be back in his right mind and in some other woman's bed to make him forget. Hadn't that been what had helped him the last time? Yes, somewhat, but it hadn't taken care of the root of his problem.

He wanted Nikki in a way a man usually wanted a woman. In his bed. Whether he'd admit it or not, kissing her a second time had pretty much changed the dynamics of their relationship. She was now under his skin deeper than before.

Jonas looked ahead and saw the flashing railroad crossings go down. He expelled an agitated breath and brought his bike to a complete stop.

"If you straddle a woman like you do that bike then you're definitely a man who knows how to ride."

Jonas rolled his eyes before glancing at the very attractive woman seated behind the wheel of a canary-yellow Corvette convertible idling beside him. His gaze first appreciated the car and then the woman. The look she was giving him made him feel naked. Unfortunately for her, he didn't experience even the faintest hint of excitement from her intense perusal.

"Yes, I know how to ride and enjoy doing so," he responded, knowing neither of them was talking about his bike.

"Then maybe you need to follow me."

He thought that maybe he did, until he saw the ring on her finger. "And maybe you need to go home to your husband."

She pouted. "He's no fun."

Your problem, not mine. "I don't encroach on another man's territory."

"Um, that's a pity," she said sarcastically.

"Probably is." *Especially since tonight I'd love to ride a woman more than this bike.*

But as he took off when the railroad crossing arms went back up, he knew the only woman he wanted to ride. But he didn't want to think about it. He didn't want to think about her.

So he continued to ride as he tried to shut off his mind to any thoughts of Nikki Cartwright. About to take a curve, he leaned in, liking the feel of power beneath his thighs. It was a thrumming sensation he couldn't get anywhere else. The vibration of the bike's engine helped to lull him into a contented mood for the time being. He felt totally in sync with the road, the bike he was riding, and the entire universe. The feeling was totally awesome.

Jonas tried to recall the last time he'd had a woman on the bike with him. It had been a while since his back had rested against a pair of plump, ripe breasts or a woman's arms had been wrapped around him while she held on tight.

At that moment the image of the only woman he wanted to share a bike ride with loomed in front of him. And he was suddenly filled with arousal that had his erection pressing hard against his zipper. He drew in a deep breath and adjusted his body on the seat. As much as he wished otherwise, it was evident that Nikki would not be eradicated from his thoughts anytime soon. The woman was one sensual piece of art.

It was only when he came to a stop at a red light that he took in his surroundings. He was only a block away from where Nikki lived. What had possessed him to come this way when he lived in the other direction? What was this madness? He should be putting as much distance between them as he could. That kiss was proof enough that when it came to her he couldn't think straight.

And maybe that was the reason he should have a face-off with her once and for all. Granted, Nikki was a challenge to his sensibilities, but he refused to run in the opposite direction whenever he saw her, like he'd been doing for the past eighteen months. He would face her like a man and do what he knew he needed to do and be done with it.

Hell, the way he saw it, he would be doing her a favor. Like he told her, she was approaching thirty and it was time to put all that nonsense of a forever love out of her head. Being a romantic was one thing. Being a hopeless, incurable romantic was another.

He checked his watch. It was late, close to one in the morning. But there was someone he needed to call now. Pulling to the side of the road, he killed his engine and removed his helmet. He took his cell phone out of his pocket to make a call.

"Hello."

"Stan. I figured you would still be up."

"Jonas? Kind of late for you to be calling. Is there a party somewhere that I'm missing?"

Jonas chuckled. "No. Just calling to collect a favor."

"Okay, buddy. I owe you so many of them I won't waste my time asking which one. Just tell me what you need."

"Your brother Jeremy is campaign manager for Senator Joseph, right?"

"Yes, that's right."

Jonas nodded. "Someone made a job offer to a photographer by the name of Nicole Cartwright. I want them to pull the offer."

"Pull the offer?" Stan asked, surprised.

"Yes."

"All right. I'll see what I can do."

"Thanks. I appreciate it."

Satisfied for the time being, Jonas returned the cell phone to his pocket and put the helmet back on his head. Firing up the bike's engine, he headed for home.

Chapter 5

"Senator Joseph's campaign actually withdrew their offer to hire you as a photographer?" Brittany Steele asked as she gazed across the table at her best friend.

"Yes," Nikki said, still somewhat annoyed at the call she'd received yesterday.

"Why?"

"They said something about reevaluating the budget. It was definitely bad timing since I had planned to call them to accept." Nikki glanced around Samantha's Café where she had met Brittany for lunch. A popular place to dine, the establishment was crowded.

She looked back at Brittany. "Now I need to look at other opportunities. Weddings, anniversary parties and family portraits are nice to do on the side, but they won't pay the bills."

"So what are you going to do?"

After taking a sip of her coffee, Nikki answered, "Not sure, especially since I turned down Jonas's offer."

Brittany raised an arched brow. "Jonas offered you a job?"

Nikki nodded. "Yes. It was a chance to work with him on that Fulton project. And he was going to pay twice as much as the Joseph campaign."

"Then why did you turn down Jonas? I would think being a part of that Fulton project would be a dream come true."

Nikki's cheeks warmed. There were certain things she had withheld from her best friend, and now it was time to come clean. "Do you recall that day we ran into each other when you first arrived in Phoenix and you were bidding on your mother's property?"

Brittany smiled as she cut into her salad. "Yes, that was over a year ago, but I remember. It was short of a miracle that we ran into each other after all those years."

"Yes, and that night we dined at Malone's and played catch-up on what's been going on with us over the past twelve years."

Brittany's smile deepened. "I was stressed out about Galen's outlandish proposal for my mother's property."

"Yes, well, I wasn't completely forthright about a few things."

Brittany stopped what she was doing and stared. "About what?"

"My relationship with Jonas, for starters."

Surprise lit Brittany's features and she set down her fork and knife by her salad bowl. "You and Jonas were involved?"

Nikki chuckled. "Only in my dreams. But when I brought him up, I made it seem as if the two of us had merely worked together once or twice and hadn't gotten all that close."

"But you and he had been close?"

"Not sexual or anything like that. But we had kissed. The reason I didn't say anything was that I was too embarrassed to admit it, especially since it was a kiss that led nowhere. And one I took more seriously than he did. We were at my office one day and had gotten excited over this deal he'd clinched and got caught up in the moment."

Nikki leaned back in her chair. "Trust me. He regretted the kiss soon enough and made sure he kept his distance whenever we would run into each other after that. In fact, the first time we came in breathing space of each other again was at your wedding."

She could remember that day like it was yesterday. She had been one of the bridesmaids and he one of the groomsmen. She had avoided him like he'd been determined to avoid her.

"And I saw him again when I was the photographer at Eli's wedding," she said, stirring her soup. She shook her head. "It's funny we only seem to run into each other at weddings."

Nikki paused, remembering that day at Eli's wedding. She could have sworn more than once Jonas's gaze had been on her, but when she would glance over at him he would be either engaged in deep conversation with someone or looking someplace else. "I was surprised when I got a call from him three days ago asking that we meet to discuss a business proposition."

"The Fulton deal?"

"Yes. We met, he made the offer and I turned him down."

"Why?"

Nikki met Brittany's gaze. "Because I knew I would not be able to control myself around him…which leads to my next confession."

"Which is?"

"I'm not living in the fast lane like I led you to believe on that night. I gave you the impression that I'd given up believing in a knight in shining armor and that I was independent, empowered, a woman on the move. A woman who wanted nothing more than a casual affair with a man. I wanted to believe I was all those things and had convinced myself I could be. But…"

"But what?"

"I blew a big chance to prove myself with Jonas this week, which leads me to believe that I might not be as ready to move out of my comfort zone as I thought. Deep down a part of me is still programmed to believe in happy endings and everything that goes along with it—love, happiness and commitment. But then there's another part that knows such things no longer exist for most women and that I need to stop reaching for a fantasy and accept reality. I can't have it both ways."

She pushed her soup bowl aside. "So all that advice I gave you that night was all talk, and nothing that I would have had the courage to try myself."

A smile touched Brittany's lips. "All talk or not, it was good advice and if I hadn't taken it, I wouldn't have Galen." She leaned back in her chair and eyed Nikki squarely. "Sounds to me like there's a battle going on inside of you. Your head against your heart.

Your head is filled with notions of how today's woman should act and the things she should want, versus the things that your heart—the heart of a romantic—wants. That old-fashioned happy ever after."

Brittany chuckled. "And don't you dare ask me which one you should listen to. That's a decision only you can make, and you'll know when it's the right one."

Nikki shook her head. "Not sure about that, and I might have muddied the waters even more. Jonas and I kissed again the other night."

The expression on Brittany's face showed she wasn't surprised. "And?"

"For me it was better than the first time, and there's no doubt in my mind that he enjoyed it as much as I did. But I know the score, Britt. Jonas is a bona fide player who doesn't have a serious bone in his body."

"And you want to become a female version?"

Nikki shrugged. "Not to that degree, but you know what they're saying. Good men are extinct, and more and more women aren't depending on a man for their happiness."

"*They're* saying. And just who are *they*?"

"Magazine articles, talk shows, reality shows, anybody you ask. Finding love, happiness and commitment is as unlikely as walking down the street and finding a million-dollar bill."

Brittany chuckled. "There aren't million-dollar bills."

Nikki giggled. "See there, another reason not to waste your time looking."

Brittany shook her head. "Seriously, in the end you have to do what makes you happy."

"But what happens if what makes me happy is something not good for me?"

"Then you'll know it and eventually reject it. In the end, either your head or your heart will win." Brittany paused a second and then asked, "So what are you going to do about Jonas and that job offer? Is it too late to tell him you've changed your mind and want it after all?"

Did she want it after all? Nikki nibbled on her bottom lip. Nothing had changed since two nights ago. She still didn't feel comfortable working so closely with Jonas again. But in reality she realized that something had changed. She no longer had choices with her employment situation. She needed a job.

She was still attracted to him and it seemed he was attracted to her. But for how long? She couldn't forget his reputation when it came to women. "Not sure what I'm going to do yet. To go back and tell Jonas that I've changed my mind and will work for him is easier said than done. The issues I had with it then are the same issues I have now. And it wouldn't hurt if he wasn't so cynical."

Brittany laughed. "Yes, he's definitely that. I love my brothers-in-law, but they're hard-core players. However, look at Galen and Eli—so were they once. So maybe there's hope."

Nikki didn't know about the others but figured that hope was on the other end of the spectrum when it came to Jonas. However, at some point she needed to see it as his problem and not hers. She had allowed his way of thinking and acting to rain on her parade, and that wasn't fair. She should not have been afraid of taking that job for fear of how she would act based on his actions.

She sighed upon realizing she had turned down what could have been her big break because of him. Instead of taking his offer and taking him on in the process, she had given in to her fears and backed away.

She glanced up at Brittany and took a deep breath. "My financial needs outweigh my emotional ones right now. And you're right. It will be a battle between my head and my heart. I just hope I can survive the fight."

3 days later

"Mr. Steele, Nikki Cartwright is here to see you."

Jonas looked up from the document he was reading when his secretary's voice came across the intercom. *Finally*, he thought. It had taken Nikki almost a week to come calling, and for a minute he'd gotten worried that perhaps he'd misplayed his hand and there was some other job she had lined up that he hadn't known about. He tossed what was left of his Tootsie Pop in the trash can by his desk, leaned back in his chair and smiled. Evidently that wasn't the case.

"Give me a few minutes to wrap up this report, Gail, and then send her in," he said, standing to straighten his tie. He didn't have any report to wrap up. He needed the extra time to prepare himself mentally for the woman he couldn't get out of his mind. He sniffed the air; he inhaled her scent already.

He checked to make sure his shirt was neatly tucked into his pants while thinking that he would discount the fact it had taken manipulation on his part to get her here. After their second kiss, it had become extremely clear to him just how much he wanted Nikki in his bed, and at that point he had decided he would do whatever it took to get her there. Sleeping with her once should do it. He was convinced of it.

He was marveling over the brilliance of that supposition when he heard the soft knock on his office door. "Come in."

His gaze connected with hers the moment the door opened. He swallowed tightly and immediately thought he might need to sleep with her more than once. It would be breaking a rule, but some rules were made to be broken. "Nikki, this is a surprise." Like hell it was. He'd been expecting her. Hoping she would take the bait and decide she needed to work for him after all.

"I hope I didn't catch you at a bad time, Jonas. I thought about calling but figured it would be best if we talked in person."

"Sure, have a seat."

He watched her cross the room to the chair he offered, and thought she looked fresh in her jeans and pretty blue blouse. He liked how the denim fit over her soft curves. Seeing her in a dress that night had taken the guesswork out of what her legs looked like, and he hated that she'd covered them up today.

"You can have one of those," he said of the Tootsie Pops in a candy jar on a table near Nikki's chair.

"No, thank you. I don't normally have a sweet tooth."

He had to bite back from saying sweet tooth or not, what he'd tasted of her so far was simply delicious. He went to sit on the edge of his desk to face her, inhale her scent, recall the fantasies he'd had of her just last night. They'd been hot, lustful, erection-throbbing fantasies of him riding her. Her riding him. Oral sex. Can't-walk-the-next-day sex. When his stomach clenched he figured he better get his thoughts under control and out from under the bedcovers.

"So what can I help you with, Nikki?"

She began nibbling on her bottom lip, which meant she was nervous. He felt his erection throb, which meant he was horny. With effort, he pushed from his mind the thought of just what those two things might have in common.

"The other night you offered me the chance to work with you on the Fulton project."

He nodded slowly. "Yes, and you turned me down."

She looked good today, sexy as hell. Innocent and hot all rolled into one. There was something about that curly hair of hers and the way it crowned her face. It teased the primal maleness inside of him. And that errant curl that seemed to always be out of place, falling just so between her brows, was hammering something fierce below his belt.

"Yes, but later you said you would hold the offer for at least a week, in case I changed my mind," she reminded him.

He held back from telling her he didn't need reminding. He knew just what he said, how he'd said it and why he'd said it. It was right after deciding, that whether he liked it or not, eighteen months hadn't rid him of his desire for her and he would risk any feelings of vulnerability that bedding her would bring on. The main thing was to get her out of his system so things could go back to normal for him.

"Yes, I did say that. So, have you changed your mind, Nikki?"

"Yes. Does that mean the job is still available and you'll consider me for it?"

"Like I told you, I want the best and I consider your skill with a camera unsurpassed." That was the truth and had nothing to do with his plan to get her in his bed. The bedding part was a done deal as far as he was concerned.

"Thanks." She began nibbling on those lips again and there was silence between them. There was more she wanted to say, he knew, but she was hesitating.

"I take it that there's something else you need to clear the air about before you make your final decision." He couldn't let her sit there and gnaw her mouth off. He couldn't afford for her to do that, not when he had plans for that luscious-looking mouth of hers.

She sat up straight in her chair. "Yes, there is. We've kissed. Twice now."

He nodded, fighting back the urge to tell her that was for starters and didn't come close to all the other things he intended for them to do now that he'd made up his mind about a few things regarding her. "Yes, that's twice now."

"It can't happen again. You did say you're willing to keep your hands to yourself."

Yes, he had said that. But that didn't necessarily mean he'd meant it. "Is that what you want?"

He'd seen it. She hadn't been quick enough to disguise that flash that had appeared in her eyes. He knew what it meant so whatever she said now didn't matter one iota.

"Yes, that's what I want."

Yeah, right. "Okay, I'll give you what you want." And he meant every word. She was going to discover soon enough that a hands-off policy between them was the last thing she really wanted.

He pushed away from his desk. "So, are you going to work for me?"

When she hesitated, he lifted a brow and a smile touched his lips. "What? Do you need me to put the strictly business policy in writing or something?"

She stood as well. "Of course not."

"Then what is it?"

"Nothing."

He tilted his head. "I think there is something bothering you."

She adjusted the straps of her purse on her shoulder. He couldn't resist breathing in her scent and almost groaned.

"No, I'm fine."

You definitely are. "If you're sure, we can shake on it for now and then Gail will have your contract ready in a few days. Like I told you there's a launch party to attend in Las Vegas."

She nodded. "I'll be there. I just need the itinerary."

"Gail will call you when that's prepared as well."

He crossed the room to her, refused to consider the very real fact that he hadn't been completely honest with her about everything and that she probably wouldn't like it one damn bit when she found out how he'd manipulated things to get what he wanted.

Jonas reached his hand out to her and she took it, and he immediately felt his body's reaction to the feel of her smaller hand in his. "Welcome aboard, Nikki. I'm looking forward to working with you again."

He knew she felt something as well, although she was struggling hard not to. She tried not to make eye contact with him. Tried not to glance down at their joined hands. "Thanks, Jonas."

When she began nibbling on her lips again he figured it was time to release her hand. "You still have my mobile number, right?" he asked.

"Yes."

"Use it to contact me if you have any questions. I'm attending a wedding this weekend in New York, and from there I'm flying out for Vegas." A smile touched his lips. "I plan to have a little fun in Sin City before work begins."

He saw another flash that flitted in her eyes before she had time to hide it. Um, was the mention of his fun time in Vegas causing her worry? Should he take that as a red flag that the forever-after side of her had a tendency to show every once in a while? Hell, he hoped not since that sort of thinking was a waste of time with him.

"Enjoy yourself."

His grin was mischievous. "I intend to."

She tilted her head slightly and the mass of dark curls hid one eye so he couldn't completely figure out what she was thinking. "We'll be in Vegas a few days before flying to Los Angeles," he said while leading her to the door. "That's where we'll board the *Velocity*. And from there our two-week adventure begins."

What he didn't add was how much he was looking forward to that time. He intended to work hard and play even harder. "Any questions, Nikki?"

She shook her head. "No questions. I'll see you in Vegas, ready to work."

Every muscle in his body reacted to the thought of them working closely together. In the conference room. In the bedroom.

Chapter 6

Nikki clutched her hand to her chest as she stared out the taxi's window. For as far as her eyes could see, there were tall elegant hotels, neon signs, glitter and glitz. Sin City. She could just imagine all the transgressions being performed and knew all of it wasn't at the slot machines. She shook her head. What had she expected from a state where prostitution was legal?

"Your first time in Vegas?"

She glanced up at the driver. Truth be told, it might be her last time as well. She was feeling overwhelmed. "Yes, and I doubt I've ever seen anything like it."

She figured there was no decline in the economy here, at least there shouldn't be. The casinos never closed. And just how many Elvis impersonators had she seen since leaving the airport?

"You haven't seen anything yet. Just wait until this

place lights up at night. That's when everything looks spectacular."

She could only imagine. Twice in the past she'd made plans to come to Vegas, but each time those plans had fallen through for some reason or another, leading her to believe there was a bad omen between her and this city.

Nikki didn't want to consider the possibility that her being here now didn't bode well, either. She had gotten a call from Jonas's secretary a few days ago letting her know there had been a change and she was needed in Vegas earlier than originally planned. In addition to rearranging her schedule, she had rushed to do some shopping to make sure she had all the appropriate outfits she would need beside her usual jeans and blouses. She couldn't help wondering what turn of events had made Jonas decide she needed to be here ahead of her scheduled time.

As the cab continued to whisk her along the Vegas Strip, a part of her tried downplaying her excitement in seeing Jonas again. She should really get over it— and him, to boot. Wasn't he the same man who'd kissed her twice already and then told her he planned to leave for Vegas a few days early to have fun—no doubt with other women? Not that she thought those kisses had meant anything to him, mind you. But it was the principle of the thing.

But that's just it, Nikki. Men like Jonas have no principles. When will you finally see that?

She let out a frustrated sigh. It's not that she didn't know it, because she did. It was her heart side—the one still filled with idealistic hopes and dreams—working against her, refusing to accept what her head already knew *but just refused to accept on most good days.*

She looked down at the camera around her neck and was reminded of the real reason she was here. It wasn't about Jonas. It was about her doing a good job and making a name for herself. If she didn't succeed at this project she would have no one to blame but herself.

But still…

And there was that but in there, although she wished otherwise. There was nothing wrong with enjoying herself while she was here, if time allowed. Her brother always said if you work hard then you should reward yourself and play harder. Truthfully, she couldn't recall the last time she'd had some "let your hair down" fun. Maybe it was about time she did.

Nikki settled back against her seat's cushion. She had a feeling that before she left Vegas she was going to have an eye-opener as to just how sinful this city really was.

Gannon Steele stared across the hotel room at his brother. "Now tell me again why Nikki Cartwright is arriving in Vegas earlier than planned?"

Jonas rolled his eyes as he continued to button his shirt. He wasn't surprised the youngest of the Steele brothers was questioning why he'd sent for Nikki to come to Vegas early. Gannon was pouting, disappointed that the two of them wouldn't be hanging together as originally planned. That meant Gannon would have to visit some of the Vegas hot spots on his own, including the Doll House, a gentlemen's club owned by one of Galen's friends, Quinton Hinton.

Gannon, who'd turned thirty a few months ago, was

determined not only to blaze a trail for himself, but also to follow in his older brothers' footsteps by doing the wild and the reckless. Over the years Gannon had heard about their outlandish escapades and exploits, and figured what was good for the goose was also good for the gander.

"I told you already. She needs to get set up, and I need to make sure Fulton knows we're on the job," Jonas replied.

"Yes, but her flying in means you'll be working and really, man, nobody comes to Vegas to work."

"I did, and you knew that when you followed me here, so stop whining."

Gannon frowned. "Hell, I'm not whining."

Jonas rolled his eyes. "Yes, you are, so get over it already or I'll send you back home to Mama."

Jonas chuckled when he saw Gannon's frown. Brother number six hated being reminded he was the baby in the family. Jonas loved his youngest brother, but at times he really wondered about him and hoped to hell he didn't end up being the worst of the lot where women were concerned. Their mother would never forgive them if he did. Gannon was still easily influenced by his older brothers and Eden had accused them more than once of corrupting Gannon's mind.

If only she knew. Gannon might be the youngest and he might be impressionable, but he could hold his own in ways Jonas didn't want to even think about. Back in the day there was no such thing as social media. And now Gannon had taken internet dating to a whole new level. Hell, he had even come up with his own form of speed dating.

"Checking out one of those brothels is on my to-do list today."

Jonas nodded. He wasn't surprised and figured that visiting one of those would probably make Gannon's day…and probably his night as well. He wouldn't complain if it kept Gannon busy for a while and out of his hair. "Sounds like a good plan. And I'll give Quinton a call to let him know you'll be dropping by the Doll House sometime later and to make sure you have a good time."

Gannon's face lit up. "Hey man, that will be great. I appreciate it."

Jonas chuckled. "Hey, that's what brothers are for."

It was only after Gannon left that Jonas took a moment to sit down, unwrap a Tootsie Pop and stick it in his mouth as he reflected on the real reason he had asked Nikki to come to Vegas early. As much as he assumed he would have fun in Sin City, he'd discovered that instead he had spent his time thinking about her, counting the days, the hours—hell, even the minutes—when she was to fly in. And for a man who was usually on top of his game, he hadn't been involved with any woman since the night they kissed. He hadn't a desire to do so. Hell, what was that about?

Instead of heeding these red flags, he took an even deeper plunge by summoning her earlier. At one point it was as if he couldn't get her here fast enough. He was tired of waking up from dreams in which she had a leading role and which had left him hornier and even more frustrated. He could only smile at the depth of his manipulations. He'd seen it as the only way to take care of those pent-up frustrations that had begun taking over his senses. If things went as planned, his photographer would be arriving any minute.

In all honestly, he had lied. There was nothing they needed to do before the launch party, but there was definitely something he needed to do. Bed her. Get her out of his system. And do it sooner than he'd anticipated.

He checked his watch. He would give Nikki time to rest up from her flight and then he would seek her out.

Nikki brushed back a curl from her face as she glanced around the spacious hotel suite. Decorated in the most vibrant colors and prints, it was simply beautiful. She hadn't expected a suite. A standard room in this hotel would have been enough considering the hotel's extravagance. But she had no complaints and liked the fact that Ideas of Steele was being more than generous.

She had a sitting room separate from the bedroom, which had a bed that was bigger than any she'd ever seen. *Leave it to Vegas*, she thought. But what really caught her eye was the flower arrangement on the coffee table. Thinking it was a gift from the hotel, she crossed the room and pulled off the card.

Nikki, welcome to Vegas. We need to have dinner later to go over a few new developments. I'll call you. Jonas

Her brow furrowed. *New developments?* Placing the card on the table she headed toward the bedroom to unpack, certain she would find out soon enough just what those new developments were.

A short while later, after she had unpacked and

taken a shower, she stood looking out the huge floor-to-ceiling window in the sitting room. Already she was anticipating nightfall when she would see the Strip light up. She figured she should have an awesome view from her suite on the thirtieth floor.

She tightened the belt of her bath robe—courtesy of the hotel—and was about to go back into the bedroom when the hotel phone rang. Crossing the room, she picked it up. "Yes?"

"Nikki, this is Jonas."

She drew in a deep breath. Why did he have to sound so darn sexy? And why did the fact that that sexy voice also belonged to a man with a sexy body and a drop-dead gorgeous face have her heart beating like crazy in her chest? She didn't even have to close her eyes to envision the tall, dark and handsome mass of sensual masculinity on her phone. Just once she would love to run her fingers through his wavy hair, nibble at the corners of his lips before sliding her tongue between them.

Feeling overheated and knowing those thoughts were out of line, she cleared her throat. "Jonas, thanks for the flowers. They're beautiful."

"You're welcome and I'm glad you like them. I felt it was the least I could do for having you come out sooner than we discussed. I appreciate your flexibility."

"No problem. You mentioned something about new developments."

"Yes. I'll cover everything over dinner. Is six o'clock okay?"

"Six will be fine. Do you want us to meet in the lobby?"

"No, I thought we could have dinner in my suite."

She paused and immediately the intimate setting flashed right before her eyes and sent feathered sensations down her spine. She forced her heart to stop pounding while she tried to restrain her thoughts. The thought of just the two of them in his hotel room was—in addition to everything else—causing heat to form between her thighs.

"Nikki?"

Girl, get that head of yours out of the gutter. Can't you tell by the sound of his voice he's all about business and nothing else? He's gotten two kisses off you and figures that's enough, so chill. He hasn't been the least bit unprofessional since you and he agreed on your terms. He probably wants to have an early dinner with you so he'll have time for some hot date later tonight.

"Yes, I'm still here," she said, finally responding to her name

"Will dinner in my hotel room at six work for you? If not, I could squeeze some time in for us to go out if you prefer."

Squeeze some time in? Please. Don't do me any favors. "Dinner in your suite will work fine, Jonas. That way I can get out and tour the city later." She stayed on the line long enough to get his room number before hanging up.

She glanced at her watch. She had four hours and figured she might as well take a nap. After she had dinner with Jonas she would take a stroll down Las Vegas Boulevard. It was bound to be a long night and she wanted to be well-rested.

Jonas paced his hotel room while sucking on a Tootsie Pop. He glanced at his watch again. He had another fifteen minutes and he didn't know any woman who would arrive early to anything, so why was he tripping?

Oh, he had an easy answer for that one. He wanted Nikki. Now if the evening would only go according to his plans. They would enjoy dinner and then enjoy each other—all night long. He was no longer worried about the outcome of any type of vulnerability on his part. Since seeing her in Phoenix he had convinced himself he was dedicated to bachelorhood, and there was no woman alive who could make him think differently, no matter how deep his desire for her went.

Then what was with the flowers, Steele?

"So okay, I sent them," he muttered under his breath to the imaginary mocking voice he heard in his head. He had played on her romantic side in sending those flowers but didn't feel the slightest bit of regret doing so. When it came to women the only time he played fair was when she belonged to someone else.

So as far as he was concerned, the lines were free and clear with Nikki. A few months ago, without giving anything away, he'd gotten Galen into a conversation about her, figuring Galen and Brittany probably told each other everything. He'd been right.

Although Galen didn't know a whole hell of a lot, he was positive Nikki wasn't seriously involved with anyone. Jonas had figured that much out on his own after they'd kissed that first time. And the second time, he hated to admit he hadn't really thought about whether she'd gotten involved since then or not. Her dating status had been the last thing on his mind that night when he'd all but begged her for that kiss.

He paused in his pacing to toss the finished pop in

the trash. And speaking of that kiss—hell, not just one but both—he couldn't get it out of his mind. It didn't take much to remember the feel of her enticing curves plastered against him while he took her lips with a hunger that he could remember even to this day, at that very moment. His gut clenched and his heart began beating like crazy in his chest. There had to be a reason he wanted her so badly, and why even now his heart was racing while he waited for her arrival.

He was about to start pacing again when he heard the knock on his hotel room door. He checked his watch and saw Nikki was seven minutes early. His mother, who was the epitome of punctuality, was seldom early. She would use every single minute to make sure she was well together, as she would say.

Inhaling deeply he moved toward the door, feeling the way his heart was kicking with each step he took. He tried to prepare himself, figuring he was making a big deal out of nothing. Nikki probably wasn't wearing makeup—not that she needed any. More than likely she was wearing jeans—although he thought she looked good in them, too. And chances were she had her camera around her neck since he'd only seen her without it a few times.

He opened the door and swallowed deeply as his gaze ran all over her. She was wearing makeup, a skirt that showed off her beautiful legs, and instead of a camera, she had a beaded necklace around her neck.

She looked simply gorgeous.

Chapter 7

"**Y**ou did remember we had a meeting, didn't you?" Nikki asked Jonas when he stood there and stared as if he hadn't been expecting her. He was wearing dark dress slacks and a crisp white shirt, as if he was about to go out for the evening.

"Of course. What makes you think otherwise?" he asked, stepping aside for her to enter.

"You're all dressed up."

His gaze roamed her up and down, then returned to her face. "So are you."

No, she wasn't really, she thought, glancing down at herself. Little did he know the few times she did get dressed up, she cleaned up pretty well. "I'm checking out the Strip after our dinner meeting."

He closed the door and leaned back against it. "You do that a lot, don't you?"

She lifted a brow. "Do what?"

"Go out alone. Why? I'm sure getting dates isn't an issue for you."

They'd had this conversation before so why was he bringing it back up again, she wondered. Evidently he'd forgotten their discussion. "I like male company, don't get me wrong, but once in a while I like just doing things solo. I don't have to impress anyone or—"

"Play the kind of games you think men like me are so good at playing," he broke in to say.

So he had remembered. "Um, yes, something like that." Not wanting to get into a debate with him about the tactics he used with women and just what she thought of them, she glanced around. "I thought my room was nice—thanks, by the way—but this one is even nicer. But that's expected since you're *the man*."

"Am I?"

She grinned. "Yes, my bank account will definitely proclaim such in six weeks."

He threw his head back and laughed. The sound was both surprising and heartwarming, sending hot shivers escalating up her body. In addition to the busy zipper on his pants, it seemed Jonas knew how to let down his hair and he had enough locks on his head to do it. "Glad to know I'm doing my part to stimulate the economy," he said when he finally stopped laughing.

She fought back the urge to tell him that he was doing his part in stimulating other things as well. Like that inner part of her that was feeling arousing sensations just from listening to his voice. And her eyes were appreciating the sight of him as well. His slacks covered muscled thighs, long legs and a trimmed waist, and his shirt couldn't conceal well-defined abs and broad shoulders.

She drew in a deep breath and then released it slowly. "Your note said something about a new development, which is why you wanted me in Vegas earlier than planned."

"Yes, we need to talk about that. Dinner will be here any minute."

She followed him to the sitting room, and when he gestured to the sofa, she sat down. Then she watched him ease his body into the chair across from her. He picked up a folder from the coffee table. It was then she noted the bag of Tootsie Pops. Evidently he liked the things.

"It's nothing major, just a change in how we're presenting *Velocity* this weekend," he said. "We're still providing the brochures as planned, but I've come up with something I think will add dimension to our presentation."

"What?"

"The use of JumboTrons, strategically located at different places in the ballroom, running simultaneously to give attendees an idea of what to expect when they board the *Velocity*."

She immediately envisioned such a thing in her head and could see it working to their benefit. "But will we have time to work on the video?"

"Yes, my videographer, Rick Harris, is in Los Angeles now, putting together everything on his end. It'll arrive on Friday. I'd like you and Rick to make sure everything is ready by Saturday night's launch party."

He paused a moment and then asked, "What do you think of that idea?"

"I think it's fantastic. Rick and I have worked together before on other projects and he's good."

Adding those JumboTrons really wasn't a big deal and wouldn't account for her having to drop everything and fly in to Las Vegas three days earlier than planned. There had to be more "new developments" they had yet to discuss. She tilted her head to the side and gazed over at him. He had unwrapped one of those Tootsie Pops and placed it in his mouth.

The muscles between her legs clenched at the way Jonas was sucking on the lollipop. You could tell he was getting sheer enjoyment out of doing so. And there was something about how the pop was easing in and out of his mouth, being worked by his tongue, leaving a sweet glaze all over his lips.

He caught her staring and held her gaze. "Would you like one?"

She swallowed. "No, thank you. Is there anything else to discuss?"

He shook his head and put the unfinished pop aside. "No, that's about it."

"You seem to like those," she said, motioning to the bag of Tootsie Pops on the table in front of him.

Jonas smiled. "Yes, they have definitely grown on me. They started out as a supportive measure from my brothers when I quit smoking some years back. They figured the pops would replace the cigarette. Basically they have."

He checked his watch. "Dinner should be here soon."

Nikki nodded. If the JumboTrons were the only new development then her coming to Vegas early made no sense, especially when Rick wouldn't be arriving until

Friday. That meant she had two whole days to do practically nothing.

She was about to point that out to Jonas when there was a knock on the door. He stood. "I'll get that. I think that's our dinner."

Jonas took a deep, steadying breath while watching Nikki leave to go to the powder room to wash her hands. He had seen the look in her eyes when she'd asked if there were any other new developments. She was an intelligent woman and was probably wondering why he'd sent for her three days before she was actually needed. Adding those JumboTrons was no big deal. She knew it as well as he did.

"Will there be anything else, sir?"

He glanced over at the waiter who had wheeled in the table set for two. "No, that will be all," he said, signing the invoice.

He was closing the door behind the man when Nikki returned. "Whatever it is smells good," she said.

Not as good as you smell and look, sweetheart, he thought, turning around and scanning her up and down. He really liked that outfit on her, admired the way the material clung to her hips and her rounded bottom and accentuated her curves. And then there were the shoes she was wearing. The sling backs did some serious business to her shapely legs.

He then recalled what she'd said earlier about walking the Strip after their dinner. Not by a long shot. Little did she know he had plans for her after they ate. Um, he could easily switch the timing of those plans to before dinner without much hassle. The food would keep and they would definitely have worked up an appetite for it later.

"I took the liberty of selecting something off the menu. I hope you don't mind. I understand you're a seafood lover and shrimp is your favorite."

"Yes, that's right. How did you know?

A smile touched his lips. "That's my secret."

He decided not to tell her he made it his business to know about any woman in whom he was interested. However, he would admit he had taken more interest in finding out things about her than any other woman before.

Before she could ask him to divulge those secrets, he said, "Now it's my turn to wash my hands. I'll be back in a minute."

Nikki watched Jonas walk away. All the Steele men had a sexy walk—even the old man—but she thought Jonas's was the sexiest. And the way his shoulders moved while the thick wavy hair flowed around his shoulders was eye-catching. She had never thought she would be attracted to a man who had more hair on his head than she did, but Jonas had proved her wrong.

He had also proved her wrong about something else as well—that she couldn't want him any more than she had before. And that surprised her, especially after that pep talk she'd given herself on the plane and most recently the one she'd had before stepping onto the elevator that had brought her to his penthouse suite. The look on his face when he had opened the door had reminded her of that night at Mavericks, when he had stared at her that same way.

She must be imagining things, especially since

they'd reached an agreement. And they had reached an agreement, hadn't they? He would be keeping his hands to himself. No more kisses, no more intense attractions or talk of an affair, right? Then why did she feel he was stripping her naked with his gaze each and every time he looked at her? And why was she stripping him naked with hers? Her mind was envisioning what he was packing underneath his slacks and shirt. And why did she want to see it for herself just for the hell of it?

She drew in a deep breath, not believing the way her thoughts were going tonight. But then why was she so surprised? Brittany had warned her about the battle—her head versus her heart. Her head wanted Jonas, the man, with all his flaws. Even if it was just to say she'd gotten a taste of the forbidden and was able to enjoy it and move on.

But her heart was singing another song—one of Love and Happiness—and intended to give Al Green a run for his money. Her heart didn't want her to waste her time on a man like Jonas, a man who could take that same heart, if given the chance, and break it. A man who would get what he wanted and then walk away without looking back.

Her heart wanted more. It felt it deserved more, and although there was no sign of a Mr. Right out there for her just yet, her heart didn't want her to give up too soon.

"Ready?"

She blinked upon realizing Jonas had returned. When she felt intense heat stir the lower part of her belly, she tore her gaze away from his, thinking of all the things she could be ready for. Those mesmerizing green eyes had an unnerving effect and were messing with her mind. They were hypnotic, spellbinding and luring her not to think straight.

"So are you going to stand over there, or will you join me over here, Nikki?"

The impact of his question had her staring at him. They were still talking about sharing dinner, weren't they? Then why were emotions she always downplayed around him suddenly forcing their way to the forefront? Confusing her mind? Suffusing her with heated warmth at the juncture of her thighs?

Nikki slowly crossed the room to where he stood beside the table. She had thought he would pull out the chair for her, and when he just stood there and stared at her, she felt her heart almost racing out of control. He moved and stepped closer, not just to crowd her space but to get all into it and take command. Hot shivers flowed through her.

And why was he wearing the scent of a man, a sensual aroma that was inebriating her senses? Her heart was being pushed to the background, where only her head was speaking, and what it was saying wasn't good. Definitely not smart.

Get real, girl! You claim you want to make the transition from a woman who believes in fantasies to a woman who realizes the real fantasies are the ones you make for yourself. There are no knights in shining armor, just rogues in aluminum foil. At least you know where this one stands and there won't be any expectations on your part. Cross over to the desire side by doing a smash and grab. Smash what has proved to be idealistic baloney once and for all, and grab what could be an experience of a lifetime.

She swallowed, hearing all the things her head was saying, but still, when he took a step even closer, her heart fought back and she couldn't stop the words. "If I remember correctly, things were going to be strictly business between us, Jonas."

A smile curved his lips. "Um, that's not how I remember things."

She narrowed her gaze. "And just what do you remember?" His scent was driving her crazy, breaking down her defenses even more.

He inched closer, and she felt him, his aroused body part pressed against her middle. Instead of recoiling from it, she felt fire rush through her veins and race up her spine. That same head that was trying to fill her mind with naughty thoughts began spinning. It was kicking out her common sense and replacing it with a whole lot of nonsense. Making her wonder such things as how it would feel to slide her fingertips along that aroused member, cup him in her hand, taste him in her mouth and—

"I distinctively recall a promise to give you what you wanted," he said, interrupting her thoughts and lowering his head down to breathe the words across her lips. "And I intend to push you over the edge, Nikki Cartwright, and make sure you want me."

And when he captured his mouth with hers, she knew she didn't stand a chance because she was a goner the minute he slid his tongue inside her mouth.

Chapter 8

Jonas had developed a taste for Nikki from their first kiss. That had to be the reason he was taking her mouth with an urgency that was stirring all kinds of emotions within him. It didn't matter that her mouth felt like pure satin beneath his or that her lips were a perfect fit. The only thing that mattered was the way they were connecting so intimately to his as he sank deeper and deeper into the warmth of her mouth.

Tangling with a woman's tongue had never driven him to the point where lust ruled his senses. The fire that had built up inside of him was blazing out of control, and that was the one thing he never lost with a woman. Control. And he knew at that moment there was no way he could regain it.

There was nothing he could do to stop the flow of adrenaline that was rushing through his body, drowning his pores and playing hell with his molecules. And his erection was throbbing fiercely, sending a sensual warning that if he didn't pull back now, there would be no pulling back later.

If he didn't ease his shaft inside of her, penetrate her deep while she moaned, thrust in and out and make her cream all over him, he would lose his mind. He wanted to make love to her so badly he could hardly stand it, and the thought of doing so sent shivers through him.

What he felt wasn't just desire, it was hard-core desire. And he refused to waste his time trying to figure out why. He'd done so for eighteen months and still didn't have a clue.

He continued to kiss her as if her tongue had been created just for him to enjoy. And he could tell she was enjoying it too from the way her fingertips were digging into his shoulders. Her moans sounded so starkly sexual they were tapping into his emotions, both physical and mental, and he knew of no way to stop them.

The need to breathe made him break off the kiss, and he stared up at her while every muscle in his body tightened in yearning. "I suggest that you tell me to stop now, Nikki, because if you don't, I plan to mate with you all over this place."

He paused a moment and then decided to add, "And just so you'll know, when I finish with you, the last thing you'll have energy for is a walk down Vegas Boulevard."

He'd been so brutally honest, but he felt that she deserved to know what she was up against. He had a fierce sexual appetite, and with her it would take a long time to be appeased. There was something about her that was tempting everything male inside of him. And there could only be one possible outcome.

Jonas watched the rise and fall of her breasts as she tried getting her breathing under control. He saw by the V-neckline of her shirt that she was wearing a pink bra. He couldn't help wondering if her panties were pink as well. That curiosity had him shifting his gaze back to her eyes and what he saw in them almost made it difficult to breathe.

Although she might never admit it to him or to herself, she wanted him as much as he wanted her. There was no if, and, or but about it. The eyes looking back at him were full of fire. As much fire as he felt thrumming through his loins right now. And at that moment, he planned on making good on what he'd told her. He intended to push her over the edge. Right onto her back with him on top.

He leaned in and slanted his mouth over hers again. His hands moved from her waist, slid down to cup her bottom and squeezed it gently before bringing it closer to the fit of him. Without releasing his hold on her mouth, he shifted to bring his hard erection closer to the juncture of her thighs, eliciting an automated sigh from deep within her throat. He liked the sound.

And he especially liked how she arched her back, bringing the firm tips of her breasts into his chest like heated darts, and sending shock waves of pleasure riveting through him. He felt hot inside and was burning in places that had never burned before. He moved closer, needing her curvaceous body even closer to his.

This time she was the one who pulled back from the kiss. But before she could draw in a quick breath he was unbuttoning her shirt as swiftly as his fingers could move to do so, trying like hell not to rip any in his haste. She hadn't told him to stop so he planned to make good on his threat. There was no way he could walk away from this, from her, even with all those red warning signs flashing him all in the face.

Without wasting time he went to the front clasp of her sexy, pink lace bra and unhooked it, freeing the most luscious-looking breasts he'd ever seen and soliciting a growl that erupted from deep in his throat.

His hands went still as he lifted his gaze from her breasts to her eyes. It seemed as if time stood still as their gazes connected, held, fused in a way that just wasn't rational. But at that moment, he couldn't break eye contact even if he wanted to.

Silence surrounded them and the air seemed electrified, charged, pricked with an element so sensual, the components were unknown to mankind. There was this unexplained and undefined chemistry between them. They'd gotten primed, ready, saturated in lust, and there was no turning back. No letting mere kisses suffice any longer. No more denying what they both truly wanted, although they should be fighting it. That was no longer an option. They wanted the real deal and wouldn't waste any more time getting it.

Nikki hadn't expected this, an odd surge of passion that splintered everything within her—every logical thought, every ounce of common sense. Instead she was feeling a burst of freedom that she'd never felt before and it was rejuvenating her all through her bones. She wanted this. She wanted him. She no longer cared that her head was winning the battle and her heart was losing this round. The main thing was that there was another war going on inside of her and it had nothing to do with logic, and everything to do with need.

And what she needed at that moment was to make love with Jonas. No matter how many regrets she might have in the morning, she needed him to touch her, make love to her all over the place just like he'd threatened to do. So she stood there and watched him. Waited with bated breath.

Now she understood the reputation he had attained. In the confines of the sauna rooms, ladies' clubs and sorority meetings, the feminine whispers discreetly echoed around town that when it came to lovemaking, bad-boy Jonas Steele had a finesse that could be patented. She'd never doubted it then, and she was seeing it in action firsthand now.

He slowly lowered his gaze to travel down her body, and she felt the heat of his green orbs on her breasts. Her hardened nipples seemed to tighten even more before his eyes. She felt it and knew he had to be seeing it.

"I need to suck on them, Nikki. I need to let my tongue wrap around them. I need to lick them."

His words broke the silence and suddenly the air oozed with need. A need that was unbearable and fueled by a lusty craving. Her gaze followed the masculine hands that reached up to push both her shirt and bra from her shoulders, bearing the upper part of her breasts to him. From the look in his eyes, he more than liked what he saw.

Before he could make a move she decided to play the Jonas Steele game by reaching out and all but snatching the shirt off his body, ripping buttons in the process and ignoring the fact that replacing the shirt would cost a pretty penny. At the moment she didn't care.

Nikki saw the tattoo on his stomach, a huge, raging bull. It was appropriate since he had the stamina of one. She was tempted to lick his stomach to soothe as well as tame such a fierce-looking animal. Then she would move lower and let her tongue wrap around him like he planned to do her.

Do her.

The thought of him doing her made the juncture of her thighs cream. And she felt the thickening moisture drench her panties. She tightened her legs together as sensations flared in her womanly core.

If he was surprised by the way she'd torn the shirt from his body he didn't show it. It seemed he was just as pushed over the edge as she was. And like her, he had inwardly conceded there was no turning back. No more discussions. From here on out there would only be action.

Her head had taken over big-time, filling her mind with thoughts of doing him, and acting out the part of the vixen she'd bragged to Brittany she was but had never truly been. She suddenly wanted to see if she could handle the role.

"You've done it now, sweetheart."

His words, laced with hot caution, spoken in that deep baritone of his, didn't scare her any. If anything they sent shivers of anticipation racing through her body at the same time they kicked her courage and confidence levels up a notch.

Before Nikki could dwell on anything else, Jonas reached out and pulled her to him in a way that had them tumbling to the carpeted floor, though he made sure his body cushioned her fall. Trying to regain the breath that had been snatched right from her lungs, she glanced down at him at the same moment she realized she was sprawled on top of him, her limbs entwined with his. She was shirtless and her skirt was hiked high enough she could feel air hitting her almost bare bottom. She felt her womanly core react to the hard erection pressing against it.

"Kiss me," he rasped before pulling her mouth down to his and immediately sliding his tongue between her lips. Sexual energy between them was surging out of control and she felt it in the sensual mating of their mouths.

Her senses were overwhelmed with the scent and feel of him at almost every angle. Their bodies writhed against each other, as if they couldn't get close enough, and his hands lifted her skirt even higher to palm her backside. His fingers traced a sensuous path along the crevice as if to verify she was actually wearing a thong. And then he released her mouth to latch on to a nipple, sucking it between his lips the way she'd seen him do that Tootsie Pop earlier.

Nikki moaned deep in her throat and felt her inner muscles contract with the sucking motion of his mouth on her breasts. He wasn't just trying to taste her, he was consuming her and propelling her body into quivers that rammed all through her. She had made love before, but never like this and never with this intensity or greed. And what frightened her even more was knowing there was pleasure still yet to be fulfilled. Areas yet to be discovered.

She moaned again when his mouth moved to her other breast, sucked another nipple between his teeth as if his very life depended on it. And now his hands were no longer torturing her bottom but had traveled to the front, eased between their connected bodies, slid underneath the waistband of her thong to begin toying in her now drenched feminine folds, stirring up the air with her scent.

He suddenly released her breast and gave her only a second to see the smile that curved his lips before he flipped her on her back so she was staring up at him. Before she could blink he had removed the shoes from her feet, and proceeded to jerk her thong and skirt down her hips and toss them aside, leaving her completely bare. Naked as the day she was born.

She held her breath as his gaze roamed up and down her body from head to toe, and she actually felt the hot path his gaze took and knew what areas it concentrated on before moving on to another. Then he was lifting her legs, hoisting them high up on his shoulders and bringing his face up close and personal to her bikini-cut feminine mound.

He leaned forward and she felt intense heat from his nostrils when he took his nose and pressed it against her, rubbed it up and down in her as if to inhale her scent as deep into his nasal cavity as he could. And then his nose was replaced with the tip of his tongue that jabbed through her folds, straight for her clit.

His mouth latched on to her, and then it was on. Every single rumor she'd heard whispered about him and his deadly steady, lickity-split, seemingly mile-long tongue was true. The man definitely knew how to give pleasure while he enjoyed the ultimate feast. Somehow he seemed to close his mouth in a way that made his jaws lock on her as his tongue greedily devoured her like it was a treat he'd developed a sweet tooth for, a craving he couldn't get enough of.

Never had she been sensually mauled this way before. Never had any man used his tongue to pleasure her to this degree. His tongue went deep, stroked hard, and she couldn't stop the moans as tension built within her, making her already electrified senses reel.

"Jonas!"

She screamed his name when her body fragmented into tiny pieces with the most intense climax she'd ever experienced. Instead of letting her go, he slid his hands beneath her, lifting her hips, pressing her more firmly to his mouth while his greedy tongue possessed her mega-stimulated mound. The sensations surging through her were over the top, off the charts, mind-boggling and earth-shatteringly explosive.

And before her heart rate could slow down, he quickly shifted positions and pulled her up in front of him, on her knees with her back to him. She heard the sound of him tearing off the rest of his clothes and ripping into a condom packet with his teeth.

Before she could recover from the orgasm that still had her mind reeling, her teeth chattering, he grabbed hold of her hips, spread her thighs and proceeded to slide his hard shaft into her from behind.

She continued to shudder as he began riding her, locking his hips to hers with every hard thrust. The sound of flesh beating against flesh as his skin slapped hard against her, his testicles hitting her butt cheeks, made her senses start reeling all over again. He glided his hands under them and cupped her breasts as he rode her. Each stroke into her body was long, sure and done with a purpose and not a wasted effort.

And when she threw her head back and tilted her hips at an angle to give deeper penetration, Nikki heard

Jonas's deep groan before he frantically bucked against her body while using his hands to keep the lower part of her locked tight against him.

"Nikki!"

At that moment she didn't want to think of how many other names he'd screamed or that she would be added to the list. Another notch on his infamous bedpost. What mattered most at that moment was that they were in sync, connected with his engorged sex planted deep within her womanly core while her inner muscles clenched, relaxed and then clenched mercilessly again, draining him like he was draining her. He was once again showing her just how hot and explosive lovemaking could be, and she felt deep satisfaction all through her bones.

She came again as fire consumed her, raged out of control and compelled her to cry out his name once more as she enjoyed every last moment of the experience. And before she could fully recover, she felt him pulling her up off the floor and gathering her into his arms.

"Now I'll feed you and then we'll do this all over again in my bed."

And she knew at that moment he would make good on his warning that before he was finished with her they would do it all over his suite.

Chapter 9

The ringing of the hotel room's phone stirred Jonas from a deep and peaceful sleep. He slowly opened his eyes and squinted against the bright sunlight shining in through the window. It took a split second to recall where he was and why his body felt so achy. He couldn't stop the smile that touched his lips when the memories of the night before came flooding through his hazed mind.

He glanced at the spot beside him and saw it was empty. Except for the ringing of the phone there wasn't another sound. He didn't need to be told he was alone and his bedmate of the night before had vanished. Pulling up in bed, he reached out to answer the phone. "Yes?"

"Hell, I was about to hang up. What took you so long to answer? I tried calling your cell phone all night. Where the hell were you?"

Jonas rubbed his hand down his face, frowning at all the questions Gannon was firing at him. "The reason it took me so long to answer the phone was because I was asleep," he growled.

"And the reason you couldn't get me last night was because I was busy." That was all his brother needed to know. There was no way he would admit that he'd been trying to screw Nikki's brains out. Which made him wonder how she had gotten out of the hotel room. After the intensity of their lovemaking, he was surprised she could still walk.

"Well, since you're up you can join me for breakfast. I can't wait to tell you about all that went on at the Doll House."

Jonas rolled his eyes. Gannon might be bursting at the seams, but personally, he could wait. Besides, he was very familiar with the gentlemen's club so nothing Gannon told him would come as a surprise. "I'm not up yet, Gan, so do breakfast without me. I need at least another three hours of sleep."

"Uh-oh. That means you scored last night. I have a feeling you didn't sleep in your bed alone and probably aren't alone now."

Jonas had no intention of appeasing Gannon's curiosity about his sexual activities, especially when they involved Nikki. "Goodbye, Gannon. I should be well-rested by lunchtime."

"I'm visiting that brothel today."

Jonas shook his head. "Make sure you have plenty of condoms."

"Dammit, Jonas, I'm not a kid. I know how to handle my business, thank you very much. Just make sure you're handling yours."

Jonas blinked when the sound of Gannon's phone clicked loudly in his ear. He drew in a deep breath. Okay, the kid was thirty now, but old habits were hard to break. The five of them were so used to looking out for their baby brother they sometimes forgot he was now a man. And Jonas had to constantly remind himself that he was only two years older than Gannon. Two years but with a hell of a lot more experience.

He glanced around the room. One thing was for certain: Gannon was right, he needed to take care of his own business. And the first thing that topped the list was Nikki. The first order of business was to find out why he'd awakened alone in bed this morning. He was usually the one to decide at what point a woman left his bed and couldn't recall when it was ever the other way around.

But then he couldn't ever recall having sex with any woman with the intensity of last night's session. Nikki had drained him dry. He hadn't stood a chance against the contractions of her inner muscles. He had come more times than he could remember and had been putty in her hands. But then, she'd also been putty in his. He couldn't recall the last time he'd enjoyed getting between a pair of spread legs so much. And they hadn't been just any woman's legs. They had been Nikki's.

And then there had been his obsession with tasting her. He had gone down on her more times in a single night than he'd done all year. It seemed that once he'd tasted her, he hadn't been able to get enough. It was as if her clit had been created just for his mouth. At least his tongue had evidently thought so. Even now he was convinced the taste of her had lingered, and a part of him was glad that he could taste her again. He licked his lips and found her there. His curly-headed, jeans-wearing, tasty-as-hell fantasy girl.

He closed his eyes, not wanting to think of any female as being his fantasy girl. He hoped like hell that last night had effectively cleansed his desire for her from his system and that he wouldn't get hard each and every time he thought about her.

He frowned. If she was out of his system then why were shivers racing through him at the thought of seeing her and making love to her again? And why couldn't the memories go away? The memories of him on top of her. Her on top of him. Their bodies mating, moving together in an urgency that took his breath away just thinking about it. The feel of being inside of her, and how her inner muscles would clench him tight, while he took her with a hunger that bordered on desperation and greed.

He shook his head, trying to free himself of the memories and saw that he couldn't. The vision of her naked body, the intense look on her face when she came and the sound of her letting loose in pleasure were things he couldn't forget, so there was no use trying.

But he knew he eventually would forget when he moved on to another woman. He frowned at the thought that he didn't want another woman right now. He liked her well enough and there was no reason to move on. Surely one more night with her wouldn't hurt anything. A powerful force of pleasure rushed through him at the thought.

He would grab a few more hours of sleep and then he would get up, get dressed and get laid.

* * *

As the sunlight slashed its way through the curtains, Nikki lay in bed and stared up at the ceiling. Each time she moved she felt aches from muscles she hadn't used in years. But thanks to Jonas, she had certainly used them last night.

Granted she'd only made love but twice in her entire life—once in college and the other when she'd thought she'd met the man of her dreams four years ago, only to find out he'd shown interest just to make his old girlfriend jealous. She'd thought both times were okay, decent at best. However, what she'd shared with Jonas last night went beyond decent. In fact, there was nothing decent about any of it. They'd gotten downright corrupt. Never in her wildest dream had she expected to share something that naughty with any man. Did couples actually go that many rounds, try out all those positions even on a good night? She'd never experienced anything so amazing, so hot and erotic. And so spine-tingling sensational. Her dreams and fantasies hadn't come close to the real thing.

She remembered how she had checked out his body, studied all his tattoos. She had liked the fierce-looking bull on his stomach, but her favorite had been the Libra sign on his side.

She pulled in a deep breath thinking he had certainly given her fair warning. Nothing could have been closer to the truth. She wondered if other men had that much energy and enjoyed sex that much. And she knew that's what it had been, nothing but sex. He hadn't made love to her. She had made up her mind to stop equating sex with love.

So where did that leave her?

She knew the answer to that one. It left her right where she had lied about being for the past two years. She could remember the day she had looked herself in a mirror and decided to give up on marriage and babies and instead join the ranks of the single ladies. There was no man out there to put a ring on it so she'd decided to live her life, have fun and not have any regrets.

She closed her eyes to fight off the regrets. She really shouldn't have any. Any other woman would be smiling this morning from ear to ear. But then, any other woman probably would not have sneaked out of Jonas Steele's bed and fled to her own hotel room, where she'd slid into bed and eased her overly sore body beneath the covers.

Now it was morning and she was awake, her body still sore, and her heart fighting a losing battle against the memories stored in her head. And they were memories that made her blush just thinking about them.

After having sex that first time—on the floor of all places—Jonas had planted her naked body into the chair to eat dinner. And then he proceeded to sit across from her—naked as well—while they ate. He had carried on a conversation with her as if it was the most natural thing to share dinner with a woman in the nude.

Probably a natural thing for him, but it had definitely been odd for her. At least it had been at first. That was before dessert time when he had crawled under the table to where she sat, told her to spread her legs and then used his tongue on her like she was an ice cream cone, slowly licking her before plunging in deep with long, penetrating kisses. She had lifted the tablecloth to look down, observing the way his mouth was paying very special attention to that part of her, watching how he would flick his tongue left to right, right to left and then to the center before gently scraping against her clit with his teeth. Moments later, she couldn't help but lean back in her chair and stretch out her legs to spread them farther apart while he made her moan and groan. Never had she experienced anything so scandalous.

Nikki closed her eyes and drew in his scent, which wasn't hard to do since he'd left an imprint on every inch of her. She couldn't stay in bed all day. Besides, she knew from her workout classes at the gym that the best way to ease soreness out your body was to get a move on.

She glanced out the window. It was daytime now, but last night she had seen the brightly lit Strip from Jonas's hotel room. She had stood at his window. Well... actually, she had been leaning toward his window while he'd gotten her from behind.

Knowing if she continued to lie there she would eventually drown in all those tantalizing memories, she moaned at her sore body as she eased out of bed.

She would take a shower, get dressed and do what she had planned to do last night but had not gotten around to doing. She would walk the Strip.

"Just who do you keep trying to call, Jonas?"

"None of your business." Jonas frowned, putting his cell phone back in his pocket as he glanced across the table at his brother.

They were sitting downstairs in one of the hotel's restaurants waiting on the waitress to bring their food. He had slept five hours instead of the three, and would have slept longer if Gannon hadn't called, waking him up again.

Gannon smiled. "Yeah, right. You found another woman and you're trying to make a hit, aren't you?"

Jonas stared at his brother as he took a sip of his lemonade. Gannon would probably fall out of his chair if Jonas admitted he was trying to make a hit on the same woman from last night. He seldom did repeats and most people knew it. It wasn't in his makeup to spend time doing just one woman. Not when there were so many of them out there to do.

Instead of answering Gannon, he asked, "You've spent most of the time talking about the naughty happenings over at the Doll House. I noticed you didn't have much to say about your visit to the brothel."

"I haven't gone there yet. I got sidetracked with Nikki."

Jonas swung his head around so fast it was a wonder his neck hadn't snapped. He stared over at Gannon. "Nikki?" He was grateful Gannon had pulled out his iPhone to check messages, otherwise there was no way he would have missed what Jonas knew had to be an intense look on his face.

"Yes, Nikki," Gannon said, studying his phone. "You know, Brittany's best friend. Your photographer who flew in a couple days early because you needed her to start work." Gannon glanced up. "Well, I hate to tell you but she wasn't working today."

Jonas arched his brow, forcing his features to an expressionless state when he asked, "What was she doing?"

"Shopping. Walking the Strip. Having lunch. Shopping some more."

Jonas tilted his head to the side and stared at his brother. "And how do you know this?"

Gannon shrugged as he placed his phone back in his pocket. "I ran into her on the Strip and we spent some time together. I helped her carry her bags and later we had lunch together at The Glades."

Jonas frowned so hard he was certain anger lines appeared in his face. "You had lunch with Nikki?"

"Yes, and if you're getting mad because I woke you up to have lunch again, it was because I was still hungry. You aren't the only one who might have worked up an appetite last night. I met this woman at the Doll House and she was something else."

Jonas glared. Little did Gannon know that his anger had nothing to do with the fact that Gannon was making a pig out of himself by eating two lunches. His anger solely rested on the fact that he'd been trying to reach Nikki and hadn't been able to do so. Was she deliberately avoiding his calls?

"Did Nikki say what she would be doing after lunch?"

Gannon rolled his eyes. "Jesus, Jonas, give the woman a break. Do you really expect her to be on the time clock 24/7? When we parted she was on her way to do more shopping."

He simply stared at his brother knowing Gannon didn't have a clue as to his real interest in Nikki and that was a good thing. He picked up his water, took a sip and tried to ask as inconspicuously as possible, "So, how was she?"

"Who?"

Jonas let out a frustrated breath. "Nikki."

"Oh." Gannon then gave him a rakish smile. "She

looked good as usual. Those tight jeans hug that rounded backside of hers like nobody's business."

Jonas frowned, not liking the fact that Gannon had been ogling Nikki's backside.

"Oops. I better not let Mercury hear me say that.'"

Jonas lifted a brow. "Say what?"

"Anything about Nikki's body." Gannon chuckled. "He told me at Eli's wedding that she was off-limits, so I can only assume our brother has the hots for her. He's probably already scored."

At that moment the waitress returned with their food and Jonas wondered if Gannon noticed the steam coming from his ears.

Jonas felt his jaw tighten as he stepped off the elevator onto the thirtieth floor. He hadn't been able to end lunch with Gannon quickly enough. The good thing was that Gannon had been in too much of a hurry to get over to that brothel to notice Jonas's bad mood. Or too busy helping himself to the steak Jonas had ordered but had been too pissed to eat.

He had tried calling Mercury, but according to his brother's secretary, he was in a meeting. But Jonas wanted answers and if he couldn't get them from Mercury, he would get them from Nikki. If she thought she was playing him and his brother against each other she was sorely mistaken. If she was involved with Mercury then why in the hell had she slept with him last night? The one thing the Steele brothers didn't do was share women.

He knocked on her hotel room door. Hard. Inwardly he told himself to calm down, but he was too angry to do so. If he had known something was going on be-

tween her and Mercury he would not have touched her.
Dammit. Now he couldn't help but wonder when had
she'd become involved with his brother. Had it been
before or after their kiss eighteen months ago?

The door opened and he saw the surprised look on
her face. "Jonas? Is anything wrong?"

He leaned in the doorway, drew in a deep breath and
stared at her without saying anything for a moment.
Then he silently asked himself why he was there. He
had never run behind a woman, gotten upset when he
couldn't reach one after a night of sex. It'd always been
out of sight and out of mind for him. He'd found it so
easy to move on to the next woman.

So why had he gotten so pissed at the thought he
hadn't been able to reach her today? And why was the
thought of Mercury having dibs on her eating away at
his gut? He shouldn't even be here without first talking to Mercury to find out what was going on. But he
couldn't wait. He had to see her. He had to know the
truth.

"Jonas?"

"What?"

"I asked if anything is wrong."

The urge to reach out and pull her into his arms
and kiss her was overpowering. He straightened and
tightened his hands into fists at his side. He needed to
know if she was involved with his brother. "Yes, something is wrong."

Instead of asking him what, she took a step back to
let him into her hotel room.

Chapter 10

Nikki stared across the room at Jonas. He'd said something was wrong, which meant there could be only one logical reason for him to seek her out. Swallowing deeply, she asked, "Did Fulton not like the idea about using the JumboTrons?"

He stared at her for a second, and then instead of answering he rubbed his hand down his face. He then stared at her again and it appeared his green eyes had darkened in anger. "Well, is that it, Jonas?"

He shook his head. "Do you think I'm here to talk about JumboTrons, or that I'm here to discuss business period?"

She really didn't know how to respond to his question, or what answer he was looking for. So she asked a question of her own. "What other reason would you be here?"

He stared at her for a moment. "I slept with you last night," he all but growled.

She wondered what that had to do with anything. He was a Steele. He slept with women all the time. "And?"

"And you were gone this morning and I haven't been able to reach you all day."

She lifted a brow. He had tried reaching her? Why? "My phone battery was dead. I had it on the charger all day. So what's wrong? Why were you trying to reach me?"

He stared at her for a moment and then shrugged. "Doesn't matter now. I need to ask you something."

"Okay. What?"

"Why didn't you tell me that something is going on between you and my brother?"

She stared at him, wondering where he'd gotten an idea so ridiculous. She then recalled she had run into one of his brothers while walking the Strip and he'd offered to help her with the bags she'd collected from shopping. Afterward they'd had lunch together. Had someone seen them together and jumped to the wrong conclusions?

"Gannon was merely kind enough to help me carry a few packages," she said. "Then we—"

"I'm not talking about Gannon," he said in a low voice that was as hard as nails.

Now she knew he really had lost it. "Then what brother are you talking about?" she asked.

"Don't you know?"

"If I knew I wouldn't be asking," she responded smartly.

He paused a moment, narrowed his gaze and then said, "Mercury."

She expressed disbelief in her features. "Mercury! I barely know him."

"Are you saying the two of you are not involved?"

She placed her hands on her hips and glared at him. "That's exactly what I'm saying. Where did you get such a crazy idea?"

"He told someone you were off-limits."

"Then whoever he told that to must have misunderstood." She sighed, shaking her head. "You actually thought I'm banging your brother and still slept with you last night?"

"I honestly didn't know what to think."

Her frown deepened and she lifted her chin. "In that case, it's nice to know the kind of woman you think I am. Please leave."

Jonas stared across the room at Nikki suddenly feeling lower than low. It didn't take much to see she was pretty damn mad. And he could also tell his accusation had come as a blow. He could see the hurt in her face although she was trying like hell to hide it.

He drew in a deep breath when he thought of what he'd all but accused her of. He had listened to Gannon, who'd evidently heard Mercury wrong like she'd said. And instead of waiting to talk to Mercury about it first, he had stormed up here to Nikki's hotel room and confronted her about something that was undoubtedly not true. He couldn't blame Gannon for relaying false info. He could only blame himself for acting on it the way he had.

"I'm sorry," he said, knowing she had no idea the degree of his remorse. He had been quick to think the worst, mainly to disprove this theory that there was something about her that was different from other women he'd messed around with.

"Is there a reason you're still standing there?"

He met her gaze. Held it for a long while before saying, "I'm here because I can't think of being anywhere else."

She stiffened her spine and lifted her chin. "Then think harder while my door hits you in the back."

Boy, she was cruel, but no crueler than he'd been to her with his accusations. "You won't accept my apology?"

"Right now I don't want anything from you. Not even an apology." She paused for a second, drew in what he knew was an angry breath and then asked, "Do you know what your problem is, Jonas?"

Not waiting for him to answer, she said, "You want to judge every woman on the basis of your own sleazy behavior."

He couldn't say anything to that because maybe he probably did. And he wasn't even offended that she thought his behavior was sleazy. It had been described as worse on more than one occasion. Knowing there was nothing he could say or do to redeem himself at the moment, he crossed the room, and before reaching the door, he turned and looked back at her. The intensity of her glare had burned a hole in his back, he could feel it. But he would make it up to her.

Without saying anything else, he opened the door and walked out of it.

Jonas had made it to his room when his cell phone went off and he saw it was Mercury. He answered it in a frustrating voice. "Mercury."

"Hey, Jonas, Nancy said you called. Don't you have

enough to do in Vegas without trying to keep up with me? I hear Gannon visited the Doll House yesterday and that you missed all the fun."

Jonas frowned, not wanting to talk about anything with his brother but Nikki. "Look, Mercury, I want to know about Nikki."

"Nikki?"

"Yes, Nikki Cartwright. Did you or did you not warn Gannon she's off-limits?"

There was a brief pause, and then Mercury said, "Yes, I warned him off."

Jonas's stomach twisted, and it was like the breath had been sucked from his lungs. According to Nikki she and Mercury weren't involved. So did that mean Mercury was interested in her but she just didn't know it? "So you're interested in her?"

Mercury chuckled. "No."

"Then why in the hell would you tell Gannon she is off-limits?"

"Because she is. But I'm not the one who wants her."

Jonas's jaw hardened. "Then who the hell wants her?"

"You do."

"What?"

He could hear Mercury laughing. "Oh yeah, *you* do. I noticed it first at Galen and Brittany's wedding. You couldn't keep your eyes off her when you thought no one else was looking. And then at Eli's wedding when she was taking all those pictures, you were taking her in, angle by angle, every time that cute little body of hers moved around the room. You were all but salivating."

Jonas frowned. "I hate to burst that overimaginative mind of yours, but you're wrong."

"Umm, I don't think so, and now after this phone conversation, I know so. So the way I see it, telling Gannon and Tyson that Nikki was off-limits was actually doing you a favor. You can thank me for it later."

He heard the click as Mercury ended the call.

Nikki stood at the window looking out at the Strip, drawing in deep breaths and then expelling them slowly, tasting the anger still lodged deep in her throat. A part of her still couldn't believe it. The man who had passionate sex with her last night had stood in the middle of her hotel room less than ten minutes ago, all but accusing her of sleeping with one of his brothers? Just because he'd heard Mercury had said she was off-limits? Of all the nerve. If her career wasn't on the line she would pack up and return to Phoenix in a heartbeat.

But then again, when it came to Jonas, she never thought with her heart. She couldn't. She always thought with her head and that's where the trouble lay. Her head was trying to tell her he'd been more jealous than pissed, but with Jonas that didn't make any sense. He could have any woman he wanted. He'd certainly gotten her last night and big-time. And why had he seemed upset when he hadn't been able to reach her today? What was that all about?

She shook her head. Jonas, jealous over her? She chuckled, knowing nothing could be further from the truth. So they had shared lusty, heated, make-you-holler sex last night, through most of the night. For her it might have been a night to remember, but she figured for him it was business as usual.

When she recalled how he had stared her down, accusing her of being involved with his brother, she couldn't help but feel a resurgence of anger. But she needed this job, so the best thing for her was to do what she was being paid to do and leave everything else alone. Jonas fell in the category of everything else.

Okay, she would be a notch on his bedpost, but then he would be a notch on hers as well. Her notches may not get carved as often as his, but she could deal with that. What she couldn't deal with was an involvement with Jonas, so the best thing to do would be to keep her distance.

And that's what she intended to do.

Chapter 11

Jonas's gaze sought out Nikki the moment he walked into the launch party. She had her camera in hand, as she moved around the room and worked it like the professional photographer that she was. Even though she was only wearing a pair of silky-looking slacks and a matching blouse he thought she stood out over all of the women dressed in expensive designer gowns.

Although this was a working event for her, she looked just as elegant and refined as anyone else. And those slacks she was wearing showed what a curvy little backside she had, just as much as her jeans always did. Which was probably why several men were ogling her as she moved around the room, shifting, twisting and bending that cute rounded bottom all around, snapping one picture after another.

One man in particular was Curtis Rhinestone, a

reporter for CNN. Jonas and he had attended college together in Michigan and had been frat brothers. He could recall that back in the day while at the university, more than once he and Curtis had competed for the same girl. And now he didn't like the way Curtis all but licked his lips while staring at Nikki. It wouldn't take much for Jonas to cross the room and bust those same lips with his fist.

He drew in a deep breath wondering why it bothered the hell out of him to think of Curtis—or any other man for that matter—checking out Nikki. Why even now the temperature in the room seemed to have risen a few degrees since he'd seen her, and why while looking at her fully clothed he vividly recalled her naked. Beneath him…on top of him…

He took another sip of his drink. Why was he so fixated on her? Hell, she was just a woman. And he'd slept with more than he could ever count. But he'd always had the ability to move on without any problems. Why was moving away from Nikki causing him so much grief? Why couldn't he get a friggin' handle on those emotions she could so effortlessly stir within him?

"Well, if it isn't Jonas Steele."

Jonas looked up into the face of a woman by the name of Chastity Jenkins. He had met the PR firm owner while on a business trip to L.A. three years ago. He'd found her first name amusing since there was no part of her that came with a lock of any sort. It had been a one-night stand and that was all it was ever meant to be. He had made that clear in the beginning and at the end. So he had been surprised at the call he'd gotten a few months later saying she would be visiting Phoenix and preferred crashing at his place instead of a hotel.

As nice as he could, he'd told her he really didn't give a damn what she preferred, but staying at his place, even for a few days, wasn't going to happen. She hadn't liked his response and after expressing that dislike in a few choice words, she hadn't contacted him since.

"Chastity," he said dryly. "It's been a while."

She smiled up at him. "It wasn't my choice, Jonas."

No, it hadn't been her choice. Her comment let him know she still hadn't gotten over things. At least someone hadn't. He glanced over at Nikki. She hadn't looked his way since he'd arrived, which meant evidently she had. The realization annoyed the hell out of him.

Chastity began talking, namely about her favorite subject. Herself. He really wasn't listening, only pretending he was since for the moment, he didn't have anything else to do.

Click.
Click.

Nikki moved around the room, taking pictures of one celebrity after another. This was her first assignment where so many famous people in the same place. And when it came to smiling for the camera they weren't shy.

She fought to ignore the kicking of her heart, which signaled Jonas was somewhere in the room. They had avoided each other for the past two days and that had been fine with her. They'd had their one-night stand—as brief and meaningless as it could get—and had moved on. The decision had evidently been a mutual one. But they did have to work together, so they couldn't avoid each other forever.

She twisted and bent her body, snapping one picture after another and as if her camera was responding to the call of the wild…and the reckless: it unerringly zeroed on him. She sucked in a deep breath when he was captured within the scope of her camera's lens. Oh, God, he looked good in his dark suit with his hair flowing around his shoulders.

Her camera continued to snap away, as it moved all over him, from his expensive leather shoes to those fine-as-a-dime muscled thighs beneath his slacks. And it didn't take much for her to recall how those same thighs had held her within their tight grasp while riding her.

Her camera continued snapping, moving upward to Jonas's broad chest and the designer jacket he was wearing, to the handsome features that still haunted her dreams. They were dreams she couldn't restrict from her mind. She knew she was taking more pictures of him than any other person there tonight. It was as if she couldn't help it. And then as if he suspected he was the object of someone's attention, he shifted his gaze from the woman he was talking to and looked straight into the lens of her camera.

She swallowed deeply and her mind suddenly scrambled when she felt the full-fledged intensity of his stare directly on her. She forced herself to stay unruffled because she had no reason to lose her composure. She was merely doing her job. Besides, instead of looking at her, he should be concentrating on the woman he was talking to—the one with the heavily made-up face, over-the-top weave job, way-too-long French-tipped nails and blood red lips. She was talking a mile a minute, and all but demanding his attention. Would she be the one to share his bed tonight? The one who would be scratching his back this time? Getting the ride of her life? And should Nikki even care? Her heart began pounding viciously and she knew she cared although she shouldn't.

"Hey, you've been at it long enough. Shouldn't you be ready to take a break about now?"

She turned toward the deep, masculine voice and couldn't help but force a smile. It was the same guy who'd tried hitting on her earlier. He'd introduced himself as Curtis Rhinestone and said he worked for CNN. It was as if he'd singled her out since she had felt the heat of his gaze on her most of the night. He wasn't bad-looking. In fact most women would probably consider him downright gorgeous. She would too, if he could in some way hold a candle to Jonas. Unfortunately, he couldn't.

She lowered her camera, thinking she'd focused on Jonas too much already. She checked her watch. "You're in luck. Starting now I'm free for the rest of the night."

He smiled. "Good. I think it's time we got to know each other."

Out of the corner of his eye Jonas watched Nikki move around the room with Curtis and felt his anger rising. How dare Rhinestone try to take something that was his?

He drew in a sharp breath. When had he ever thought of any woman as his? No matter how many women he bedded, he'd never claimed one. What made Nikki different? What had there been about having sex with her that still had him breathless? He took a sip of his drink, his last for the night, as he continued to track Nikki and Curtis while trying not to be too damn obvious.

"Excuse me if I'm boring you."

He shifted his gaze back to Chastity. Why was she still there, taking up his time? A better question to ask was why was he letting her? He knew the reason. He was allowing her to do so because she was so into herself she wouldn't notice that he was into someone else. At least he figured she wouldn't notice. Evidently he'd been wrong.

"You aren't boring me," he said, taking another sip of his drink.

"Then why are we still here? The last time we attended a party together we'd left within minutes."

She didn't have to remind him. They'd split the party in L.A. and he'd taken her up to his hotel room. He was just about to respond, explain that it had been three years ago, tons of women ago…especially one in particular. But then he saw Curtis lead Nikki outside on the patio and knew he had to put a stop to *that* foolishness once and for all.

"It was good seeing you again, Chastity. Now if you will excuse me…" Not waiting to see if she would excuse him or not, he walked off.

"It's a beautiful night, isn't it?"

The cool air hit Nikki in the face as she glanced over at Curtis. He was nice enough and for the time being, had taken her mind off Jonas, which was a good thing. Whether she liked it or not, the sight of Jonas and that woman who kept touching his arm, batting her false lashes up at him while giving him a toothy smile, had irked her. So when Curtis had suggested they step out on the patio, she had been more than raring to go.

She glanced around. They were high up on the fortieth floor, where she could see the brightly lit Vegas Strip with all the flashing neon signs. "So you're going to be a passenger on the *Velocity*?"

She smiled up at him. "Yes, and you will, too. Right?"

"Yes, I'm doing the coverage for CNN and looking forward to the next two weeks."

She took a sip of her wine. "So am I. Although I'll be working a lot of the time, I'll have time to relax and enjoy myself."

He smiled down at her. "And I hope I'll be someone that you'll enjoy your leisure time with."

Nikki wasn't caught off guard by his suggestion. In fact, she had been preparing herself for it. For the past twenty minutes he had been tossing out hints that he would love to spend time with her. The man sure didn't know the meaning of taking things slow.

"Are you sure you want to do that?" she asked.

"I'm more than sure. You're a very sexy woman and any man in his right mind would want to show you a good time."

In the bedroom, of course, Nikki thought. *Been there, done that just three days ago, and the memories are still too potent for me to even consider doing it with another man anytime soon...or ever.*

She was about to open her mouth, to tell him that she wasn't sure that was a good idea, when a masculine voice behind her spoke up.

"I don't know how that will be possible, Rhinestone, when she's with me."

Nikki spun around so fast she almost spilled her drink. She drew in a deep breath and watched as Jonas emerged from the shadows and strolled into the light. The muscle that was ticking in his jaw indicated he was angry, and if looks could kill both she and Curtis would be dead. What was his problem, and why had he made such an outrageous claim just now?

"Steele, I wasn't aware she was with you tonight."

Curtis's words jerked her from her dazed moment. What was Jonas trying to pull? She wasn't with him. He knew good and well that they didn't have that kind of relationship.

She was about to open her mouth to say just that when Jonas came to stand beside her and said in a voice with a hard edge to it, "Well, now you know."

Curtis met her gaze and gave her a chance to refute Jonas's claim. She would have if the vibes she was picking up off Jonas weren't infused with just any excuse to go upside the man's head. Did they know each other? Was something going on between the two men that she wasn't aware of? She decided the best thing to do for now was to put as much distance between the two men as possible before they came to blows. Based on their expressions, a fight wasn't far off. The friction between them appeared that intense.

When she didn't say anything Curtis turned his attention back to Jonas. The looked that passed between them verified what she'd assumed earlier. They did know each other, and there was something going on that she wasn't privy to, but at the moment felt caught in the middle of.

It was Curtis who finally broke the silence. "Then maybe I should back off."

"Yes, I would highly suggest that you do," Jonas said in what sounded like a low growl. "Now if you will excuse us."

And then he grasped her arm beneath the elbow and leaned close and whispered in her ear in that same low growl, "We need to talk."

She narrowed her eyes at him, and when Curtis walked off, leaving them alone on the patio, she snatched her arm back from Jonas and swirled to face him. "We most certainly do. I want to know what that was about."

Jonas stood staring at Nikki, not sure himself just what that was about. Never in his thirty-three years had he stood before a man and claimed a woman was with him. But a few minutes ago, he had done just that.

"Jonas?"

He drew in a deep breath and said the first thing that came to his mind. "I don't like him."

She frowned. "And you not liking him affects me… how? I believe he stated he wanted to show *me* a good time, not you."

His features suddenly hardened again and he leveled his gaze at her. "He's not getting near you, dammit."

She placed her hands on her hips. "Says who?" she snapped.

"Says me," he snapped back, advancing on her.

She didn't have the good mind to back up and his body pressed against hers. She felt crowded and it was at that moment her temper exploded. "And who the hell are you supposed to be? You're someone I slept with one time. And that's your famous motto—'one and done'—isn't it? Or have you forgotten? In case you have, then let me remind you. One and done, Jonas. And that one time doesn't give you any rights and *you* of all men wouldn't want them if it did. So what in God's name is your problem?"

He rubbed his hand down his face, inwardly acknowledging that he honestly didn't know what his problem was. The only thing he knew was that he wanted her again. Here. Right now. "You, Nikki Cartwright, seem to be my problem," he said in a low steely tone, seconds before grabbing her around the waist, lowering his head and sinking his mouth down on hers.

Chapter 12

Nikki saw it coming and had intended to resist. But all it took was for Jonas to take her mouth with a hunger that sent shivers all through her. Without letting up on her mouth, he drew her closer into the fit of his body, into the juncture of his thighs and right smack into the heat of the hard erection pressing against her.

His hands were no longer on her waist but had moved to her backside as his fingers skimmed sensuous designs all over her bottom while pressing her closer still. She released a tiny whimper from deep in her throat when his tongue seemed to plunge deeper.

Needing to touch him with the same degree of fervor, she placed the palms of her hands at the back of his neck and pulled him closer, locking her mouth even more to his. The silky, soft feel of his hair flowing her over hands as their mouths mated sent intense heat flaring through every part of her body.

Jonas had a way of making her feel both feminine and wantonly wicked at the same time, and there was nothing she could do but slide deeper into his embrace as he continued his sensual assault on her mouth. He was also assaulting her senses, battering them until he had her entire body trembling.

Then suddenly, she felt her legs moving, noted in the hazy part of her mind that he was walking her backward as the cool night air ruffled her curls. She wasn't sure just where he was luring her, but knew as long as he continued to plunder her mouth this way, she was game.

She heard the sound of a glass door sliding open and when he pulled her inside, she pulled her mouth away from his to glance around while drawing in several deep breaths. They were in a small room Ideas of Steele had reserved to store their equipment and supplies for the party.

Before she could say anything, reclaim her senses, he leaned forward and began brushing heated kisses around the corners of her lips. At that moment the only thing she wanted to reclaim was how he was making her feel. She didn't want to do anything but feel his warm breath against the contours of her mouth.

"I want you again, Nikki," he whispered softly before tracing the tip of his tongue along a path down the side of her ear. "I want you so damn bad. I'm going to burst out of my zipper if I don't have you."

Her heart began racing at his words, at the thought that he wanted her that much. But there was something she couldn't let go of and that was why they'd been at odds with each other over the past couple of days. He thought the worst of her. He thought she was someone capable of sharing brothers. And that was unacceptable to her.

She pushed back out of his arms. "I think we need to return to the party. Who knows? Mercury might have surprised us both and arrived in town and is there waiting for me."

He didn't say anything for a second, and then he reached out and took her hand in his, gently held it in his larger one. He stared down at her and met her gaze. "I told you I was sorry about that. It was miscommunication that I acted on without thinking. Don't ask me why I did it, but I did. I acted hastily and I regret it. Deep down I know your character is nothing but wholesome, above reproach."

He paused a moment, released her hand to rub the back of his neck and then said, "And what you said that day is probably true. I'm such a jaded ass that I overlook the decency in others at times. Again, I'm sorry."

"I didn't call you a jaded *ass.*"

He chuckled. "No, actually you accused me of sleazy behavior and in my book it practically means the same thing." He got quiet and his expression became serious. "So, will you forgive me?"

She studied his features for a moment. "Will it matter to you if I do or don't?"

He stared at her, as if his gaze was touching every inch of her features, and she could barely breathe under the intensity. Then he finally said, "Yes, it will matter. I like you."

Nikki could only shake her head. Did he actually like her or like sleeping with her? They'd only done so once, but he wanted them to do so again. Tonight. And unfortunately, she wanted to make love with him again as well.

There was just something about the feel of being in his arms, having him planted deep inside of her, intimately connected to her, that made her insides quiver just remembering how it was between them. And it was a way she wanted to be with him again. But what about that "one and done" policy he was known for? Taking her again would be breaking one of his rules. She shrugged. He would be breaking it, not her. The thought of being his "exception" was sending spikes of pleasure through her and making her feel wild and reckless.

"I'm waiting for you to say that you accept my apology and that you like me too, Nikki."

She stared up at him and saw he was serious. There were sober lines etched under his eyes, slashed across his face, and she was tempted to smooth them away with her fingers. Instead, feeling bold, she leaned up on tiptoe and used the tip of her tongue to erase the lines.

Moments later she whispered against his lips, "I accept your apology and I do like you."

And then she went back to licking his sober lines away. Unable to stay mobile under her ministrations, he reached up and began running his fingers through the mass of curls on her head. The feel of his hands in her hair sent her pulse escalating.

And then when her tongue got inches from his mouth, licked his lips from corner to corner, he steadied her head to look at him and whispered, "You're welcome to come inside for a visit."

She did, easing her tongue into his mouth and that's when he crushed her to him and took over the kiss.

He could kiss her forever, Jonas thought as he plundered Nikki's mouth. This was heaven. At least it felt like it anyway. Like he'd told her, he wanted her and he wanted her bad. He wanted to suck on her breasts, lick them all over. Lick her all over. Taste her honeyed warmth again, a taste he hadn't been able to get over.

And then he wanted to make love to her, pump inside of her while her inner muscles clamped down on him. Pulled everything out of him. But he wasn't sure they had time to do all that now. If not now, definitely later. At this moment he would gladly get what he could.

All those thoughts made him slowly pull back from their kiss to look down at her. "Rick is handling things so don't worry about us being missing in action."

"You sure?"

He smiled. "Well, Curtis might miss you, but I won't be missed, trust me."

She chuckled against his lips. "You keep it up and I'm going to start thinking that you're jealous."

He knew she was teasing, but little did she know she had hit pretty close to home. He had gotten jealous. It wouldn't have taken much for him to rip Rhinestone in two. Instead of commenting on what she'd said, he reached out and took her hand in his. He leaned in and murmured against her lips. "Come here, I know just where I want to take you."

He'd said that literally and every cell in his body was ready, invigorated, fully charged. He pressed her hand lightly as he led her around a crate of boxes toward the east side of the room where another set of doors led to a private balcony.

They didn't have a whole lot of time, but he planned to relish to the fullest what they had.

Nikki drew in a deep breath the moment the cool air hit her in the face and shivers ran through her body. Jonas was standing directly behind her and she could feel his heat, his hard erection pressing against her backside. He reached his arms around her and held her around the waist.

"Look up at the stars, baby, and pretend it's just me and you out here in the universe," he whispered. "We are going to make the most of it with a very satisfying, mind-blowing quickie."

She glanced up at the sky. It was clear, with a full moon and twinkling stars. In a few days they would be up there in the sky, flying around in *Velocity*. The thought of them making love while up there sent ripples through her. She knew that she and Jonas would give new meaning to the mile-high club.

"I like this," he murmured close to her ear while his hand moved from her waist to cup her backside. "I like how you twist and bend it while stooping down taking pictures."

His touch felt good and anticipation ran through her when he slowly began easing her pants down her legs, followed by her thong. She stepped out of her shoes and glanced over her shoulder when she saw he had taken off his jacket and tossed it on a nearby bench. The sound of a packet being ripped open let her know he was putting on a condom. She heard the moment he unzipped his pants, and then she felt the long, hard heat of him touching the cheeks of that backside he said he liked so much.

"I love making out with you this way. The feel of being connected to you like this."

Nikki didn't think any man could arouse her the way Jonas did. With both his words and his actions. He liked to talk while seducing a woman and she liked hearing what he had to say. His words were blatant, erotic and usually provided an image that would take her breath away.

"Now for your blouse. We need to take it off as well."

She lifted a brow and under the moonlight she saw him smile. "I locked the door, baby, and this is a private balcony. Nobody is out here but you and me and what you see overhead."

"But you said it would be a quickie."

He took a step toward her, reached out and traced a path along the lacy hem of her blouse. "After the other night you should know that my quickies are also thorough."

He began unbuttoning her blouse as he held her gaze. "Besides, I don't care how quick I intend to be. There's no way I can penetrate you without tasting you all over first."

With the last button undone, her blouse fell open to reveal a black lacy bra. And with a flick of his wrist to the front clasp, the bra came undone and her twin breasts poured forth. "You won't need this for a while," he said, peeling the straps from her shoulders and easing them down her arms, before tossing the bra on the bench to join his jacket and the rest of her things he'd picked up and placed there.

She stood before him totally naked and she hoped everything he said was true. First, that with Rick in charge they wouldn't be missed at the party and secondly, that this was a private balcony.

"Do you know just how beautiful you are?"

She met his gaze and the awe in the depth of his green eyes—eyes that roamed up and down and zeroed in on certain body parts—made her breath catch in her throat.

That night they'd spent together he'd told her a number of times he thought she was beautiful. She had taken his words as those men would typically say to the women they sleep with. But there was a look in Jonas's eyes that made her think that perhaps he really thought so and he wasn't just feeding her a line.

Nikki knew she wasn't bad-looking, but she was far from a gorgeous babe. And she definitely wasn't the sleek and sophisticated type of woman Jonas's name was usually associated with. He probably just found the novelty of her amusing. Yes, that had to be it.

That thought didn't bother her. Things were what they were, and just as long as she kept on a straight head and did not put any more stock into this short, meaningless and oh, so brief affair—if she dared to call it that—then she would be okay.

Whatever other thoughts she wanted to dwell on suddenly flew from her mind when his tongue snaked out and licked around the areola before it wrapped around a nipple, slowly drawing it into his mouth. She could feel the aroused nub swell even more in his mouth. She closed her eyes and felt her inner muscles clench, and she tightened her thighs together to stop the ache starting to build there.

"Not so fast, baby," he said, reaching out and sliding his hand up her thighs to her center. "I want to feel how wet I can make you get."

She recalled how he would intentionally get her wet just to taste her. She had found out that oral sex was something he definitely enjoyed, and by the time he'd finished with her, she had enjoyed it as well.

She moaned the minute his fingers slid inside of her, moved around and plunged deeper as if seeking her moist heat. He touched her clit and began stroking it with his fingertips. Without missing a beat with his fingers, he released one breast and went to the other, giving it the same torment and pushing her even deeper into an aroused state.

He placed her back against the rail as he released her and she didn't open her eyes. She didn't have to. She knew he had lowered to his knees in front of her to make good on what he'd said he intended to do. And when she felt the tip of his hot tongue slide inside of her, locking on to the clit his fingers had tortured earlier, she couldn't stop the whimper that escaped her lips.

She wondered how a man's tongue could go so deep inside a woman. How did it know just what spots to hit to make her moan, whimper and groan?

He released her, leaned back on his haunches and held her gaze. "You like that?"

She drew in a deep breath, not once, but twice before she could answer. "Yes, and I see that you do, too."

He nodded slowly while he licked his lips. "Yes, but just with you." And before she could decide whether he was telling the truth or not, he grabbed hold her of thighs once again, leaned forward and plunged his tongue back into her depths.

She screamed when he began making circular motions with his tongue that had her grabbing his head to hold him there. Right there. How could he make the tip of his tongue feel so hot and find all her erotic places? Her G-spot was definitely taking a licking and then some.

And then suddenly, he did something with his tongue when it caught hold of her clit, wiggled in such a way that made her scream. Luckily the sound was muffled by the noise from the party. She clutched his head tighter to her and he clenched her thighs, locking his mouth to her as a way to let her know he didn't plan on going anyplace.

And only when the last orgasmic spasm flowed from her body did he unlock his mouth from her. She was still whimpering uncontrollably when he gathered her up into his arms and carried her over to the chaise longue. She kept her eyes closed, listening to his erratic breathing.

When she heard him removing his clothes, she drew in enough strength to open one eye and saw him moving toward her like she was his prey. Her gaze latched on to his aroused shaft embedded in a thatch of dark hair. It was so thick, so hard and so big the thought that he was about to use it on her sent sensuous shivers racing through her. She wasn't worried about not being able to fit it in, since she'd done it before. But then she had been pretty sore the next day. Um, maybe now was not the time to—

Before she could finish that thought, he reached out and effortlessly lifted her off the lounger. "Wrap your legs around me," he said in a deep, husky voice. As if he'd spoken to her body and her body alone, it complied and her legs wrapped themselves around him, crossing her ankles at his back.

"Mmm, I like your scent," he said, nuzzling her neck before licking it, then moving from the base of her throat up toward her chin.

"And I like yours," she responded, throwing her head back to give him better access to her neck and throat. This had to be the longest quickie on record. But she had no complaints, especially when she was on such a pleasurable receiving end. She would have to do something extra special to him the next time, and for some reason she had a feeling there would be a next time, at least until she was no longer a novelty.

She felt him spreading her thighs and when he eased the head of his manhood inside of her she couldn't help but moan. "Mmm, we fit perfectly," he said when he grabbed a hold of her buttocks and gripped them tight, pressing them closer into the curve of him.

She was convinced the head of his engorged penis had worked its way right smack into her womb. "What's next?" she asked, like there could be any other ending to what they were doing.

He smiled and she thought he looked so doggone handsome, the way his lips tilted at the corners, and the way that mass of wavy hair on his head made him look wild and untamed. "Now, I'll let your body know who I am."

She chuckled as she tightened her legs around him when he began walking. "I think you did that the last time. I could barely walk the next day."

A huge smile touched his lips as if he was pleased

to hear that. She was tempted to pop him upside the head. But injuring him in any way was not at the top of her list. She needed him to finish this. She desperately needed him to finish this.

"Let's sit a spell," he said, easing down on the padded bench.

Sit? She raised a brow. Hadn't he planned to take her against a wall or something? Evidently not as he eased down on the bench, their bodies still connected and facing each other.

"Mmm, now I can look at you," he said, staring into her face. "I want to see you come."

"Do you?"

"Hell, yeah. And I want to see what I can do to you to get you prepared."

No sooner had he finished his sentence, his hands began rubbing her all over, starting at her thighs and then lifting her legs to move down her calves.

He unwrapped her legs from around his back and lifted them high on his shoulders. And their bodies remained connected during the entire process. "How did you know my legs could get raised so high?"

He shifted a little to spread his legs as she sat straddling his lap. "Umm, I figured as much when I saw how you moved around snapping pictures. Anyone who moved the way you did has to have agility down to a science. And you verified my assumptions the last time we made love."

She didn't have to ask how she'd done that. It was during one of those positions he'd sprung on her. She had almost flexed her body into a bow to make sure he didn't miss a thing.

Jonas intruded on her thoughts when he began massaging her legs, kneading her knees and stroking her calves. "You're tense," he said softly. "Relax."

Nikki looked at him. She thought she was relaxed. Maybe he'd gotten her eagerness mixed up with tension. "I'm fine," she said, when she really wasn't.

She was straddling his lap with her legs high on his shoulders while their bodies were connected…and she meant *connected*. If anyone were to see them now they would assume they were glued together, joined at the hips, thighs and definitely the reproductive organs.

"Wiggle a little bit closer."

She didn't think such a thing was possible, considering how close they were already. But she did so, which elevated her legs at a higher angle. "Oh." She felt it. Elevating her legs made her pelvis tilt in a way that stimulated her G-spot. She felt it, all the way to her toes. The sensations had her slanting her bottom for another sensual hit.

"Okay, let's not get carried away, Nikki."

She met his gaze and giggled. "I like you, Jonas."

He threw his head back and laughed. "You would now. But we've wasted enough time. I want to be looking in your face when you scream my name."

And without further ado, he began moving, lifting his hips off the bench as he began thrusting into her, holding her hips in place for every deep, concentrated stroke. She watched him the same way he watched her and saw the intensity in his features as he made love her, increasing the pace with hurried precision, going deeper and deeper, faster and faster with piston speed.

She screamed again when it became too much, the pleasure overtaking her, exploding inside of her and sending her entire body in a tailspin. And he didn't take his eyes off her. She held his gaze and saw when it got to be too much for him as well as he bucked, once, twice and a third time, gripping her thighs tight, holding her body in place as he exploded inside of her.

He ground his hips against hers as a groan was ripped from his throat, but he kept thrusting and she came a second time, calling his name as he continued to rapidly stroke her pulsing flesh. And the erotic waves finally washed over her, cutting her loose from such an intense ride of pleasure. She leaned in and wrapped her arms around him while fighting to regain her breath.

"You are beautiful when you come," he whispered while gently stroking her back.

At that moment she didn't care if he was lying and all he'd seen was an ugly face. On two different occasions he had surpassed all her expectations in the bedroom. He'd proved the real thing was a heck of a lot better than fantasy, but mostly that maybe her head knew what it was talking about when it would tell her to enjoy today and put away the foolish ideas of yesterday.

"If we continue to stay connected like this, I'll be tempted to go another round," he whispered in her ear. The heat of his breath sent blood rushing through her veins.

Nikki knew he was telling the truth. The man had the stamina of a bull. Like the one tattooed on his stomach. She was a living witness to how many orgasms he could get and give in one night. She shifted and noted he was still hard, probably hadn't gone down. She looked at how her legs were hoisted up high on his shoulders and knew if she was going to get them down she needed his help. After all, he had helped get them up there.

"Will you help get my legs down?"

He smiled and she knew she'd made a big mistake. "Sure you want to go back to the party? Our contribution to tonight's affair is over by now."

He shifted positions a little and she felt just how hard he still was. "We need to go back," she said, not using too much of a convincing tone. But then how could she when he was still buried deep inside of her to the hilt and she was feeling him growing bigger and bigger. Her insides were already weeping in joy.

"No, we don't." And then he leaned forward and took her mouth and the only thing she could think of at that moment was that she hoped the noise from the party continued to drown out her screams.

Chapter 13

"So where were you last night, Jonas? I looked around the party and didn't see you anywhere."

Jonas paused in his packing to glance over at Gannon. "I was there, Gan. The only time I was missing was when I had to step out a few minutes for a bit of fresh air."

There was no need to tell his brother that air wasn't the only thing he'd left the party for. And it hadn't been for a few minutes. He'd been missing in action for a little more than an hour. After convincing Nikki to go one more round for the road, he had helped her redress before sending her back to the party ahead of him. He had remained behind to get his bearings and screw his head back on straight. He'd done neither. What he'd done was to remain on that padded bench, stretched out naked as a jaybird while staring up at the

sky and remembering every vivid detail of their supposed "quickie."

He had closed his eyes at the memory of how good
it had felt being inside of her, how her features took
on a whole other look right before an orgasm hit her.
He'd never seen anything so gorgeous in his life. Her
gaze had held his, and his senses had almost gone on
overload at the pleasure he'd seen radiating from her.
All the while her inner muscles had clenched him,
demanded from him something he'd never given any
woman.

And that's when he'd come, exploding all over the
place inside of her. Their union had been so explosive,
so damn amazing, just thinking about it now had shivers running all through his body. When had mating
with a woman done that to him? He should have been
prepared for the strength of their lovemaking from the
last time, but when it hit him again—that overpowering force that had practically transported him into another place and time—his mind, body and soul had
been taken for one hell of a ride. It'd been one damn
sexual transportation that had taken him to a whole
new hemisphere, maybe another universe.

When he had returned to the party a while later,
he hadn't had to worry about being missed. The place
was packed. People were everywhere, wall-to-wall,
with more trying to get in. He had looked around, but
Nikki was nowhere to be found. He would have left
the party in search of her if it hadn't been for Mr. Fulton, who'd wanted to talk his ear off.

By the time he'd been able to get rid of the man—
who'd had one drink too many and was more than
happy with how things had turned out—it was past

three in the morning, and too late to go knocking on Nikki's door. He figured she had to be as drained as he was. Instead he had gone to his own room, stripped naked for the second time that night and fallen in bed with Nikki's scent still clinging to him. Not surprisingly, he had been awakened by a phone call from Gannon, who'd reminded him he had a flight to L.A. that morning. For once he had appreciated his brother's call. Otherwise, he probably would have missed his flight.

"Jonas?"

He blinked when Gannon snapped his fingers in front of his face. He glared at his brother. "What?"

"Damn, man, where were you just now? I was talking to you and you zoned out like you were in another world and you had this downright stupid look on your face."

Jonas frowned as he zipped up his luggage. "You're imagining things." He checked his watch. "Look, I got to go. Thanks for coming and hanging out with me a few days on the Strip."

Gannon chuckled. "The visits to the Doll House and that brothel were worth the trip. Besides, other than those two days before the party, we really didn't spend time together."

Jonas nodded. And only because those were the two days he had been trying to avoid Nikki. "Yeah, but we had fun."

Gannon would be returning to Phoenix later that day. Jonas would be catching a plane to L.A. in time to board the *Velocity*. That's where he and Nikki would be meeting up again. She had an earlier flight, he knew, since she had a meeting with some Hollywood producer about a possible freelancing gig.

He couldn't wait to see her again. There was no reason to ask why. Didn't matter. The woman was so in his system. And what they'd shared last night out on that balcony beneath the moon and the stars was nothing short of spectacular.

He reached out to grab handfuls of his hair to bind it into a ponytail. He had decided at eighteen, much to his mother's dismay, that he would not let another barber do anything more than give him a slight trim. It hadn't mattered that his brothers had teased him mercilessly by calling him Samson. They still did on occasion.

"Have fun while traveling the globe, Jonas."

His thoughts went to Nikki, and he couldn't help but smile. "I'm going to try. What time does your plane take off?"

"Around two. I'm going back to the Doll House to hang out with Quinton. He's quite a character."

Jonas rolled his eyes. Yeah, that wasn't all Quinton Hinton was. A damn bad influence topped the list. Gannon was a grown-ass man, but still, he couldn't help warning his brother. "Don't get into any trouble, Gan."

He didn't particularly like the smile on his brother's face when he responded, "Trust me, I won't."

Nikki walked into the cabin she'd been assigned, still in a daze. She had read everything Jonas had given her on the *Velocity*, but never in her wildest dream had she seen anything so spectacular, magnificent and brilliant. It was as if she was on board the starship *Enterprise* for a taping of *Star Trek*. Everything she saw was not just state-of-the-art; it had to be part of the future.

Even this cabin, for instance, with an octagonal window that was right over the bed, giving her a sky view anytime she wanted it. There wasn't a lot of space, but it was used efficiently, right down to the bed that conformed to the person's size and weight. She'd heard the mattress was comprised of special fibers blended together that guaranteed a perfect sleep each and every time. Good, because she needed a good rest, she thought, yawning. She was still tired from last night.

She couldn't recall what happened without thinking about Jonas. The man was screwing up her head big-time, and her heart didn't stand a chance of getting any talking points into the mix. Each time her heart tried reminding her that Jonas was not her Mr. Right, her head would counter, *Maybe not, but he's definitely a hot and tantalizing Mr. Wrong.*

Deciding she needed sleep more than anything, she was glad the aircraft wouldn't be taking off for another three hours and that she wasn't due to make an appearance until the dinner meeting in another five.

Most of the other people who were on board—who'd been just as fascinated as she about the airship—were still walking around in awe. She had left the group to escape to her cabin the first chance she got. She knew Jonas was scheduled to be on board in a couple of hours, and she needed to pull herself together before seeing him again.

Although she didn't want to listen to her heart at the moment, she knew things couldn't continue like this. Did she really want to become some man's booty girl, a woman he could go to and get laid whenever he wanted? Granted, there was always something in it for her, but still. Didn't she want more? Besides, booty girls weren't the kind men wanted for wives.

And that's the point, Nikki, her head was saying. *When are you going to accept that most men don't want wives? If they did they would be knocking down your door. You're everything any man would want, but that never put you at the top of their list, so chill. Have fun. Stop looking for Mr. Right because he's not out there. Be smart and take what you can get. You don't need a degree in psychology to know most men have issues that you wouldn't want to be bothered with anyway, so why are you so stuck in that forever-after mind-set? Live today and let tomorrow take care of itself.*

Nikki drew in a deep breath and placed her hands to her ears. She didn't want to listen to either her head or her heart right now. All she really wanted was more sleep and she was determined to get it.

Jonas glanced at his watch. Where was Nikki? Granted the dinner meeting didn't start for another ten minutes, but he wanted to see her now. He'd made it to the L.A. airport just in time to catch the shuttle that took him over to the gate were the *Velocity* had been docked. Already the media were on it and the place had been jam-packed. It was obvious everyone was in awe of the huge zeppelin that Fulton intended to be the first of many. But first, he had to make sure the *Velocity* was well-received, and it seemed from how things were going so far, it was.

Fulton himself was hosting this dinner meeting, personally welcoming everyone on board. There was no doubt he would wine and dine the media for positive news coverage and already Jonas could tell the man had them eating out of his hands.

Jonas glanced around the room, fought the urge to

check his watch again and frowned when he met Curtis Rhinestone's gaze. He didn't trust him one bit. He had a feeling that although he'd managed to get Nikki away from the man last night, Rhinestone would still try and sniff behind her today, and if the bastard thought for one minute that Jonas would let him, then he had another think coming.

Getting agitated just thinking about it, he decided to move around the room, stretch his legs and appreciate the view. Unlike the others, this wasn't his first time aboard the airship, although this would be the first time he'd been in flight and so far it was smooth flying. He hadn't felt any turbulence, which was one of the *Velocity*'s strong points he would market. Because of the airship's structure it could easily hold its own, even in the most unruly of winds.

The last time he'd been on the *Velocity* had simply been an exclusive tour to see just what sort of marketing scheme he was getting himself into. Then, like now, he'd been truly amazed. There was no doubt in his mind that the *Velocity* would be a huge success. Already the naysayers were questioning the ship's safety and performance but he was certain by the end of this voyage everyone would see just what a remarkable airship this was. That was one of the reasons this trip was so important.

"I was wondering when you were going to get here, Nikki."

He turned at the sound of Curtis's voice and immediately felt his blood boil when Nikki entered the room and Rhinestone got all up in her face. Jonas was tempted to cross the room and smash the man's face in just for the hell of it, but he figured for now he needed to keep his cool. Working for Fulton was an opportunity of a lifetime and he wouldn't jeopardize it with drama. And what was pissing him off more than anything was that Rhinestone knew it.

He took a sip of his tonic water and studied Nikki. Even wearing her signature jeans and shirt she looked beautiful and he absolutely loved the soft-looking curls crowning her face. She had a camera in her hand, ready for business. But all he could think about at that moment was her, naked, straddling him while he thrust in and out of her, making out with her in a way he'd never made out with another women. Not with the same degree of passion, greed or urgency.

He suddenly felt a tingling in his fingers when he remembered them inside of her, stoking her heat, preparing her for his entry. Remembered how when he'd made it in he'd whispered naughty words to her, words that had made her blush while she had creamed some more. The warmth of her skin—whether it had been when their thighs had connected or when her legs had rested high on his shoulders—had wrapped him in a cocoon of sensuality he'd never felt before. She had done more than touch his body last night. She had somehow touched his soul.

Hell, how had that happened?

Had it occurred during those two days he'd tried to avoid her, only to go bonkers when he'd seen her again? Or had it been when they'd made out that night when she'd arrived in Vegas, right on the floor in his suite? For some reason he believed it had been that time when he'd kissed her, and then tried avoiding her for eighteen months. During that time he'd tried to convince himself she was just a woman and he had them anytime he wanted and whenever he wanted. What he hadn't counted on was her being different from all the others. He hadn't thought any woman capable of drawing out emotions in him, some of which he hadn't known he was capable of having. Like the need to do bodily harm to anyone who looked at her for too long.

Rhinestone glanced over his way with a smirk on his face. Jonas forced back the anger that tried rising to the top, well aware of the game the man intended to play. And if he thought he would play that game with Nikki then he was sorely mistaken.

Jonas inhaled deeply He refused to stand on the sidelines and let Curtis, or any man, make a move on Nikki. Curtis knew how he operated and until he made a public claim for a woman, the man wouldn't be backing off. And anyone who knew Jonas knew his hard and steadfast rule against ever doing such a thing. There were too many women out there to ever lay claim to just one.

He tried ignoring Rhinestone standing so close to Nikki. That resolve lasted all but two seconds. He placed his glass on the tray of a passing waiter and headed across the room after deciding it was time to break his own rule yet again.

Chapter 14

Nikki did the polite thing and nodded a few times while Curtis and another reporter conversed about how fascinated they were with the *Velocity*. She was surprised at the way Curtis had greeted her, especially after the obvious tension between him and Jonas last night.

She scanned the room, deliberately not allowing her gaze to wander where Jonas was standing. She'd seen him the moment she'd arrived and her heart had skipped a beat when he'd turned and their gazes had connected.

He was wearing his hair back in a ponytail and anytime he did so it only highlighted the angular lines of his face and showed a handsomeness that would take any woman's breath away. Dressed casually in a pair of jeans and a shirt, he was the epitome of masculine perfection.

She'd seen his frown when Curtis had stopped her. It was obvious he didn't like it. She really shouldn't care what he liked or didn't like because no matter how many times they came together, it was just for sex. He knew it as well as she.

"So what are your plans when we reach Beijing?" Curtis asked her, pulling her back into the conversation. "Surely you won't be expected to work while we're docked."

She opened her mouth to respond when a shadow crossed her path just seconds before a pair of lips brushed across hers in a kiss. Then a deep, masculine voice said, "Hello, sweetheart. I've been waiting for you and as usual, you were worth the wait."

For the hell of it, Jonas decided to brush a second kiss across her lips just to wipe the shocked look off her face. He stood by her side and wrapped his arms around her waist, ignoring the tension he felt flowing through her. He then turned to the two men and reached out for handshakes. "Rhinestone. Loggins. Good seeing you guys again. I hope you're enjoying yourselves."

He inwardly smiled at the way Rhinestone was recovering from a dropped jaw. The man was just as shocked as Nikki. He and Rhinestone weren't just fraternity brothers, they'd pledged on the same line. Kissing Nikki in front of everyone was a public claim to show their relationship was more than just casual. For Curtis to trespass on a fellow frat brother was a social taboo, a violation of the code of honor, something he wouldn't do.

"So how long have the two of you been involved?"

Rhinestone asked, taking a sip of his drink and holding Jonas's gaze.

Jonas was quick with a response, which was a question of his own. "Why do you want to know?"

"Curious."

He was tempted to tell Rhinestone just what he could do with his curiosity, but instead said, "Long enough. Now if you gentlemen will excuse us, I think Fulton is ready for dinner to begin."

Taking Nikki's arm beneath the elbow, he led her to one of the tables in the room. He sensed her anger and knew she was holding her peace longer than he'd expected. Eventually she would let him have it but wouldn't do it here.

He leaned closer, considered her a moment and then asked, "You okay?"

She inclined her head and the gaze staring at him was filled with fury. "What do you think?"

He forced his lips to form a thin smile. "I don't know. That's why I asked. And no, I'm not trying to be a smart-ass."

"Then what are you trying to be?" she asked as they sat down at a table set for two. He'd deliberately chosen this one for privacy.

When they'd taken their seats, he leaned closer and whispered to her, his breath fanning the side of her face, "What I intend to be is the only man who's going to pleasure you on this air voyage."

Less than six hours later Nikki walked down the corridor that led to her hotel room. The *Velocity* had docked at the Beijing Airport without any problems. Everything at the dinner party had gone well. Fulton had welcomed everyone on board and introduced his twelve flight attendants—males and females who looked like they had stepped off the covers of *GQ* and *Cosmo*. But she had to hand it to them, they had been true professionals and their customer service skills had been superb.

The meal they were served at dinner would rival that at any five-star restaurant. It was hard to believe they had dined while flying more than forty thousand feet in the air. Except for during takeoff and landing, they had been free to roam about the airship to enjoy the shopping boutiques, casino, library, game room and restaurant.

Jonas hadn't left her side the entire evening, clinging on to her like a grape to a vine. But she'd refused to indulge in private conversation with him. She ignored his air of possession whenever they conversed with others and got annoyed at how easily he would slide his arms around her waist and bring her closer to his side whenever another male got near, becoming territorial. When she hadn't been able to stand it anymore, she had feigned a migraine and gone to her cabin. He had offered to go with her to make sure she was okay, but she had turned down his offer and made it quite clear that she wanted to be alone. He'd called later to check on her, but when she answered the phone she had told him they had nothing to say to each other.

Reservations had been made for each passenger at several hotels in Beijing, where they would remain for three days on their own. She was grateful for that decision since she definitely needed to put distance between her and Jonas, even if only for three days.

As soon as the airship had docked, she had switched

groups with another passenger and ridden off in a different limo from the one she'd been assigned. She felt good knowing Jonas had no idea where she was and wouldn't be seeing her again until they returned to the *Velocity* to continue their air voyage to Australia. As far as she was concerned, he could play his little game all by himself.

She rubbed her temple after entering her hotel room and closing the door behind her. What had she done in going along with Jonas's deception that they were involved in an affair? Sleeping with a man twice didn't constitute an affair, and considering his reputation, Jonas of all people knew that. So what if he'd transitioned from one-and-done to twice-is-nice? The only thing he'd accomplished was to gain triumph over Curtis, a man who evidently was his adversary. And he had used her to do it.

She glanced at her watch. It was in the middle of the day in Beijing, but her body was still in the Pacific time zone. She would sleep the day through and then tomorrow she would go out and do some sightseeing. By the time she returned to the *Velocity*, she would be able to handle the likes of Jonas Steele and set the record straight once and for all. They were not involved.

Jonas stared at the smiling flight attendant. "What do you mean Ms. Cartwright departed the *Velocity* a few hours ago?"

The young woman nodded. "Yes, sir. She requested a change in her itinerary and we were able to work something out with another passenger. She was in the first group that departed."

He drew in a deep agitated breath. He should have

followed his mind and checked on her although she'd told him she wanted to be left alone. But he'd figured he would let her get some rest and then talk to her later. When she hadn't come out of her cabin for a while, he'd figured she had decided to grab a few more hours of rest, since they were the last group scheduled off the airship.

His gaze went back to the woman. "Then I'd like to know where she's gone since obviously she's no longer in my group and won't be staying at my hotel."

The woman's smile remained in place. "Yes, sir, but we can't divulge that information."

He of all people should know that. A high degree of privacy was one of *Velocity*'s strongest marketing points. He would have to use another approach. "Ms. Cartwright works for me and I need to get a message to her."

He knew before he'd finished talking that the woman wasn't buying it. She was one of the attendants who had worked the dinner meeting last night and had seen how he'd been all over Nikki. No matter what he said, the woman knew their relationship wasn't all business and if he couldn't find his woman then there must be trouble in paradise and she wasn't getting involved.

His woman.

Where had that thought come from? He shook his head. Damn. For the time being Nikki *was* his woman. He had pretty much claimed as much last night in a public display. And hadn't he made it clear to her that he intended to be the only man who would pleasure her on this voyage? Evidently she was still upset about last night and what he needed to do was talk to her as soon as possible. Hopefully, the two of them could reach some sort of an agreement.

"Do you not have her cell phone number, sir?"

"Yes, but I can't reach her." What he wouldn't say was that Nikki wasn't answering her phone.

"Sorry to hear that. Is there anything else, sir?"

He looked down at the woman, seeing she wasn't going to bend. He glanced down at her name tag. "No, Mandy, there's nothing else."

Jonas moved on as his mind began working. He'd always had ways of finding out whatever it was he wanted. One person who would know where Nikki had run off to was Brittany. However, he doubted his sister-in-law would tell him anything. He could turn to Galen to coax the info from his wife, but that would mean spilling his guts as to why he wanted to know. It was one thing to give a handful of strangers the impression he was enamored with a woman, but to give his brothers that same impression was another. He would never live it down.

That meant he would have to go to plan B and he had no qualms doing so. He had seen the way Mandy had ogled Rick last night and Rick's reputation as a ladies' man was just as bad as his. Jonas felt certain Rick could make more strides with Mandy than he had.

Rick owed him a favor and it was time for him to collect.

Nikki shifted in bed to drown out the insistent knocking at her hotel room door. Why was the cleaning service bothering her? Hadn't they seen the do-not-disturb sign on her door? "Go away," she called out before burying her head beneath her pillow.

When the knocking continued, she threw back the bed covers and stormed out of the bedroom to the door, pausing only to grab her robe off a chair. Customer service would definitely hear about this. She had wanted to rest for at least twelve hours. Jet lag was a bitch.

Nikki stopped halfway to the door when it opened. She crossed her arms over her chest, ready to take the person to task for disturbing her sleep. Her mouth dropped open when the person who walked across the threshold was not someone from housekeeping.

It was Jonas.

Chapter 15

"What are you doing here?"

After closing the door behind him, Jonas stood there, almost dazed, staring at her and thinking that with her curls tossed all over her head, bare feet and in a short robe showing a luscious pair of thighs, Nikki looked absolutely breathtaking.

She also looked absolutely mad. Furious was more like it.

"I asked what you're doing here, and what gives you the right to just come into my hotel room?"

He tossed his jacket on a chair. "I'm here to spend time with you. Someone from housekeeping heard me banging on your door, was fearful I'd wake up the whole floor, so she unlocked your door for me."

Nikki glared at him. "Wrong move on her part. I'm going to make sure she doesn't have a job much longer."

"Boy, you're mean."

"And you're leaving. Goodbye."

He shook his head and pushed his hair back from his face. He hadn't had time to bind it back after finding out Nikki's whereabouts. It hadn't taken Rick long to discover what hotel she'd gone to, and Jonas had caught the first taxi here. "I'm not leaving, Nikki."

"Fine, then I'll call security," she tossed over her shoulder as she headed for the phone.

"I wouldn't if I were you. Things could get pretty messy. More than likely your actions will generate gossip, fodder for the tabloids. I can see our faces plastered in the papers back home. Should be interesting reading."

She crossed her arms over her chest and stared him down. "You have more to lose than I do, Jonas. So what's it going to be?"

He crossed his arms over his own chest, stood with his legs spread apart and glared right back at her. "I'll tell you what it's going to be. You. Me. We have it out now, Nikki. You're still mad at me for what I did at that dinner party. Why? I thought women preferred knowing a man was interested in them. Last night I did something I've never done before, and that was to claim you as mine in front of everyone. So what's the problem?"

Nikki was convinced he really didn't have a clue. The man was so used to being in control, doing whatever the hell he wanted to do where women were concerned, that he thought *claiming* her was doing her a favor. Well, she had news for him. She didn't want to be claimed. She wanted to be loved.

Yes, yes, it was her heart talking again and she couldn't help it. The truth had hit her full force in the face at dinner. He had pampered her with attention, given her a taste of how things could be between them if they were in love. He hadn't left her side and had touched her easily, sliding his arms around her waist like it had been the most natural thing.

And every time he'd looked at her, although she'd tried to stay mad, her heart would leap in her chest, making her realize that without a doubt she had fallen in love with him. Though she had probably been in love with him for a while, at dinner she had opened her eyes and given in to her heart.

Giving in to her heart was one thing she could not abide. Admitting her love for Jonas had no place in this argument and there was no way he would ever know how she felt. There was no use. The man wasn't capable of loving a woman. That wasn't part of his makeup. He had probably figured out in that player mind of his that kissing her in front of everybody would entitle him to unlimited access to her bed. Well, she had news for him.

"I don't want to have it out with you, Jonas. I just want to be left alone."

"Do you?" he threw back. "I don't think so."

"I don't care what you think."

"Then maybe you should," he said, slowly moving toward her like a hunter who'd targeted his prey.

Nikki drew in a deep breath, convinced the man was mad. He was also sexy as hell. How could he not be when he was unbuttoning his shirt with every step he took? She backed up. "I don't want you, Jonas."

"Then I guess I'm going to have to change your mind about that."

She refused to back up any farther, deciding to stand her ground. She placed her hands on her hips and stared him down. "What is it with you Steeles? Why do you assume you can get any woman you want?"

He shrugged. "I can't speak for my brothers, but as for myself, the only woman I want is you."

She looked up at him. "Why?"

"I can give you a number of reasons. No woman can wear a pair of jeans like you do. Seeing your curvy bottom in them makes me hard each and every time. Then there are those soft curls on your head that frame your face. It's such a beautiful face."

His gaze went to her chest. "And then there're your breasts that fit perfectly in my hands."

His gaze shifted lower to the juncture of her thighs. He smiled. "The only thing I can say about *that* part is that I think I'm addicted to it. I love tasting it, touching it and getting all into it any way I can."

She lifted her chin. "Sounds all sexual to me."

"Probably because I'm a sexual kind of guy. But no matter how much I enjoy it, you're the only woman who has me wanting to come back for more, wishing there was a way I could stay locked inside you forever, make you a permanent taste bud on my tongue."

She knew it had to be a deliberate move on his part because her body was ripening with every word he said. Her panties were getting wet, her nipples felt sensitive against her robe and her lips were tingling. She should be fighting his assault on her senses, but she was getting pulled into a stream of mindless pleasure. The kind she knew he could deliver.

He slowly began advancing upon her again and she still held her ground, feeling the charged energy radiating between them that was breaking down her defenses, playing havoc with her senses one turbulent sensation at a time. She drew in a deep breath and filled her nostrils with his masculine scent and felt intense desire flood her middle.

"Why do you want to fight me, Nikki, when all I want to do is make love to you?"

His words were like ice water being dumped on a heated surface. She took a step back and narrowed her gaze. "You wouldn't know how to make love to a woman if it killed you, Jonas. All you know how to do is have sex with one. There is a difference."

He came to a stop in front of her. "Then show me how to make love. In fact I have a proposition for you. I propose that we enter into a private arrangement where for the rest of our trip on the *Velocity*, we don't have sex, but we make love."

She rolled her eyes. Those words just confirmed what she already knew. He didn't have an idea of what love was if he thought the arrangement he was proposing was possible. "Love isn't anything you can speak into existence. People can only *make* love when they are *in* love."

He reached out, wrapped an arm around her waist, drawing her closer. "In that case, let's pretend we're in love, then. You know that I don't love you and I know that you don't love me, but if it makes you feel better, we can pretend."

A part of Nikki couldn't believe he would suggest such a thing, but then another part of her did believe it. Although his parents were still happily married and he had two brothers who were also in happy marriages, Jonas just didn't get it, mainly because he'd never felt that emotion himself, and she wondered if he ever would. Who knew, maybe if he got a taste of it, he might like it.

She shook her head. Her thoughts were beginning to be just as insane as his, which meant her head was filling up with crazy ideas and ludicrous notions. Men like Jonas didn't fall in love. They didn't even know the meaning of it. But maybe if he were to pretend long enough…

There was that silly thought again. Besides, it wouldn't be any pretense on her part, so what would that do to her heart when he decided he didn't even like the pretend version? But then if she did enter into such a private arrangement with him, it would help her to move on and accept that the man she loved would never love her back.

She hadn't told anyone yet about the job offer she'd gotten from the L.A. producer who'd interviewed her before she boarded the *Velocity*. He'd been so impressed with her portfolio that he had called just minutes before the airship had taken off and made her a job offer as set photographer. The salary he'd offered had almost made her fall out of the bed in her cabin. And since he'd be directing a miniseries that would take three years of filming, it would be steady work for a long while.

The only drawback she'd seen at the time was moving from Phoenix to L.A. for those three years. But now, considering everything, the move to L.A. wouldn't be a drawback but a blessing. If she considered Jonas's offer of a private arrangement, the next two weeks would be all she would ever have before she left Phoenix to start a new life on the coast.

Jonas placed his finger beneath her chin so their gazes could connect. "So, baby, are you game?" he asked in a low tone, the depths of his green eyes holding hers. "Women are into this love thing more so than men, so if you want to pretend that you got me all strung out for you then that's fine. And just so we're clear, our arrangement ends when the *Velocity* docks back in L.A."

He moved closer still, so close his thighs were touching hers, and she could feel the hardness of his erection press against her stomach. And it felt so good resting there. So hot. So tempting.

"I can see you're hesitant. Maybe I need to give you something to help you make up your mind," he murmured, lowering his head to lick her lips.

"Something like what?" she asked, feeling her senses ooze away from her.

"Something like this."

He pushed the robe from her body and quickly removed her short baby-doll nightie as well. Then, as effortlessly as any man could do, he lifted her up off her feet and stood her naked body on the edge of the couch with her thighs spread apart.

"Jonas, I think that we—"

"Shh," he whispered, stepping back to remove his clothes and put on a condom although she knew she was on the pill. He then moved back to the couch to stand in front of her. "Bend your knees a little, baby, so I can ease inside you," he said in a deep husky tone.

She did as he asked and then glanced down to watch how the head of his engorged penis penetrated her flesh and slid deep inside of her. It fascinated her that something that large could fit inside of her so perfectly. Reaching out, he grabbed her hips to hold her body steady as he made the journey in. As deep as he could go. Then he reached out to lave her breasts with his tongue, licking all over the areola before sucking a turgid nipple into his mouth.

"You're starting to cream all over me and I like it," he said as he released her nipple. "It's hot and thick. Just the way I like to feel it. Just the way I love to taste it. But for now I want to pump you up. Give you reason to want to pretend we're in love."

And then the lower part of his body began moving as he captured her mouth, mating with it the same way he was mating with her womanly core. She moved to his rhythm as their bodies rocked and rolled, and she met his every thrust. And then he picked up speed and power, beginning to pound into her while he gripped her backside to hold her in place while he went deeper still, as if carving out his place inside of her.

"I can't get enough of you," he growled and she knew what he meant, mainly because she couldn't get enough of him, either. She widened her legs and the moment she did so, her senses spun out of control as he hit her G-spot.

She lifted her legs off the couch to wrap them around his waist as tight as they could get. He deepened the kiss and moved from the sofa to the nearest wall, where he pressed her back against the solid surface and continued to pound into her like the world would be ending tomorrow and he needed every thrust to count.

And they did.

Only with him was her body this sharp, keen, capable of feeling every single sensation he evoked. This was crazy. This was madness. And in the back of her mind she was reminded this was just sex. For him, yes, but not for her. He might be having sex with her, but she was definitely making love to him.

And then her body exploded under his forceful thrusts and she screamed his name as an orgasm ripped solidly into her, almost blinding her. It not only assaulted her body, it beat up on her senses. Whipped them to the point of no return. At that moment nothing mattered but this and how he was making her feel. She ignored that little chat from her heart that she deserved better. Instead she listened to her head. *You can't get any better than this.*

Jonas followed suit, roaring loudly on the heels of a deep masculine growl. He gritted his teeth while the lower half of his body continued to grind into her nonstop. He was pulling everything out of her and was still demanding more. And he was doing it in such a way that she felt every single movement. Never had she felt more connected to any man than right now.

She wrapped her arms around his neck and met his gaze. No words were exchanged between them. None was needed. And then their mouths joined again in a long, sensuous kiss.

Yes, she would agree to the private arrangement that he wanted, and when they returned to Phoenix she would be ready to move on with her life in another city.

It would be far away from the heartbreak she knew awaited her if she were to stay.

Chapter 16

"Okay, I give up," Jonas said, staring at the item on the serving tray that a waiter had just placed in front of them. "What is it?"

Nikki chuckled. "It's the carcass of the duck we had for dinner. The Chinese don't believe in letting anything go to waste so they fried it for us."

He arched his brow. "And we're supposed to eat it?"

"Yes."

He wiped his mouth and tossed his napkin on the table and leaned back in his chair. "I'll pass. I'm full already. What about you?"

She smiled over at him. "I'm full as well. Dinner was wonderful."

He would have to agree with her. The staff at their Beijing hotel had recommended this restaurant, and he had selected items off the menu that he recognized and had gone along with Nikki to try a few dishes he hadn't been familiar with and had enjoyed them as well. But he would draw the line with duck carcass.

Jonas studied Nikki as she sipped her tea, finding it hard to believe they'd spent the last two days together in perfect harmony. At first he had questioned his sanity in suggesting their private arrangement. To pretend to be in love with a woman had to be one of the craziest notions he'd ever come up with. But so far things were working.

He enjoyed watching her sleep and how her curls would fan her face and the soft snoring sounds she would occasionally make. And then in the mornings when she would wake up, he liked how she would smile up at him before reaching out for what had become their good-morning kiss. Of course that kiss would lead to other things.

"So, what will we do today?"

Her question pulled him from his thoughts and he glanced across the table at her. Her eyes were just as bright as her smile. "I'll let you decide today since yesterday's activities were my idea."

"Yeah, and you whined the entire time."

He looked offended. "I did not whine."

She leaned in closer across the table. "You did too, Jonas Steele."

He laughed. "Okay, maybe I did."

It had been his idea for them to climb the Great Wall of China, but halfway up he was ready to go back down. He hadn't known the place would require so much energy—energy he preferred using for other things like making love to her. Even now he was still overwhelmed by the power of what they shared in the bedroom. They were doing things the same way, but he could swear he was beginning to note a difference. A difference he couldn't quite put his finger on.

"In that case, since you're letting it be my decision, I suggest we take a cooking class."

He sat up straight in his chair. "A cooking class?"

She chuckled. "Yes."

He crossed his arms over his chest. "Why would I want to attend a cooking class? I have a woman who comes in twice a week to clean and cook enough food to last me all week. Then there are my weekly Thursday dinners at my parents' home. I don't need to know how to cook."

"I think it will be fun."

"Whatever," he said, taking a sip of his own tea. "I guess I'm game if that's what you really want to do."

Her smile brightened even more. "Yes, that's what I really want to do."

He smiled, enjoying the smile that curved her lips. "Okay. Where's my apron?"

With shopping bags in each hand, Nikki entered her hotel room and used her feet to shut the door behind her. All the passengers would return to the *Velocity* later that day and she had wanted to get some shopping in before the limo arrived to transport her and Jonas to the airport. Their next stop was Sydney, Australia, where they would be spending another three days.

Earlier that morning after making love, she and Jonas had toured a Chinese palaces and Tiananmen Square. Afterward, they'd shared lunch at, of all places, Friday's. Jonas had been tickled to see an American chain restaurant and insisted on going. She had invited him to go shopping with her in the afternoon, but he declined, saying he wanted to return to the hotel for a quick nap.

Nikki glanced at her watch. That had been three hours ago and from the soft hum of his snoring, it seemed he was still at it. Quietly placing her bags on the sofa, she tiptoed out of the sitting area into the bedroom. She leaned in the doorway and stared across the room at the man she loved.

His upper torso, not covered by the bed linens, was bare, as she was certain the rest of him was since he loved sleeping in the nude. She blushed when she recalled how he now had her sleeping in the nude as well, something she had learned was an enjoyable experience. Especially since Jonas had a tendency to wake up during the crazy hours of the night wanting to make love.

Nikki stepped into the room, closer to the bed. With his mass of hair all over the pillow, the man was pure temptation even while asleep. She drew in a deep breath. These would be the only days she would have with him this way, trouble free, filled with fun and excitement, and both beginning and ending with them connected in a way that took her breath away just thinking about it. It always felt good being wrapped in his embrace, held by him, hearing whispered erotic words that could make her come just listening to them.

She was about to move away from the bed when suddenly his hand snaked out and grabbed her around the wrist. She looked down at him and saw his eyes were open and the depth of his green eyes had her holding her breath.

His hold on her hand tightened when he continued

to stare at her. Then he said in a deep husky tone, "I want you, baby. And I want you now."

He pulled her into the bed with him, almost tore off her clothes, and it seemed within seconds after donning a condom he retrieved from the night stand, he was straddling her, easing between her legs, slowly penetrating her, deep and sure.

Gracious! Him inside of her felt so right. Why couldn't he see it? Why couldn't he feel it? Why couldn't he love her as much as she loved him? There were too many whys for her to concentrate on at the moment. Not when he was thrusting inside her so hard the whole bed was shaking.

"Come for me, baby. I want you to cream all over me," he said, breathing the words against her neck.

And she did, calling out to him while lifting her hips to take him in as far as possible. Their days were numbered, but she was determined to collect as many memories as she could.

"Brittany is pregnant?" Jonas asked, not believing what his brother Galen had just told him.

"Yes, and I'm so happy about it I can't stand it."

Jonas nodded, hearing that excitement in his brother's voice. And then he couldn't help but chuckle when he recalled what he'd suggested to his mother a few weeks earlier about hitting Galen and Brittany up for a grandchild. He could just imagine his mother's happiness and excitement as well.

"Have you told Mom yet?" he asked.

"No, we're telling her tonight when we go to the folks' place for dinner."

Jonas would give anything to be there to see the

expression on Eden's face when they did. Expecting a grandbaby should definitely keep her busy and out of her single sons' business for a while.

"If you see Nikki, don't mention anything to her. Brittany wants to be the one to tell her. I think she's going to ask Nikki to be our baby's godmother."

Jonas nodded thinking Nikki would make a good choice for godmother. They had spent a lot of time together over the past two weeks, and he had been exposed to a side of her he hadn't seen before. He saw she was generous to a fault, liked to have fun and was loyal to those she considered friends. Like him she was close to her family, and like his, her parents had been married for a long time.

A part of him was trying to forget that tomorrow they would be returning home. At least he would. She mentioned that she had a meeting with someone in L.A. and wouldn't be back in Phoenix until the end of the week.

Jonas knew that everyone traveling on the *Velocity* could say that it had been one hell of a voyage and that they had had the experience of a lifetime. There was no doubt in his mind the reviews written by the media on board would be favorable, and it would be up to his staff to capitalize on the good publicity and roll out the marketing campaign that would guarantee a sellout as soon as *Velocity* took its next voyage.

He couldn't help but think of this one. After Beijing they had traveled to Australia, from there to Dubai and finally to Paris. They had covered four continents in fourteen days. Tomorrow they would leave Paris for L.A.

"Jonas?"

It was then that he recalled his brother's request. "Okay, I won't say anything to Nikki," he answered.

No one knew he and Nikki were involved other than those who saw them together on the airship. But he didn't care if the whole world knew it. The only thing was their affair would be ending soon so sharing the information was a moot point now.

Moments later he ended his call with Galen to walk over to the window and look out. This hadn't been his first visit to Paris and wouldn't be his last. He loved the place, with its elegant architecture, beautiful countryside and majestic castles. Everyone was staying at Chateau d'Esclimont, which was an hour outside of Paris. The place was simply breathtaking and nestled in the Loire Valley. He had discovered Nikki could ride a horse and the two of them had ridden two Thoroughbreds around the countryside. And then later they'd had a picnic near a picturesque lake.

Australia had been just as magnificent. It been somewhat strange knowing it was winter in the States and arriving in Sydney during the heart of their summer. He and Nikki had totally enjoyed themselves, taking a tour of the city and flying over the Great Barrier Reef. Seeing one of the seven wonders of the natural world had been totally captivating, something he would never forget.

And Dubai was certainly a place he would return to. There was nothing like sailing on the Persian Gulf and taking a camel ride across the desert. He couldn't help but smile when he recalled how Nikki had blushed profusely at the sight of camels mating. And then later that night, back in their hotel room, they'd done a little camel-like mating of their own.

He moved away from the window. The time he'd spent with Nikki was something he couldn't forget, either. She had brought something into the last two weeks that he hadn't expected. Namely, the kind of companionship he hadn't expected to find with any woman. She was someone he could talk to about anything, and he definitely enjoyed their conversations. Considering their rocky beginning, he was simply amazed at how well they got along. That didn't mean they agreed on anything, far from it. But they had a very satisfying way of compromising when they did disagree.

He was finding out that pretending to love a woman had its benefits, although he wouldn't want to do that with any other woman. Besides, he couldn't imagine any other woman agreeing to such a deal. But Nikki had. She had agreed to this private arrangement between them, and he didn't regret making it.

The only thing he regretted was that tomorrow things would come to an end. There was no doubt in his mind that he and Nikki would run into each other on occasion, but he would resume his life as he knew it and she would resume hers.

Yesterday he had viewed all the photographs she'd taken and of course he hadn't been disappointed. She had done an excellent job and he couldn't wait for the marketing campaign to move forward.

Once she emailed him all the photographs, her employment with Ideas of Steele would cease. He would pay her for her services and that would be it.

His hands shook when he tried pouring coffee from the pot in the room. After spending two such glorious weeks with Nikki, how was he supposed to get back into the swing of things without her? At that moment, the thought of becoming involved with another woman, going back to his "one and done" rule just didn't have the appeal it had once had.

Even worse, the thought of his manhood sliding between any woman's legs other than Nikki's, or his head being buried between any other woman's thighs, or his mouth mating with any other woman's, was leaving a bad taste in his mouth.

He put down his coffee cup and ran his fingers over his chin, feeling the stubble there. What in the hell was wrong with him? No woman had ever made him feel this way and, dammit, he didn't like it one bit. He needed to get ready to get his groove on once again, be the player he was. There were all those models, socialites and party girls who wanted to share his bed. He was certain any one of them could get him back on the right track, put his mind back in check. And put Nikki way in the back of it.

She'd been fun, enjoyable, but now it was time for them to move on, and they would because when the *Velocity* landed in Los Angeles, their private arrangement as they knew it would be over.

Tears of happiness sprang into Nikki's eyes. "Oh, Britt, that is so wonderful. Congratulations. I am so happy for you and Galen."

And she truly was. She knew Galen and Britt's relationship was solid and they loved each other very much. To Nikki, having a baby, one conceived in love, had to be the most rewarding thing that could happen to a woman.

"I can't wait until you get back. We're going to have to celebrate," Brittany cut into her thoughts and said.

Nikki agreed. "Yes, we will. I'll be back in the States later today, but I've got another meeting with Martin Dunlap before I come back to Phoenix."

"So you are going to take that job in Los Angeles?"

"Yes, I think it will be for the best. I'm at a place in my life where I need to make a change."

She drew in a deep breath. In less than two hours the *Velocity* would be leaving its docking station in Paris to return home. Everyone was on board and accounted for, and Jonas was in a private meeting with Fulton. She knew the man was pleased with how this trial voyage had turned out, and so far all the media coverage had been positive. She'd heard that people were already clamoring to get tickets for the next trip, which was scheduled in two weeks.

"I hate that we're going to be separated again, Nikki."

Nikki hated that, too. She and Brittany had lived across the street from each other while in their early teens, and when Nikki's military dad had received orders to move to another port, Nikki and Brittany had lost touch. They had found each other a year and a half ago when Brittany had come to Phoenix on business. She and Galen had met and the rest was history.

"We'll never be separate, Britt. I'll just be a plane ride away. Besides, now that you've asked me to be the baby's godmother, you'll be seeing me more than you think."

Brittany chuckled. "Yes, and I believe that one day you'll have all those babies of your own that you've always wanted."

Nikki wished that was true but wouldn't be holding her breath for that to happen. "Maybe. But in the meantime, I'll spoil my little goddaughter or godson rotten."

A short while later, after she ended her call with Brittany, Jonas returned to the cabin. After their decision regarding their private arrangement, they had begun sharing a cabin. They'd decided to use his since it had been the larger of the two.

He glanced over at her the moment he entered the room. He must have seen her red eyes, because he crossed the room and pulled her into his arms. "Hey, you okay?"

She nodded and looked up at him. "Yes, I just finished talking to Brittany. She told me about her and Galen's good news. She also told me that you were sworn to secrecy."

He chuckled. "Yes. That kind of news definitely made my parents happy. Galen and Brittany told them last night. I hear my mother is already buying out the baby stores."

Nikki could just imagine. She remembered how her mother had behaved when her brother and sister-in-law presented her parents with their first grandbaby.

Jonas stroking her back felt good. Being in his arms felt good as well. Boy, she was definitely going to miss this. Neither of them had broached the subject of what would happen when the *Velocity* arrived in Los Angeles. They didn't have to. It had been part of the agreement. He would go his way and she would go hers.

Of course their paths would cross in Phoenix from time to time. There was no way around it, and there was always the chance they might work together again. But the intimacy they'd shared would become a thing of the past. Their relationship would move from friends with benefits to just friends.

She pulled out of his arms and looked up at him. "I'm fine. How did things go with Fulton?"

"Great. He had a chance to look at the portfolio you put together and said you did a wonderful job. He told me to tell you that."

"Thanks." Their relationship was changing already. She could feel it. Although they had made love that morning, she had felt him beginning to withdraw. Her heart was breaking inside, but a part of her understood that that's the way things were to be. Nothing lasted forever, even if it was pretend.

Their gazes held and she felt the yearning stir within her as it always did. He had that effect on women. He certainly had that effect on her. But did they have time now? They would be docking in L.A. in less than four hours. There was a part of her that wished time could stand still.

"Nikki, I—"

She reached out and placed her finger to his lips. "I know and it's okay. I had a good time and I hope you did, too."

He nodded. "I did."

He pulled her back to him and lowered his head toward hers. She had gotten her answer. They would make love one last time. This would be their goodbye. And despite everything, she had no regrets.

Chapter 17

Three weeks later

"You're awfully quiet tonight, son. Usually you're the life of the party."

Jonas glanced up at his dad, a man whom he highly admired and respected. Over forty years ago Drew Steele had taken his small trucking company and turned it into a million-dollar industry that had routes all over the United States.

Another one of his father's accomplishments was always making time for his six sons, no matter how busy he'd been. And although he and his brothers would moan and groan about his parents' Thursday-night chow-down, where their attendance was expected, deep down they appreciated it as a way to stay connected, no matter how busy their schedules were.

Jonas forced a smile to his lips. "I'm fine. Besides, I decided to take a backseat to Gannon tonight since he seems to have a lot to say."

Drew chuckled. "Yes, I can see that." He paused a moment, then said, "I understand that the four-continent air voyage was a huge success and your company's marketing campaign was instrumental in getting it over the top. Congratulations."

"Thanks." Deep down he felt the credit should go to Nikki. Those photographs she'd taken had helped to introduce the *Velocity* into the market. His social media guru had taken Nikki's pictures and had done a fantastic job in incorporating them in the Ideas of Steele marketing plan.

Nikki.

He gazed down into his glass of wine wondering how she'd been doing. More than once he'd been tempted to pick up the phone to call her and ask. But each time he had talked himself out of doing so. Something was going on with him and at the moment he didn't have a clue as to what. All he knew was that as of yet he hadn't been able to get back into his game. Hell, the thought of kissing another woman had almost made him gag, and the thought of sharing a bed with one sent negative shivers through his body.

"And you sure you're okay?"

He met his father's gaze again. "Yes, I'm sure, but I'd like to ask you something."

"What?"

"That time when you and Mom were dating and you let her run off to Paris and almost lost her. Why did you do that?"

Over the years Jonas and his brothers had heard the

story of their parents' tumultuous love affair. They'd heard how Drew had refused to accept Eden as his fate and ended up pushing her away. By the time he'd come to his senses, she had left the States for Paris. Drew had freaked out at the possibility of losing Eden forever and had followed her and asked her to marry him.

His father met his gaze for a long moment and then said, "Because I was convinced I was not ready to love her or any woman. I honestly assumed I was above falling in love. I loved women too much to settle down with just one."

Jonas nodded. That pretty much sounded like the story of his life. "What made you see things differently?"

"I asked myself what I thought would be a simple question. Would my life be better without Eden in it? Was chasing women more important than making memories of waking up to the same woman, one who could connect to me on all levels? One who made me think about her when I should be working? One who made me think of having several little girls who would look just like her, even when I thought I didn't even want kids? When I finally was honest with myself and answered those questions, then I knew that whether I wanted to be or not, I was in love. And then I knew there *was* no way I could let her go."

Drew released a chuckle from deep within his chest. "Hell, I had it so bad for her and didn't even know it. I was pure whipped." He paused a moment, then threw in an extra piece of sage advice. "I believe a smart man not only recognizes when he's whipped but actually loves the thought of it, especially if the woman is worth it. There's nothing wrong with falling in love if it's a woman you can't live your life without."

Drew then glanced across the room at his wife, who was sitting down on the sofa talking to their daughters-in-law. "And for me, your mother is that woman. She always will be."

He then met Jonas's gaze again. "So if you're ever lucky to meet such a woman, whatever you do, please don't make the mistake your old man almost made."

Drew smiled then. "Come on. Your mom is beckoning us to dinner."

Jonas drowned out the conversation around him at the dinner table as he ate his food. Everyone seemed to be in a festive mood, so why wasn't he? Fulton had called today to congratulate him on an outstanding marketing campaign. Already voyages on the *Velocity* had sold out for the next six months and they were working on a waiting list that extended well into the next three.

However, what had really consumed Jonas's thoughts for the past three weeks hadn't been the success of *Velocity*'s marketing campaign. It had been Nikki. His Nikki. The woman who'd enticed him to push for a private arrangement with her for two weeks. It was an arrangement he still had memories about today. Never had a woman been so loving, so giving, so downright sexy.

Even now he could recall them dancing together in a nightclub in Sydney, him finally being talked into going shopping with her in Dubai, and the two of them viewing the Eiffel Tower in Paris. Their time together had been so ideal, so perfect. Exactly how it should feel for a couple who cared about each other.

Who had pretended to.

There were times when he was alone in his bed, at work or just riding in his car when he would remember and wish there was a way he could recapture those moments, a way he could book another flight on the *Velocity* and relive every single second. But he knew there was no way he could do that. So all he had was memories.

He felt an ache in the lower part of his gut just remembering all those sexy outfits she'd purchased on her shopping spree and how she would give him a personal fashion show, which ended with him removing every single item, stitch by stitch. Then they would make love all through the night and the early-morning hours.

Jonas glanced up when Tyson asked him a question about the *Velocity*. Moments later Eli and Galen asked him a few more questions. He knew his brothers had noted he was quieter than usual and were trying to draw him into the family's conversation. He appreciated their efforts, but he truly wasn't in a talkative mood tonight.

"So, Jonas, what happens if you get another big account like Fulton's and need a photographer?" Mercury asked.

Jonas frowned, wondering where the hell that question came from and why Mercury was asking. He glanced across the dinner table at his brother. "I'll do like I've always done and use a freelancer. Of course I'll approach Nikki Cartwright first. She's the best." Jonas then quietly returned to his meal.

"Yeah, but that won't be possible now that she's moving to L.A."

Jonas's head snapped back up and his green eyes slammed into his brother's. "What did you just say?" His tone had such a deadly and hard edge to it that everyone at the dinner table stopped eating and stared at him.

Mercury pretended not to notice Jonas's steely disposition when he answered with an insolent smile on his lips. "I said Nikki is moving to L.A. She got this job offer from some big-time producer and I understand she's moving away at the end of the month."

Jonas shifted his gaze from Mercury to Brittany, who was sitting at Galen's side. "Is that true?"

She nodded slowly. "Yes. I thought you knew."

Jonas drew in a deep breath. No, he hadn't known. For some reason he looked at his father, and when their eyes met, Jonas clearly remembered the conversation they'd shared before dinner.

He pushed his plate back and stood. "Please excuse me. I need to leave. There's some business I need to tend to."

Eden, who was completed dumbfounded, spoke up. "Surely whatever it is can wait, Jonas. You haven't finished dinner."

He shook his head. "No, Mom, it can't wait."

And then he headed for the door, only pausing to grab his motorcycle helmet off a table in the foyer on his way out.

Nikki couldn't sleep, but then that was the story of her life since she returned home. Too bad she couldn't get thoughts of Jonas out of her mind. She wondered if he ever thought about her with the same yearning and intensity that she thought about him. Probably not. The only good thing was that his name hadn't been linked with any woman in the tabloids since they'd gotten back, but she knew it was just a matter of time.

She thought about her move to L.A. Of course her parents and brother who lived in San Diego were happy with her decision, since that meant she would be closer to them. She hadn't lived in California since leaving home for college so perhaps the move would do her some good.

And then maybe she would be able to forge ahead with her life and forget about Jonas. Then she wouldn't have to worry about the possibility of running into him unexpectedly or worry whether he was with another woman. Not that it mattered, really. Just remembering all they'd shared was enough to shatter her these days.

And then there was another problem she'd encountered because of Jonas. Her body was going through sexual withdrawal. This time of night when she couldn't sleep, she would remember everything they'd shared, especially the time she'd spent in his arms, making love with him, using all those positions. And during those last fourteen days they *had* made love. She wondered if he'd been able to tell the difference. Probably not.

After a few more tosses and turns she finally sat up in bed. She clicked on a lamp and looked around. For the first time since she moved here she realized just how lonely this house was. Lonely and empty. Her bedroom was prettily decorated in her favorite colors of chocolate and lime green, and she'd hired a professional decorator to make sure things were just how she'd wanted them. But something was missing.

It really didn't matter now since she was moving away. Already her realtor had found a buyer so there was nothing or no one to hold her to Phoenix any longer. She would miss Brittany and their weekly lunch dates, but like she'd told her best friend, they were just an airplane flight away.

Galen had promised to call her the minute Brittany went into labor. More than anything she wanted to be around when her goddaughter or godson was born.

Since it seemed like sleep was out of the question for her at the moment, she slid out of bed and slipped into the matching robe to the baby-doll nightgown she was wearing. Both had been items she'd purchased while in Paris.

She had made it downstairs when she heard the sound of a motorcycle. One of her neighbors had recently purchased a Harley and she figured he'd taken it out for a late-night ride.

Nikki was headed for her kitchen to raid her snack jar. Thanks to Jonas she liked Tootsie Pops and always kept a bag on hand. Whenever she plopped one in her mouth she thought of him.

She stopped walking when she heard a knock on her door. Who on earth would be visiting her at this hour? She tightened her robe around her and went to the door, pausing to take a look out the peephole. Her breath caught in her throat when she saw her late-night caller.

She quickly entered the code to disarm her alarm system before opening the door. "Jonas? Why… What are you doing here?"

He was standing under her porch light in a pair

of jeans, a T-shirt that advertised Ideas of Steele, and biker boots. In his hand he held his bike helmet. "Would it be okay if I come inside so we can talk?"

Although she had no idea what they had to talk about, she nodded and took a step back. "Sure. Come in."

Once he entered and closed the door behind him, she watched as he glanced around and saw the boxes already packed and sealed, ready to be picked up by the movers.

"I heard tonight that you're leaving town. I didn't know," he said.

She nodded. So he didn't know. Would it have mattered if he had? She doubted it. "Yes, I got a job offer in L.A."

"Why didn't you tell me you were moving away, Nikki?"

His question surprised her. Why would she tell him? It's not like they meant anything to each other. Those two weeks on board the *Velocity* had been nothing but a game of pretend that he'd initiated under the disguise of a private arrangement. She'd gone along with it because she loved him. And she had no regrets.

"Nikki?"

She met his gaze, suddenly feeling angry when she recalled how he'd started withdrawing from her the last day of their trip. They'd made love true enough, but she'd felt he was pulling back in ways he hadn't before. Now she placed her hands on her hips and lifted her chin to glare at him.

"I really didn't think you'd want to know, Jonas. We had an agreement and you made sure I understood the terms. I did. When we returned to Phoenix, things would go back to the way they were between us. So excuse me, but did I miss something?"

He blew out a long breath and rubbed his hand across his face; then he looked back at her. "Yes, you missed something, and so did I."

She lifted a brow. "Really? Then please enlighten me because I have no idea what *we* could have missed."

"The fact that I have fallen in love with you."

His words took the wind out of Nikki's sail. She sucked in a deep breath, and it seemed that every muscle in her body tensed. She stared at him, saw his unreadable green eyes staring back at her. She slowly shook her head. "Impossible. You don't know how to love."

"I do now. You taught me, remember? For two weeks you taught me there's a difference between having sex with a woman and making love to one. I know that difference now, Nikki. I've always made love to you because I've always loved you. Since our first kiss, and possibly before it. But I fought it tooth and nail."

He paused a moment and then said in a low voice, "I probably would still be fighting it if I hadn't heard you were leaving. Once I heard I knew I couldn't let you go without telling you how much you mean to me. Just how much I love you."

Nikki closed her eyes, fearful when she opened them he would be gone and his presence would have been only a figment of her imagination. Evidently he'd read her mind, because when she opened her eyes, he said, "I'm still here."

Yes, he was still there, standing in the middle of her living room with his helmet clutched to his hand, his feet braced apart and his hair tied back in a ponytail. He looked like a rebel, a rogue, a man determined to defy the odds. A man who'd managed to claim her heart.

"Why do you love me, Jonas?" she asked, wondering if he really knew or if he only assumed he was in love with her.

"Why *don't* I love you?" he countered. "But to answer your question, I love everything about you. But I especially like how you handle your business. I admire that. And I love the way you make me feel when I'm inside of you, lying beside you in bed, or sitting across from you at a table. I think I fell in love with you that day we met at my office and you came in from the rain. I was so totally captivated by you then, but I tried denying it. And then that day we kissed in your office, I was so taken aback I couldn't think straight. That's why I tried avoiding you for eighteen months. You pulled out emotions in me that I wasn't use to feeling, and I was afraid that you would encompass my whole world. In fact, you do. My only question is how do you feel about me?"

She drew in a deep breath, fighting back tears and thinking only a man like Jonas would have to ask. Anyone else would have been able to see it on her face. "I love you, too, Jonas. I think I fell in love with you that rainy day as well, but I knew for certain how I felt while on the *Velocity*. But I thought loving you was a hopeless case on my part, although I wanted to use those two weeks to show you what love was about."

"You did, sweetheart. I know the difference between sex and making love. Each and every time I touched you, we made love."

"Oh, Jonas."

He placed his helmet on the table and then slowly crossed the room and pulled her into his arms. "Just so you know, me loving you is not about making any demands. More than anything I want you to follow your dream. Move to L.A. if you have to, but I'll be coming with you. I can set up a satellite office and work from just about anywhere."

Nikki's eyes lit up. "You would do that for me?"

"I would do that for *us*. I don't want to be away from you. I got used to having you around on the *Velocity*, and I've been miserable these past three weeks without you."

He paused a moment and then said, "And I need to be completely honest about something, confess to something I did just to keep you around me."

She lifted a brow. "What?"

He reached out, captured her finger and wrapped his bigger one around it. "That night you turned down my job offer I took measures into my own hands."

"How?"

"By playing a favor card. I called a guy I knew whose brother is closely tied with Senator Joseph's election campaign. I had him renege on your job offer."

She stiffened in his embrace. "You did?"

"Yes. I did."

She didn't say anything for a minute, just stared at him. The multitude of emotions revealed in his eyes nearly took her breath away. Even then he had wanted her and had even been willing to play dirty to get her. But she would have to admit that the end result had been worth it.

"I hope you know doing something like that is going to cost you," she said, making sure he heard the lightness in her voice when she began seeing a wary look in his gaze.

"Hmm, what's the charge?"

She paused as if thinking about it and then said, "You're going to have to love me for the rest of your days."

He drew her closer. "Baby, I had planned on doing that anyway."

And then Jonas lowered his mouth to hers, kissing Nikki with the hunger he had only for her and no other woman. Only with her did he want to feel free, be loved and give love. Only with her did his emotions rise to the top. And only with Nikki was he not afraid to want more than what he'd been getting. He wanted commitment. He wanted to abolish his one-and-done policy and replace it with one-and-only, because that's what Nikki was to him.

He broke off the kiss and swept her off her feet and into his arms. "I need to make love to you. And just so you know, I haven't touched another woman since you. I couldn't because they weren't you and I didn't want anyone else."

He leaned down and kissed her again. When he released her lips, he asked, "Let's go to the bedroom?"

He slowly carried her there, kissing her intermittently along the way. When he reached her bedroom he placed her down in the middle of her bed. He glanced around. "Nice room."

She looked him up and down and smiled. "Mmm, nice man."

He chuckled and likewise, let his gaze travel all over her. "Nice woman."

And then he began removing his clothes, and she

watched as he removed every single piece. He then moved back to the bed and with a couple flicks of his wrists, he had removed the robe and gown from her body.

"You're pretty good at that, aren't you?" she said when he'd gotten her naked.

"Only for you, sweetheart," he said against her throat before trailing a path with his tongue past her ear. "And there is something else I'd like to ask you."

"What?" She was barely able to get the word out before his hand lowered between her legs and he quickly moved to the honeyed warmth he knew awaited him there.

"Will you marry me?"

It seemed she had stopped breathing, and he leaned back and stared into her face. She returned his stare and he knew what she was doing. She had to see the sincerity of his question in his features, in his eyes, in the lips he then eased into an earnest smile.

He saw the single tear that fell from her eye before she smiled and said, "Yes, yes. I'll marry you. I'd almost given up hope that I would find him."

He lifted a brow. "Find who?"

"My knight in shining armor." She chuckled. "Little did I know he would be riding a motorcycle instead of a horse, but I'll take him any way I can. My Mr. Wrong became my Mr. Right. I love you so much."

"And I love you, too."

And then he was kissing her again, pulling her into his arms while their limbs entwined. And then he eased over her, slid between her legs, lifted her hips and stared down at her while he penetrated her. He'd never tire of looking down at her while they made love.

"Damn, I miss this. Damn, how I miss you," he said in between deep, languid thrusts. He didn't intend to rush. Instead he made love to her with the patience of a man who had all day and all night. He wondered if she noticed the difference in their lovemaking and figured eventually she would. She wrapped her legs around him and, lifting her hips off the bed, met his thrusts, stroke for stroke.

"Oh Jonas, I miss this, too," she said, as her inner muscles clenched him hard, trying to pull everything out of him.

He threw his head back and screamed her name at the same moment she screamed his. He gripped her hips tightly, needing as much of a connection with her as he could get.

And that's when he knew she felt him, felt him in a way no other woman had felt him before. He was exploding inside of her, christening her insides with his release.

Her shocked eyes looked up at him with delight when she realized he hadn't put on a condom. He didn't intend to use one ever again. This was the woman he would marry, and he wanted babies with her. No other man who would be her babies' daddy. With her he would share everything.

Moments later, when they were both spent, he slumped down in the bed and gathered her into his arms. They would sleep, wake up and make love, sleep and then make love some more. Later. Tomorrow. They would talk and lay out a strategic plan to tackle how they would make things work with her new job in L.A. They were and always would be a team.

"You forced me to realize I wanted the very things

I thought I would never desire, Nikki," he whispered, emotions clogging his voice. "But I can see so clearly now and I know what I want, sweetheart. More than anything I want you."

And then he leaned down and slanted his mouth over hers, knowing this was the beginning, and for them there would never be an end.

Epilogue

A beautiful day in June

Nikki glanced around the ballroom that was filled with over five hundred guests who'd come to witness one of Phoenix's most notorious bachelors tying the knot. It had been the kind of wedding she'd always dreamed of having, with her mother and her mother-in-law working together. Her dream had come true.

She glanced across the room at her husband, who was talking to his father and some of his cousins. There were a lot of Steeles, more than she'd known existed, and now she was a part of the family. She and Jonas had decided to alternate living in L.A. and Phoenix. His idea for a satellite office had been a good one.

"You're such a beautiful bride," one of Jonas's female cousins, Cheyenne, the mother of triplets, told her, pulling her back into the conversation. They were standing there talking with Brittany and two more of Jonas's female cousins from Charlotte. Brittany was showing already, and she and Galen had found out a few months ago they would be having twins. Everyone in the Steele family was excited at the thought of multiple births again.

"Thanks." And she felt beautiful, because of Jonas. When she had walked down the aisle to him at the church, it was as if the two of them were the only ones there. The gaze that had held hers spoke volumes and had sent out several silent messages, ones that only she could decipher. That was a good thing. If anyone else had read his thoughts, they would have been scandalized.

"Ladies, I need to borrow my wife for a minute."

She glanced up when Jonas suddenly appeared by her side, sliding his hand into hers. He looked devastatingly handsome dressed in his white tux with his wavy hair flowing about his shoulders. His green eyes were sharp when he glanced down at her. "We'll be leaving in a few minutes and I thought we should say goodbye to our parents before we took off."

She beamed up at him. "Okay."

As a wedding gift, Mr. Fulton had given them the honeymoon suite on board the *Velocity*. They would remain in Dubai for two weeks and would return to the States on the *Velocity* when the airship came back through, making its rounds.

Halfway over to where their parents stood, Jonas stopped and pulled her into his arms and kissed her. She ignored the catcalls and whistles as she sank closer into her husband's embrace. When he finally released her, she smiled up at him. "And what was that for?"

He grinned. "I thought it was time for me to make another public claim. You're mine and I want the whole world to know it."

Nikki was filled with intense happiness. Her head and her heart were no longer at battle. Now they were on the same page, reading from the same script and the writing said *Jonas loves Nikki. Nikki loves Jonas. And they will live happily ever after.*

* * * * *

Reese Ryan writes sexy, emotional romance with captivating family drama, surprising secrets and a posse of complex characters.

A Midwesterner with deep Southern roots, Reese currently resides in semi-small-town North Carolina, where she's an avid reader, a music junkie and a self-declared connoisseur of cheesy grits. Reese is the author of the Bourbon Brothers and Pleasure Cove series.

Connect with her via Instagram, Facebook, Twitter or at reeseryan.com. Join her VIP Readers Lounge at bit.ly/vipreaderslounge.

Books by Reese Ryan

Harlequin Desire

The Bourbon Brothers
Savannah's Secret
The Billionaire's Legacy
Engaging the Enemy

Dynasties: Secrets of the A-List
Seduced by Second Chances

Texas Cattleman's Club: Inheritance
Secret Heir Seduction

Visit the Author Profile page at Harlequin.com for more titles.

SAVANNAH'S SECRETS

Reese Ryan

To my parents, who instilled a love of reading in me at an early age. To the teachers who fostered that love. To my childhood friends who felt reading was as cool as I did—both then and now. To my husband and family, who sacrifice precious time with Babe/Mom/Nonni so that I can share the stories in my head with the world. And to the amazing readers who are kind enough to come along for the ride. Thank you, all.

Chapter 1

Blake Abbott rubbed his forehead and groaned. He'd rather be walking the floor of the distillery, preparing for their new product launch, instead of reviewing market research data. Out there on the floor was where the magic of making their world-renowned bourbon happened.

His assistant, Daisy, knocked on his open office door. "Blake, don't forget the interview for the new event manager position… It's in fifteen minutes."

Blake cursed under his breath. His brother Max had asked him to handle the interview. The new position fell under Max's charge as marketing VP. But he was at a trade show in Vegas. Probably partying and getting laid while Blake worked his ass off back at the office.

Their mother—who usually handled their special events—was in Florida helping her sister recover from surgery.

Tag, I'm it.

But Blake had more pressing matters to deal with. Production was two weeks behind on the limited-edition moonshines they were rolling out to commemorate the upcoming fiftieth anniversary of King's Finest Distillery. Once an illegal moonshine operation started by his great-grandfather in the hills of Tennessee, his grandfather had established the company as a legal distiller of premium spirits.

What better way to celebrate their golden anniversary as a legitimate enterprise than to reproduce the hooch that gave them their start?

Getting the project back on track took precedence over hiring an overpriced party planner.

Blake grunted, his eyes on the screen. "Too late to reschedule?"

"Technically? No," a slightly husky voice with an unfamiliar Southern drawl responded. "But then, I am already here."

Blake's attention snapped to the source of the voice. His temperature climbed instantly when he encountered the woman's sly smile and hazel eyes sparkling in the sunlight.

Her dark wavy hair was pulled into a low bun. If she'd worn the sensible gray suit to downplay her gorgeous features, it was a spectacular fail.

"Blake, I'm sorry." Daisy's cheeks flushed. Her gaze shifted from him to the woman. "I should've—"

"It's okay, Daisy." Blake held back a grin. He crossed the room, holding the woman's gaze. "I'll take it from here, thanks."

Daisy shoved a folder into his hands. "Her résumé. In case you can't find the copy I gave you earlier."

Blake thanked his assistant. She knew him well and was unbothered by his occasional testiness. It was one of the reasons he went to great lengths to keep her happy.

"Well, Miss—"

"Carlisle." The woman extended her hand. "But please, call me Savannah."

Blake shook her hand and was struck by the contrast of the softness of her skin against his rough palm. Electricity sparked on his fingertips. He withdrew his hand and shoved it in his pocket.

"Miss… Savannah, please, have a seat." He indicated the chair opposite his desk.

She complied. One side of her mouth pulled into a slight grin, drawing his attention to her pink lips.

Were they as soft and luscious as they looked? He swallowed hard, fighting back his curiosity about the flavor of her gloss.

Blake sank into the chair behind his desk, thankful for the solid expanse between them.

He was the one with the authority. So why did it seem that she was assessing him?

Relax. Stay focused.

He was behaving as if he hadn't seen a stunningly beautiful woman before.

"Tell me about yourself, Savannah."

It was a standard opening. But he genuinely wanted to learn everything there was to know about this woman.

Savannah crossed one long, lean leg over the other. Her skirt shifted higher, grazing the top of her knee and exposing more of her golden-brown skin.

"I'm from West Virginia. I've lived there my entire

life. I spent the past ten years working my way up the ranks, first at a small family-owned banquet hall. Then at a midsize chain hotel. In both positions, I doubled the special events revenue. My recommendation letters will confirm that."

She was confident and matter-of-fact about her accomplishments.

"Impressive." Regardless of how attractive Savannah Carlisle was, he would only hire her if she was right for the job. "You're a long way from West Virginia. What brings you to our little town of Magnolia Lake?"

"Honestly? I moved here because of this opportunity."

When Blake narrowed his gaze in response, she laughed. It was a sweet sound he wouldn't mind hearing again. Preferably while they were in closer proximity than his desk would allow.

"That wasn't an attempt to sweet-talk you into hiring me. Unless, of course, it works," she added with a smile. "This position is the perfect intersection of my talents and interests."

"How so?" Blake was intrigued.

"I've been fascinated by distilleries and small breweries since I worked at a local craft brewery my senior year of college. I led group tours."

Blake leaned forward, hands pressed to the desk. "And if you don't get the position?"

"Then I'll work my way up to it."

Blake tried not to betray how pleased he was with her unwavering conviction. "There are lots of other distilleries. Why not apply for a similar position elsewhere?"

"I believe in your products. Not that I'm a huge drinker," she added with a nervous laugh. "But as an event professional, King's Finest is my go-to. I also happen to think you have one of the smoothest finishes out there."

He didn't respond. Instead, he allowed a bit of awkward silence to settle over them, which was a device he often employed. Give a candidate just enough rope to hog-tie themselves, and see what they'd do with it.

"That's only part of the reason I want to work for King's Finest. I like that you're family-owned. And I was drawn to the story of how your grandfather converted your great-grandfather's moonshine operation into a legitimate business to create a legacy for his family."

She wasn't the first job candidate to gush about the company history in an attempt to ingratiate herself with him. But something in her eyes indicated deep admiration. Perhaps even reverence.

"You've done your homework, and you know our history." Blake sat back in his leather chair. "But my primary concern is what's on the horizon. How will you impact the future of King's Finest?"

"Excellent question." Savannah produced a leather portfolio from her large tote. "One I'm prepared to answer. Let's talk about the upcoming jubilee celebration. It's the perfect convergence of the company's past and present."

"The event is a few months away. Most of the plans are set. We don't expect anyone to come in, at this late hour, and pull off a miracle. We just want the event to be special for our employees and the folks of Magnolia Lake. Something that'll make them proud of their role in our history. Get them excited about the future."

A wide grin spanned her lovely face. "Give me two months and I'll turn the jubilee into a marketing bonanza that'll get distributors and consumers excited about your brand."

An ambitious claim, but an intriguing one.

King's Finest award-winning bourbon sold well in the States and was making inroads overseas. However, they faced increased competition from small batch distilleries popping up across the country in recent years.

"You have my attention, Savannah Carlisle." Blake crossed one ankle over his knee. "Wow me."

Savannah laid out a compelling plan to revamp their jubilee celebration into an event that was as reflective of the company's simple roots as it was elegant and forward thinking.

"I love your plan, but do you honestly think you can pull this off in two months?"

"I can, and I will." She closed the portfolio and returned it to her bag. "If given the chance."

Blake studied the beautiful woman sitting before him. No wonder their HR manager had recommended the woman so highly. Impressed with her after a joint telephone interview, Max and their mother had authorized him to make her an offer if she was as impressive in person.

Savannah Carlisle was clever and resourceful, everything they needed for their newly minted event manager position. There was only one problem with hiring the woman.

He was attracted to her. More than he'd been to

any woman in the two years since his last relationship imploded.

Blake was genuinely excited by the possibility of seeing Savannah every day. Of knowing she occupied an office down the hall from his. But there was the little matter of their family's unwritten rule.

No dating employees.

Problematic, since he'd spent the past half hour preoccupied with the desire to touch her skin again. But he had something far less innocent than a handshake in mind.

Blake wouldn't hire her simply because she was attractive. And it wouldn't be right not to hire her because of her beauty, either.

His feelings were his problem, and he'd deal with them.

"All right, Savannah Carlisle. Let's see what you can do."

They negotiated her salary, and then Blake sent her off to complete the requisite paperwork. His gaze followed her curvy bottom and long legs as she sashayed out of the office.

Blake shook his head and groaned. This time, he may have gotten himself in over his head.

Chapter 2

Savannah had never relied on sex appeal for a single, solitary thing in her life.

But today was different.

If her plan succeeded, it would correct the course of her family's lives. Money wouldn't be an issue. Not now, nor for generations to come.

Her grandfather would get justice and the recognition he deserved. Her sister wouldn't have to struggle under the crushing weight of student loans.

So failure wasn't an option. Even if it meant playing to the caveman instincts of a cretin like Blake Abbott.

He hadn't been obvious about it. She'd give him credit for that. But the smoldering intensity of his gaze and the sexy growl of his voice had made the interview feel a lot like a blind date.

His warm brown gaze penetrated her skin. Made

her feel something she hadn't expected. Something she couldn't explain. Because despite the charm of the man she'd just met, she knew the truth about Blake Abbott and his family.

They were thieves, plain and simple.

The kind of folks who would cheat a man out of what was rightfully owed to him. Who didn't have the decency or compassion to feel an ounce of regret for leaving such a man and his family twisting in the wind, floundering in poverty.

So despite Blake's warm smile and surprisingly pleasing demeanor, she wouldn't forget the truth. The Abbotts were heartless and cruel.

She would expose them for the snakes they were and reclaim her grandfather's rightful share of the company.

Once she'd exited the parking lot in her crappy little car, she dialed her sister, Delaney, back in West Virginia.

"I'm in," Savannah blurted as soon as her sister answered the phone. "I got the job."

Laney hesitated before offering a one-word response. "Wow."

"I know you don't agree with what I'm doing, Laney, but I'm doing this for all of us. You and Harper especially."

"Vanna come home!" her two-year-old niece said in the background.

"Listen to your niece. If you're doing it for us, pack up and come home now. Because this isn't what we want."

"It's what Granddad deserves. What we all deserve." Savannah turned onto the road that led back to town.

"This will alter our family's future. Make things better for you and Harper."

"This isn't about Harper or my student loans. You're playing to Grandpa's pride and yours."

Savannah silently counted to ten. Blowing up at Laney wouldn't get her sister on board. And deep down she wanted Laney's reassurance she was doing the right thing.

Their grandfather—Martin McDowell—had raised them after the deaths of their parents. He'd made sacrifices for them their entire lives. And now he was gravely ill, his kidneys failing.

"Grandpa's nearly ninety. Thanks to the Abbotts, his pride is all he has, besides us. So I say it's worth fighting for."

Laney didn't answer. Not surprising.

When they were kids, Savannah was mesmerized by her grandfather's stories about his days running moonshine in the Tennessee hills as a young man. But even as a child, Laney took a just-the-facts-please approach to life. She'd viewed their grandfather's stories as tall tales.

Their positions hadn't changed as adults. But Laney would come around when Savannah proved the truth.

Joseph Abbott, founder of the King's Finest Distillery, claimed to use recipes from his father's illegal moonshine business. But, in reality, he'd stolen their grandfather's hooch recipe and used it to parlay himself into a bourbon empire. And the tremendous fortune the Abbotts enjoyed.

"If the Abbotts are as heartless as you believe, does it seem wise to take them on alone? To get a job with them under false pretenses and snoop around in search of…what? Do you think there's a vault with a big card in it that says, 'I stole my famous bourbon recipe from Martin McDowell'?"

"I didn't get this job under false pretenses. I'm extremely qualified. I'm going to do everything I can to help grow the company. We're going to be part owners of it, after all." Savannah navigated the one-lane bridge that crossed the river dividing the small town.

"You're risking jail or maybe worse. If something were to happen to Granddad…" Her sister's voice trailed. "You're all Harper and I would have left. We can't risk losing you. So, please, let it go and come home."

She didn't want to worry Laney. School, work, taking care of a two-year-old and seeing after their grandfather was strain enough. But this was something she had to do.

If she succeeded, it would be well worth the risk.

"I love you and Harper, Laney. But you need to trust that I'm acting in all of our best interest. And please don't rat me out to Grandpa."

"Great. I have to lie to him about it, too." Laney huffed. "Fine, but be careful. Remember, there's no shame in throwing in the towel and coming to your senses. Love you."

"Love you, too."

After hanging up, Savannah sighed heavily and focused on the road as the colorful shops of the quaint little town of Magnolia Lake came into view.

She parked behind the small building where she was staying. It housed a consignment and handmade jewelry shop downstairs and two apartments upstairs.

The shop and building were owned by Kayleigh Jemison, who was also her neighbor.

Inside her furnished, one-bedroom apartment, Savannah kicked off her heels and stripped off her jacket. Her thoughts drifted back to Blake Abbott. He was nothing like the cutthroat, ambitious jerk her grandfather had described. Blake was tall and handsome. His warm brown skin was smooth and practically glowed from within. He was charming with a welcoming smile and liquid brown eyes that made her stomach flip when they met hers.

Her grandfather had only known Joseph Abbott personally. The rest of the Abbotts he knew only by reputation. Maybe he was wrong about Blake.

"You are *not* attracted to him. Not even a little bit," Savannah mumbled under her breath. "He's the enemy. A means to an end."

But Blake was obviously attracted to her. A weakness she could exploit, if it came to it.

An uncomfortable feeling settled over her as she imagined Laney's thoughts on that.

The solution was simple. Avoid Blake Abbott, at all costs.

Chapter 3

Savannah signed her name on the final new hire form and slid it across the table.

Daisy was filling in for the HR manager, who was out sick. She studied the document and gave it a stamp of approval. Her thin lips spread in a big smile, her blue eyes sparkling. "You're officially a King's Finest employee. Welcome to the team."

"Fantastic." Savannah returned the smile. "So, what's next?"

The conference room door burst open.

Blake Abbott.

He was even more handsome than she remembered. The five o'clock shadow crawling along his square jaw made him look rugged and infinitely sexier. Uneasiness stirred low in her belly.

"Daisy, Savannah… I didn't realize you were using

the conference room." His hair, grown out a bit since their initial meeting, had a slight curl to it.

"We're just leaving anyway." Daisy collected her things. "Did I forget there was a meeting scheduled in here?"

"No, we decided to have an impromptu meeting about the changes Savannah proposed for the jubilee celebration. We can all fit in here more comfortably. Come to think of it—" he shifted his attention to Savannah "—this would be a great opportunity for you to meet my family…that is…our executive team."

She wasn't in a position to refuse his request. Still, there was something endearing about how he'd asked.

It took her by surprise.

"I've been looking forward to meeting the company's founder." Savannah forced a smile, unnerved about meeting the entire Abbott clan. Especially Joseph Abbott—the man who'd betrayed her grandfather.

"I'm afraid you'll have to wait a bit longer." He sounded apologetic. "We want the changes to be a surprise. Speaking of which… I know it's last-minute, and I hate to throw you into the fire on your first day, but do you think you could present your ideas to the rest of our team?"

Savannah's eyes went wide. "Now?"

"They're all really sweet." Daisy patted her arm and smiled. "You're going to love them. I'm just sorry I can't stay to hear your presentation. Got another new hire to process. Good luck!" Daisy called over her shoulder as she hurried from the room.

"I've been telling everyone about your proposal. Got a feeling my father and brother will be more easily persuaded if you wow them the way you did me."

Savannah had anticipated meeting every member of the Abbott family, eventually. But meeting them all at once on her first day was intimidating. Particularly since she had to refrain from saying what she wanted.

That they were liars and thieves who'd built their fortune by depriving her family of theirs. But she couldn't say that. Not yet, anyway. Not until she had proof.

"I've got my notes right here." Savannah opened her portfolio. "But with a little more time, I can create a formal presentation."

"What you presented to me is fine. They'll love it." Blake slid into the seat across from her.

Her belly did a flip.

"Hey, Blake, did you eat all of the…? Oh, I'm sorry. I didn't realize you were meeting with someone," came a voice from the doorway.

"It's all right." Blake waved in the woman Savannah recognized as his sister. "Zora, this is our new event manager, Savannah Carlisle. Savannah, this is our sales VP, Zora Abbott—the baby of the family."

"And they never let me forget it." Zora sat beside her older brother and elbowed him. The woman leaned across the table and shook her hand. "Welcome aboard, Savannah. We need you desperately. You've certainly impressed my big brother here. Not an easy feat."

A deep blush of pink bloomed across Blake's cheeks. He seemed relieved when another member of the Abbott clan stepped into the room.

"Max, this is your new event manager, Savannah Carlisle," Zora informed the handsome newcomer, then turned to Savannah. "Max is our marketing VP. You'll be working for him and with our mother—who isn't here."

There was no mistaking that Max and Blake were brothers. They had the same square jaw capped by a cleft chin. The same narrow, brooding dark eyes. And the same nose—with a narrow bridge and slightly flared nostrils.

Max wore his curly hair longer than Blake's. And where Blake's skin was the color of terra-cotta tiles, his brother's skin was a deeper russet brown. Max was a little taller than his brother, with a leaner frame.

"I look forward to working with you, Savannah." Max sat beside her and shook her hand, his grip firm and warm. His smile seemed genuine. "I'm excited to hear more of your ideas for the anniversary celebration."

"That's why I invited her to join us. She can relay them much better than I can."

Two more men walked into the room. "Didn't realize we were having guests," the younger of the two said, his voice gruff.

"My brother Parker." Zora rolled her eyes. "Chief financial officer and resident cheapskate."

Parker was not amused, but the older man—whom Zora introduced as their father, Duke—chuckled and gave Savannah a warm greeting.

Parker offered a cursory greeting, then shifted his narrowed gaze to Blake.

"I thought we were going to discuss the proposal honestly." Parker sat at one end of the table. Duke sat at the other.

"We will." The intensity of Blake's tone matched his brother's. He nodded toward Savannah. "No one is asking you to pull any punches. She might as well get accustomed to how we do business around here. Besides, she can best respond to your questions about the kind of return on investment we should expect."

"Welcome, then." Parker tapped something on his phone. "I've been described as…no-nonsense. Don't take it personally."

"I won't, if you promise not to take my tendency to shoot straight personally, either." Savannah met his gaze.

Parker nodded his agreement and the other siblings exchanged amused glances.

"You found someone Parker can't intimidate." Zora grinned. "Good job, Blake."

The Abbotts continued to tease each other while Zora or Blake filled her in on the inside jokes. Savannah smiled politely, laughing when they did. But an uneasiness crawled up her spine.

The Abbotts weren't what she'd expected.

Her grandfather had portrayed them as wild grizzly bears. Vicious and capable of devouring their own young.

Don't be fooled by their charm.

"Ready to make your presentation?" Blake asked.

Parker drummed his fingers on the table and glanced at his watch.

Don't show fear.

"Absolutely." Savannah stood, clutching her portfolio.

Blake's warm smile immediately eased the tightness in her chest. Her lungs expanded and she took a deep breath.

Savannah opened her portfolio and glanced around the room.

"All right, here's what I'm proposing…"

Blake typed notes into his phone as Savannah recapped her presentation. She'd won over everyone in the room. They were all on board with her plan—even penny-pinching Parker.

The event had graduated from the "little shindig" his mother had envisioned to a full gala. One that would retain a rustic charm that paid homage to the company's history. Savannah had also suggested holding anniversary events in other key cities.

The upgrades Savannah proposed to the old barn on his parents' property to prepare for the gala would significantly increase its rental income. They could charge more per event and would draw business from corporations and folks in nearby towns. All of which made Parker exceedingly happy.

"There's one thing I'm still not sold on," he interjected. "The majority of our market share is here in the South. Why invest in events elsewhere?"

"It's the perfect opportunity to deepen our reach outside of our comfort zone," Savannah said.

Parker folded his arms, unconvinced.

"She's right." Blake set his phone on the table and leveled his gaze on his brother. "I've floated the idea with a few distributors in the UK, California and New York. They love our products and they're eager to introduce them to more of their customers. I'm telling you, Parker, this could be a big win for us."

Savannah gave him a quick, grateful smile. A knot formed low in his gut.

"Savannah and Blake have done their homework," his father said. "I'm ready to move forward with Savannah's proposal. Any objections?"

Parker shook his head, but scowled.

"Excellent. Savannah, would you mind typing up your notes and sending them to the executive email list so my wife can get a look at them?"

"I'll do my best to get them out by the end of the day, Mr. Abbott."

"Duke will do just fine. Now, I'm late for a date with a five iron."

"The gala is going to be sensational." Zora grinned. "Right, Max?"

"It will be," Max agreed. "I wasn't sure that turning Mom's low-key, local event into something more elaborate and—"

"Expensive," Parker interrupted.

"Relax, El Cheapo." Zora's stony expression was a silent reminder that she wasn't just their baby sister. She was sales VP and an equal member of the executive team. "The additional sales will far exceed the additional expenses."

"Don't worry, lil' sis. I'm in." Parker tapped his pen on the table. "I'm obviously outnumbered. I'm as thrilled as you are to expand our market and rake in more cash. I just hope Savannah's projections are on target."

"I look forward to surprising you with the results." Savannah seemed unfazed by Parker's subtle intimidation.

"C'mon, Savannah." Max stood. "I'll show you to your office. It isn't far from mine."

Blake swallowed back his disappointment as she

left with Max, Zora and their father. So much for his plan to give Savannah a tour of the place.

"Watch yourself," Parker warned.

"What do you mean?" Blake stuffed his phone in his pocket and headed for the door.

"You know *exactly* what I mean. You've been stealing glances at Savannah when you think no one is looking. Like just now." Parker followed him.

"You're exaggerating."

"No, I'm your brother." Parker fell in step beside him. "I know the signs."

"Of what?" Blake turned to face his brother. "A man very impressed with his new hire?"

"It's worse than I thought." Parker shook his head. "Look all you want, just don't touch. She's our employee. A subordinate. Don't cross the line with her. And for God's sake, don't get caught up in your feelings for this woman."

"Good advice." Blake resumed the walk to his office. "Too bad you haven't been good at following it."

"That's why I know what a horrible idea it is."

"Don't worry, Parker. I won't do anything you wouldn't." Blake went into his office and shut the door.

He didn't need Parker to remind him that Savannah Carlisle was off-limits.

Chapter 4

Savannah surveyed the gleaming copper stills and the pipes running between them that filled the distillation room. "They're beautiful."

She was home. Exactly where she was meant to be, had it not been for Joseph Abbott's treachery.

"I guess they are." Daisy checked her watch again.

Blake's assistant was a nice enough woman, but her limited knowledge wasn't helpful to Savannah's cause. If she was going to take on the powerful Abbott family and prove they'd stolen her grandfather's bourbon recipe and his process for making it, she needed to learn everything there was to know about the making of their signature bourbon.

Daisy gave the stills a cursory glance. "I never really thought of them as beautiful."

"I do. I just didn't think anyone else did," a familiar, velvety voice chimed in.

Blake again.

The man seemed to pop up everywhere. Hopefully, it wouldn't be a daily occurrence.

"Didn't mean to scare you, Dais." Blake held up a hand. "Just met with Klaus—our master distiller," he added for Savannah's benefit. "I'm surprised you're still here. Doesn't Daphne's softball game start in an hour?"

"It does." Daisy turned to Savannah. "Daphne's my ten-year-old daughter. She's pitching as a starter for the first time."

"I'm sorry." No wonder Daisy had tried to rush her through the tour. "I didn't realize you had somewhere to be."

"Get out of here before you're late." Blake nodded toward the exit. "Tell Daph I'm rooting for her."

"What about the tour? We're nowhere near finished. Savannah has so many questions. I haven't done a very good job of answering them."

"You were great, Daisy," Savannah lied, not wanting to make her feel bad. "Your daughter's pitching debut is more important. We can finish the tour another day."

"Go." Blake pointed toward the exit. "I'll finish up here. In fact, I'll give Savannah the deluxe tour."

Daisy thanked them and hurried off.

"So you want to know all about the whiskey-making process." Blake turned to Savannah. He hadn't advanced a step, yet the space between them contracted.

"I mentioned that in my interview." She met his gaze, acutely aware of their height difference and the broadness of his shoulders.

His fresh, woodsy scent made her want to plant her

palms on his well-defined chest and press her nose to the vein visible on his neck.

"Thought that was just a clever bit to impress me." The edge of his generous mouth pulled into a lopsided grin that made her heart beat faster.

"Now, you know that isn't true." Savannah held his gaze despite the violent fluttering in her belly.

She was reacting like a hormonal high-school girl with a crush on the captain of the football team.

Blake was pleasant enough on the surface, and certainly nice to look at. Okay, that was the understatement of the year. His chiseled features and well-maintained body were the stuff dreams were made of.

But he wasn't just any pretty face and hard physique. He was an Abbott.

E-N-E-M-Y.

Her interest in this man—regardless of how good-looking he was or the sinful visions his mouth conjured—needed to stay purely professional. The only thing she wanted from Blake Abbott was insight into the history between their grandfathers.

"So you promised me the deluxe tour."

"I did." His appraising stare caused a contraction of muscles she hadn't employed in far longer than she cared to admit. "Let's go back to the beginning."

"Are you sure?" Savannah scrambled to keep up with his long, smooth strides. "I've nearly caused one family crisis already. I don't intend to start another today. So if you have a wife or kids who are expecting you—"

"That your not-so-subtle way of asking if I'm married?" He quickly pressed his lips into a harsh line. "I mean… I'm not. None of my siblings are. Our mother is sure she's failed us somehow because we haven't produced any grandchildren."

"Why aren't you married? Not you specifically," Savannah added quickly, her cheeks hot.

"We're all married to this place. Committed to building the empire my granddad envisioned nearly half a century ago."

Blake held the door open and they stepped into the late-afternoon sunlight. Gravel crunched beneath their feet, forcing her to tread carefully in her tall spike heels.

They walked past the grain silos and onto a trail that led away from the warehouse. The property extended as far as she could see, a picturesque natural landscape that belonged on a postcard.

"Someone in town mentioned that you have another brother who isn't in the business."

"Cole runs the largest construction company in the area. With the explosion of high-end real estate around here, he's got the least time on his hands."

"Doesn't bode well for those grandchildren your mother wants."

"No, it doesn't," Blake agreed. "But she's convinced that if one of us finally takes the plunge, the rest will fall like dominoes."

"So then love is kind of like the plague?"

Blake's deep belly laugh made her grin so hard her cheeks ached.

"I can't disagree with that." He was smiling, but there was sadness in his eyes. There was a story there he wasn't willing to tell, but she suddenly wanted to hear.

The gravel gave way to a dirt path that was soft and

squishy due to the recent rain. Her heels sank into the mud. "I thought we were going to start at the beginning of the tour."

"We are."

"But we already passed the grain silos." She pointed in the opposite direction.

He stopped, turning to face her. "Do you know why most of the storied whiskey distilleries are based in Kentucky or here in Tennessee?"

Savannah shook her head. She'd noticed that the industry was concentrated in those two states, but hadn't given much thought to why.

"A whiskey with a smooth finish begins with the right water source." He pointed toward a creek and the hills that rose along the edge of the property. "See that limestone shelf? Springs deep in these limestone layers feed King's Lake—our sole source of water. The limestone adds calcium to the water and filters out impurities like iron that would make the whiskey bitter."

She studied the veins in the limestone shelf. "So it wouldn't be possible to produce bourbon from another water source with the same composition and flavor?"

"Not even if you used our exact recipe." He stood beside her, gazing reverently at the stony mountain and the waters that trickled from it. "Then there's the matter of the yeast we use for fermentation. It's a proprietary strain that dates back to when my great-grandfather was running his moonshine business seventy-five years ago."

"Most distilleries openly share their grain recipe. King's Finest doesn't. Why?"

"My grandfather tweaked the grain mixture his father used. He's pretty territorial about it." Blake smiled.

"So we keep our mash bill and yeast strain under tight control."

The fact that Blake's grandfather had stolen the recipe from her grandfather was the more likely reason.

"I'm boring you, aren't I?"

"No. This is all extremely fascinating."

"It's a subject I can get carried away with. Believe me, no other woman has ever used the word *fascinating* to describe it."

"You still think I'm feigning interest." Something in his stare made her cheeks warm and her chest heavy.

His lips parted and his hands clenched at his sides, but he didn't acknowledge her statement. "We'd better head back."

They visited the vats of corn, rye and malted barley. Next, they visited the large metal vat where the grain was cooked, creating the mash. In the fermentation room there were large, open tubs fashioned of cypress planks, filled with fermenting whiskey. The air was heavy with a scent similar to sourdough bread baking.

In the distillation room, he gave her a taste of the bourbon after it passed through the towering copper still and then again after it had made another pass through the doubler.

"It's clear." Savannah handed Blake back the metal cup with a long metal handle he'd used to draw a sample of the "high wine."

Her fingers brushed his and he nearly dropped the cup, but recovered quickly.

"The rich amber color happens during the aging process." He returned the cup to its hook, then led her through the area where the high wine was transferred to new, charred white oak barrels.

They walked through the rackhouse. Five levels of whiskey casks towered above them. Savannah fanned herself, her brow damp with perspiration, as Blake lowered his voice, speaking in a hushed, reverent tone.

"How long is the bourbon aged?"

"The signature label? Five years. Then we have the top-shelf labels aged for ten or more years." Blake surveyed the upper racks before returning his gaze to hers. "My grandfather made so many sacrifices to create this legacy for us. I'm reminded of that whenever I come out here."

Blake spoke of Joseph Abbott as if he were a self-sacrificing saint. But the man was a liar and a cheat. He'd sacrificed his friendship with her grandfather and deprived him of his legacy, leaving their family with nothing but hardship and pain.

Tears stung her eyes and it suddenly hurt to breathe in the overheated rackhouse. It felt as if a cask of whiskey was sitting on her chest. She gasped, the air burning her lungs.

"Are you all right?" Blake narrowed his brown eyes, stepping closer. He placed a gentle hand on her shoulder.

"I'm fine." Her breath came in short bursts and her back was damp with sweat.

"It's hot in here. Let's get you back in the air-conditioning. Our last stop is the bottling area." His hand low on her back, he guided her toward the exit.

"No." The word came out sharper than she'd intended. "I mean, I promised your father I'd get that presentation out today."

"You told him you'd try. Do it first thing tomorrow. It'll be fine."

"That's not the first impression I want to make with the company's CEO. Or with his wife, who's eagerly awaiting the information." Savannah wiped the dampness from her forehead with the back of her hand. "I gave my word, and to me, that means something."

Chapter 5

It was clear Blake had offended Savannah.

But how?

He replayed the conversation in his head. Before she'd looked at him as if he'd kicked a kitten.

They'd been talking about how his grandfather had built the company. The sacrifices he'd made for their family. How could she possibly be offended by that? Especially when she'd already expressed her admiration for his grandfather's entrepreneurial spirit.

"If sending the presentation out tonight is that important to you, I won't stop you. All I'm saying is…no one will hold it against you if we receive it tomorrow."

Savannah turned on her heels, caked in dry mud from their earlier walk. She headed back toward the main building.

Even with his longer strides, he had to hurry to catch up with her. "You'd tell me if I upset you?"

"You didn't. I'm just—" Her spiked heel got caught in the gravel, and she stumbled into his arms.

He held her for a moment, his gaze studying hers, enjoying the feel of her soft curves pressed against his hard body.

Her eyes widened and she stepped out of his grasp, muttering a quick thank-you.

"I'm angry with myself for not remembering the presentation earlier."

"You've been busy all day. That's my fault."

"It's no one's fault." She seemed to force a smile. "I appreciate the deluxe tour. What I've learned will be useful as I prepare my presentation. It's given me a few other ideas."

"That's good, then." Blake kneaded the back of his neck. "I'll walk you back to your office."

"I'd like to find it on my own. Test my sense of direction." Savannah's tepid smile barely turned up one corner of her mouth. She headed back to the building, calling over her shoulder. "See you tomorrow."

When she was too far away to hear it, Blake released a noisy sigh. He returned to his office by a different route.

Despite what Savannah said, he'd clearly upset her. He couldn't shake the gnawing need to learn why. Or the deep-seated desire to fix it so he could see the genuine smile that lit her lovely eyes, illuminating the flecks of gold.

Blake gritted his teeth.

You do not feel anything for her.

He said the words over and over in his head as he trekked back inside, past her office and straight to his.

You're full of shit, and you know it.

Why couldn't his stupid subconscious just cooperate and buy into the load of crock he was trying to sell himself?

There were a million reasons why he shouldn't be thinking of Savannah Carlisle right now. Long-legged, smooth-skinned, caramel-complexioned goddess that she was.

He shouldn't be thinking of her throaty voice. Her husky laugh. Her penetrating stare. Or the way she sank her teeth into her lower lip while in deep thought.

Blake shut his office door and loosened his tie. He dropped into the chair behind his desk, trying not to focus on the tension in his gut and the tightening of his shaft at the thought of Savannah Carlisle…naked. Sprawled across his desk.

He opened his laptop and studied spreadsheets and graphs, ignoring the most disconcerting aspect of his growing attraction for Savannah. What scared him… what was terrifying…was how Savannah Carlisle made him feel. That she'd made him feel anything at all.

Especially the kind of feelings he'd carefully avoided in the two years since Gavrilla had walked out of his life.

Since then he'd satisfied his urges with the occasional one-night stand while traveling for business. Far away from this too-small town, where every single person knew the private affairs of every other damned person.

In painful detail.

He hadn't been looking for anything serious. Just

a couple of nights in the sack. No feelings. No obligations beyond having safe, responsible sex and being gentlemanly enough never to speak of it.

But from their first meeting, he'd been drawn to Savannah. She was bold and confident. And she hadn't begged for a shot with the company. She'd simply laid out a solid case.

He would've been a fool to not hire her.

Her indomitable spirit and latent sex appeal called to something deep inside him. In a way that felt significant. The feelings were completely foreign and yet deeply familiar.

He didn't believe in love at first sight or soul mates. But if he had, he'd have sworn that Cupid had shot him the second Savannah Carlisle sashayed her curvy ass into his office.

Blake loosened the top two buttons of his shirt. Parker's admonition played on a loop in his head. It could be summed up in five words: *Don't think with your dick.*

If Parker recognized how perilous Blake's attraction to Savannah was, he was in big trouble. He needed to slam the lid on those feelings. Seal them in an indestructible steel box fastened with iron rivets and guarded by flaming swords and a den of rattlesnakes.

Because he could never go back there again. To the pain he'd felt two years ago when Gavrilla had walked out. She'd left him for someone else. Without warning or the slightest indication she'd been unhappy.

Without giving him a chance to fix things.

In retrospect, she'd done him a favor. Their stark differences—so exciting in the beginning—had been flashing red lights warning of their incompatibility.

Blake sighed. It'd been a while since he'd taken a

business-meets-pleasure excursion. Experienced the adrenaline of tumbling into bed with a stranger.

He'd have Daisy schedule a meeting with a vendor in Nashville or maybe Atlanta. Somewhere he could blend in with the nameless, faceless masses.

Anywhere but Magnolia Lake.

Blake hit Send on his final email of the night—a response to a vendor in the UK. He checked his watch. It was well after seven and Savannah's proposal hadn't pinged his inbox.

She'd been determined to send it before she left for the night. That meant she was still in her office working on it.

Blake rubbed his unshaved chin. Perhaps she'd encountered a problem. After all, it was her first day. He should see if she needed help.

Blake packed up his laptop, locked his office door and headed down the hall. He almost kept walking. Almost pretended he didn't hear the tapping of computer keys.

He groaned, knowing he was acting against his better judgment.

"Hey." He gently knocked on Savannah's open office door. "Still at it?"

"Finished just now." Her earlier uneasiness appeared to be gone. "You didn't wait for me, did you?" She seemed perturbed by the possibility.

"No. Just finished up myself. But since I'm here, I'll walk you to your car."

"I thought small towns like Magnolia Lake were idyllic bastions of safety and neighborliness." Savannah barely contained a sarcastic grin as she grabbed her bags.

"Doesn't mean we shouldn't practice courtesy and good old-fashioned common sense." He opened the door wider to let her out, then locked it behind them.

They made the trip to her small car in near silence. She stopped abruptly, just shy of her door.

"About earlier." She turned to him, but her eyes didn't meet his. "Sorry if I seemed rude. I wasn't trying to be. I just…" She shook her head. "It wasn't anything you did."

"But it was something I said." He hiked his computer bag higher on his shoulder when her eyes widened.

"It won't happen again."

"Good night, Savannah." Blake opened her car door. He wouldn't press, if she didn't want to talk about it.

They weren't lovers, and they needn't be friends. As long as Savannah did her job well and played nice with others, everything would be just fine.

He stepped away from the car and she drove away.

Blake made his way back to his truck, thankful Savannah Carlisle had saved him from himself.

Savannah let herself into her apartment, glad the day was finally over.

When she got to the bedroom, she pulled a black leather journal from her nightstand. It held her notes about the Abbotts.

Savannah did a quick review of what she'd learned on the job today and jotted down everything she could remember.

Their processes. The grains used in their bourbon

composition with a question mark and percentage sign by each one. The industry jargon she'd learned. Next, she outlined her impressions of each member of the Abbott family—starting with Blake.

Finished with the brain dump, she was starving and mentally exhausted. She scarfed down a frozen dinner while watching TV.

Her cell phone rang. *Laney.*

"Hey, sis." Savannah smiled. "How's my niece? And how is Granddad doing?"

"They're both fine. How was your first day?"

"Long. I just got home." Savannah shoved the last bite of processed macaroni and cheese into her mouth, then dumped the plastic tray into the recycle bin. "I made my proposal to the entire family—"

"You met all the Abbotts?"

"Everyone except their mother, Iris, and Joseph Abbott." Savannah was both angry and relieved she hadn't had the chance to look into the eyes of the coldhearted bastard who'd ruined her grandfather's life.

"What were they like?"

Savannah sank onto the sofa. Blake's dreamy eyes and kind smile danced in her head. The vision had come to her in her sleep more than once since they'd met.

In her dreams, they weren't from opposing families. They'd been increasingly intimate, holding hands, embracing. And last night she'd awakened in a cold sweat after they'd shared a passionate kiss.

She'd struggled to drive those images from her head while spending a good portion of her day in his company.

"The Abbotts aren't the ogres you expected, are

they?" There was a hint of vindication in Laney's question.

"No, but I met most of them for the first time today. They were trying to make a good first impression. After all, even a serial killer can have a charming facade."

Laney didn't acknowledge her logic. "Tell me about them, based on what you observed today. Not on what you thought you knew about them."

Savannah removed her ponytail holder and shook her head. Her curly hair tumbled to her shoulders in loose waves from being pulled tight.

"It was hard to get a read on their dad—Duke. He's personable, but all business."

"What about the rest of them?"

"I met Blake, Parker, Max and Zora—the four siblings who run the distillery. There's a fifth—Cole. He has his own construction company."

"Why didn't he go into the family business?"

"Don't know." Savannah had wondered, too.

"Quit stalling and tell me more."

"Zora is sweet. Max is funny. Parker is kind of an asshole."

"And what about Blake Abbott? This was your second encounter. Did your impression of him improve?"

"Yes." She hated to admit that it was true. But Blake's genuinely warm interactions with his employees during the tour made him appear to be an ideal boss.

"So now that you see you were wrong about the Abbotts, will you please let this thing go?"

So much for Laney being on board with the plan.

"The congeniality of Joseph Abbott's grandchildren isn't the issue here."

"Savannah—"

"If they're genuinely innocent in all of this...well, I'm sorry their grandfather was such a bastard. It isn't like I plan to steal the company from under them the way he did from Granddad."

"Then what exactly do you want, honey? What's your grand plan here?"

"Our family deserves half the company. That's what I want. And if they don't want to share, they can buy us out. Plain and simple."

Laney made a strangled sound of frustration. A sound she made whenever they discussed their grandfather's claims regarding King's Finest.

"I couldn't do what you're doing." Laney's voice was quiet. "Getting to know people. Having them come to like and trust you. Then turning on them."

Savannah winced at the implication of her sister's words. "I'm not 'turning' on them. I'm just standing up for my family. As any of them would for theirs. Besides, I'm not harming their business in any way."

"You're spying on them."

"But I'm not taking that information to a competitor. I'm just gathering evidence to support Granddad's ownership claim." Savannah tamped down the defensiveness in her tone.

"And what about Blake?"

"What about him?"

"You like him. I can tell. What happens when he learns the truth?"

A knot twisted in Savannah's belly. "If he's as good a man as everyone seems to think, he should want to make this right. In fact, I'm counting on it."

Chapter 6

Savannah smiled in response to the email she'd just received from Max, who was away at another trade show. They'd secured the endorsement of a local boy who'd become a world-famous actor. With his rugged good looks and down-home, boyish charm, he was perfect.

Her plans for the jubilee were in full swing. The rustic gala, to be held in the Abbotts' old country barn, would celebrate the company, its employees and distributors and attract plenty of media coverage. The renovated barn would provide King's Finest with an additional revenue stream and create jobs in the small town.

Savannah had been working at the distillery for nearly a month. The residents of the small town had done their best to make her feel welcome—despite her desire to hang in the shadows and lie low.

Every Friday she turned down no less than two invitations to the local watering hole for drinks after work. One of those invitations always came from Blake.

An involuntary shudder rippled down Savannah's spine when she thought of Blake with his generous smile and warm brown eyes. Savannah shook her head.

She would *not* think of how good Blake Abbott looked in the checkered dress shirts and athletic-fit slacks he typically wore. Each piece highlighted the finer points of his physique. A broad chest. Well-defined pecs. Strong arms. An ass that made it evident he was no stranger to lunges and squats.

His clothing was designed to torture her and every other woman with a working libido and functioning set of eyes. It tormented her with visions of what his strong body must look like beneath that fabric.

A crack of thunder drew her attention to the window. She checked the time on her phone. It was barely after seven, but dark clouds and a steady downpour darkened the sky, making it feel later.

Savannah worked late most nights. The gala was quickly approaching and there was so much to do.

Plus, being the last member of the administrative team to leave each night gave her a chance to do some reconnaissance. She could access files she didn't feel comfortable perusing when Max, Blake or Zora might pop into her office at any minute.

Then there was the surprising fact that she thoroughly enjoyed the work she was doing. She was often so engrossed in a task that time got away from her.

Like tonight.

Outside the window, increasingly dark clouds

loomed overhead. The steady, gentle rain that had fallen throughout the day was now a raging downpour.

Another flash of light illuminated the sky. It was quickly followed by a peal of thunder that made Savannah's heart race.

It was lightning that posed the real danger. Savannah knew that better than most. The thunder was just sound and fury.

She loathed driving in inclement weather. Tack on the steep hills, narrow roads, one-lane bridge and her vague familiarity with the area, and it was a recipe for disaster.

One wrong turn, and she could end up in a ditch, lost in the woods, undiscovered for months.

Stop being a drama queen. Everything will be fine. Just take a deep breath.

Savannah took a long, deep breath.

She'd hoped to wait out the storm. Her plan had backfired. Engrossed in her work, she hadn't noticed that the rain had gotten much heavier. And it didn't appear to be letting up anytime soon.

After composing and sending one final email, Savannah signed off her computer. She gathered her things and headed for the parking lot, as fast as her high-heeled feet could carry her.

Shit.

She was without an umbrella, and it was raining so hard the parking lot had flooded. No wonder the lot was empty except for her car.

If it stalled out, she'd be screwed.

A flash of lightning lit the sky like a neon sign over a Vegas hotel.

Jaw clenched, Savannah sucked in a generous

breath, as if she were about to dive into the deep end of the pool. She made a mad dash for her car before the next bolt struck.

Despite the warm temperatures, the rain pelted her in cold sheets as she waded through the standing water. Her clothing was wet and heavy. Her feet slid as she ran in her soaking-wet shoes.

Savannah dropped into the driver's seat and caught her breath. Her eyes stung as she wiped water from her face with the back of her hand, which was just as wet.

She turned her key and gave the car some gas, grateful the engine turned over.

There was another flash of lightning, then a rumble of thunder, followed by a heavy knock on the window.

She screamed, her heart nearly beating out of her chest.

A large man in a hooded green rain slicker hovered outside her window.

She was cold, wet, alone and about to be murdered.

But not without a fight.

Savannah popped open her glove compartment and searched for something…anything…she could use as a weapon. She dug out the heavy tactical flashlight her grandfather had given her one Christmas. She beamed the bright light in the intruder's face.

"Blake?" Savannah pressed a hand to her chest, her heart still thudding against her breastbone. She partially lowered the window.

Even with his eyes hidden by the hood, she recognized the mouth and stubbled chin she'd spent too much time studying.

"You were expecting someone else?"

Smart-ass.

If she didn't work for the Abbotts, and she wasn't so damned glad not to be alone in the middle of a monsoon, she would have told Blake exactly what she thought of his smart-assery.

"What are you doing here? And where'd you come from?"

"I'm parked under the carport over there." He pointed in the opposite direction. "Came to check on the building. Didn't expect to see anyone here at this time of night in the storm."

"I didn't realize how late it was, or that the rain had gotten so bad. I'm headed home now."

"In this?" He sized up her small car.

She lifted a brow. "My flying saucer is in the shop."

Savannah knew she shouldn't have said it, but the words slipped out of her mouth before she could reel them back in.

Blake wasn't angry. He smirked instead.

"Too bad. Because that's the only way you're gonna make it over the bridge."

"What are you talking about?"

"You're renting from Kayleigh Jemison in town, right?"

"How did you know—"

"It's Magnolia Lake. Everyone knows everyone in this town," he said matter-of-factly. "And there are flash-flood warnings everywhere. No way will this small car make it through the low-lying areas between here and town."

"Flash floods?" Panic spread through her chest. "Isn't there another route I can take?"

"There's only one way back to town." He pointed toward the carport. "The ground is higher there. Park behind my truck, and I'll give you a ride home. I'll bring you back to get your car when the roads clear."

"Just leave my car here?" She stared at him dumbly.

"If I could fit it into the bed of my truck, I would." One side of his mouth curved in an impatient smile. "And if there was any other option, I'd tell you."

Savannah groaned as she returned her flashlight to the glove compartment. Then she pulled into the carport as Blake instructed.

"Got everything you need from your car?" Blake removed his hood and opened her car door.

"You act as if I won't see my car again anytime soon."

"Depends on how long it takes the river to go down."

"Seriously?" Savannah grabbed a few items from the middle console and shoved them in her bag before securing her vehicle. She followed Blake to the passenger side of his huge black truck.

She gasped, taken by surprise when Blake helped her up into the truck.

"I have a couple more things to check before we go. Sit tight. I'll be back before you can miss me."

Doubt it.

Blake shut her door and disappeared around the building.

Savannah waited for her heartbeat to slow down. She secured her seat belt and surveyed the interior of Blake's pickup truck. The satellite radio was set to an old-school hip-hop channel. The truck was tricked out with all the toys. High-end luxury meets Bo and Luke Duke with a refined hip-hop sensibility.

Perfectly Blake.

A clean citrus scent wafted from the air vents. The

black leather seats she was dripping all over were inlaid with a tan design.

A fierce gust of wind blew the rain sideways and swayed the large truck. Her much smaller car rocked violently, as if it might blow over.

Another blinding flash of lightning was quickly followed by a rumble of thunder. Savannah gritted her teeth.

She'd give anything to be home in bed with the covers pulled over her head.

Everything will be fine. Don't freak out.

Savannah squeezed her eyes shut. Counted backward from ten, then forward again. When she opened them, Blake was spreading a yellow tarp over her small car.

Damn you, Blake Abbott.

She'd arrived in Magnolia Lake regarding every last one of the Abbotts as a villain. Blake's insistence on behaving like a knight in shining armor while looking like black Thor made it difficult to maintain that position.

He was being kind and considerate, doing what nearly any man would under the circumstances. Particularly one who regarded himself a Southern gentleman.

That didn't make him Gandhi.

And it sure as hell didn't prove the Abbotts weren't capable of cruelty. Especially when it came to their business.

But as he approached the truck, looking tall, handsome and delicious despite the rain, it was impossible not to like him.

Relax. It's just a ride home.

The storm had Savannah on edge. Nothing a little

shoo-fly punch wouldn't soothe. She just needed to endure the next twenty minutes with Blake Abbott.

Blake stood outside the truck with the wind whipping against his back and his soaking-wet clothing sticking to his skin. He forced a stream of air through his nostrils.

Parker's warning replayed in his head.

Don't think of her that way. It'll only get you into trouble.

He'd come back to the plant after dinner with his father to make sure everything was okay. But he'd also come back looking for her, worried she'd spent another night working late, not recognizing the dangers of a hard, long rain like this. Something any local would know.

He would have done this for any of his employees—male or female. But he wasn't a convincing enough liar to persuade himself that what he was doing tonight... for her...wasn't different. More personal.

Something about Savannah Carlisle roused a fiercely protective instinct.

Keep your shit together and your hands to yourself.

Blake took one more cleansing breath and released it, hoping his inappropriate thoughts about Savannah went right along with it.

When he yanked the door open, Savannah's widened eyes met his. Shivering, she wrapped her arms around herself.

"You're freezing." Blake climbed inside the truck and turned on the heat to warm her, wishing he could take her in his arms. Transferring his body heat to hers would be a better use of the steam building under his collar. "Is that better?"

Savannah rubbed her hands together and blew on them. "Yes, thank you."

Blake grabbed a jacket off the back seat and handed it to her. "Put this on."

There was the briefest hesitance in her eyes before Savannah accepted the jacket with a grateful nod. It was heavy, and she struggled to put it on.

Blake helped her into it. Somehow, even that basic gesture felt too intimate.

"Let's get you home." Blake put the truck into gear and turned onto the road that led across the river and into town.

They traveled in comfortable silence. It was just as well. The low visibility created by the blowing rain required his complete focus.

They were almost there. Savannah's apartment was just beyond the bridge and around the bend.

Shit.

They were greeted by a roadblock and yellow warning signs. The water had risen to the level of the bridge.

"There's another way into town, right?" Savannah asked nervously.

Blake didn't acknowledge the alarm in her brown eyes. If he didn't panic, maybe she wouldn't, either, when he broke the bad news. "That bridge is the only route between here and your place."

"I can't get home?" Her voice was shaky and its pitch rose.

"Not tonight. Maybe not tomorrow. The bridge is in danger of washing out. I could possibly make it across in my truck, but the weight of this thing could compromise the bridge and send us downriver."

"So what do I do for the next couple of days? Camp out in my office until the bridge is safe again?"

"That won't be necessary." Blake groaned internally. Savannah wasn't going to like the alternative. "My house is up the hill a little ways back."

"You think I'm staying at your house? Overnight?" She narrowed her gaze at him. As if he'd orchestrated the rain, her staying late and the bridge threatening to wash out.

"You don't really have another choice, Savannah." He studied her as she weighed the options.

She pulled the jacket around her tightly as she assessed the road in front of them, then the road behind them. "Seems I don't have much of a choice."

A knot tightened in the pit of Blake's stomach. He'd hoped that she would be stubborn enough to insist on returning to the office. That he wouldn't be tortured by Savannah Carlisle being off-limits *and* sleeping under his roof.

"Okay then." He shifted the truck into Reverse, turned around and headed back to the narrow road that led to the exclusive community where he and Zora owned homes.

As they ascended the hill, the handful of houses around the lake came into view. A bolt of lightning arced in the sky.

Savannah flinched once, then again at the deafening thunder. She was trying to play it cool, but her hands were clenched into fists. She probably had nail prints on her palms.

Why was she so frightened by the storm?

He wanted to know, but the question felt too personal. And everything about Savannah Carlisle indicated she didn't do personal. She kept people at a safe distance.

She'd politely refused every social invitation extended to her since she'd joined the company. Some of his employees hadn't taken her repeated rejections so well.

He'd tried not to do the same. After all, distance from her was exactly what he needed.

When they arrived at his house, he pulled inside the garage.

"You're sure this won't cause trouble? I mean, if anyone found out…" A fresh wave of panic bloomed across her beautiful face. "It wouldn't look good for either of us."

"No one else knows. Besides, any decent human being would do the same," he assured her. "Would you prefer I'd left you in the parking lot on your own?"

"I'm grateful you didn't." Her warm gaze met his. "I just don't want to cause trouble…for either of us."

"It's no trouble," Blake lied. He hopped down from the cab of the truck, then opened her door.

She regarded his extended hand reluctantly. Finally, she placed her palm in his and allowed him to help her down.

Blake stilled for a moment, his brain refusing to function properly. Savannah was sopping wet. Her makeup was washed away by the rain, with the exception of the black mascara running down her face. Yet she looked no worse for the wear.

Her tawny skin was punctuated by a series of freckles splashed across her nose and cheeks.

Something about the discovery of that small detail she'd hidden from the world thrilled him.

His gaze dropped to her lips, and a single, inappropriate thought filled his brain.

Kiss her. Now.

She slipped her icy hand from his, slid the jacket from her shoulders and returned it to him.

"Thank you." He tossed it into the back seat and shut the door.

When he turned to Savannah she was shivering again.

He rubbed his hands up and down her arms to warm her before his brain could remind him that was an inappropriate gesture, too.

Her searing gaze made the point clear.

"Sorry... I..." Blake stepped away, his face heated. He ran a hand through his wet hair.

"I appreciate the gesture. But what I'd really love is a hot shower and a place to sleep."

"Of course." Blake shrugged off his wet rain slicker. He hung it on a hook, then closed the garage door. "Hope you're not afraid of dogs."

"Not particularly."

"Good." Blake dropped his waterlogged shoes by the door to the house. When he opened it, his two dogs surrounded him, yapping until he petted each of their heads. They quickly turned their attention to Savannah.

"Savannah Carlisle, meet Sam—" He indicated the lean Italian greyhound who, while peering intently at Savannah, hadn't left his side. "He's a retired racing greyhound I rescued about five years ago."

"Hello, Sam."

"And that nosy fella there is Benny the labradoodle."

Blake indicated the rust-and-beige dog yapping at her feet, demanding her attention.

"Hi, Benny." Savannah leaned down and let the dog sniff her hand, then petted his head. "Pleasure to meet you."

Benny seemed satisfied with her greeting. He ran back inside with Sam on his heels.

"Did you rescue Benny, too?"

"No." Blake swallowed past the knot that formed in his throat when he remembered the day he'd brought Benny home as a pup.

He'd bought Benny as a surprise for his ex. Only she'd had a surprise of her own. She was leaving him for someone else.

"Oh." Savannah didn't inquire any further, for which he was grateful.

Blake turned on the lights and gestured inside. "After you."

Chapter 7

Stop behaving like the poor girl who grew up on the wrong side of the tracks. Even if you are.

Savannah's wide eyes and slack mouth were a dead giveaway as Blake gave her an informal tour of his beautiful home.

She realized the Abbotts were wealthy. Still, she'd expected a log cabin with simple country decor. Maybe even a luxurious bachelor pad filled with gaming tables and the latest sound equipment.

She certainly hadn't expected this gorgeous, timber-built home overlooking a picturesque lake and offering breathtaking mountain vistas. The wall of windows made the pastoral setting as much a feature of the home as the wide plank floors and shiplap walls.

Rustic charm with a modern twist.

It was the kind of place she could imagine herself

living in. The kind of home she would be living in, if not for the greed and betrayal of Joseph Abbott.

Her shoulders tensed and her hands balled into fists at her sides.

"You must be tired." Blake seemed to sense the shift in her demeanor. "I'll show you to your room. We can finish the tour another time."

Blake always seemed attuned to how she was feeling. A trait that would be endearing if they were a couple. Or even friends.

But they weren't. It was a reality she couldn't lose sight of, no matter how kind and generous Blake Abbott appeared on the surface.

She was here for one reason. But she'd learned little about Joseph Abbott and nothing of his history with her grandfather. If she opened up a little with Blake, perhaps he'd do the same, and reveal something useful about his family.

Maybe Blake didn't know exactly what his grandfather had done. But he might still provide some small clue that could direct her to someone who did know and was willing to talk.

But none of that would happen if she couldn't keep her temper in check. She had to swallow the bitterness and pain that bubbled to the surface whenever she thought of Joseph Abbott's cruel betrayal.

At least for now.

"I'm tired. And wet. And cold. So I'm sorry if I'm cranky." Her explanation seemed to put him at ease.

"Of course." He led the way through the house and up an open staircase to the second floor. Sam and Benny were on his heels.

"I hate to ask this, but do you think I could borrow a T-shirt and some shorts?"

"Don't think I have anything that'll fit you." Blake stopped in front of a closed door. His gaze raked over her body-conscious, black rayon dress. Soaked through, the material shrank, making it fit like a second skin. Blake made a valiant effort to hold back a smirk.

He failed miserably.

"I'll see what I can find."

He opened the door to a spacious guest room with a terrace. The crisp, white bedding made the queen-size bed look inviting, and the room's neutral colors were warm and soothing. The angle of the windows provided a better view of a docked boat and an amphibious plane.

Maybe being a guest chez Blake won't be so bad after all.

"Thanks, Blake. I'll be out of your hair as soon as I can, I promise."

Her words drew his attention to her hair, which was soaking wet. A few loose strands clung to her face.

He reached out, as if to tuck a strand behind her ear. Then he shoved his hand into his pocket.

"It's no trouble. I'm just glad I came back to check on you… I mean, the plant." His voice was rough as he nodded toward a sliding barn door. "The bathroom is there. It's stocked with everything you need, including an unopened toothbrush."

"Thank you, again." Savannah set her purse and bag on the floor beside the bed.

Neither of them said anything for a moment. Blake dragged his stare from hers. "I'll find something you can sleep in and leave it on the bed. Then I'll rustle up something for us to eat."

With the violent storm crackling around them, she hadn't thought about food. But now that he mentioned it, she was starving. She hadn't eaten since lunch.

"All right, cowboy." She couldn't help teasing him. She hadn't ever heard the word *rustle* used outside of a cowboy movie.

Blake grinned, then slapped his thigh. "C'mon, boys. Let's give Savannah some space."

The dogs rushed out into the hall and Blake left, too, closing the door behind him.

Savannah exhaled, thankful for a moment of solitude. Yet, thinking of him, she couldn't help smiling.

She shook her head, as if the move would jostle loose the rogue thoughts of Blake Abbott that had lodged themselves there.

Don't you dare think about it. Blake Abbott is definitely off-limits.

"Hey." Blake was sure Savannah could hear the thump of his heart, even from where she stood across the room.

She padded toward him wearing his oversize University of Tennessee T-shirt as gracefully as if it was a Versace ball gown. Her black hair was chestnut brown on the ends. Ombre, his sister had called it when she'd gotten a similar dye job the year before.

Savannah's hair hung down to her shoulders in loose ringlets that made him want to run the silky strands between his fingers. To wrap them around his fist as he tugged her mouth to his.

Absent cosmetics, Savannah's freshly-scrubbed,

freckled skin took center stage. She was the kind of beautiful that couldn't be achieved with a rack of designer dresses or an expensive makeup palette.

Her natural glow was refreshing.

Seeing Savannah barefaced and fresh out of the shower felt intimate. She'd let down her guard and bared a little of her soul to him.

Blake's heart raced and his skin tingled with a growing desire for this woman. His hands clenched at his sides, aching to touch her.

He fought back the need to taste the skin just below her ear. To nip at her full lower lip. To nibble on the spot where her neck and shoulder met.

Blake snapped his mouth shut when he realized he must look like a guppy in search of water.

"Hey." Savannah's eyes twinkled as she tried to hold back a grin. "Where are Sam and Benny?"

"I put them downstairs in the den. Didn't want to torture them with the food or annoy you with Benny's begging. One look at that sad face and I'm a goner." He nodded toward the orange-and-white University of Tennessee shirt she was wearing. "I see the shirt fit. Kind of."

Savannah held her arms out wide and turned in a circle, modeling his alma mater gear. "It's a little big, but I think I made it work."

That's for damn sure.

The hem of the shirt skimmed the tops of her thighs and hugged her curvy breasts and hips like a warm caress.

Blake was incredibly jealous of that T-shirt. He'd give just about anything to be the one caressing those undulating curves. For his body to be the only thing covering hers.

The too-long sleeves hung past her fingertips. Savannah shoved them up her forearms. She lifted one foot, then the other, as she pulled the socks higher up her calves. Each time, she unwittingly offered a generous peek of her inner thigh.

Blake swallowed hard. The words he formed in his head wouldn't leave his mouth.

"Smells good. What's for dinner?" She didn't remark on his odd behavior, for which he was grateful.

"I had some leftover ham and rice." He turned back to the stove and stirred the food that was beginning to stick to the pan. "So I fried an egg and sautéed a few vegetables to make some ham-fried rice."

"You made ham-fried rice?"

There was the look he'd often seen on her face. Like a war was being waged inside her head and she wasn't sure which side to root for.

"Yep." Blake plated servings for each of them and set them on the dining room table, where he'd already set out a beer for himself and a glass of wine for her. He pulled out her chair.

She thanked him and took her seat. "I didn't realize you cooked. Did your mom teach you?"

Blake chuckled. "There were too many of us to be underfoot in the kitchen."

"Not even your sister?"

Blake remembered the day his mother decided to teach Zora to cook.

"My sister was a feminist at the age of ten. When she discovered Mom hadn't taught any of us to cook, she staged a protest, complete with hand-painted signs.

Something about equal treatment for sisters and brothers, if I remember correctly."

"Your mother didn't get upset?"

"She wanted to be, but she and my dad were too busy trying not to laugh. Besides, she was proud my sister stuck up for herself."

"A lesson your sister obviously took to heart." Savannah smiled. "So if your mother didn't teach you to cook, who did?"

"I became a cookbook addict a few years back." A dark cloud gathered over Blake's head, transporting him back to a place he didn't want to go.

"Why the sudden interest?" She studied him. The question felt like more than just small talk.

Blake shrugged and shoveled a forkful of fried rice into his mouth. "Got tired of fast food."

"I would think there's always a place for you all at Duke and Iris's dinner table." Savannah took a bite, then sighed with appreciation.

What he wouldn't give to hear her utter that sound in a very different setting: her body beneath his as he gripped her generous curves and joined their bodies.

"There is an open invitation to dinner at my parents' home," he confirmed. "But at the time I was seeing someone who didn't get along with my mother and sister." He grunted as he chewed another bite of food. "One of the many red flags I barreled past."

"You're all so close. I'm surprised this woman made the cut if she didn't get along with Zora or Iris."

This was not the dinner conversation Blake hoped to have. He'd planned to use the opportunity to learn more about Savannah. Instead, she was giving him the third degree.

"We met in college. By the time she met any of my family… I was already in too deep. A mistake I've been careful not to repeat," he added under his breath, though she clearly heard him.

"Is that why things didn't work out? Because your family didn't like her?"

He responded with a hollow, humorless laugh. "She left me. For someone else."

The wound in his chest reopened. Not because he missed his ex or wanted her back. Because he hadn't forgiven himself for choosing her over his family.

Though, at the time, he hadn't seen it that way.

After college, he'd moved back home and worked at the distillery, and he and Gavrilla had a long-distance relationship. But when he'd been promoted to VP of operations, he'd asked her to move to Magnolia Lake with him.

The beginning of the end.

Up till then, his ex, his mother and sister had politely endured one another during Gavrilla's visits to town. Once she lived there full-time, the thin veneer of niceties had quickly chipped away.

Blake had risked his relationship with his family because he loved her. She'd repaid his loyalty with callous betrayal.

She'd taught him a hard lesson he'd learned well. It was the reason he was so reluctant to give his heart to anyone again.

"I'm sorry. I wouldn't have brought it up if I'd known it would stir up bad memories." Savannah frowned.

"You couldn't have known. It's not something I talk about." Blake gulped his icy beer, unsure why he'd told Savannah.

"Then I'm glad you felt comfortable enough to talk about it."

"That surprises me." He narrowed his gaze.

"Why?"

"You go out of your way not to form attachments at work."

Savannah's cheeks and forehead turned crimson. She lowered her gaze and slowly chewed her food. "I don't mean to be—"

"Standoffish?" He did his best to hold back a grin. "Their words, not mine."

"Whose words?"

"You don't actually think I'm going to throw a member of my team under the bus like that, do you?" Blake chuckled. "But that fence you work so hard to put around yourself… It's working."

"I don't come to work for social hour. I'm there to do the job you hired me to do." Savannah's tone was defensive. She took a sip of her wine and set it on the table with a thud.

"That's too bad." Blake studied her. Tension rolled off her lean shoulders. "At King's Finest, we treat our employees like family. After all, we spend most of our waking hours at the distillery. Seems less like work when you enjoy what you do and like the people you do it with."

"Am I not doing my job well?" Savannah pursed her adorable lips.

"You're doing a magnificent job." He hadn't intended to upset her. "I doubt anyone could do it better."

She tipped up her chin slightly, as if vindicated by his statement. "Has anyone accused me of being rude or unprofessional?"

"No, nor did I mean to imply that." He leaned forward. "All I'm saying is…you're new to town. So you probably don't have many friends here. But maybe if you'd—"

"I didn't come to Magnolia Lake to make friends, Blake. And I already have a family."

Savannah had given him a clear signal that she didn't want to discuss the topic any further, but she hadn't shut the conversation down completely. There was something deep inside him that needed to know more about her.

"So tell me about your family."

Chapter 8

They'd talked so much about his family. Savannah shouldn't be surprised he'd want to know about hers.

Not in a getting-to-know-you, we're-on-a-date kind of way. In the way that was customary in Magnolia Lake. One part Southern hospitality. One part nosy-as-hell.

Had she not been determined to keep her personal life under wraps, she might've appreciated their interest.

She didn't want to discuss her family with Blake or any Abbott. But she hadn't gotten anywhere in her investigation. If she didn't want to spend the rest of her natural life in this one-horse town, she needed to change her approach.

If the quickest route to getting answers was charming the handsome Blake Abbott, she'd have to swallow her pride, put on her biggest smile and do it. At the very least, that meant opening up about her life.

"I have a sister that's a few years younger than me."

"That your only sibling?"

"Yes."

"What's she like?"

"Laney's brilliant. She's been accepted as a PhD candidate at two different Ivy League schools. All of that despite being the mother of a rambunctious two-year-old." A smile tightened Savannah's cheeks whenever she talked about Laney or Harper. "Someday my sister is going to change the world. I just know it."

"Sounds like Parker." Blake grinned. "While the rest of us were outside running amok, he had his nose in a book. For him, being forced to go outside was his punishment."

"Seems like his book obsession paid off."

"A fact he doesn't let any of us forget. Especially my mother." Blake chuckled. "You and your sister..."

"Delaney." No point in lying about her sister's name. He could find that out easily enough.

"Are you close?"

"Very. Though with our age difference and the fact that we lost our parents when we were young, I sometimes act more like her mother than her sister. Something she doesn't appreciate much these days."

"Sorry to hear about your parents. How'd you lose them, if you don't mind me asking?"

She did mind. But this wasn't about what she wanted. She needed Blake to trust her.

"The crappy little tenement we lived in burned down to the ground. Lightning hit the building and the whole thing went up in no time." She could feel the heat and smell the smoke. That night forever etched in her brain. "A lot of the families we knew growing up lost their lives that night."

"How'd you and your sister get out?" There was a pained expression on Blake's face. It was more empathy than pity.

A distinction she appreciated.

"My dad worked second shift. When he arrived home the building was in flames. He saved me and my sister and a bunch of our neighbors, but he went back to save my mother and…" A tightness gripped her chest and tears stung her eyes. She inhaled deeply and refused to let them fall. "He didn't make it back out."

"Savannah." Blake's large hand covered her smaller one. "I'm sorry."

The small gesture consoled her. Yet if not for what Blake's grandfather had done, her life would be very different.

She couldn't know for sure if her parents would still be with her. But they wouldn't have been living in a run-down housing project that had been cited for countless violations. And they wouldn't have lost their lives that stormy night.

"Thank you." Savannah slipped her hand from beneath his. "But it was such a long time ago. I was only nine. My sister was barely four. She hardly remembers our parents."

"Who raised you two?"

"My grandfather." She couldn't help smiling. "I didn't want to go live with him. When my parents were alive he'd always seemed so grumpy. He didn't approve of my dad. He'd hoped my mother would marry someone who had more to offer financially. But after my dad gave his life trying to save my mom… He realized too late what a good guy my father was." She shoved the last of her food around her plate. "He's been trying to make it up to them ever since."

They ate in silence, the mood notably somber.

"Sorry you asked, huh?" She took her plate to the kitchen.

"No." Blake followed her. "I understand now why you don't like to talk about yourself or your family."

"I'd rather be seen as polite but aloof than as Debbie Downer or the poor little orphan people feel sorry for."

A peal of thunder rocked the house, startling Savannah. The storm had abated for the past hour only to reassert itself with a vengeance.

"It's raining again." Blake peered out the large kitchen window. When he looked back at her, a spark of realization lit his eyes. "Your parents… That night… That's why you're so freaked out by thunderstorms."

Savannah considered asking if he wanted a cookie for his brilliant deduction. The flash of light across the night sky turned her attention to a more pressing issue.

"Where do you keep the bourbon around here?"

Blake chuckled. "I was saving it for after dinner."

"It's after dinner." Savannah folded her arms. "After that trip down memory lane, I could use something that packs a punch."

"You've got it."

She followed him down to the den. Sam and Benny greeted them, their tails wagging.

This was the game room she'd anticipated. But instead of having a frat-house quality, it was simple and elegant. There was a billiards table, three huge televisions mounted on the walls, a game table in one corner and groupings of chairs and sofas throughout the large room.

One bank of windows faced the mountains. The other faced the lake with more mountains in the distance.

Savannah sat on a stool at the bar. "This place is stunning. It isn't what I expected." She studied him as he stepped behind the bar. "Neither are you."

A slow grin curled one corner of his generous mouth. Her tongue darted out involuntarily to lick her lips in response. There was something incredibly sexy about Blake's smile.

He was confident, bordering on cocky. Yet there was something sweet and almost vulnerable about him. When he grinned at her like that, she felt an unexpected heaviness low in her belly. Her nipples tightened, and she mused about the taste of his lips. How they would feel against hers.

Blake produced a bottle of King's Finest top-shelf bourbon. Something she'd only splurged on for high-end, no-expenses-spared affairs when she'd planned events at the hotel.

"If you're trying to impress me, it won't work." She lowered her voice to a whisper. "I happen to know you get it for free."

"Not the premium stuff. I buy that just like everyone else." He chuckled. "Except for the bottle we give employees every year at Christmas. But I did use my employee discount at the gift shop."

Savannah couldn't help laughing. She honestly didn't want to like Blake or any of the Abbotts. She'd only intended to give the appearance of liking and admiring them. But then, she hadn't expected that Blake would be funny and charming in a self-deprecating way. Or that he'd be sweet and thoughtful.

Blake was all of that wrapped in a handsome package that felt like Christmas and her birthday rolled into one.

And that smile.

It should be registered as a panty-obliterating weapon.

"How do you take your bourbon?" Blake set two wide-mouth glasses on the counter.

"Neat." She usually preferred it in an Old Fashioned cocktail. But with the sky lighting up and rumbling around her, drinking bourbon straight, with no fuss or muss, was the quickest way to get a shot of courage into her system.

Before the next lightning strike.

Blake poured them both a fourth of a glass and capped the bottle.

Savannah parted her lips as she tipped the glass, inhaling the scent of buttery vanilla, cherries and a hint of apple. She took a sip, rolling the liquor on her tongue. Savoring its smooth taste.

Light and crisp. Bursting with fruit. A finish that had a slow, spicy burn with a hint of cinnamon, dark cherries and barrel char absorbed during the aging of the bourbon.

Savannah inhaled through both her nose and mouth, allowing the scent and flavors of the twelve-year-old bourbon to permeate her senses. She relished the burn of the liquor sliding down her throat.

"You approve, I take it." Blake sat beside her and sipped his bourbon.

"Worth every cent." She raised her glass.

"My grandfather would be pleased."

Savannah winced at the mention of Joseph Abbott. It was like being doused with a bucket of ice water.

She took another sip of the bourbon that had catapulted King's Finest to success. Their King's Reserve label had quickly become a must-have for the rich and famous.

Her grandfather's recipe.

"I look forward to telling him in person." Savannah smiled slyly as Blake sipped his bourbon. Her grandfather always said liquor loosened lips. She couldn't think of a more suitable way to induce Blake to reveal his family's secrets.

"Up to watching a movie or playing a game of cards? We could play—"

"If you say 'strip poker,' I swear I'll—"

"I was thinking gin rummy." The amusement that danced in his dark eyes made her wonder if the thought hadn't crossed his mind.

"Since you, and the entire town, are hell-bent on getting to know me, I have another idea." She traced the rim of her glass as she studied him. "'Truth or dare?'"

Blake laughed. "I haven't played that since college."

"Neither have I, so this should be fun." She moved to the sofa. Benny sprawled across her feet and rolled over for a belly rub. Savannah happily complied.

Blake studied her as he sipped his bourbon. He still hadn't responded.

"If 'truth or dare?' is too risqué for you, I completely understand." Having satisfied Benny's demands, Savannah crossed one leg over the other, her foot bouncing. Blake's gaze followed the motion, giving her an unexpected sense of satisfaction.

He sat beside her on the couch, and Sam settled at his feet.

"My life is an open book. Makes me fairly invincible at this game." He rubbed Sam's ears.

"A challenge. I like it." The bourbon spread warmth through Savannah's limbs and loosened the tension in her muscles. She was less anxious, despite the intense flashes of light that charged the night sky.

Thunder boomed and both dogs whined. Benny shielded his face with his paw.

Savannah stroked the dog's head. "By all means, you go first, Mr. Invincible. I'll take truth."

A grin lit Blake's dark eyes. "Tell me about your first kiss."

Chapter 9

Blake had always considered himself a sensible person. Sure, he took risks, but they were usually calculated ones. Risks that would either result in a crash and burn that would teach him one hell of a lesson or pay off in spades.

Sitting on his favorite leather sofa, drinking his granddaddy's finest bourbon and playing "truth or dare?" with the sexiest woman who'd ever donned one of his shirts was the equivalent of playing with fire while wearing a kerosene-soaked flak jacket.

Or in this case, a bourbon-soaked one. They'd both had their share of the nearly empty bottle of bourbon.

Their questions started off innocently enough. His were aimed at getting to know everything there was to know about Savannah Carlisle. Hers mostly dealt with character—his and his family's. But as the game went

on—and the bourbon bottle inched closer to empty—
their questions grew more intimate.

Too intimate.

Savannah was an employee and he was part owner
of King's Finest. He shouldn't be sitting so close to
her, well after midnight, when they'd both been drinking. While she was wearing his shirt, her skin smell-
ing of his soap.

Savannah folded her legs underneath her, drawing
his eyes to her smooth skin.

They were playing Russian roulette. Only the six-
shooter was loaded with five bullets instead of one.

Neither of them was drunk, but they were sure as
hell dancing along its blurry edge.

"What's your favorite thing to eat?" he asked.

"Strawberry rhubarb pie. My sister makes it for my
birthday every year in lieu of a cake." She grinned.
"Your turn. Truth or dare?"

"Truth."

Savannah leaned closer, her gaze holding his, as if
she were daring him instead. "Tell me something you
really wanted, but you're glad you didn't get."

The question felt like a sword puncturing his chest.
His expression must have indicated his discomfort.
"Married."

Savannah's cheeks turned crimson and she grimaced. "If it's something you'd rather not talk about—"

"I wanted to surprise my ex with a labradoodle for
her birthday." He got the words out quickly before he
lost his nerve. "Instead, she surprised me. Told me
she'd fallen for someone else, and that it was the best
thing for both of us."

"That's awful. I'm sorry."

"I'm not." He rubbed Sam's ears, then took another sip of bourbon, welcoming the warmth. "She was right. It was the best thing for both of us. Marrying her would've been a mistake."

They were both quiet, the storm crackling around them.

He divided the remainder of the bottle between their two glasses and took another pull of his bourbon. "Truth or dare?"

"Truth." Her gaze was soft, apologetic.

"Why'd you *really* come to Magnolia Lake?" It was a question he'd wanted to ask since he'd learned she moved to town prior to being offered the position.

He couldn't shake the feeling there was more to the story than she'd told him that day. Savannah Carlisle was an organized planner. And too sensible a person to move to an area with very few employment options on the hope she'd be hired by them.

"Because I belong at King's Finest." Something resembling anger flashed in her eyes. "It's like I told you—I was compelled by the company's origin story. I want to be part of its future." She shifted on the sofa. "Now you. Truth or dare?"

"Truth." He studied her expression and tried to ignore the shadow of anger or perhaps pain she was trying desperately to hide.

"If you could be doing anything in the world right now, what would it be?"

"This." Blake leaned in and pressed his mouth to hers. Swallowed her little gasp of surprise. Tasted the bourbon on her warm, soft lips.

A soft sigh escaped her mouth and she parted her lips, inviting his tongue inside. It glided along hers as

Savannah wrapped her arms around him. She clutched his shirt, pulling him closer.

Blake cradled her face in his hands as he claimed her mouth. He kissed her harder and deeper, his fingers slipping into her soft curls. He'd wanted to do this since he'd first seen the silky strands loose, grazing her shoulders.

He reveled in the sensation of her soft curves pressed against his hard chest and was eager to taste the beaded tips straining against the cotton.

Blake tore his mouth from hers, trailing kisses along her jaw and down her long, graceful neck.

"Blake." She breathed his name.

His shaft, already straining against his zipper, tightened in response. He'd wanted her in his arms, in his bed, nearly since the moment he'd laid eyes on her.

He wanted to rip the orange shirt off. Strip her down to nothing but her bare, freckled skin and a smile. Take her right there on the sofa as the storm raged around them.

But even in the fog of lust that had overtaken him, his bourbon-addled brain knew this was wrong. He shouldn't be kissing Savannah within an inch of her life. Shouldn't be preparing to take her to his bed. Not like this. Not when they were both two glasses of bourbon away from being in a complete haze.

He wouldn't take advantage of her or any woman. His parents had raised him better than that.

Blake pulled away, his chest heaving. "Savannah, I'm sorry. I can't... I mean...we shouldn't—"

"No, of course not." She swiped a hand across her kiss-swollen lips, her eyes not meeting his. She stood abruptly, taking Benny by surprise. "I...uh... Well, thank you for dinner and drinks. I should turn in for the night."

Blake grasped her hand before he could stop himself. "You don't need to go. We were having a good time. I just got carried away."

"Me, too. But that's all the more reason I should go to bed. Besides, it's late." She rushed from the room, tossing a good-night over her shoulder.

"Benny, stay," Blake called to the dog, who whimpered as Savannah closed the door softly behind her. "Come." The dog trotted over and Blake petted his head. "Give her some space, okay, boy?"

The dog clearly didn't agree with his approach to the situation. Neither did certain parts of Blake's anatomy.

"Way to go," he whispered beneath his breath as he moved about the room, gathering the glasses and the empty bottle.

I shouldn't have kissed her. Or brought her here. Or given her that damn shirt to wear.

He could list countless mistakes he'd made that evening. Missteps that had inevitably led them to the moment when his mouth had crashed against hers. When he'd stopped fighting temptation.

Blake shouldn't have kissed her, but he wished like hell that he hadn't stopped kissing her. That Savannah Carlisle was lying in bed next to him right now.

Sam's howl and Benny's incessant barking woke Blake from his fitful sleep at nearly three in the morning.

"What the hell, guys? Some of us are trying to sleep." Blake rolled over and pulled the pillow over his head.

A clap of thunder rattled the windows and the dogs intensified their howls of distress.

Benny hated thunderstorms, but Sam usually remained pretty calm. Blake sat up in bed and rubbed his eyes, allowing them to adjust to the darkness.

"Guys, calm down!" he shouted.

Benny stopped barking, but he whimpered, bumping his nose against the closed door.

Blake strained to listen for what might be bothering the dogs. Maybe Savannah had gone to the kitchen.

He got out of bed, his boxers sitting low on his hips, and cracked open his bedroom door.

No lights. No footsteps. No running water. Aside from the storm and the rain beating against the house, everything was quiet.

"No! No! Please! You have to save them."

"Savannah?" Blake ran toward her room at the other end of the hall. He banged on the guest bedroom door. "It's me—Blake. Are you okay?"

There was no response. Only mumbling and whimpering.

"Savannah, honey, I'm coming in."

He tried the knob, but the door was locked. He searched over the door frame for the emergency key left by his brother's building crew.

Blake snatched down the hex key, glad he hadn't gotten around to removing it. He fiddled with the lock before it finally clicked and the knob turned.

He turned on the light and scanned the room.

Savannah was thrashing in the bed, her eyes screwed shut, tears leaking from them.

"Savannah, honey, you're okay." He touched her arm

gently, afraid of frightening her. "You're right here with me. And you're perfectly fine."

"Blake?" Her eyes shot open and she sat up quickly, nearly head-butting him. She flattened her back against the headboard. "What are you doing here?" She looked around, as if piecing everything together. "In my room."

"You were having a bad dream. The dogs went nuts. So did I." He sat on the edge of the bed, his heart still racing from the jog to her room. "I thought you were hurt."

Her voice broke and her breathing was ragged. "Sorry I woke you, but I'm fine."

"No, you're not. Your hands are shaking, and you're pale."

"Thank you for checking on me." She wiped at the corners of her eyes. "I didn't intend to be so much trouble tonight."

"I'm glad you're here." Blake lifted her chin so their eyes met. "I'd hate to think of what might've happened if you'd been out there alone on that road tonight. Or home alone in this storm." He dropped his hand from her face. "Do you always have these nightmares during a storm?"

"Not in a really long time." She tucked her hair behind her ear. "Talking about what happened that night probably triggered it." Savannah pressed a hand to her forehead.

"I shouldn't have pushed you to talk about your family. I just wanted to…" Blake sighed, rubbing Benny's ears.

"What were you going to say?" For the first time since he'd entered the room, her hands weren't trembling. Instead of being preoccupied with the storm, she was focused on him.

"There's this deep sadness behind those brown eyes."

Savannah dropped her gaze from his.

"You try to mask it by throwing yourself into your work. And you ward off anyone who gets too close with that biting wit. But it's there. Even when you laugh."

"Let's say you're right." She met his gaze. "Why do you care? I'm just another employee."

"I would think that kiss earlier proved otherwise."

"So what…are you my self-appointed guardian angel?" Savannah frowned.

"If that's what you need." He shrugged.

Silence stretched between them. Conflicting emotions played out on her face. There was something she was hesitant to say.

Blake recognized her turmoil. He'd been struggling with it all night. Wanting her, but knowing he shouldn't. He struggled with it even now.

"Thank you, for everything, Blake. For coming to check on me." She scanned his bare chest.

Blake was suddenly conscious that he was sitting on her bed. In nothing but his underwear.

Good thing he wore boxers.

"Sorry. You sounded like you were in distress, so I bolted down here after Benny woke me up."

Savannah turned her attention to Benny's wide brown eyes and smiled for the first time since Blake had entered the room. She kissed the top of the dog's furry head.

"Were you worried about me, boy?" She laughed when Benny wagged his tail in response.

Blake chuckled softly. Benny was a sociable dog, but he'd never been as taken with anyone as he seemed to be with Savannah.

"You've earned at least one fan here." Blake's face grew hot when Savannah's gaze met his.

"Thank you both." She gave Benny one last kiss on his snout. "I won't keep you two up any longer. Good night."

"Good night." Blake turned out the light.

Savannah flinched in response to the lightning that flashed outside the window.

"Look, why don't Benny and I sleep in here tonight?"

"With me?" The pitch of her voice rose and her eyes widened.

"I'll sleep in the chair by the window."

She scanned the chair, then his large frame. "I don't think you'd be very comfortable contorting yourself into that little chair all night. Don't worry about me. Seriously, I'll be fine."

A bolt of lightning flashed through the sky, followed by a loud cracking sound.

Savannah screamed and Benny whimpered and howled, hiding underneath the bed.

"It's all right." Blake put a hand on Savannah's trembling shoulder. He went to the window and surveyed the property.

Lightning had hit a tree just outside the bedroom window. A huge section had split off. The bark was charred, but the tree wasn't on fire.

Blake turned back to Savannah. Her eyes were filled with tears, and she was shaking.

"It's okay." He sat beside her on the bed. "There was no real damage, and no one was hurt."

Blake wrapped an arm around her shoulders. He pulled her to his chest, tucked her head beneath his chin and rocked her in his arms when she wouldn't stop crying.

"You're fine, honey. Nothing's going to happen to you, I promise."

"What if I want something to happen?" She lifted her head. Her eyes met his, and suddenly he was very conscious of the position of her hand on his bare chest.

The backs of her fingertips brushed lightly over his right nipple. "What if I want to finish what we started earlier?"

Electricity skittered along his skin and the muscles low in his abdomen tensed as his shaft tightened.

He let out a low groan, wishing he could just comply with her request and give in to their desire. He cradled her face in his hand.

"Honey, you're just scared. Fear makes us do crazy things."

"Wanting to sleep with you is crazy?" She frowned.

"No, but getting into a relationship with a member of the management team is ill-advised."

"I'm not talking about a relationship." She seemed perturbed by the suggestion. "I'm just talking about sex. We're adults, and it's what we both obviously want. I'm not looking for anything more with you."

He grimaced at the indication that it was him specifically she didn't want more with. For once in his life, he longed for a good *It's not you, it's me*.

"That won't work for me." He sighed heavily. "Not with you."

They were way past the possibility of meaningless sex. He felt something for her. Something he hadn't allowed himself to feel in so long.

"Why not with me? I'm here, and I'm willing." She indicated his noticeable erection. "And unless you're hiding a gun in your boxers, it's what you want, too."

"Savannah…" Blake gripped her wrists, holding her hands away from his body. "You aren't making this easy for me."

"I thought I was." She grabbed the hem of the shirt and tugged it over her head, baring her perfect breasts. The brown peaks were stiff. Begging for his mouth. Her eyes twinkled. "Can't get much easier than this."

Blake's heart raced as the storm raged around them. He wanted to take the high road. But right now, it wasn't his moral compass that was pointing north.

Blake tightened his grip on Savannah's neck and something about it sent a thrill down her spine. Her core pulsed like her heartbeat.

The cool air tightened the beaded tips of her breasts. His gaze drifted from the hardened peaks back to her.

"You're scared. You've been drinking. You're not thinking clearly right now. Neither am I."

"We slept off the bourbon hours ago," she reminded him, pressing a kiss to his jaw. His body stiffened in response. "Besides, you kissed me last night." She kissed his neck, then whispered in his ear, "And don't pretend you haven't thought about us being together before tonight."

Savannah relished Blake's sharp intake of breath when she nipped at his neck. She wanted his strong, rough hands to caress her skin. And she longed to trail her hands over the hard muscles that rippled beneath his brown skin.

Adrenaline rushed through her veins, her body hummed with energy and her brain buzzed with all of the reasons she shouldn't be here doing this.

Just for tonight, she wanted to let go of her fear and allow herself the thing she wanted so badly.

Blake Abbott.

Sleeping with him would complicate her plans, but weren't things between them complicated anyway? Whether they slept together tonight or not, things would never be the same between them.

Maybe she didn't want them to be.

If it turned out her grandfather was confused about what had transpired all those years ago, she need never tell Blake why she'd really come to Magnolia Lake. And if her grandfather was right...and Blake's family had used him cruelly...why should she feel the slightest ounce of guilt? The Abbotts certainly hadn't.

Either way, she wanted him. And she had no intention of taking no for an answer when it was clear he wanted her, too.

Savannah wriggled her wrists free from Blake's loose grip. She looped her arms around his neck, her eyes drifting shut, and kissed him.

Blake hesitated at first, but then he kissed her back. He held her in his arms, his fingertips pressed to her back.

The hair on his chest scraped against her sensitive nipples. She parted her lips and Blake slipped his tongue between them, gliding it along hers.

Savannah relished the strangled moan that escaped his mouth. The way it vibrated in her throat. That small sound made her feel in control in a moment when she'd normally have felt so powerless.

As helpless as she'd felt when she'd watched the building burn. Unable to save her parents.

Her parents. Her grandfather. Laney.

What would they think of what she was doing right now? Giving herself to the grandson of the man who had taken everything from them?

Savannah's heart pounded in her chest as she tried to push the disquieting thoughts from her head.

They wouldn't understand, but she did. She wasn't giving herself to Blake Abbott. She was taking what she wanted…what she needed…from him.

She'd gotten lost in her thoughts. Blake was the one driving the kiss now. Both of them murmured with pleasure as his tongue danced with hers. Then he laid her back and deepened the kiss.

Savannah glided her hands down Blake's back and gripped his firm, muscular bottom.

His length hardened against her belly and he groaned, his mouth moving against hers.

Savannah kept her eyes shut, blocking out the lightning that periodically illuminated the room, and the thunder that made poor Benny whimper. Instead, she focused on the beating of her own heart. The insistent throb and dampness between her thighs.

Savannah couldn't control what was happening outside. But she could control this. How he felt. How he made her feel.

Powerful. Alive. In control.

She slipped a hand beneath his waistband and wrapped her fingers around the width of his thick shaft. Blake moaned against her open mouth, intensifying the heat spreading through her limbs. She circled the head with her thumb, spreading the wetness she found there, relishing the way his breathing became harder and faster in response.

He grabbed her wrist, halting her movement as she glided her fist up and down his erection.

"Neither of us is ready for what happens next if you keep doing that, sweetheart." His voice was low and gruff.

"Then we should stop wasting time and get down to business."

Blake shooed the dogs from the room and locked the door behind them before returning to bed. He cradled her cheek.

"Savannah, you know I want you. But I don't want you to do this for the wrong reasons."

"Does it matter why?"

"Yeah, baby. In this case, it does." He swept her hair from her face. "Because this isn't a typical one-night stand for me."

"Why not? I'm sure you've done this lots of times before." She tried to rein in her frustration. In her limited experience, it had never been this difficult to get a guy to have sex with her.

"Not with someone who works for me."

Suddenly an Abbott is worried about being ethical?

"It'll be our little secret. And it'll be just this once." She hated that an Abbott had reduced her to groveling.

"I can't promise that, because I'm already addicted to your kiss." He kissed her mouth. "Your taste." He ran his tongue along the seam of her lips. "And if I get more…and make no mistake about this—I do want more…there is the definite risk of becoming addicted to having you in my bed."

It was the sweetest, sexiest thing any man had ever said to her.

She wanted to hear more of it while Blake Abbott moved inside her, making her forget her worries and fears and replacing the tragic memory associated with thunderstorms with a pleasurable one.

"I can't promise what's going to happen tomorrow." She kissed him again, trying to convince him to let go of his worries, too. "I can only tell you that this is what I want. It isn't the liquor or my fear talking. It's me. I want you. Period."

His body tensed, and his eyes studied hers there in the dark. Then he claimed her mouth in a kiss that shot fireworks down her spine, exploding in her belly. Her core throbbed with a desire so intense she ached with the emptiness between her thighs.

An emptiness only he could fill.

Blake trailed kisses down her neck and ran his rough tongue over one sensitive nipple. He gripped the flesh there and sucked the hardened nub. Softly at first, then harder. She moaned as he licked and sucked, the sensation tugging at her core.

"Oh, Blake. Yes." She arched her back, giving him better access. His eyes met hers and he smiled briefly before moving on to the other hardened peak, making it as swollen and distended as its counterpart.

He trailed kisses down her belly and along the edge of the waistband of her panties. Suddenly, he pulled aside the fabric soaked with her desire for him and tasted her there.

Gripping a handful of his short, dark curls, Savannah gasped and called out his name. She spread her thighs, allowing her knees to fall open and providing Blake with better access to her swollen folds and the hardened bundle of nerves he was assaulting with that heavenly tongue.

He reached up, pinching one of her nipples as she rode his tongue. Every muscle in her body tightened as a wave of pleasure rolled through her hard and fast.

She was shivering and trembling again. This time, it wasn't because of the storm. It was because Blake Abbott had given her an orgasm that had struck her like a lightning bolt.

And left her wanting more.

Chapter 10

Blake groaned as the sunlight filtered through the window of the guest bedroom. He peeked one eye open and lifted his arm, which had been draped across Savannah as she slept. He looked at his watch.

It was well after seven. Normally he would've worked out and walked the dogs by now. He was surprised Sam and Benny weren't already…

His thoughts were interrupted by Benny's moaning and scratching at the door.

Savannah sighed softly, her naked bottom nestled against the morning wood he was sporting.

Hell, his erection had probably never gone away after his night with Savannah. A night in which he'd brought her to pleasure with his mouth and fingers so many times that her throat was probably raw from calling his name.

He hadn't made love to her, and he hadn't allowed her to give him so much as a good hand job. A decision his body—strung tight as a piano wire—bemoaned. But he had to be sure her head was in the right place. That she wasn't just acting out of fear.

Blake sucked in a deep breath, inhaling the scent of her hair. He wanted to run his fingers through the silky curls again, brush her hair back so he could see her lovely face.

But he didn't want to wake her. He wasn't ready to burst the bubble they'd been floating in.

He couldn't bear for her to wake and regret their night together. A night he didn't regret in the least.

Blake slipped out of the room, got dressed, fed the dogs and took them for their usual walk, avoiding all the waterlogged areas. He surveyed the damage to his property and the neighborhood. There were a few downed branches and lots of upended lawn furniture. A tree had fallen through one neighbor's roof. Shingles littered their front lawn, and a yellow tarp, draped over the roof, billowed in the wind.

But for Blake, the storm hadn't been a bad thing. It'd brought Savannah to his home and into his bed.

Blake hoped she hadn't been serious about making this a one-off. He liked her. A lot.

Dating Savannah would ruffle his family's feathers. He wouldn't tell them right away. Not until he knew whether this was serious. If it was, he'd just have to deal with the consequences of breaking their unwritten rule.

Blake opened the side garage door and let the dogs in, wiping their muddy paws on a rag. As they went back into the house, he paused to listen.

The house was silent. Savannah was evidently still sleeping. He washed his hands and checked the kitchen for breakfast food. He cursed under his breath for putting off grocery shopping.

Every Southerner knew you stocked up on basic goods when there was an impending storm of any kind.

Luckily, there were his mother's and sister's refrigerators to raid. Both of them kept their pantries and deep freezers well stocked. His mother's deep freezer likely contained a side of beef and enough chicken to feed the entire company. Zora's would be filled with frozen meals and store-bought goodies.

Right now, he'd settle for either. But since Zora lived closest, he'd start with her.

"You two be good." He patted Sam's and Benny's heads. "I'll be back before you know it. And don't bother Savannah. She's sleeping." He headed back toward the garage. "That means you, Benny."

Benny whimpered, dropping on the floor in the corner and resting his head on his paws.

Blake hopped in his truck and drove the five minutes to his sister's home on the other side of the lake. She was outside gathering broken tree limbs.

"If you came to help, you're too late. I'm just about done here." Zora stepped on a long branch, snapping it in two. Then she snapped each piece in half again.

Blake hugged his sister. It didn't surprise him that she hadn't asked for assistance. Since she was a kid, Zora had been determined to prove her independence.

"Well, since you've already got everything under control, maybe you can help me out. I don't have anything for breakfast back at the house. I was gonna go grocery shopping this weekend but the bridge is out."

He shoved his hands in his pockets, hoping to avoid his sister's usual forty questions.

Zora stopped breaking branches and eyed him. "Why don't you fix breakfast here for both of us?"

"Because."

"I'm not twelve, Blake. That doesn't work anymore." Zora propped a hand on her hip.

Blake sighed. "Okay, fine. I have company."

Zora stepped closer. "Female company?"

Blake tried to keep his expression neutral.

"You don't have women over to the house. Ever. Not since you broke up with Godzilla."

"Gavrilla." But he didn't correct the part about him initiating the breakup. They both knew it wasn't true, but saying it seemed to make his family feel better.

"Whatever." She waved her hand. "This must be serious if you brought one of your out-of-town hook-ups home."

"How did you—"

"I didn't, but I always suspected that's why you never take Daisy when you travel." Zora looked more proud of herself than she had when her team had posted record sales numbers the previous quarter.

"Don't you have anything better to do than to worry about who I'm sleeping with?"

"People around here talk. If they're not talking, nothing's happening. I haven't heard about you hooking up with anyone around here and…well…you are a guy."

"Zora, *enough*."

He was *not* going to have a conversation with his sister about his sex life. Though Zora was an adult, she'd always be his baby sister.

"I can't help it if I'm smarter than you." She shoved him playfully.

"You're the Jessica Fletcher of who is doing who in this town. Congratulations, Brat." He dug up her childhood nickname. "Now, can we get back to my request?"

"Right. You need to shop my pantry."

Zora removed her work gloves and headed toward the garage of her colonial. The place was newer than his, though a bit smaller and far more traditional-looking.

"Let's find something you and your girlfriend can eat for breakfast."

"Didn't say she was my girlfriend." Blake gritted his teeth.

Zora turned to him. "She woke up at your house, presumably in your bed. Just let that sink in for a minute."

"I'm seriously starting to wish I'd gone to Mom and Dad's house. Besides, they have real food. Not just crap that comes out of a box."

"That hurts." Zora punched his arm. "Besides, that's no way to talk to someone you want a favor from, big brother."

Zora opened her well-stocked fridge. She cut an egg carton in half and gave him half a dozen eggs. Then she took out a mostly full package of thick-cut maple bacon and an unopened jug of orange juice. She arranged everything in a reusable shopping bag.

"Please tell me you at least have the basics…cheese, milk, maybe an onion and some mushrooms."

"I'm the one who actually cooks for myself," Blake reminded her. "But I think I used my last onion making fried rice last night."

"You cooked dinner for her, too?" Zora's eyes lit up like a Christmas tree that had just been plugged in. "After you left Mom and Dad's last night?"

Ignoring her question, Blake accepted two sweet onions from his sister and dropped them in the bag, careful not to crack the eggs. "Thanks, Brat."

"You're not even going to give me a hint who I'm feeding?" She leaned one hip against the fridge.

"I don't kiss and tell." He hoisted the bag. "And I didn't sleep with her."

"Then why won't you tell me who it is?"

"Because it's none of your business."

"Speaking of business…your mystery guest wouldn't happen to be a certain not-so-Chatty-Cathy employee who you can't seem to keep your eyes off, would it?"

Blake froze momentarily, but recovered quickly. Zora was fishing, hoping to get a reaction out of him. If he played it cool, she'd move on to another theory.

"Thanks for the food," he called over his shoulder. "Holler if you need help with the yard."

"Only if you'll bring your girlfriend over."

Blake shook his head and climbed back in his truck. *Brat.*

He waved and backed out of his sister's drive. As he headed toward home, his neck tensed in anticipation of seeing Savannah.

Savannah's eyes fluttered open. She was floating on a warm cloud of indescribable bliss, and her entire body tingled with satisfaction. Her mouth stretched in an involuntary smile.

Last night, Blake had given her mind-blowing pleasure, and he'd done it without removing his boxers.

He'd focused on making their encounter special for her. Even if it meant denying himself.

No one had ever given her such intense pleasure or focused solely on her needs. Savannah groaned. She'd finally met a man who made her want *things*. Things she hadn't allowed herself the luxury of wanting.

God, why does he have to be an Abbott?

Because apparently the universe hated her.

As she'd given in to her desire for him, she'd convinced herself she could remain detached and keep their encounter impersonal. Transactional.

But when he looked into her eyes, all she'd seen was Blake. Not his family versus hers. Not the history of their grandfathers. Nothing but him.

For a few hours, she'd allowed herself to buy into the delusion that she could have him and still get justice for her family.

But she couldn't have both. At some point, she'd have to choose. And her allegiance was to her own family.

Savannah sighed and rolled over. Blake wasn't in bed. She got dressed and went down to the kitchen.

No Blake.

She walked through the house, calling him without response. His truck wasn't in the garage. When she returned to the kitchen, she saw his note.

Gone to rustle us up some breakfast.

She couldn't help smiling. *Smart-ass.*

Why couldn't he stop being funny and thoughtful

and all-around adorable? He was making it difficult to focus on her mission. Which was the only thing that mattered.

She was alone in Blake Abbott's house. She'd never get a better opportunity to see if there was anything there that could shed light on what had happened between their grandfathers.

She went to Blake's office. The door was unlocked, but the moment she opened it, the dogs ran down the hall and greeted her.

Savannah shut the door and stooped in front of the dogs, petting them and giving Benny a peck on his nose.

"Stay here. I just need to take a quick peek." Savannah slipped inside, shutting the door behind her. The dogs yipped in protest.

A loud thump nearly made her jump out of her skin. One of the dogs had jumped against the door.

Benny. The thud was too heavy to be Sam.

She glanced around. The neat, organized room was flooded with sunlight.

She had no idea how long it would be before his return. There was no time to waste.

Savannah searched the bookshelves. She looked through drawers and scanned files for anything related to the company's origin. She sifted through his desk drawers, hoping to find something…anything.

There was nothing out of the ordinary.

She spotted his laptop. The same one he used at work.

Frustrated, Savannah sat down at the large oak desk and groaned. She bumped the mouse and the screen woke.

It was unlocked.

He'd obviously used it that morning and hadn't been gone long. Savannah rummaged through the computer directories. All she found were the same files she accessed at work.

Savannah pulled open the desk drawer again and lifted the organizer tray. A photo of Blake, Sam and a woman was wedged in back.

The ex.

She was pretty, but something about her didn't feel real.

Hypocrite.

She was under Blake's roof, sleeping in his bed and trying to stage a coup at his family's company.

At least his ex had been up-front with her treachery.

Guilt gnawed at Savannah's gut. She replaced the photo and then put the drawer back in order.

There were few personal photos elsewhere in the house, but the office walls and shelves were filled with family pictures and photos of King's Finest employees—many of whom had worked for the Abbotts for decades.

Savannah was struck with deep, painful longing for her own family. The parents she'd never see again. The ailing grandfather who'd raised her. Her sister and young niece. They were the reasons she was doing this.

She had no desire to hurt Blake, but this was war. And in war, there were always casualties.

Her family hadn't started it. But she sure as hell would finish it.

Even if it meant hurting Blake.

She was a spy working on the side of right. Sometimes trickery and deceit were required. And sometimes people got hurt. Good people. People you liked. But wasn't getting justice for her family more important than hurting Blake Abbott's pride?

He was a big boy. He'd get over it. Just as he'd gotten over his ex.

Or had he?

Savannah glanced at the drawer where the woman's photo was hidden.

She sighed softly. He'd never forgive her once he learned that she was the granddaughter of his grandfather's enemy.

But maybe he'd eventually understand.

Joseph Abbott hadn't given her a choice. This was what she had to do, even if what she really wanted now was Blake Abbott.

The garage door creaked. Savannah peeked through the window. Blake's big black pickup truck was approaching.

Savannah made a quick sweep of the room, ensuring everything was as she'd found it. She hurried into the hall past the dogs.

"Stay." She held up a hand when they tried to follow her. Benny's paw prints were all over the door, but there was no time to clean them.

Savannah hurried upstairs and got into the shower. She pressed her back against the cool tiles and reminded herself she'd done what she had to do.

So why was her chest heavy with guilt? And why did her eyes sting with tears?

Because she couldn't stop wishing last night had been real and that she could have Blake Abbott for herself.

Chapter 11

Their tails wagging, Sam and Benny ambushed Blake when he stepped through the garage door.

"Calm down, you two." Blake set the grocery bag on the counter and unloaded it.

The house was quiet, but the note he'd left for Savannah had been moved, so she'd been downstairs.

Blake put the bacon in the oven and set up an impromptu omelet bar. When the bacon was done, he grabbed another shirt for Savannah and headed toward the guest room. The room where he'd awakened with her in his arms.

He knocked on the door. "Savannah, you up?"

She opened the door wearing a bath towel wrapped around her curvy frame. Her hair was wrapped in another. "Sorry. I just hopped out of the shower."

"Then you'll be needing this." He handed her another shirt, this one a gray short-sleeve T-shirt.

"Thanks." She clutched the garment to her chest. "That was thoughtful of you."

"Breakfast is set." He shoved his hands into his pockets, feeling awkward, as if they were strangers who hadn't been intimate the night before. "Hope you like omelets and bacon."

"I love them." Her smile was polite. Distant. "Be down in a sec."

"Okay then." Blake rubbed the back of his neck. He wasn't sure where things stood between them, but their awkward morning-after conversation didn't bode well.

He jogged down the steps and paused, head tilted, noticing paw marks on the office door. He obviously hadn't done a thorough job of cleaning Benny after their walk.

Blake grabbed a rag and some wood cleaner and wiped the door down. Then he cleaned Benny's paws again and tossed the rags into the laundry room.

Why was Benny trying to get into the office?

He wouldn't unless someone was in there. The muddy prints weren't on the door when Blake left. That meant Savannah had been inside.

But why?

Blake returned to his office. Everything was exactly as it had been that morning. Still, she'd been there. He was sure of it.

He returned to the kitchen and cut up some fruit, his mind turning.

"Smells delicious." Savannah stood at the entrance of the kitchen with Sam and Benny at her feet.

Traitors.

They dropped him like a bad habit whenever Savannah was around, Benny more so than Sam.

"Thanks. I made bacon, set up an omelet bar and made a fruit salad." Blake poured himself a glass of orange juice. He lifted the container. "Juice?"

"Please." She sat at the breakfast bar. "But let me make the omelets. I insist."

"The stove is all yours." He handed her a glass.

Savannah sipped her juice, then melted butter in a pan and sautéed vegetables.

"I hope you were able to get some sleep," Blake said finally. He wanted to ask why she'd been in his office.

"Didn't get much sleep." She flashed a shy smile. "But I certainly have no complaints."

"Glad to hear it." The tension in Blake's shoulders eased. He parked himself on a stool.

"One other thing…" Savannah pulled an ink pen from the breast pocket of her T-shirt and handed it to him. "I borrowed a pen from your office. Hope you don't mind."

"Of course not." Blake breathed a sigh of relief. Savannah did have an innocent reason for being in his office. It was good he hadn't accused her of snooping. "Glad you found what you were looking for."

He tapped a finger on the counter after an awkward silence fell over them. "About what happened last night," he began.

Her posture stiffened. She didn't turn around. "What about last night?"

"It was amazing."

"For me, too. Believe me." Savannah's cheeks were flushed but she seemed relieved. She moved to the counter and cracked eggs into a bowl.

"I like you, Savannah. I have since the day you

walked into my office and called bullshit on me for trying to reschedule your interview."

She looked at him briefly and smiled before washing her hands at the sink with her back to him. "But?"

"But I shouldn't have kissed you or let things get as far as they did."

She turned off the pan with the vegetables, then heated butter in another pan.

"I get it. I work for your family. Last night was my fault. You tried to show restraint. I should apologize to you." She glanced over her shoulder at him. "It won't happen again."

"That's the thing." Blake stood, shoving his hands into his jean pockets. "I don't want it to be over. I don't think you do, either."

Savannah turned to him slowly. She worried her lower lip with her teeth.

"It doesn't matter what we want. You're an Abbott, and I'm…" She sighed. There was something she wouldn't allow herself to say. "I'm your subordinate. If anyone knew about what happened last night…it wouldn't look very good for either of us."

She wasn't wrong.

Blake groaned, leaning against the counter. "I've never been in this position before."

"You've never been attracted to one of your employees before?" she asked incredulously.

"Not enough to risk it."

Her teasing expression turned more serious. She returned to her task. "You're worried I'll kiss and tell, like everyone else in this gossipy little town."

"That isn't it at all."

"Then there's no problem. Once the bridge opens,

you'll take me back to my car and we'll pretend this never happened."

Blake wanted to object. But Savannah was right. It would be best if they pretended last night never happened.

But that was the last thing he wanted to do.

"Thanks for breakfast," Savannah said as she ate the final bite of her omelet. "Everything was delicious."

They'd endured the awkward meal, both acting as if walking away from each other was no big deal. The heaviness in the air between them indicated otherwise.

"Your omelet especially." Blake gathered their plates and took them to the sink. "Good thing I raided my sister's refrigerator."

"You told Zora I was here?"

"Of course not." He turned to scrape the plates. "She hinted that she thought it was you, but she was just fishing. Trust me."

Savannah joined him at the sink. "What did she say *exactly*?"

"I don't recall her exact words."

Savannah was supposed to be a fly on the wall. Working in the background, hardly noticed. Now she had the full attention of Blake and she'd be on Zora's radar, too.

And if Zora suspected, did that mean she'd already told the rest of his family?

"But your sister asked specifically if it was me you were entertaining for breakfast?"

"She didn't mention your name. And if she had any real reason to believe it was you, she would've told me. There's nothing to worry about."

"Maybe for you. Your family won't fire you over this."

"No one is getting fired. I promise." He dried his hands on a towel and gripped Savannah's shoulders. "Look at me."

She did, reluctantly.

"I'd never let you get fired because of me. Trust me. All right?"

Savannah nodded, her breath coming in quick, short bursts. She'd come so far, and she was so close. She wouldn't let anything derail her plans—not even Blake Abbott.

"When do you think I'll be able to leave?"

"Got a weather alert on my phone." Blake pulled it out of his pocket. "The bridge is still closed. According to the alert, it'll be a couple of days. My dad already emailed us to say that if the bridge isn't open by tomorrow, the plant will be closed on Monday."

"I can't stay here all weekend."

"You don't really have a choice." He held her hand. His voice was quiet and calm.

"I don't want to complicate things for either of us."

"And I don't want you to leave." Blake lifted her chin. He dragged a thumb across her lower lip, his gaze locked with hers.

"I don't want to, either." The truth of her admission shocked her. They weren't just words, and she wasn't simply playing a role. "But we've discussed all the reasons I should."

"I know." He stepped closer. His clean, masculine scent surrounded her. "But I don't care."

"I do." She stepped beyond his reach. "And one of us needs to be the adult here."

"You walking away right now won't resolve our feelings for each other."

"What do you expect me to say, Blake?"

"Say you'll stay. That you'll spend another night in my bed." He slipped his arms around her waist and hauled her against him. "This time, I know you're making the decision with a clear head. So I won't hold back."

Her belly fluttered and her knees were so weak she could barely stand. She held on to him. Got lost in those dark eyes.

"Say it." Blake pressed a gentle kiss to one edge of her mouth, then the other. Then he kissed the space where her neck and shoulder met. "Say you'll stay."

Savannah wanted Blake so badly she ached with it. Despite who his family was. Despite what she'd come there to do.

Blake Abbott was the last man in the world she should want. Yet she'd never wanted anyone more.

"Yes." Her response was a whisper.

"Yes, what?" His gaze followed his hand as it trailed down her arm.

Her skin tingled wherever he touched it. "Yes, I'll stay with you."

"Where?"

It wasn't a question. It was a demand issued in a low growl that caused a trembling in her core. Her knees wavered slightly.

"In your bed." Her eyes met his.

Blake's pull was as strong as the earth's gravity. She was too close to escape its effects. And she wouldn't want to, even if she could.

He grinned. "Good girl."

Even as she gave in to him, she needed to prove she wasn't a pushover. "But I'll only stay until—"

He covered her mouth with his, swallowing her objection as if it were a morsel that had been offered to him. Blake tugged her hard against him as he laid claim to her mouth.

Savannah gasped at the sensation of his erection pressed to her belly. She had zero willpower where this man was concerned. The dampness between her thighs and hardening of her nipples were evidence of that.

Blake tugged the T-shirt up over her hips, planted his large hands on her waist and set her on the cold quartz countertop. She shivered in response. He stepped between her legs, spreading them. Blake stripped off her shirt and dispensed with her bra. He assessed her with his heated gaze.

"Beautiful," he murmured.

He'd seen her naked the night before. So why did she feel so exposed? As if she was standing on a stage naked?

He surveyed her full breasts and tight, sensitive nipples that were hungry for his mouth, his touch. Her belly knotted and electricity skipped along her spine, ending in a steady pulse between her thighs.

Blake stepped as close as the countertop would allow him. He kissed her neck and gently nipped the skin, as if marking his territory.

He palmed the heavy mounds. Sucked a beaded tip into his warm mouth.

A soft gasp escaped her lips. She slipped her fingers into his short, dark curls as he sucked, then laved the hypersensitive nub with his rough tongue.

Her mind flashed back to how delicious it had felt

to have that tongue attending to more sensitive areas of her body. How it had felt inside her.

"Blake, please." She hardly recognized her own voice as she made the urgent plea for him to relieve the deep ache between her thighs. "I want you."

He trailed kisses down her belly as he laid her back on the cool surface. "Don't worry, babe. I know exactly what you want."

Blake slid her back on the counter and pulled her legs up so that her heels pressed against the countertop. Starting inside her knee, he kissed his way down her inner thigh to her panties.

He tugged the damp fabric to one side and kissed the slick, swollen flesh. Each kiss sent her soaring higher, making her want him more. In any way he wanted to take her.

She arched her back, lifting her hips off the cool quartz. Blake cupped her bottom and sucked on her distended clit, bringing her close to the edge. Then he backed off, lavishing the surrounding flesh with slow, deliberate licks before sucking on it again.

Savannah was falling. Hurtling toward her release. She covered her mouth and tried to hold back the scream building in her throat.

"No." He lifted his head, leaving her aching for his mouth. His hooded gaze locked with hers. "Don't hold back. Whatever you're feeling... I want to hear it. Every murmur. Every scream."

He slowly licked the swollen flesh again, his tongue moving in a circular motion, hitting everywhere but where she needed him most.

Teasing her.

"Understand?" His eyes met hers again.

She nodded. "Yes."

He went back to sucking on her slick bud. She trembled, bucking her hips and clutching his hair.

She let go of embarrassment and fear. Of her worries about what would happen next. Instead, she floated on the sea of bliss surrounding her.

She let go of every moan. Every curse.

Until she couldn't hold back the river of pleasure that flooded her senses, shattering any remaining control.

She called his name. Her back arched as she rode his tongue until she'd shattered into a million tiny, glittering pieces.

Savannah lay there afterward, her breathing rapid and shallow. Her chest heaving. Feeling both satisfied and desperate for more.

Blake placed delicate kisses on her sensitive flesh. Each kiss caused another explosion of sensation.

He kissed his way up her belly and through the valley between her rising and falling breasts, as he pulled her into a seated position. His eyes met hers momentarily, as if seeking permission. Then he pressed a kiss to her open mouth. The taste of her was on his tongue.

Blake lifted her from the counter and led her up the stairs and to the opposite end of the hall.

His bedroom.

The decor was rustic, but elegant, in keeping with the style of the house. A king-size bed dominated the space. Large windows flooded the room with light and provided a nearly unobstructed view of the lake and the mountains in the distance.

Before Savannah could admire the space, he'd taken her in his arms and kissed her again. His tongue delved into her mouth. His hands drifted over her body. Her hands explored his body, too, and traced the thick ridge beneath his jeans.

Savannah loosened his belt, eager to touch the silky head of his velvety shaft again. She slipped her hand inside his pants, gripping the warm, veiny flesh. He grunted and shuddered at her touch before breaking their kiss.

Blake turned her around abruptly and nestled her bottom tight against him. His groan of pleasure elicited a sigh from her.

Pinning her in place with one strong forearm slung low across her stomach, Blake kissed her neck and shoulder. He glided the backs of his fingers up and down her side. The featherlight touch made her knees shake. Her sex pulsed with need.

Had the few men she'd been with before been doing it all wrong?

Blake hadn't entered her. Yet he'd found countless ways to bring her such intense pleasure she wanted to give him everything.

All of her.

He slid his fingers into the hair at the nape of her neck, turning her head. His mouth crashed into hers. She gasped when Blake grazed one painfully hard nipple with his palm.

The contact was so slight. A whisper against her skin. But it made her want to drop to her knees and beg for more.

She considered doing just that, but Blake pinched her nipple, sending a bolt of pleasure to her core. She cried out, though she wasn't sure if it was from the pain or the pleasure.

He toyed with her nipple—so sensitive she could barely stand it. Then he glided his hand down her belly, dipping it beneath her waistband.

She gasped against his hungry mouth when he slipped two fingers through her wetness. He massaged the sensitive, swollen flesh, avoiding her needy clit.

Savannah moaned, moving against his hand. He swallowed her cries, intensified them with his movements.

His long fingers drifted from the back of her neck and lightly gripped her throat. Not enough to cause constriction or bruising. Just enough to let her know he was in control.

There was something about his grip there that was primal and erotic. A surprising turn-on that brought her closer to the edge.

"You like that, don't you?" His warm lips brushed her ear as he whispered into it, his voice tinged with deep satisfaction. "I knew you would."

"Blake, please, I'm so close." Her words were clipped, her tone breathy.

He used four fingers, massaging her clit and the sensitive flesh around it. His hand moved faster, until she shattered, her knees buckling as she cried out his name.

Savannah Carlisle coming apart in his arms was probably one of the most erotic things Blake had ever seen.

Her caramel skin glistened with sweat. Her small, brown nipples had grown puffy and rock-hard after his ministrations. So sensitive that the slightest touch had her ready to fall apart.

Savannah's body was perfect. Womanly curves

in all the right places. Smooth, creamy skin. Long, shapely legs.

Her responsiveness to him was a thing of beauty. The way her skin flushed, from head to toe. The slow grinding of her hips against him. The little murmurs that grew louder as she became more aroused. How wet she'd gotten for him—even before he'd laid a hand on her.

Then there was the air of mystery about her. Something Blake appreciated after living most of his life in this tiny town.

He liked that he knew very little about this woman. That he had to earn every bit of knowledge he'd gathered about her. Savannah Carlisle was an enigma he'd enjoy unraveling.

Bit by bit.

They moved to his bed, where Blake lay on his side, his head propped on his fist as he stroked her skin.

Savannah had given him her trust. Something he didn't take lightly.

Until now, he'd focused on her satisfaction. It was no selfless act. He'd relished the control. But he ached with his desire for her. His body was taut with need.

Savannah released a long, slow breath and opened her hazel eyes. Her lopsided smile was adorably sexy.

One look at her kiss-swollen lips and the vivid image of Savannah on her knees flashed through his brain. He groaned, his shaft stretching painfully.

"That was amazing. I can't wait to find out what comes next."

He dragged a thumb across her lower lip. "And I can't wait to give you what comes next."

Savannah's eyes danced. She accepted the digit, sucking it between her soft lips, her gaze locked with his.

Blake pulled his thumb from her mouth with a pop. He kissed her as Savannah removed his shirt, and he shed his remaining clothing.

The widening of her eyes, followed by an impish grin as she glided her tongue across her upper lip, made his erection swell. He swallowed hard, needing to be inside her.

Blake rummaged through his nightstand, praying he'd find at least a handful of condoms. He didn't stock them at home.

Hookups were something that happened elsewhere. Outside of this tiny town.

Blake wasn't sure how to categorize what was happening between them. But it definitely wasn't a one-off, meaningless hookup.

Finally, he found a strip of three condoms. He took one and tossed the others on the nightstand.

He fumbled with the foil packet, finally ripping it open and sheathing himself as quickly as his fingers would allow.

Blake knelt on the bed. Savannah's mouth curved in a smile, but her eyes held a hint of sadness.

Whatever it was…a painful memory, a bad experience…he wanted to wipe it away. He'd make her forget whoever had come before him. Men who probably hadn't shown her the sincerity and respect he would.

He dragged the lacy panties down her legs and pitched them on the floor. He admired her glistening pink center as she spread her thighs for him.

Blake groaned. A delicious sensation rippled through him as he slipped the head of his erection through her wetness. He pushed his hips forward, then drew his shaft back over her firm clit.

Savannah's belly tensed and she made a low keening moan. The sound became more pronounced with each movement of his hips.

He needed to be inside her. Now.

Blake pressed his shaft to her entrance. Inched his way inside her warm, tight walls.

They both murmured at the incredible sensation. He cursed as he moved inside her, his motions measured, controlled.

So. Fucking. Good.

He went deep. Hit bottom. Then slowly withdrew. Beads of sweat formed on his brow and trickled down his back as he tried to maintain control.

He refused to give in until he'd brought her to pleasure once more with him deep inside her.

Blake took her by surprise when he flipped their positions so he was lying on his back. She dug her knees into the mattress on either side of him and leaned backward, bracing her hands on his thighs. Her gaze locked with his as she moved her hips furiously, her breasts bouncing.

The sight of this beautiful woman grinding her hips against him was almost too much for him to take.

Suddenly, she leaned forward and planted her hands on his chest. Blake reached up and slipped the tie from her ponytail. Her loose curls cascaded forward, shielding her face like a dark curtain.

He gripped a handful of her hair, flipping it out of the way so he could watch as she got closer. He gritted his teeth, tried to slow his ascent as her mouth formed an O, euphoria building on her face.

She was close, and he was ready.

He rolled her onto her back again. Kneeling on the mattress, he leaned forward, increasing the friction against her hardened nub as he moved between her thighs.

Savannah cried out. Digging her heels into the mattress, she arched her back and clutched the bedding. With her eyes screwed shut, her head lolled back as she gave in to sweet ecstasy.

Pleasure rolled up his spine as her inner walls spasmed. He continued to move his hips. A few more strokes and Blake cursed and moaned as he came hard inside her. He shuddered, then kissed her softly, still catching his breath.

Savannah looped her arms around him. He settled the weight of his lower body on her and supported himself on his elbows as he kissed her. Slowly. Passionately.

It was something he'd never do with a hookup. Something he hadn't realized he missed...until now.

Blake pulled away, but Savannah tightened her grip on him.

"Can't we stay like this just a little while longer?"

Blake lay on his side and pulled Savannah against him, cradling her in his arms. He tucked her head beneath his chin and pulled the cover over them.

They lay in silence, enjoying the warmth and comfort of each other's bodies. Savoring everything they'd just shared.

As he drifted to sleep, his only thought was the need to keep Savannah in his bed.

Chapter 12

Savannah had awakened in Blake's arms for the second morning in a row. At least last night they hadn't made the mistake of falling asleep without discarding the condom, as they had the night before. To make matters worse, her birth control pills were at her apartment. She hadn't taken them for the past three days.

What if you're...?

Her heart beat furiously whenever she considered the possibility. So she couldn't allow herself to consider it. Not even for a moment.

When Blake received notice that the bridge had reopened, she was relieved. Blake had taken her to pick up her car, and she'd followed him in his truck back across the river.

Her time with Blake had been amazing, but it was a weekend fling. Two people confined together in a storm.

Shit happened.

That didn't make them a couple.

Yet Blake believed they could be more than a fling.

Savannah pulled into the parking lot behind her apartment building and got out of her car, wishing the circumstances were different.

She tugged down the hem of the too-tight, wrinkled rayon dress, ruined the night of the storm. She approached Blake, who leaned against the truck, waiting for her.

"I appreciate your insistence on seeing me home." She scanned the parking lot and a nearby street, which was a main thoroughfare in town. "But I think I'm good now."

"Don't worry. I'm maintaining my distance." His tone was laced with irritation. "But I know the history of this building." He nodded toward it. "It flooded during storms like this a few times before. Kayleigh needs a new roof, but she can't afford one and she's too damned stubborn to let my brother Cole fix it for her."

"Fine." She glanced around again. "But remember—"

"You're just an employee. Got it." He narrowed his gaze, his jaw tight. Blake headed toward the back entrance that led to her apartment, without letting her finish.

If he wanted to be that way…fine. It would absolve her of the guilt she might have felt when she finally exposed the Abbotts for who they really were.

She unlocked the main door, and Blake trailed her up the stairs to her apartment.

"Kayleigh's done a good job with the place." He

glanced around the small space. The entire apartment was probably smaller than his great room.

"It's not a house on the lake with mountain views, but it's home." Savannah closed the door behind him and dropped her bags on the sofa.

"You think I'd look down on you because you have a smaller place?" Blake's brows furrowed. "Is that why you keep trying to push me away?"

Savannah didn't respond.

"You can't convince me this weekend didn't mean anything to you."

Savannah's throat tightened and her lungs constricted. "I thought I'd been clear. I'm not looking for a relationship. That would cause problems for both of us."

"I'm not saying we should run out and tell the world."

"You don't want your family and friends to know you're slumming it."

"I never said that." The vein in his neck pulsed. He raked his fingers through his hair. "You're purposely being combative."

"But it's the truth." She sank onto the sofa. "Besides, I doubt that Iris Abbott would want any of her precious boys to fall under the spell of some poor girl from the wrong side of the river."

Blake shoved aside the magazines on the coffee table and sat in front of her. He lifted her chin, forcing her gaze to meet his. "You don't really believe that."

"Because you know me so well." She pulled free of his grip.

"I know you better than you think. I know your fears, what turns you on…" He leaned in closer, his voice low. "I know how to satisfy you in ways no one else has."

Blake was too close. He was taking up all of the air in the room, making it difficult for her to breathe.

"So what?" She shrugged. "You haven't known me long. Maybe you wouldn't like me if you really knew me."

He leaned in closer, his gaze softer. "That's something I'd like to find out for myself."

She swallowed the lump in her throat. "Why is getting to know me so important to you? Most men would be content with a no-strings weekend." She forced a laugh. "You don't even have to pretend you're going to call."

"I'm not most men. Not when it comes to you." Blake kissed her.

She held back, at first. But when he took her face in his hands, Savannah parted her lips to him and pulled him closer, needing more of the connection they'd shared.

When he pulled away, one edge of his mouth curled in a smirk. "Is that your way of admitting that this weekend meant something to you, too?"

"If I say yes, will you take me to bed?"

"No." He stood, the ridge apparent beneath his zipper. "But it does mean I'm asking you on a date."

"Around here? Are you crazy?" She stood, too. "Everyone will know before dessert."

He sighed heavily. "True."

"Then where do you propose we have this date?"

"My place for starters." He tucked her hair behind her ear. "But pack for the weekend. I've got something special in mind."

He kissed her, made a quick inspection of the apartment, as promised, and left.

Savannah closed the door behind him and exhaled.

What have I gotten myself into?

She needed to vindicate her grandfather and get the hell out of Magnolia Lake before she fell any deeper under Blake's spell.

She'd barely sat down when there was a knock at her door.

Had Blake changed his mind?

"Savannah, it's me—Kayleigh." A wall separated their apartments, though there were separate staircases leading to each.

Savannah opened the door. "Hi, Kayleigh. Is everything okay?"

"I bought too much food and I thought you might be hungry."

"Starving." She let the woman in. "Thanks for thinking of me."

"Haven't seen you around since the storm. I was worried." Kayleigh set containers of barbecue chicken, wedge fries and coleslaw on the table.

"Got caught on the other side of the river." Savannah gathered plates, napkins and silverware.

"I hope someone put you up during the storm." Kayleigh was trying to figure out where she'd spent the past few days.

"Thankfully, yes." Savannah put the dishes on the table and sat across from her landlord and neighbor.

"Well, that's a relief."

Savannah was eager to change the subject and avoid the question she knew would come next. "Everything smells delicious. Thanks for sharing."

"My pleasure." Kayleigh spooned coleslaw onto her plate.

Savannah fixed a plate for herself, hoping the other shoe didn't drop.

"I noticed that Blake Abbott followed you home today."

The other shoe dropped.

Savannah couldn't deny what Kayleigh had seen with her own eyes. But she could spin it.

"I'm about the only person in town who doesn't have a truck or SUV. Blake was nice enough to make sure I made it back across the river safely."

"And it was kind of him to see you inside."

Didn't the people in this town have anything else to do with their time?

"He mentioned that the building's roof has leaked in previous storms."

"Damn Abbotts think they're better than everyone else."

"He mentioned that you won't let his brother fix the roof."

"I'm not one of their charity cases." Kayleigh opened a jar of preserves and spread it onto her biscuit. "I can afford to get my own roof repaired…eventually."

They ate in companionable silence. But even the delicious food wasn't enough to keep Kayleigh quiet for long.

"It's none of my business what you do and who you do it with." The woman took a sip of her sweet tea. "But getting involved with an Abbott isn't too smart, if you ask me."

Savannah chewed her food. She had no intention of

confirming her involvement with Blake Abbott, but she didn't bother denying it, either.

"You've made it clear you don't like them," Savannah said. "But you've never said why."

Kayleigh's scowl briefly shifted to a pained expression. Then her mask of anger slipped back in place.

"They're always throwing their money around like they can buy anyone they want."

"Did they do something to you specifically?"

Maybe the Abbotts had a pattern of cheating business partners. If she could prove that, it would go a long way toward supporting her grandfather's claim that Joseph Abbott had done the same to him.

"I went to school with Parker." She groaned. "That one is a piece of work."

Savannah couldn't disagree with that. Parker was smart, but his people skills were nonexistent. Everyone at the distillery seemed to understand that was simply who Parker was. No one took his overly direct approach personally. She'd learned to do the same.

"Is Parker the reason you don't like the entire family?"

"Parker is only part of the reason." Kayleigh's mouth twisted. She dropped her fork, as if she'd lost her appetite. "The other reason has to do with my father."

"What happened?"

The fire that always seemed to blaze in Kayleigh's eyes faded. "When I was growing up, my dad was the town drunk. In and out of the local jail all the time. Generally horrible to my mother, my sister and me."

"That must've been difficult for you. Especially in a small town like this one."

"There wasn't a week that went by when I wasn't

humiliated by some kid talking shit about my dad's latest antics."

"Kids like Parker?"

"Not at first. At first, he and his brothers were about the only kids who didn't tease me. But then Parker started hanging with a different crowd… He wanted so badly to fit in back then."

"Doesn't sound like the Parker Abbott I know." Savannah tried to imagine the abrasive man as an impressionable kid who just wanted to fit in. She couldn't. "The guy I know doesn't care much what anyone thinks of him."

"It's true. Parker was different from the other kids. Smarter. More direct. Way too honest." Kayleigh shook her head and sighed. "So he tried to be part of the crowd. That meant embarrassing me, like all the other 'cool' kids." She used air quotes to emphasize the word.

"I see why you dislike Parker, but why don't you like the rest of the Abbotts?"

"Because Duke Abbott is a liar and a thief." The fire was back in Kayleigh's eyes. The icy tone returned to her voice.

Now we're getting somewhere.

Savannah leaned forward. "What did Duke Abbott steal from you?"

"We didn't have much, but my grandfather had left my mom a ton of property adjacent to the distillery. The old house and barn were dilapidated, but when my dad was sober we'd take a ride out there and walk around. He wanted to fix the place up. Make it a working farm again." She swiped angrily at the corner of her eye.

"In those moments when my dad was completely

hammered, those walks on my grandfather's property were the one good memory I held on to. The only hope I had that one day he'd finally come through and be a real father to us."

"What happened to the farm?" Savannah knew the answer before she asked the question. Why else would Kayleigh hate the Abbotts when everyone else in town fawned over them?

"While my sister and I were away at college, Dad got really sick. Sicker than he or my mother were telling us. His liver couldn't take any more. My mother didn't want to burden us with their financial problems. So she sold the property to Duke Abbott for a fraction of what it was worth to pay hospital bills and help with our tuition."

"Must've been a tough decision for your mother."

"Selling her dad's property for a song broke her heart. She died not a year later. That's when I learned that greedy bastard Duke Abbott had bought it." Kayleigh paced the floor. "He'd already torn down the old house and put new buildings up."

Like father, like son.

The sound of her own heartbeat filled Savannah's ears. She was getting closer to establishing a pattern of the Abbotts cheating neighbors and friends. It evidently hadn't been much consolation to Kayleigh, but at least her family had received *something* for their property. That was more than her family could say.

"Sorry—I don't want to dump my issues on you. And I don't mean to be the kind of petty person who doesn't want her friends to have any other friends." Kayleigh returned to her chair and nibbled on a wedge fry. "But I had to warn you. The Abbotts seem like sunshine and roses. But when it comes to something they want, they'd as soon stab you in the back as smile in your face."

Savannah was surprised Kayleigh had referred to her as a friend. She hadn't thought of the woman that way. Kayleigh always seemed closed off, and Savannah hadn't been eager to make new friends, either. But maybe together they could form an alliance against the Abbotts.

She opened her mouth to tell Kayleigh who her grandfather was, and the reason she loathed Joseph Abbott. But the truth was, she didn't really know Kayleigh.

What she did know was that Kayleigh was part of the town's gossip circle. If she told her the truth it would be all over town by morning. She'd lose her one advantage over the Abbotts: the element of surprise.

Blowing her cover wasn't worth the risk.

Instead, she thanked the woman for her advice and turned the conversation elsewhere, while her grandfather's advice played on repeat in her head.

Never trust an Abbott farther than you can throw one.

Not even Blake.

But that didn't mean she couldn't enjoy whatever it was that they had. For now.

Chapter 13

"Hello, darlin'. Miss me?"

Blake glanced up from his laptop to find the whirl-wind that was Iris Abbott in his office.

"Mama." He met her in the middle of the room so she could give him one of her trademark bear hugs. "Dad didn't tell me you were back."

"I wanted to surprise you."

"How's Aunt Constance?" Blake straightened his collar and sat behind his desk.

"Much better." She sat in one of the chairs across from him. "She'll only need me for a few more weeks. Then I'll be home for good."

"How long are you staying?" Blake studied his mother's face. Iris Abbott considered flying a necessary evil. If she took a voluntary plane trip, she had a damn good reason for it.

"A few days." Her eyes roamed the space, as if it were her first visit. "Just long enough to have a couple of meetings with this Savannah girl."

The hair on the back of Blake's neck stood up. "Thought you two were holding video conferences about the gala."

"We have been, and we've gotten lots done. She's sharp, and she's not just talk. She makes things happen."

Blake crossed one leg over the other. "Sounds like the arrangement is working. So why the surprise trip?"

"What, you didn't miss your mama?"

"I did." Blake leaned on the armrest. "But you haven't answered my question. Why make a special trip just to meet with Savannah?"

His mother shifted in her chair, brushing imaginary crumbs from her summery floral skirt. "Technology is great, but it doesn't replace sitting across the table from someone and getting a good read on them."

"And why do you suddenly need a better read on Savannah?"

She folded her arms. "A little birdie told me her car was here all weekend."

"We had one heck of a storm. The bridge was closed, and she lives on the other side of the river. She obviously got stuck on this side."

"And *where* do you suppose she spent all that time?"

"Why are you asking me?" Blake composed an email to Savannah, warning her of his mother's suspicions.

"Tread carefully, son." Iris flashed her you-ain't-fooling-me smirk. "I saw the video of you bringing her back to her car on Monday afternoon."

Damn blabbermouth security guards.

"What if I did?" He shrugged. "She's new to the area. Didn't know it's prone to flooding. I wanted to make sure she was all right. What's wrong with that?"

His mother hiked one brow. "You still haven't answered my question. Where did she spend that long weekend? In your bed?"

"Just so we're clear, that question will *never* be okay." His cheeks flooded with heat. "Who I sleep with—or don't—is my business."

"Except when it threatens *our* business."

"You're being melodramatic, Mother."

"Am I?" She folded her arms. "You remember how ugly things got when Parker made a mess of things with his secretary?"

Blake groaned, recalling how angry the woman had been when Parker broke it off.

"This situation isn't the same."

"So you *are* sleeping with her."

He wasn't a good liar, which was why he preferred to take the it's-none-of-your-business approach. But his mother never had trouble getting to the truth.

Still, what happened between him and Savannah wasn't up for family discussion.

"Blake, you were the one son I could count on to not break the rules. What happened? Did she seduce you?"

"I'm a grown man. Nothing happened I didn't want to happen. Let's leave it at that."

She folded her arms, pouting.

"I need you to promise me something, Mama." He moved to sit beside her.

"And what is that?"

"Don't mention this to Savannah."

"Now you want to dictate what I can say to her? This is why I made the rule in the first place, son. Can't you see the problems this is causing already?"

"Do this for me. Please."

"Fine." She stood, flipping her wrist to check the time. "I won't say anything—"

"To anyone," he added.

"For now." She leaned down and kissed him. "Come by for dinner tonight. I promise you and your little girlfriend won't be the topic of discussion."

"I'll be there around six."

Blake groaned in relief as his mother left.

His weekend with Savannah made him realize that his feelings for her were deeper than he'd imagined. Savannah evidently had feelings for him, too. Yet she was hesitant to explore them.

If she found out what his mother knew, it would only spook her. She'd pull away again.

Blake returned to his desk and discarded the email to Savannah. He could handle his mother, and what Savannah didn't know wouldn't hurt her.

Chapter 14

Savannah pulled her car into Blake's garage and parked, as he'd requested. She'd spent the previous weekend at his place out of necessity. But this was a deliberate decision.

She'd crossed the line and the guilt bored a hole in her gut. Savannah could only imagine what Laney would say, if she knew.

Her sister would be gravely disappointed in her.

But she hadn't slept with Blake as part of some grand scheme to elicit information from him. What had happened was precipitated by the very real feelings that had been developing between them.

But didn't that make what she was doing worse?

She was giving him hope. Making him believe something could come of the game they were playing. Only Blake had no idea he was playing a game.

Savannah got out of her car, her hands shaking. *This was a mistake. I should go.*

Blake stepped into the garage, a dish towel thrown over one shoulder. He seemed to know she was grappling with the decision to come inside.

His welcoming smile assured her everything would be okay.

"Hey." He took her bag and kissed her cheek.

"Hey." She slipped her hand into his and let him lead her inside. The house smelled like roasted vegetables and baked goods. "Are you sure this is a good idea? Your sister or one of your brothers could pop by at any—"

Blake set the bag on the floor and pulled her into a kiss that ended her objections. Her heart raced and warmth filled her body.

She forgot all the reasons she shouldn't be there as she tumbled into a morass of feelings she might never be able to escape.

A buzzer sounded in the kitchen. Blake reluctantly suspended their kiss.

"We'll finish this later." He gave her a lingering kiss before removing a pie from the oven.

"Smells delicious. What kind of pie is it?"

"Strawberry rhubarb." He removed his oven mitts. "Hope you like it."

He remembered.

"You made it?"

"It's my first one." He grinned. "So I want you to be brutally honest. If it tastes like crap, don't pull any punches. It's the only way I'll learn to make it the way you like it."

"You did this for me?"

"Why else?" Blake tugged her against him and kissed her again.

It was just a silly little pie. So why was she so moved by the gesture?

Because Blake cared about what she wanted. About what was important to her.

And all she cared about was getting revenge for her grandfather and hurting his family in the process.

She pulled away, tears burning her eyes.

Blake cupped her cheek. "Did I do something wrong?"

"No." Savannah's neck and face tingled with heat. She swiped away warm tears and forced a smile. "Anyone ever tell you you're a little too perfect?"

"No." He chuckled, then kissed her again. "Certainly not any of my siblings."

"Brothers and sisters are there to rein us in when we get a little too big for our britches."

"At that, they excel." Blake grinned. "But they're also there when I need someone to help me get my head back on straight. Or to remind me that things aren't as bad as they seem." He moved to the counter and uncovered the steaks. "I imagine you and your sister do that for each other, too."

"Laney does her best to keep me on the straight and narrow. Doesn't always work, but she tries."

"And what about you?"

"I'm the pit bull." Savannah sat at the counter, watching him prep the steaks. "Even when our parents were still alive, it was my job to protect my sister." She swallowed past the thickness in her throat. "It still is. Even when it requires me to make difficult choices."

"Like what?" He held her gaze.

Savannah's heart felt heavy. It was a lead weight pulling her beneath the sea of guilt washing over her. Blake's reaction to learning the truth flashed in her head. Would he be hurt or angry? Probably both.

He'd regret the day he laid eyes on her.

She'd always anticipated that the day she finally vindicated her grandfather would be the happiest day of her life. Now she could only envision heartbreak and pain.

She'd have to explain to Blake why she'd misled him about her reasons for coming to King's Finest. Her only comfort was knowing she hadn't lied to him. Which meant she couldn't answer his question now.

Blake put the steaks in a skillet and washed his hands. When he turned around, she handed him a towel.

"It's been a long week." She looped her arms around his waist, tugging his lower body against hers as she gazed up at him. "I'm not in the mood for talking or eating right now."

She guided Blake's lips to hers and kissed him.

Blake gripped her bottom, hauling her closer. She accommodated his silent request by grinding her body against his until he grew hard against her belly.

Savannah broke their kiss and whispered in his ear. "I want you, Blake. Now."

"What about dinner?" His voice was as rough as his beard, which scraped against her skin as he trailed hot kisses up her neck.

"It'll be just as good if we have it later…in bed." She unfastened his belt and slid her hand beneath his waistband. Savannah took his steely length in her palm and stroked his warm flesh.

Blake groaned against her throat, his body tensing. He pulled away just long enough to turn off the broiler and put the steaks in the fridge. Then he grabbed her bag and followed her to his bedroom as quickly as their legs would carry them.

They stripped each other naked. Blake tried to lead her to his bed, but Savannah urged him into a brown leather chair.

Her gaze fused with his as she slowly sank to her knees. She swirled her tongue around the head of his thick erection before taking just the tip in her mouth.

Blake cursed and his thighs tensed. He gripped the arms of the chair, as if it took every ounce of self-control he could muster to refrain from palming the back of her head and urging her to take him deeper.

She gripped the base of his shaft and ran her tongue lazily along the underside before taking him in her mouth again. Until she could feel him at the back of her throat.

Blake swore under his breath. He loosely gathered a handful of her hair in his fist so it wouldn't obstruct his view of her taking him deep.

"Do you have any idea what you're doing to me, Savannah?"

She ran her tongue along a bulging vein. "I'd like to think so."

"That's not what I mean." His expression became serious. "It's been a really long time since I've cared for anyone the way I care for you."

Savannah froze, her heart racing. She'd done this to remind them both that this was only sex. They were mutually satisfying each other's needs.

She hadn't expected Blake to say she meant something to him. What did it matter if she felt the same? She couldn't say it back. It would only make it hurt more once he knew the truth.

"Blake…" Her mouth went dry and her chest ached. "I can't—"

"It's okay." He pressed a kiss to her mouth. "My mother always says I'm the kid that goes from zero to a hundred in sixty seconds flat." He sighed, then stood, pulling her to her feet. "Forget I said anything."

But she couldn't forget.

It was all she could think of as he took her into his arms and kissed her.

When he made love to her.

Fire and passion spread through her limbs. Her body spasmed with intense pleasure. Her heart was overwhelmed with the emotions that sparked between them.

Blake Abbott had turned her inside out. Made her feel there was nothing in the world he wanted more than her.

He'd left her wishing desperately that this was more than an illusion, born from deception and half-truths.

Unable to sleep, Savannah lay in Blake's arms after their late-night dinner, listening to him breathe as he slept. Blake Abbott had ruined her. Her life would never be the same without him.

If only she could reclaim her grandfather's legacy and have Blake Abbott, too.

Chapter 15

Blake straightened his tie and adjusted the cuffs of the suit jacket Savannah had helped him pick out for the jubilee gala. His jaw dropped as he surveyed the barn.

He'd witnessed the slow transformation of the structure as his brother Cole's construction crew renovated and painted it over the past month. He and the rest of the team had assisted with the execution of Savannah's party plans and decor over the past three days.

Still, he was floored by the remarkable beauty of what had once been a run-down building at the edge of his parents' property. His brother's company did excellent work. But this had all been Savannah's vision.

It was everything she'd promised when she'd pitched her idea. An upscale event with down-home roots. An event that honored their past while celebrating the future.

"The place is beautiful. I had no idea this old barn had so much potential." His mother suddenly appeared beside him, dabbing the corners of her eyes with a handkerchief. "Your Savannah is a genius."

"She isn't *my* Savannah, Mother. She's very much her own woman." Blake wasn't being evasive or ambiguous. He'd spent the past month trying to convince Savannah to formalize their affair. He cared deeply for her, but he was tired of being her dirty little secret.

He and Savannah had spent lazy weekends getting to know each other better. They cooked together, ate together and spent their nights making love.

Bit by bit, he was falling for her, diving headfirst into emotions he'd spent the past two years actively avoiding.

"Women who maintain a sense of self make the best mates." Iris squeezed his hand reassuringly. "Ask your father."

They both chuckled and the tension in his shoulders eased. He squeezed his mother's hand back, appreciative of her underlying message. She wouldn't stand in the way of him being with Savannah.

Now if only he could convince Savannah it was time to take the next step.

"Can you believe this place?" Zora's eyes danced with glee as she approached. "It's incredible, and I've been dying for a good reason to dress up."

Not many occasions in Magnolia Lake called for elegant attire. The typical town event required a well-worn pair of jeans and a sturdy pair of boots.

"Will Dallas be here tonight?" Iris elbowed Zora.

"Said he wouldn't miss it for the world."

Zora's eyes sparkled when she talked about Dallas

Hamilton—her best friend since kindergarten. Though Dallas still had a home in Magnolia Lake, he and Zora didn't see each other much.

Dallas's hobby of building stunning handmade furniture pieces in his family's run-down work shed had exploded into a multimillion-dollar business. He was frequently overseas attending trade shows, visiting with vendors and presiding over the setup of new retail stores in some of the world's most glamorous cities.

Sometimes Blake envied the guy. He was a self-made millionaire who'd built an empire out of nothing with a vision and hard work.

"Make sure Dallas comes to see me as soon as he gets here." Iris beamed. "There's a spot in the entry hall just begging for one of his custom pieces."

"Dal is here as our guest, Mother. Not to work. Let him enjoy himself, please," Zora pleaded.

"That means she plans to keep Dallas to herself all night," Iris whispered to Blake loudly, fully aware Zora could hear her.

His attention shifted to Savannah as she flitted about the space. Tonight she was simply stunning.

She wore a black one-shoulder blouse and a high-waisted, long, flowing gray skirt with a bow tie at the back of her waist.

He loved her enticing curves. Had memorized them. But tonight, the cut of the blouse emphasized her bustline. Not that he was complaining. The generous flow of the skirt made her curvy bottom seem fuller, too.

Her hair, swept to one side, fell on her creamy, bare shoulder in loose curls. Blake's hand clenched at his side, his body tensing with the memory of combing his fingers through those soft curls as she lay naked in his bed.

"Seems your brother is more impressed with Ms. Carlisle than with what she's done here tonight."

Blake's cheeks warmed. He shifted his gaze back to his mother and sister. Zora giggled, likely glad their mother was temporarily distracted from her attempts to pair her and Dallas.

"I'm monitoring how she handles herself under pressure." Blake congratulated himself on his quick recovery. "Maybe you two haven't noticed who Savannah is talking to."

His mother and sister carefully assessed the tall, dark-haired man who hovered over Savannah.

"Wait a minute. Is that—"

"It's Dade Willis," Zora squealed. "I knew a couple B-and C-list Tennessee celebs had RSVP'd. I had no idea Dade Frickin' Willis would be here."

A tinge of jealousy gnawed at Blake as the man flirted with Savannah. The Tennessee native was country music's latest phenom. His single had topped the country charts for the past ten weeks. That didn't mean Blake wouldn't rearrange his pretty, surgically-enhanced face if he didn't back off Savannah.

"I'd better go greet our guest." His mother hurried toward Dade.

"Not without me you aren't." Zora caught up to their mother.

Blake went to the bar to check on their stock for the event. As Savannah rushed past him holding a clipboard, Blake stopped her with a discreet hand on her hip.

"Everything looks great, Savannah. You've done well. Take a breath and relax."

"I forgot to bring Dade's badge. He was a last-minute addition, so I made it in my office this morning."

"Not a big deal. Send one of the guys to get it."

"I need everyone here. There's still so much to do. The first band is already late and guests will arrive shortly." The words rushed from her mouth.

"Then I'll get it." Blake fought the urge to kiss her. He held out an open palm. "Give me the key to your office."

Savannah dropped her keys in his hand, her eyes filled with gratitude. "There's a small crate on the edge of my desk. My cell phone is in there, too. Thanks, Blake."

"Anything for you, babe." He lowered his voice so only she could hear him. "Now stop being such a perfectionist, or you won't get a chance to enjoy your own damn party."

Savannah seemed surprised he'd called it *her* party. She smiled gratefully, then made a beeline for the caterer.

Blake's gaze followed the sway of Savannah's hips as she crossed the room. He turned in the opposite direction when someone squeezed his shoulder.

"Gramps." Blake gave his grandfather a bear hug. "I wondered when you'd get here." He gestured around the room. "So what do you think?"

"It's remarkable." The old man removed his thick glasses and wiped them on a hankie he produced from his inside pocket. The corners of his eyes were wet with tears. "I didn't expect all this."

"But you deserve it, Gramps." Blake draped an arm

around his shoulders. "We wanted to show you what you and King's Finest mean to us and to the community. And this is only the beginning."

His grandfather's eyes widened. "What do you mean?"

"This gala kicks off a yearlong international celebration of our brand. The entire thing was envisioned by the new events manager we hired a couple of months ago—Miss Savannah Carlisle." Blake nodded in her direction.

"Oh, I see." His grandfather chuckled. "The pretty little thing you were cozied up with here at the bar. The one you couldn't take your eyes off when she walked away."

Blake didn't bother denying it, but refused to throw any more logs on the fire.

"We were discussing a small problem, which I promised to handle." Blake's gaze met Savannah's. Her mouth pinched and her eyes narrowed. "But first, let me introduce you to the woman behind all of this."

Blake walked his grandfather toward Savannah and she met them halfway, forcing a smile as she got closer.

"Don't worry—I'm headed out to take care of that errand in just a minute," Blake said quickly. "But my grandfather arrived, and I know you've been dying to meet him."

"For longer than you know." Savannah's smile was tight and her shoulders stiff. Her hand trembled slightly when she placed it in his grandfather's palm.

His grandfather clasped her hand in both of his and smiled broadly. "My grandson tells me I have you to thank for all of this. Can't begin to explain how much it means to me."

"The look on your face when everything's said and done… That's all the thanks I'll ever need." Savannah's attention turned to members of the band finally arriving. "I look forward to chatting with you at length later, but right now I need to show the musicians where to set up. Excuse me."

They both watched as she approached the band and guided them to the stage.

"I see why you're so taken with her, son." The old man chuckled. "You go on and take care of whatever it is you need to." His grandfather smiled at Zora, who was walking toward them. "My granddaughter will keep me company until you return."

Blake drove the short distance to the distillery. He retrieved the small crate from Savannah's desk and checked to make sure the badge and her phone were there.

Her phone buzzed, indicating a text message. The message scrolled across the screen, capturing his attention.

It's been two months. Give up and come home. I feel icky lying to Gramps. Giving you one week. Won't do it anymore.

Blake scanned the screen quickly before the message disappeared. It was from Savannah's sister, Laney.

A rock formed in Blake's gut.

What did Laney want Savannah to give up? Her job at the distillery? Her relationship with Blake? And why was Savannah asking her sister to lie to their grandfather?

Uneasiness skittered along his spine.

Blake couldn't ignore the text. His feelings aside, if there was a risk of Savannah leaving them in the lurch, he needed to know. They'd scheduled a year's worth of events to celebrate the King's Finest jubilee. Savannah was the point person on every one of them.

What if there was a simple, harmless explanation?

Savannah would be furious he'd read her private text message. Even if he'd done so inadvertently.

Blake had been burned before by getting involved with someone who wasn't as committed to the relationship as he was. Perhaps Savannah's reluctance to take their relationship public went beyond worries over her career.

And then there was the day she'd been in his home office, ostensibly to find a pen. Could there have been another reason?

Blake groaned.

He was being paranoid. Admittedly, her sister's text message didn't look good. But it wasn't as if Savannah had initiated a relationship with him. Or even wanted to come back to his house that night. Both had been his idea.

Blake grabbed the crate and returned to his truck. Whatever the truth was, he'd find a way to get to the bottom of it.

Chapter 16

Savannah sat down at the bar for a moment and ordered an energy drink.

Most of the night's pomp and circumstance had already played out. The Abbott family had taken the stage and thanked everyone—including the town of Magnolia Lake—for its support for the past half century. A handful of celebs, business executives and longtime employees had shared anecdotes about King's Finest bourbon.

A few other big names circulated throughout the crowd. They mixed it up with employees, townsfolk, distributors and the numerous reporters she'd invited.

Savannah had been moving at warp speed for the past seventy-two hours. It wasn't surprising she was tired. But tonight, she was unusually exhausted. And she'd felt slightly nauseous all day.

She finished her energy drink. Then she ordered a ginger ale to allay the queasiness.

"Everything okay?" Blake sat beside her.

There was something going on with him. He'd been slightly aloof since he brought the crate to her.

She'd tried to create distance between them in their public dealings. But there was something about Blake's sudden indifference that made her feel she was standing naked in a blizzard, desperate to come in from the cold.

Blake wore the expensive sand-colored suit and navy-and-white gingham-check shirt she'd selected for him during a recent visit to Nashville. It suited the man and the occasion. Serious and elegant with a bit of playfulness beneath the refined surface.

"Everything is fine. It's just been a really long couple of days. I'm a little run-down."

"Anything else wrong?" He turned slowly on the bar stool to face her. For the first time, he was sizing her up.

Judging her.

A chill ran down Savannah's spine. She wasn't imagining it. Something was wrong. Had she left an incriminating note on her desk?

Impossible.

She didn't handwrite notes about the Abbotts or the distillery. She captured digital notes in her phone.

My phone.

It'd been in the box Blake delivered to her. Had he gone through it and found her notes?

Savannah forced a smile. No point in panicking

without good reason. That would only make her seem guilty.

"Everything is good. Nearly everyone who RSVP'd made it. All of the staff and musical acts showed up. Things are running smoothly." As she spoke, Savannah inwardly ticked off possible reasons for Blake's change in attitude. "People seem to be enjoying themselves, especially your grandfather."

"Haven't seen him that emotional since my grandmother died ten years ago." Blake's stony expression softened. His eyes met hers. "I can't thank you enough for giving him all this."

Savannah's spine was as stiff as her smile. When she'd proposed this event, she'd hoped it would be the night she humiliated the Abbotts. The night when she pulled back the curtain and revealed the ugly truth that they were cruel, heartless liars and thieves who'd taken credit for her grandfather's work.

"My pleasure." Savannah finished her ginger ale and stood. "I have to go powder my nose." Her bladder was clearly unable to keep up with the amount of liquids she'd consumed throughout the day. "See you later."

Blake caught her hand in his and pulled her closer. He searched her eyes, as if seeking an answer to some burning question.

"What is it, Blake?" Savannah glanced around, her cheeks hot. She ignored the bartender's sly grin. "There's obviously something you want to say."

He averted his gaze. "Wrong place. Wrong time." He nodded toward the restrooms. "We can talk later."

Savannah made a beeline for the bathroom. But she couldn't help thinking that whatever it was Blake wanted to ask her would be the beginning of the end.

* * *

As Savannah exited the restroom, a hand reached out from the doorway of the back office and pulled her inside. She immediately recognized the scent and the hard body pressed against her.

"What on earth is going on?" Savannah whispered angrily. Blake had nearly given her a heart attack.

"We need to talk, and I'd rather do it without my mother and sister staring at us."

"Why would they be staring at us? Wait… Does your mother suspect, too?"

Blake didn't respond.

"That's why she's been looking at me like that all night. Why didn't you tell me?"

"That's not the pressing issue right now." Blake was agitated.

Her heart beat faster. "What is?"

"What's happening between us… It isn't a game for me. And regardless of what you say, this isn't just about sex for you, either." He took a deep breath. "So I want you to tell me the truth. Is there something you're keeping from me?"

Savannah's blood ran cold, and her throat was dry.

"What are you asking me, Blake?"

"Are you unhappy at King's Finest?" He frowned.

"Of course not. I told you, I belong here. I've never had a job I enjoyed more."

"Are you entertaining another job offer?"

Savannah felt a sense of relief. "How could you ask me that? Hasn't tonight's gala proven how important this company is to me?"

"It would appear so. Still—"

"Still…what?" Savannah wouldn't blink first. If

Blake thought he knew something, he'd have to ask her directly. She wouldn't volunteer information unnecessarily and compromise the mission. Not when she finally had a chance to question Joseph Abbott.

Blake gripped her shoulder, his fingers warm against her skin. His eyes demanded the truth. Something she couldn't give him.

Not yet.

"Savannah, it's been a long time since I cared this much for anyone. So if this doesn't mean the same to you, tell me now. Before I get in deeper."

Her hands trembled. Blake's expression was so sincere. It reminded her of all the things she adored about him.

Why did she have to hurt him?

"I… I…" She swallowed what felt like a lump of coal. "I can't answer that right now. Please, give me some time. This relationship is still new. What's the rush?"

"Is that what this is, Savannah? A relationship?"

"Yes." She nodded, pushing her hair behind her ear. "And it's all I can offer right now. Please, just be patient."

Blake palmed her bottom and pulled her closer. His mouth crashed against hers in a searing kiss that took her breath away.

Her body filled with heat. The hardened tips of her breasts were hypersensitive as they grazed his rock-solid chest.

"Blake…" Her objection died on his lips.

He turned her around, jerking her against him. His erection was pinned between them. Blake squeezed her full breasts. They felt tender, almost sore. Yet she craved more of his touch.

"I've never wanted anyone the way I want you, Savannah." His voice was thick as he trailed kisses along her shoulder. His beard sensitized her skin.

He kissed the back of her neck, his hand lightly gripping her throat. Blake hiked her skirt and glided his hand up her inner thigh. He palmed the drenched space between her thighs.

She moaned with pleasure as he ran firm fingers back and forth over the silky material that shielded her sex.

When Blake kissed her ear, Savannah nearly lost all control. Her knees quivered as Blake slipped his hand inside the fabric. Her flesh was so sensitive she could barely stand it.

"Blake, yes. Please."

She needed him inside her. Her mind was so clouded with lust, she didn't care about the risk they were both taking.

She only cared about Blake Abbott making love to her. Making her feel as only he could. As if there was no one in the world but the two of them.

Blake unfastened his pants and freed himself. She lifted her skirt higher to accommodate him as he shifted her panties aside and pressed his thick head to her slick entrance.

Savannah nearly lost it when he massaged her clit.

She pressed back against him, needing him inside her.

"You sure about this, baby?" Blake breathed the words in her ear.

She nodded, wanting desperately to bear down on

his thick length. She hadn't missed a single day of her birth control since the storm.

With one hand still moving over her sensitive flesh, he grabbed the base of his shaft with the other. He pressed himself inside her.

They both groaned with pleasure.

Whatever happened between them later, they would always have moments like this.

Moments in which she couldn't deny how much she cared for him. That she was falling in love with him. And maybe he was falling in love with her, too.

Savannah braced herself against a cabinet as Blake brought her closer to the edge. His hand moved over her slick flesh as he thrust inside her. Taking them both higher.

Her legs trembled and her whimpers grew louder. Blake clamped a hand over her mouth, muffling her cries as he whispered in her ear, telling her all of the deliciously dirty things he wanted to do to her once he got her back to his place.

The sounds of people laughing and talking outside the door didn't deter either of them from their singular goal: to bring each other pleasure.

Savannah was floating higher. Dizzy with her desire for him. Finally, pleasure exploded in her core. She shuddered, weak and trembling, muttering his name against his rough palm still pressed to her lips.

Soon afterward, Blake stiffened, cursing and moaning. He held her in his arms, their chests heaving and their breath ragged. Both of them seemed reluctant to be separated from the other's warmth.

He'd made her feel incredible. Yet she was quickly

overcome by a wave of sadness. Tears burned the backs of her eyelids.

Would this be the last time he'd hold her, make love to her?

"I'll leave first," he said after they'd made themselves presentable. "Wait a few minutes before you come out."

Blake reached for the doorknob. He paused and turned back to her. "Are you sure you don't need to tell me anything?"

She shook her head, her heart breaking. "Nothing at all."

It was a lie from which they would never recover.

Eyebrows drawn together and lips pursed, he turned and slipped out of the door, leaving her alone with the bitter tears that spilled down her cheeks.

When she got back to the party, Savannah hid in the shadows near the back of the room, trying to regain her composure and make sense of the change in Blake's mood. Her skin prickled and her breasts still throbbed from her encounter with Blake.

"This is quite the affair you've orchestrated, young lady."

Savannah nearly dropped her clipboard and cell phone. "Mr. Abbott."

Joseph Abbott stood beside Savannah as she surveyed the crowd, the smell of bourbon heavy on his breath. "My granddaughter tells me that even the decision to renovate this old barn was your idea."

Savannah's fists clenched so tightly she wouldn't have been surprised if blood dripped from her palms. Her throat seized, rendering her mute. She swallowed hard, forced herself to smile in the face of the devil who'd been the catalyst for every devastating thing that had happened in their lives.

"Yes, sir. It was. I'm thrilled you're pleased." Once the muscles of her larynx relaxed enough for her to speak, she oozed warmth. Like honey. Sticky and sweet. Because she was more apt to catch a fly with honey than vinegar. "I must admit, I'm obsessed with the story of how you started King's Finest all those years ago with nothing more than your father's bourbon recipe and his moonshine stills."

There was a flash of something across the old man's face. Sorrow? Regret? Whatever it was, for an instant, he looked every bit of his seventy-plus years.

"It's not that simple, I'm afraid. Nothing worthwhile ever is. I had the support of my family. Of people who helped me make this happen."

Savannah turned to the man. Her heart racing. "Like who?"

His gaze didn't meet hers. There was a far-off look in his eyes. One that would've made her feel sorry for the old man, if he hadn't destroyed her family's lives.

He didn't answer her, and for a moment they both stood in silence.

"My father died in a car accident when I was young. I wanted to revive his moonshine business, but I didn't know much about it. I partnered with someone who could teach me the ropes."

Savannah's stomach churned. Her fingers and toes tingled. Time seemed to slow.

She was finally going to get her proof from the mouth of Joseph Abbott himself. Savannah turned on the recording app on her phone.

"There's no mention of a partner in the company story on the website." Or anywhere else she'd looked.

"We dissolved the partnership before I incorporated King's Finest."

That explained why Savannah hadn't been able to find proof that her grandfather was a partner in the distillery.

But if Joseph Abbott had used her grandfather's recipe, wouldn't that still give him claim to part of the company's profits?

"Who was your partner, Mr. Abbott?"

The seconds of silence between them seemed to stretch for an eternity.

Joseph Abbott rubbed his forehead, finally raising his gaze to hers.

"Forgive me, Miss Carlisle. I'm afraid this lovely affair has been a bit too much excitement for an old man like me after my travels yesterday."

"But, Mr. Abbott—"

"Please, excuse me." The old man nodded his goodbye, then made his way across the room to where Duke and Iris stood.

Savannah's belly clenched and her hands shook. She'd been so close to learning the truth. To getting the information she needed to change her family's fortune.

She'd pushed too hard and spooked the old man. Now he'd never tell her the truth. Worse, there was a wary look in his eye before he'd fled. As if he'd seen her intentions.

Joseph Abbott wouldn't tell her anything more.

Savannah wiped away the hot tears that leaked from her eyes. Giving up wasn't an option. Not when she was this close. She'd find another way.

Her phone buzzed. It was a text message from Laney.

Did you get my previous text?

Laney knew how important the gala was to her. She'd obviously forgotten this was the night of the event. Otherwise, she wouldn't have expected a timely reply.

Savannah scrolled up the message chain.

It's been two months. Give up and come home. I feel icky lying to Gramps. Giving you one week. Won't do it anymore.

If her grandfather learned what she'd been doing, he'd insist that she stop putting herself at risk by working in what he referred to as "a den of hyenas."

Just when she was so close to finding answers.

Savannah quickly typed a reply.

Please think about what you'll be doing, Laney. I'm so close. Nearly got Joseph Abbott to admit everything just moments ago.

Savannah stared at her phone, as if that would make Laney's response come any faster.

Another alert came.

Two weeks. No more.

Savannah huffed. That didn't give her much time, but two weeks was better than one.

It was time to beat the Abbotts at their own game.

She'd have the same level of callous disregard for them as Joseph Abbott had for her grandfather. She'd be as ruthless as Duke Abbott had been when he'd acquired Kayleigh Jemison's family property for a song.

She'd do whatever it took to resolve the issue once and for all.

Even if the truth would hurt Blake.

Chapter 17

Blake stood at the window in his office, watching as a gentle breeze stirred the water on the lake. He shut his eyes for a moment, but it made no difference.

Eyes wide open or tightly shut, Savannah Carlisle had taken up residence in his head.

Blake groaned and returned to his chair. He finished his third cup of coffee and scrolled through his emails.

He'd made a couple of phone calls and answered a few emails. Otherwise, he'd gotten very little done. Instead, he'd been rehashing Laney's text message to Savannah. He imagined a dozen different scenarios her message could have alluded to. None of them good.

Blake picked up his desk phone to call Savannah. She'd been avoiding him since the night of the gala, more than a week before. And she'd made every excuse imaginable for why she couldn't come to his place.

Regardless of the consequences, they had to have this conversation. He'd confess to reading the text message and demand an explanation.

The door to his office burst open.

Blake hung up the phone. "Parker, don't you ever knock?"

His brother slipped into a chair on the other side of his desk, not acknowledging his complaint. "We need to talk."

"About what?"

"About whom," Parker corrected him. "Savannah."

Blake's spine stiffened and the muscles in his back tensed. He took another gulp of his coffee and shrugged. "What about her?"

"I'm concerned."

"About?"

Parker leaned forward, his voice lowered. "She's been asking a lot of questions."

"She's inquisitive. That's her nature." Blake had expected Parker to let him have it with both barrels over his affair with Savannah. "I'd say it's served us well."

Parker stood and paced. "It has when she's used it for us, not against us."

Blake sat on the edge of his desk. "What are you talking about?"

"She's been asking a lot of questions about our company. About how it got started and whether Gramps ever had a partner. Why is she suddenly so interested?"

"She works here." An uneasy feeling crawled up Blake's spine. Still, he folded his arms and shrugged. "That information could be useful as she prepares for the remaining jubilee events and news coverage."

"But why is she so fixated on some nonexistent business partner of Granddad's?" Parker shoved a finger in his direction.

That was odd. If she wanted to know, why hadn't she just asked him? It was one more thing they needed to discuss.

"I'll get to the bottom of it, Parker. Don't worry. Besides, it's not as if we have anything to hide." Blake studied his brother's face. "Do we?"

"No, but I still don't like it. Feels like she's got her own agenda. One that isn't aligned with ours." Parker sank into his chair again.

"Then why come to me? Dad's CEO of the company, and she reports directly to Max." Blake's eyes didn't meet his brother's.

"You hired Savannah, and I know…" Parker ratcheted down the judgment in his voice. "I know how fond you are of her."

Blake's jaw tensed. "I'd never jeopardize this company. Nor will I allow anyone else to. So if you think we have reason to be wary of Savannah…"

"That's not what I'm saying." Parker crossed an ankle over his knee.

"Then what are you saying?" Blake pressed his brother. If he was going to make an accusation against Savannah, he'd damn sure better be clear about it.

Parker tapped on the arm of the chair. "One of us needs to find out exactly what she's trying to uncover and why."

"Are you willing to possibly burn this bridge?" It was the same question he'd been forced to decide where he and Savannah were concerned.

"Dammit, Blake, none of us wants to lose her." Parker sighed heavily. "She's been good for us. Made a major impact in a short period of time. But our first job is to protect this distillery, and to protect the family. Even if that means losing Savannah."

Blake nodded. "Let's talk to Max about this when he returns from Philly tomorrow. Then we'll decide how to approach it."

The situation between him and Savannah had just become exponentially more complicated. If he gave her an ultimatum on their relationship, and she turned him down, the company's inquiry into her behavior would seem like retaliation.

That would be devastating to their reputation. Something he'd never allow.

Chapter 18

"I'm going on my dinner break now. Do you think I'll be able to clean your office when I return?" Maureen stood in the doorway in her housekeeping uniform, doing her best not to look annoyed.

"I'll try to finish up for the night before you come back." Savannah smiled at the woman, and she turned and left.

When the elevator doors closed, Savannah rushed to Maureen's cleaning cart.

Savannah had worked late every night since the gala, looking for her opportunity to search the archived files that predated the company's use of computers.

It was her last hope of finding something useful before her sister's looming two-week deadline.

Savannah retrieved the large key ring from Mau-

reen's cart and made her way down to the file room. She
tried nearly every key before she found the right one.

She slipped inside the large, windowless space and
switched on her flashlight. The room smelled stale and
dust floated in the air. Steel file cabinets lined the brick
walls in the first portion of the room. Antique wooden
furniture was pushed up against the back wall.

Savannah checked her watch. She had little more
than half an hour. She moved to the file cabinet marked
with the earliest dates and pulled out a drawer stuffed
with yellowed files. Most of the papers were typed.
Some were handwritten.

By his own admission, Joseph Abbott had dumped
her grandfather as his partner before starting the company. Maybe the files contained information about the
origin of the company's recipes and procedures.

Savannah checked her watch again and cursed under
her breath. Fifteen minutes left.

She was dirty, sweaty, and had gotten several paper
cuts during her frantic search through the files. She finally found a pad with notes written in familiar long-
hand.

Her grandfather's.

She removed the notebook and continued sift-
ing through the files. Savannah opened an envelope
marked "Old Photos." She recognized her grandfather in one of them. "Joe and Marty" was scribbled
on the back.

Savannah froze at the sound of voices in the hall.
Someone's coming.

She quietly closed the drawer and hid in the shadows, crouching between a tall bookcase and a large
antique bureau desk. She clutched her grandfather's

notebook and the photo of her grandfather and Joseph Abbott.

Keys jangled in the door, and then the hinges creaked.

"Switch on the light. I just walked into a spiderweb."

Savannah's blood ran cold.

What's Parker doing here?

He'd never been her biggest fan, but lately he'd been grumpier and questioned everything she did.

Had he followed her down here?

The light switched on.

"So where's this stuff Mom just had to have tonight?" *Max.* He'd left hours ago. Why had he returned? And what were they searching for?

Had her conversation with Joseph Abbott prompted them to destroy evidence of their theft?

"Mom had a few of the guys set the pieces she wants aside in the back."

Blake.

"Wait—do you guys smell that?" Blake sniffed, then glanced around the room. "Someone's been in here, and I know that scent."

Savannah pressed a hand to her mouth to muffle her gasp. She was wearing the perfume Blake had bought her. Her heart beat furiously as footsteps crept closer.

Blake made his way through the maze of furniture until he was standing in front of her.

"Savannah, what are you doing in here? And why are you hiding?"

Her knees shook so badly she could barely stand. Blake didn't offer to help her up, so she braced herself on the wall and climbed to her feet.

"Blake, I'm so sorry." She could hardly get enough air into her lungs to say the words.

All three brothers stood in front of her.

"I knew something was going on with her." Parker's nostrils flared. His entire face had turned crimson. She got a chill from his arctic stare. "You aren't authorized to be down here. You're trespassing. You'd better have a damn good explanation for being here or I'm calling the sheriff."

Max almost looked amused. "Don't tell me this is how you've been spending all those late nights."

"I've never been down here before tonight. I swear."

"Why should we believe anything you say?" Parker demanded. "And where'd you get these keys?"

"From Maureen's cart. I recognize her key ring." The heartbreak in Blake's voice and the pained look in his eyes were unbearable.

Blake didn't deserve this. And nothing she could say would fix it.

"What's that you're holding?" Max asked.

"They're mine." She clutched the photo and notebook, her hands shaking.

"Hand them over." Blake held out his hand, his voice jagged.

Savannah released a long, agonizing breath. She had no choice. There were three of them and one of her. They weren't going to let her leave with the notebook and photo. She handed both items to Blake, who handed them to Max.

"That's it. I'm calling the sheriff. We'll have them search her. Who knows why she was down here or what else she might be hiding." Parker gestured wildly.

"Calm down, Park. Why don't we ask her what she's

doing down here?" Max kept his voice calm. "Maybe Savannah has a logical explanation."

The three brothers turned to her.

Savannah stared at each of them, her gaze lingering on Blake's face. Tears stung her eyes and rolled down her cheeks.

"I was... I was looking for..." Savannah stammered.

She couldn't tell the Abbotts the truth. Not until she was sure she had solid documentation to support her grandfather's claim. Once they learned her reason for being there, they'd surely destroy any potential evidence.

The truth wasn't an option.

She'd tell them she was looking for info to use in the yearlong celebration of the company's inception.

"I came down here because..." Savannah snapped her mouth shut, stopped cold by the pain and disappointment in Blake's eyes.

She couldn't tell Blake the truth, but she wouldn't lie to him, either. Which left her out of options.

Savannah turned her attention to Parker. She held out the keys. "If you're going to call the sheriff, call him. I don't have anything else to say."

"Gladly." Parker pulled out his phone.

"Don't." Blake took the phone from him.

"Why not? We caught her stealing irreplaceable archival documents. Who knows what else she's taken since she's been here? She's obviously a thief." A vein twitched in Parker's forehead. "Likely a corporate spy. She was probably sent here by one of the Kentucky distilleries."

"Blake's right, Park. We don't need the bad publicity. It'll counter all the positive press we're getting now." Max clapped a hand on Parker's shoulder. "Most of it thanks to her."

"All right." Parker snatched the key ring from her open palm. "But I'm filing a complaint with the sheriff. So don't think of skipping town until everything has been accounted for."

"Of course." Savannah extricated herself from the small space, unable to bring herself to meet Blake's wounded gaze.

"Where do you think you're going?" Parker held up a hand, his large body blocking her exit. "A member of the security team will escort you to clean out your desk. It should go without saying that you're fired."

"Is that really necessary?" Blake turned to his brother.

"Very. Who knows what else she'll try to take on the way out," Parker insisted.

"No." Blake made it clear the topic wasn't up for debate. "We're not causing a scene. I'll walk her to her office, then to her car."

"Good idea." Max stuck his hand out. "Give me the key to your truck. Parker and I will load those tables and lamps Mama wanted for the barn."

Blake handed Max the truck key and took Maureen's keys from Parker. He gripped Savannah's arm and led her out the door to the elevator.

"Blake, I can't tell you how sorry I am."

"Then don't." He wouldn't look at her. The tone of his voice was icier than Parker's eyes had been moments earlier. Shivers ran down her spine.

When they got on the elevator, she plastered her back against the wall.

"I never meant to hurt you, Blake, I swear. This isn't what it seems."

"Then what is it, Savannah? Do you have a reasonable explanation for stealing the housekeeper's key, breaking into our archives and cowering in the corner? If so, I'd love to hear it."

Her eyes met his, tears spilling down her cheeks. Her answer caught in her throat.

She'd imagined the misery of the day when Blake would learn she was a fraud. But the pain in his eyes and the pain exploding in her chest were so much worse.

For an instant, she wished she'd never come to Magnolia Lake. But if she hadn't, she wouldn't have uncovered the hand-scribbled notes and photo that proved her grandfather had worked closely with Joseph Abbott.

"I wish I could tell you everything…but I can't. Not yet."

"You lied to me. Made a fool of me."

She'd misled Blake. Taken him off guard. But he wasn't the fool. She was. Because she'd fallen for him. Hard.

"I had no choice. Believe me."

"I wish I could." He stepped off the elevator and led the way to her office.

"Blake, what are you doing here?" Maureen looked up from searching her cart.

"I had to retrieve something from the archives. I forgot my key." He held out her key ring. "Hope you don't mind—I borrowed yours."

Savannah's breath hitched.

Blake was protecting her, even now. Allowing her to save face with Maureen.

"Of course not." Maureen grinned as she accepted the keys from Blake and dropped them into the pocket of her smock. "I was afraid I'd lost them some—" Maureen paused, her head tilted. She'd noticed Savannah had been crying.

"Savannah isn't feeling very well." Blake spoke up before Maureen could inquire. "We'll be ten or fifteen minutes. Then we'll be out of your way."

"Hope you feel better, Savannah." Maureen nodded and rolled her cart away.

Blake closed the door and shoved his hands in his pockets. He leaned against the wall, maintaining maximum distance between them.

"I'll help you carry your things down." His voice was stripped of the warmth and affection she'd come to adore. He was looking through her. Past her. Probably wondering what it was he'd ever seen in her.

The wave of nausea she'd been feeling for the past week rose. Savannah grabbed a half-full bottle of ginger ale from her desk and chugged it.

She dropped her planner, phone and a few other items from her desk into her bag and grabbed her purse. She held it up. "This is everything. Do you need to check it?"

Blake sighed, as if repulsed by, then resigned to, the idea of needing to search her.

He did a cursory search through the two bags she held open. Then he patted her pockets while she held her arms out wide and turned her back to him.

"One more thing." Savannah pulled a small package from her desk drawer and handed it to Blake. "I've been meaning to give this to you. It's one of those calming shirts for Benny, so he doesn't freak out during the next thunderstorm. Unfortunately, they didn't have one in my size."

Her crushed heart inflated the slightest bit when a small smile curled the edge of Blake's sensuous mouth.

The same mouth that had kissed hers. That was acquainted with her most intimate parts.

"Why didn't I see this coming?" Blake laughed bitterly as he scanned her office. "Your office is as nondescript as your apartment. No family photos. Nothing personal. You never intended to put down roots here. You used me, and I was such a fool that I begged you to do it."

Tears stung her eyes again and her nose burned. But Savannah bit her lower lip, refusing to let the tears fall. She had no right to cry. In this, she'd been the one who was heartless and cruel. Blake had been innocent.

And she'd hurt him. Just as his ex had. Only Savannah was worse. She'd always known this was inevitable. That they would both be hurt.

It was a sacrifice she'd been willing to make for her family.

As Blake's eyes searched hers, demanding an answer, her conviction that the sacrifice was worthwhile wavered.

"I know you don't believe me, but I honestly didn't intend to hurt you. I swear." She swiped angrily at her eyes and sniffed.

"Say I'm crazy enough to believe that's true." His voice vibrated with pain and anger. "Then tell me why you did this. What did you hope to gain?"

Savannah lowered her head, unable to answer him.

She'd betrayed Blake and lost the best man she'd ever known. And without the notepad and photo, she didn't have a single thing to show for it.

Chapter 19

Savannah pulled the covers over her head, blocking out the sunshine spilling through the curtains. It was nearly noon and she'd spent the entire morning in bed for the second day in a row.

She was stressed, scared, miserable and missing Blake. Her body wasn't handling the wave of emotions well. It rebelled.

She'd made countless trips to the bathroom and felt so tired and weak she could barely get out of bed. All of which was out of character for her. She prided herself on being able to endure just about anything. After watching their rattrap apartment burn to the ground with her parents inside, there was little else that could faze her.

Until now.

The attachment she felt to Blake Abbott was powerful. Unlike anything she'd experienced before.

She'd been in a handful of relationships. She'd even imagined herself to be in love once or twice before. But the end of those relationships hadn't shaken her to her core, the way losing Blake had.

She missed his intense, dark eyes, mischievous grin and sense of humor. She missed the comfort she felt in his presence—even if all they were doing was watching a movie together in silence.

Savannah clutched at the hollowed-out emptiness in her belly. She'd lost Blake and a job she actually loved. And she'd gained nothing. Except possibly an arrest record if Parker Abbott had his way.

She made another trip to the bathroom. After more retching, she rinsed her mouth and splashed cool water on her face, sure there was nothing left for her body to reject.

Savannah crawled back into bed and dialed her sister.

"Thought you weren't talking to me anymore." There was a smile in Laney's voice when she answered the phone.

Savannah was about to make a smart remark in reply, but the instant she heard her sister's voice, tears welled in her eyes. She whimpered softly.

"Savannah? What is it? What's wrong?"

Savannah told her sister about everything, including her relationship with Blake and how she'd hurt him.

"You're in love with him, aren't you?"

Savannah cried harder, unable to answer the question.

"Vanna, why would you do something so risky?"

"I only had two weeks to make something happen, so I switched to a more aggressive approach."

"Will the Abbotts press charges?"

"I don't know. Blake and Max won out against Parker that night. But in a full family meeting, I don't know if the two of them will be enough. If they don't take legal action, it'll only be because they don't want the bad publicity."

Her chest ached with the pain of letting down her family and losing Blake.

Why does it hurt so badly when he was never really mine?

Savannah hated herself for descending into a weepy, hot mess. She was the one who'd always taken care of Laney. Like she'd promised her father when she was a girl.

"What did Blake say when you told him about Granddad's claim?"

"I didn't tell him." Savannah dabbed her face with a tissue. "It would blow any chance of us getting proof down the road."

"What did you tell him?"

"Nothing. I couldn't look in his face and lie."

"You pleaded the fifth?" Laney groaned. "No wonder you nearly ended up in jail."

"And I still might."

"I'm sorry, Savannah. I know you'd hoped for a different outcome, but at least this is over and you can come back home. Harper and I miss you."

"Yeah." Savannah's response was flat. She hadn't expected to fall in love with Magnolia Lake and its town full of quirky people. But she'd begun to enjoy her life there. "Miss you, too."

"Wait… You haven't just fallen for Blake. You actually like living there, don't you? And I know you loved your job. No wonder you're miserable."

"And sick as a dog. Plus, I promised not to leave town until I get the okay from Parker and the sheriff."

Laney was silent for a few beats. "You're sick how?"

"A virus maybe. I've been run-down and exhausted. Nauseous. Haven't been able to keep my breakfast down the last couple of days." Savannah burrowed under the covers again. She felt nauseous just talking about it.

"Sweetie, you aren't late, are you?"

"For work? You do realize they fired me?"

"Not that kind of late."

"Oh!" Savannah bolted upright in bed when Laney's meaning sank in. "I can't be. We used protection and I'm on the pill."

"Protection isn't foolproof. Nor are the people who use it. Besides, if you slept with him that weekend you got trapped there by the storm...well, did you suddenly start carrying your birth control around with you?"

Savannah's forehead broke into a cold sweat. They both knew the answer to that question. She hadn't had her pills with her that weekend. And then there was that night they'd fallen asleep with the condom on.

"Shit."

"What is it?"

"I need to make a trip to the pharmacy."

"So there is a chance you might be pregnant."

"Can you at least *pretend* not to be excited about the prospect?" Savannah paced the floor. "This entire situation is already a disaster. How on earth would I explain this to Blake?"

"Tell him the truth."

"Everything?" The thought made Savannah nauseous again. "Once he learns the truth, he'll never believe I didn't plan this."

"It's your only play here."

Savannah's chin trembled and tears flowed down her face. "Blake will never forgive me for what I've done. For how I hurt him."

"Calm down, honey. It isn't good for the baby if you're stressed out."

"Pump your brakes, sister." Savannah stopped pacing. "We don't know there is a baby."

The grin returned to Delaney's voice. "Well, it's time you find out."

"Did the lessons on knocking before entering begin and end with me?" Blake looked up from his computer as his brother Max slid into the seat on the other side of his desk.

"I need to tell you something, and it couldn't wait." Max's brows drew together with concern.

It had to be about Savannah.

"Did Mom and Dad decide whether to press charges?"

"Not yet, but I discovered something and I wanted to tell you before I tell the rest of the family."

"What is it?" Blake's heart thumped against his rib cage.

"Since Savannah wouldn't tell us why she was in the archives or why she wanted that photo and notepad, I did some digging."

"And?"

"The photo was of Gramps and a man named Martin McDowell. The notepad was his, too. Did she ever mention the name to you?"

"No." Blake shrugged. "Who is he, and why would she want his old stuff?"

"This is only a copy." Max handed him a file. "But I'm sure Gramps has the original locked away somewhere safe."

Blake quickly scanned the document, reading it three times. It felt like a cannonball had been launched into his chest. Blake fell back against his chair, speechless.

"Marty McDowell was Granddad's partner in the moonshine business. *Before* he opened the distillery," Max said.

"I had no idea he had a partner." Blake rubbed the back of his neck. "But that still doesn't explain why Savannah would want the guy's old stuff."

"I couldn't explain it, either, so I looked at her employee file. Take a close look at her birth certificate." Max indicated the file folder he'd given Blake earlier.

Blake studied the birth certificate carefully.

"Her mother's maiden name was McDowell." His heart thundered in his chest. "She's Martin McDowell's granddaughter."

Blake dragged a hand across his forehead. He really had been a fool. Savannah Carlisle wasn't interested in him in the least. She'd used him to get information about the distillery and their processes. And to gain access to his grandfather—the company's founder. She'd talked to him the night of the gala.

"McDowell must've sent her here to spy on us." Max leaned forward, his elbows on his knees.

"But why? What did they hope to gain?" Blake racked his brain for a reason.

"Sabotage?"

Blake rubbed at his throbbing temples. Savannah was clever and resourceful. If she'd come to work for them with a plan to sabotage the distillery and its reputation, there were any number of ways she could've done it. Yet she hadn't. Why?

"If sabotage was their aim, they're playing the long game. Because everything Savannah has done since she's been working for us has boosted our sales and gotten us good press."

"Hmm…that's difficult to explain." Max leaned back in his chair and perched his chin on his fist. "Guess there's only one way to find out exactly why she came here."

"You want me to talk to Savannah?"

"If you can't handle it…no problem." Max shrugged nonchalantly. "I'm sure Parker would be happy to do it."

"No." Blake shot to his feet, then cursed silently when Max chuckled. He sighed. "You knew I wouldn't let Parker do it."

"You care for Savannah, and she obviously cares for you. Maybe you can turn up that charm you think you have and get some straight answers from her."

Blake sank into his chair again and blew out a long, slow breath. He'd spent the past two days trying to scrub every happy memory of Savannah Carlisle from his brain.

It was an abysmal failure.

Her laugh and broad smile crept into his daydreams. At night, he'd been tormented by memories of her body—naked, in all its glory. Her gentle touch. The sound she made when she was close. The way she'd called his name.

Blake had cared deeply for Savannah. He'd been willing to break the rules for her. But she'd used him and was ready to toss him aside, while he'd been prepared to give her his heart.

"Look, I don't know what's been going on with you two." Max's voice stirred Blake from his thoughts. "Frankly, I don't need to know. But if talking to Savannah would be too difficult for you, it's okay. I'll talk to her."

"No." Blake's objection was much softer this time. "I'll try to get the truth out of her."

"Sorry things didn't work out." Max clapped a hand on his shoulder. "We all liked Savannah. Even Parker, in his own way. That's why he's so angry."

"Thanks, Max. I'll let you know what I find out."

When Max left, Blake loosened his top button and heaved a sigh. He was ready to face Savannah again. Only this time, he was the one who held all the cards.

Chapter 20

Savannah sat on the edge of the tub, rooted to the same spot she'd been in for the past ten minutes. She'd taken three different pregnancy tests. Each had given her the same answer.

I'm pregnant.

Savannah got up and stood in front of the mirror, staring at her image. Red, puffy eyes. Hair pulled into a frizzy, low ponytail.

She looked a hot mess, had no job and had let down everyone who cared about her. Her grandfather, Laney, Harper and Blake.

Now she was growing a human being inside of her. A tiny little person for whom she'd be responsible.

Savannah braced her hands against the sink, her head throbbing and her knees unsteady.

I'm going to be a mother.

Being a parent wasn't something Savannah had ever really considered. Not the way Laney had. Yet the moment she'd seen the word *Pregnant* on that third test, she knew instantly she wanted this baby.

Suddenly, nothing was more important than her child. And there was one thing Savannah knew for sure. She'd never use this child as leverage against Blake and his family.

She'd tell Blake about the baby, because he deserved to know. But only once a doctor had confirmed the test results.

She owed Blake the truth. And she owed her child the chance to know its father—if that was what Blake wanted.

After Savannah called her sister to relay the news, she stared at the phone in her hand. She wished she could call Blake and tell him they were going to be parents. And that he'd be genuinely happy about it.

She decided to call her grandfather instead. She wouldn't tell him where she'd really been or about the baby. Not until she was 100 percent sure. But she needed the comfort of hearing his voice.

Still, she couldn't help thinking about her grandfather's reaction when he learned the identity of his great-grandchild's father.

How do I explain this to him?

Savannah screwed her eyes shut. Her grandfather would be hurt and angry. Of all the men in the world, she'd chosen to make a child with an Abbott.

His mortal enemies.

Savannah wiped angrily at the tears that wouldn't stop falling. No matter how much the truth would hurt her grandfather, she wouldn't lie.

She was exhausted by deception. Weary from trying to walk the line between truth and an outright lie.

When she returned to West Virginia, she'd tell her grandfather everything.

Before she could dial his number, there was a knock at the door.

Kayleigh.

Savannah hadn't moved her car or left the apartment in two days. Until this morning, when she'd made her run to the pharmacy looking a disheveled mess. Kayleigh would have noticed and been worried.

Plus, it was Magnolia Lake. News of her firing was probably all over town by now.

Savannah counted to three and opened the door.

"Blake?" Her heart nearly stopped.

He was as handsome as ever in a pair of gray dress pants and a baby blue checkered shirt. Yet there was something in his face and eyes. He looked tired and as miserable as she felt.

"What are you doing here? Did your family decide to—"

"Nothing's been decided yet." His response was curt. "That's why we need to talk. Now."

Savannah let him in. "Have a seat."

"No, thank you. I won't be long."

Another wave of nausea rolled over her. She sat on the sofa, her legs folded beneath her as Blake paced the floor.

Finally, he turned and glared at her.

"I'm so angry with you, Savannah. I don't know where to begin."

She chewed on her lower lip. "Then let me start by

saying I am truly sorry. I honestly never meant to hurt you. Even before I knew——"

"How easily you could manipulate me?"

That hurt.

"Before I knew what an incredible man you are. That you'd never purposely hurt anyone. I was wrong about you."

"Not as wrong as I was about you." He dropped into the chair across from her, as if his legs had buckled from the weight of the animosity he was carrying.

"I deserve that."

"You're damn right you do." His eyes blazed. "You're not the first corporate spy we've encountered. But none of them seemed willing to take things as far as you did."

"I didn't intend to get involved with you. I came here to do a job. And maybe in the beginning, I didn't care who got hurt. But then I got to know you. All of you. Suddenly, things weren't so simple."

"Not that you let that stop you."

"There was too much at stake. I couldn't let my feelings for you get in the way."

His steely gaze cut through her. "You still haven't told me why you did this. What was your endgame?"

"You wouldn't understand." Savannah went to the kitchen and poured herself a glass of ginger ale.

He stood, too, and turned to her, his arms folded. "Try me."

"Why does it matter?" She put the glass down roughly. "What I did was wrong, but I swear to you, I did it for an honorable reason."

They stared at each other in silence. They were playing a game of chicken and waiting for the other person to blink.

Savannah walked around Blake, back toward the couch.

"How's your grandfather?"

She froze, then glanced over her shoulder at him. The hair stood on the back of her neck and her hands trembled. He wasn't making a friendly inquiry about her family.

Blake knew who she really was.

Still, she wouldn't blink first. "I was about to call him before you arrived."

"Why? To tell him his little spy got pinched?" Blake shook his head. "What kind of man would send his granddaughter to do his dirty work for him?"

"My grandfather didn't send me." She folded her arms over her chest. "He'd never have allowed me to put myself in jeopardy this way."

"You expect me to believe Martin McDowell didn't send you here? That he was oblivious to your little plan?"

"It's the truth."

Blake stepped closer. "Your word doesn't hold water around here anymore."

Savannah lowered her gaze. Her voice was softer. "Grandpa didn't know, I swear."

"Maybe we're going after the wrong person." Blake folded his arms and rocked back on his heels. "The marionette instead of the puppet master."

"No, please…my grandfather didn't have anything to do with this. It was all me. My sister can testify to that."

"And was she involved, too?"

"Laney never wanted me to come here, and she's been begging me to give up and come home."

Blake rubbed his chin. "You want to keep them out of this? Then tell me the truth. Why did you come here? What does Martin McDowell have against our family?"

Savannah fought back tears. If she showed her hand to the Abbotts, she'd lose the element of surprise and jeopardize any chance of making a claim against them. If she didn't, her sister and grandfather would be pulled into the mess she'd made.

"Tell me the truth, Savannah, or I swear I'll do whatever it takes to make your grandfather pay for this."

"It isn't my grandfather who needs to pay for his sins." She blinked back the tears that made Blake a blur. "It's yours."

Chapter 21

"What are you talking about?" Blake returned Savannah's defiant gaze. Her expression had morphed from fear and concern to righteous indignation.

"I'm talking about how he betrayed my grandfather. Cheated him. Is stealing from him even now."

Now Blake was furious. He knew his grandfather well, had worked beside him as long as he could remember, learning the business of making premium bourbon. He had so much affection for the old man. Joseph Abbott was a generous and loving man, and a pillar in his adopted community of Magnolia Lake, where he'd raised his children and grandchildren.

"How dare you accuse my grandfather of being—"

"A thief."

"That's a lie. My grandfather didn't steal anything from anyone. Why would he need to? He's a wealthy man. He can buy whatever he wants."

"He's a wealthy man *because* he's a thief." Savannah stepped closer. "Why don't you ask him where he got that recipe for his world-renowned bourbon?"

"That's what you were looking for? The recipe for our bourbon."

"Unlike most distilleries from here to Kentucky, you've taken great pains to conceal your grain bill." Her tone was accusatory.

"Even if you had our mash bill, that's only part of the recipe. There's the water source, our proprietary yeast strain and so many other factors."

"Then why is it so top secret, Blake? Ask yourself, and really, truly allow yourself to consider the answer. No matter where it leads you."

"No." Blake ran a hand through his hair. "Gramps would never do that. He'd never steal someone else's work. If you knew anything about him, about his work ethic, you'd know that's not possible."

"Let's forget about your grandfather for a minute. Tell me how your father acquired the land you expanded on."

Blake narrowed his gaze. "The Calhouns' old place?"

"How'd your father acquire the property?" She repeated the question.

"Ownership fell to Mae Jemison—Kayleigh's mother. She was the last of the Calhouns still living around here. She sold the place to my father."

"You mean your father swindled her out of it. Paid her pennies on the dollar because Kayleigh's father was dying, and her mother needed the money to help her girls finish college."

"Who told you—" The question answered itself

when he remembered he was standing in the middle of an apartment owned by Kayleigh Jemison.

That explained why Kayleigh had been so cold toward his family since she'd returned to town a few years earlier. Not that she'd had any great love for them before. She and Parker had bumped heads for as long as he could remember.

Still, he had no idea Kayleigh harbored such ill will against them. Especially since they'd barely broken even at the time of the purchase, with the amount they'd had to invest in it.

"That property was an overgrown mess. It was littered with rusted, broken-down machinery and a couple of run-down shacks. Large tanks had been leaking fuel onto the property for years. It cost us a fortune to clean it up and make it usable again."

"Of course you'd say that." Savannah folded her arms.

The move framed her breasts, which looked fuller than he remembered. Or maybe it was his brain playing tricks on him. Making him want her even when he knew he shouldn't.

"It's true."

"Why would Kayleigh lie about it?"

He shrugged. "Maybe that's what her parents told her. Or maybe that's just what she chooses to believe. I don't know, but I do know my father. And he wouldn't have cheated them."

"You're just blind where your family is concerned." Savannah propped her hands on her hips. "The mighty Abbotts can do no wrong."

"Never said that. No one is perfect, and we've all made our fair share of mistakes."

He narrowed his gaze at her, chastising himself. Even now, what he regretted most was that he couldn't be with her.

"Maybe you should talk to your grandfather and father before you dismiss what I'm saying. Find out what they have to say to these accusations. You might not like what you hear."

Savannah turned around and bumped into the table, knocking her glass onto the floor, where it shattered.

She stood there, her hands shaking.

"Where do you keep the broom and dustpan?"

Savannah shook her head, as if she were coming out of a daze. She stooped to clean up the mess. "I've got it."

"You're in your bare feet." He gestured toward her. "You're going to—"

"Ouch." She lifted her bleeding foot; a shard of glass was embedded in it.

"Sit down," he instructed, glad she complied without further argument. "There must be a first-aid kit around here. Where is it?"

"In the linen closet in the hall." She drew her foot onto her lap and examined it.

Blake went to the hallway and opened the closet. He spotted the white metal box with red lettering on the top shelf. He pulled it down and looked inside. There were bandages, gauze, alcohol wipes and a few other items. He grabbed a clean washcloth and went to the bathroom to wet it. When he wrung it out, he knocked something to the floor.

Blake froze, his eyes focused on the white-and-blue stick.

A pregnancy test.

His heart thudded against his rib cage. He retrieved it from the floor and read the word on the screen over and over. As if it would change if he read it one more time.

Savannah is pregnant.

Blake swallowed hard, his mouth dry. Was that the whole point of this game? For Savannah to bear an Abbott heir?

His head was in a dense fog and the room was spinning. He returned to the living room, his steps leaden.

He handed her the first-aid kit and washcloth. "You still haven't told me. What was your objective in coming here?"

Savannah seemed to sense the anger vibrating off him. She pulled a set of tweezers from the first-aid kit and tugged the piece of glass from her foot.

"To restore my grandfather's legacy and get what's owed to him."

"Money. That's what this is all about." He'd encountered lots of women whose only interest in him had been his family's fortune and name. Until now, he'd never imagined Savannah Carlisle was one of them. "That's all it's ever been about for you."

Her chin dropped to her chest and her eyes—already red and puffy—looked wet.

"Don't look at me as if I'm some moneygrubbing gold digger. I'm not here for a handout. I only want what's owed to my grandfather."

"You want King's Finest." His gut churned as the realization dawned on him. "That's why you've worked so hard to grow the company's sales. You hope to acquire it."

"Only the half that belongs to my grandfather." She

sat taller, meeting his gaze. "We don't want anything we didn't earn."

"And how exactly is it that you *earned* half of King's Finest?"

"By providing your grandfather with the recipe he's used to build his fortune." She narrowed her gaze at him. "And I think I'm being generous in saying we're only entitled to half the company. A jury might make the argument that all of the profits should go to our family."

"Bullshit." Blake's face was hot and his heart beat like a war drum. "If you thought you had a legitimate claim, why not take it to court? Why all of the cloak-and-dagger corporate espionage?"

"My grandfather doesn't have any proof."

"If the recipe is his, it should be easy enough to prove." He gestured angrily. "Take a bottle of King's Finest to a chemist to see if his recipe and ours are the same."

"It isn't that simple." Savannah lowered her gaze, focusing on cleaning her wound and opening a bandage. "He no longer has the recipe. It got lost in the fire at our apartment."

"Why would your grandfather have entrusted something so important to someone else?"

Her cheeks reddened. "I… I don't know."

"Then how did you intend to prove that our bourbon recipe is his?" He stepped closer.

She bit her lower lip and avoided his gaze.

"Remember our deal? Tell me the truth, in its entirety. Or we'll go after your grandfather and sister, too."

Savannah repositioned herself on the sofa. "I hoped

to find evidence that would corroborate Granddad's story."

"That's why you were in the archives that night. Looking for proof of your grandfather's involvement in creating the original recipe." Her expression confirmed his theory. "And did you find anything besides the photo and notepad?"

"No, but maybe if I'd had more time to search the files or to talk to more people—"

"Like my grandfather." Blake swallowed hard, remembering that his grandfather had looked perturbed and had gone home soon after his conversation with Savannah.

"What did my grandfather tell you?" Blake had an unsettling feeling in his gut.

"That he did have a partner in the moonshine business before he started King's Finest. I was *this* close to getting him to name my grandfather as the partner he left behind."

"I don't know what role your grandfather played, but my grandfather inherited that moonshine business from his father. And he kept his father's recipe."

"Your grandfather knew nothing about the business when his father died. He was too young. My grandfather taught him the business and tweaked the recipe."

"Even if that was true, you just said he helped tweak my great-grandfather's recipe. That still makes it *our* recipe."

Savannah blinked rapidly. It seemed she hadn't considered that before. "The courts will determine that."

"If you've known about this story all your life, why wait until now to try and get proof?"

"My grandfather is gravely ill." Her eyes filled with

tears. "I couldn't bear the thought of him never realizing his dream. Never getting the recognition he deserved."

Blake sighed. For all he knew, they were a family of grifters who'd pulled this stunt on other wealthy families.

He could hear his mother's voice in his head. *And that's why we don't date employees, son.*

Savannah shoved her feet into a pair of shoes and got a broom and dustpan to clean up the glass.

She stooped to the floor, her short shorts providing an excellent view of her firm, round bottom.

He had zero self-control, which was exactly how he'd ended up in this mess in the first place.

She's a liar and a user. Best not forget that.

"Anything else you need to tell me?"

Savannah's shoulders stiffened. She shook her head and finished sweeping up the glass before returning to the sofa.

Blake's heart contracted in his chest. His limbs felt heavy.

He was desperate to believe some part of Savannah's story. To believe she'd been sincere in their moments of intimacy, which had evidently led to the conception of a child.

His child.

He wanted a reason to believe their relationship hadn't been part of Martin McDowell's calculated effort to swindle his family out of half their fortune.

But even now, when she'd agreed to put all her cards on the table and level with him, she wasn't capable of telling the complete truth.

Blake pulled the blue-and-white indicator from his

back pocket. The one that declared the truth in a single, devastating word.

"Then how the hell do you explain this?"

Savannah gasped, her fingers pressed to her lips. "What are you doing with that?"

He ignored the question, asking one of his own. "Is it mine?"

Her head jerked, as if she'd been slapped. "Of course."

"You say that like I can just believe you, no questions asked." The pained look in his eye hurt even more than his question had. "How do I know this isn't part of the sick game you're playing?"

She felt the tears rising. "I'd never lie to you about this…about our child."

"You just did. I asked if there was anything else you needed to tell me and you said no. I'm pretty sure the fact that I might be a father qualifies as something I'd need to know."

"I wanted to be sure."

"There were two more of these in the garbage." His voice boomed, making her jump. "That wasn't confirmation enough?"

"I wanted indisputable confirmation from a doctor. I didn't think you'd believe me otherwise. I was afraid you would think—"

"That this was your backup plan all along?"

Hot tears burned a trail down her face. She wiped at them angrily. "You don't honestly believe I'm capable of that."

Blake huffed, sinking onto the sofa beside her. "A few days ago, I wouldn't have believed you were capable of any of this. I was stupid enough to think you actually cared for me."

"Oh, Blake, I do." Savannah placed a hand on his arm, but pulled it away when he glared at her. "I never intended to get involved with you. But there you were. Handsome and funny. Sweet. Persistent." She wrapped her arms around herself, an inadvertent smile playing on her lips. "I honestly couldn't help falling in love with you."

She'd admitted she'd fallen in love with him, and he hadn't so much as blinked.

"Did you know about the baby the night we found you in the archives?"

"No." Her voice was barely a whisper. "I only found out this afternoon. I have the receipt from the drugstore across the street, if you don't believe me."

"I can't believe anything you've said, since the moment we met." Blake shot to his feet and paced.

"Everything I've told you is true. About my grandfather and parents. About my sister. Even my résumé. All of it's true. Check."

"Believe me, I will." He tossed the pregnancy test on the table in front of her and left, slamming the door behind him.

Chapter 22

Blake left a trail of burned rubber in his wake as he exited the parking lot behind Savannah's apartment.

He was a complete idiot.

Savannah Carlisle had played him like a fiddle from the moment she'd first sashayed into his office.

She'd been smart and confident with just the right amount of Southern sass. She'd flirted with him, then feigned a lack of interest, posing a challenge he simply couldn't resist.

Then the storm had given him the opportunity to ride in like the hero on a white horse and save her.

She didn't ask to be rescued. You insisted on it.

A little voice in the back of Blake's head refused to let go of the belief that, on some level, what he and Savannah shared had been real. He was hurt by what she'd done. Furious that she and her grandfather had taken aim at their company. And still, something deep inside of him couldn't accept that she'd purposely used him as a pawn.

Martin McDowell had obviously filled his grand-daughter's head with lies her entire life. Built up some crazy fantasy that they were the rightful owners of King's Finest.

Maybe Savannah really hadn't intended to get involved with Blake. But once she had…how could she allow things to escalate, knowing how he felt about her?

How could the woman he thought he knew use him that way?

Blake pulled into the drive of his grandfather's log cabin by the lake and knocked at the door.

"Well, this is a surprise." The old man chuckled. "Didn't expect to…" He shoved his glasses up the bridge of his nose. "What's wrong, son? You look like you've lost your best friend."

"We need to talk, Granddad." Blake followed his grandfather into the house and sat beside him on the plaid sofa in the den.

"About what?"

Blake was embarrassed to relate Savannah's accusations. Afraid there may actually be some truth to them.

"Blake, whatever you need to tell me…it isn't the end of the world." His grandfather gave him a faint smile. "So just say it. We'll get through it."

"You already know what happened with Savannah."

"Yes." His grandfather nodded gravely as he rubbed his whiskered chin. "Shame. I liked the young lady quite a lot. Seems you did, too."

Is there anyone who doesn't know what a fool I was?

"Max did some digging. He discovered that Savannah is the granddaughter of Martin McDowell."

The man's mouth fell open, his large eyes widening. He seemed to be staring into the past. "There was something familiar about her. Couldn't put a finger on it then, but now...now it all makes sense. She has her grandfather's nose and eyes. His boldness and spirit. But she has more business acumen than Marty ever had."

A knot clenched in Blake's belly. "I thought you inherited the business from your father when he died in his accident. When did you have a partner?"

"I was quite young when your great-grandfather died. Barely even a teen. Papa had wanted to teach me the business, but Mama wouldn't hear of it. White lightning was the reason she was so unhappy, despite the money and comforts we had. Eventually, it was the reason my father died."

"He'd been drinking." Why hadn't he realized that before?

"Wrapped his car around a tree coming home from a juke joint in the wee hours of the morning." His grandfather groaned. "Not the kind of thing I was proud to talk about."

"So you learned the business from Martin McDowell."

"He was a bit older than me, but he'd worked with my father. A couple years after my father died, we were just about broke. I found Martin, and I made a deal with him for a sixty/forty partnership split if he taught me everything he knew...everything my father had taught him. He was the muscle and he negotiated deals for us. Together we tinkered a bit with Papa's recipes."

Blake could barely hear over the sound of blood rushing in his ears. "Granddad, Martin is claiming that our bourbon recipe is his. That you stole it."

"That's a goddamned lie." His grandfather shot to his feet, his forehead and cheeks turning bright red. "That was Papa's recipe."

"But you just said…"

"I said we tinkered with the recipe while he was my partner. But I kept perfecting it, even after I bought him out."

"You bought him out as your partner?"

"Still got the paperwork in my safe-deposit box at the bank."

"That's good. You have proof." Blake heaved a sigh of relief.

"Why do I need it?" His grandfather raised a wiry, white brow.

"Because Martin's got it in his head that half of King's Finest should be his. That's why Savannah came to work for us. To find proof that her family should be part owners."

The old man averted his eyes and grimaced.

"What is it, Granddad?" Blake gripped his grandfather's wrist and the old man shifted his gaze to him. "Like you said, whatever it is, we'll get through it. We always do."

Joseph Abbott groaned and sank down on the sofa again. He dragged a hand across his forehead.

"By the time I was twenty-one, I got tired of Martin trying to boss me around. The business had belonged to my father, and I wanted it back."

"So you bought him out."

His grandfather nodded. "Even as a kid, I dreamed

big. But Marty wanted to stick to what we'd always done. I wanted to start a proper distillery. Become a respectable citizen with no need to dodge the law. Martin had no interest in doing that."

"If you bought him out fair and square, he has no claim," Blake pointed out.

"True." His grandfather's voice lacked conviction. "But I wasn't very fair to him, either." He lowered his gaze. "He was a heavy gambler, and I knew he'd go for a lump-sum payout, despite it being less than half of what was probably fair at the time."

His grandfather ran a hand over the smooth skin of his head. "Always felt bad about that. Especially after he gambled most of it away. Got in debt to some pretty shady characters. He and his wife left town in the dead of the night. Haven't heard from him since."

"If you felt so bad, why'd you…?" Blake stopped short of using the word *cheat*. "Why'd you shortchange him?"

"Didn't have enough saved to buy him out at a fair price. Not if I was going to buy my building, get new equipment and hire workers. I used his vice against him. It's not one of my prouder moments, son."

"So Martin was aware you wanted to start a legal distillery?"

"Like I said, he didn't have the vision his granddaughter has. Martin thought it was a terrible idea. He expected the venture to go up in flames, as it had for a few other moonshiners who'd tried to take their business legit."

"So he made a choice." Blake needed to believe his grandfather was the upstanding man he'd always thought him to be. That he hadn't wronged Savannah's grandfather. Joseph Abbott had always been his hero. Even more than his own father.

"He did. And when he signed the contract, he relinquished everything. Including the right to take up a similar business in the state for at least fifty years."

The answer to the question he'd posed to Savannah earlier. Why now?

"So legally, he has no claim to King's Finest."

"No. Got myself a damn good lawyer to draw up that contract." His grandfather's voice was faint and there was a faraway look in his eye. "It's airtight."

"But?"

"But I do feel I owe him something. I was a young man making gobs of money. I got a little bit full of myself, and I wasn't as fair as I should've been to Marty after everything he'd done for me." His grandfather rubbed his chin. "We certainly wouldn't be what we are today without him."

"But technically, Martin sold all of the recipes, all of the processes to you."

"Legally, yes." His grandfather nodded. "Morally… I've always felt like I gave the guy a raw deal."

"There's something else you need to know." Blake sighed. "Savannah…she… I mean, we…"

"Go on, son." His grandfather prodded. "At this rate, I'll be called home before you get the first sentence out."

"She's pregnant."

"And you're the father, I assume."

"Yes." The word was a harsh whisper.

"Sounds like we both need a drink." His grandfather moved to the bar and poured two glasses of their top-shelf bourbon. The same drink Blake had shared with Savannah the night of the storm. Joseph handed him a glass and returned to the sofa.

"Congratulations are in order, I suppose." His grandfather sipped his bourbon.

"It hasn't sunk in yet." Blake sipped from his glass.

"So you didn't know who Savannah was or why she was here?"

Blake shook his head. "I only learned the truth today."

His grandfather stared into his glass for a moment before meeting his gaze. "Do you love her, son?"

"I think I do. At least, I did before I realized it was never about me. It was about the money and restoring her grandfather's legacy."

"Can't it be about both?"

"Sir?"

"Maybe she did come here with the sole purpose of getting what she felt her family was owed…a noble thing, in my mind. But that doesn't mean she didn't fall for you along the way."

"What makes you believe that, Granddad?"

"Explains the tortured look in her eyes the night we met. When she was grilling me about the history of the company. Now I understand what I saw in her eyes. She probably hated me. Wanted revenge. But then there were her feelings for you. Must've been a mighty struggle for her."

Blake didn't directly address his grandfather's conjecture. "Do you think Martin McDowell is the kind of man who would've sent her here, hoping that one of us would get her pregnant? It'd be a slam-dunk way to ensure their family got a stake in the company."

"Never. In fact, I'm shocked he would've agreed to

her coming here at all. He was too proud a man to let his granddaughter fight his battle."

Blake sighed in relief. "She claims he doesn't know she's here or what she's been up to."

"Does Savannah seem to you like the kind of person who'd trick you into getting her pregnant?" His grandfather took another sip of his drink.

"No." Blake finished his bourbon and put the glass down. "Then again, I wouldn't have thought her a spy. So what do I know?"

"You know you care about the girl and that she, like it or not, is carrying the first of the next generation of Abbotts." His grandfather's mouth curled in a reserved smile.

Blake's head spun. Not from the bourbon, but from the idea that he would be a father. It certainly wasn't under the circumstances he would've wished, but still…he was going to be a father.

He poured himself another glass and topped off his grandfather's drink before settling on the sofa again. He studied the ceiling, his mind spinning.

"The question is, is it possible for you two to get past this? If you really care for this girl, maybe you can salvage it," his grandfather said. "If not, you still need to have an amicable relationship for the sake of the child."

"I don't know if I can get past what Savannah did. I know she felt she had good reason, but how can I ever trust her again?"

"Only you can answer that, son." His grandfather's voice was filled with regret. "I'm sure Marty will probably always distrust me, too."

"What are you going to do?"

"Not sure. I find it best to sleep on decisions like

this." Joe tapped a finger on his glass. "But call your parents, brothers and sister. Tomorrow morning, we need to have a family meeting."

Chapter 23

Savannah was going stir-crazy.

It'd been nearly a week since Blake had learned of her pregnancy. Two days of silence since she'd left him a message informing him a doctor had confirmed the test results. And still no word as to whether they planned to press charges.

There was a knock at her door and she answered it.

"Got a surprise for you." Kayleigh beamed, opening the signature pink box from the local bakery. "Sticky buns."

"My favorite. Thank you. C'mon in and I'll make you a cup of coffee. I can't eat these all by myself."

Savannah gave the woman whom she'd fast become friends with a grateful smile. She'd told Kayleigh the truth about why she'd come to Magnolia Lake and about the Abbotts discovering her plot. But she hadn't told Kayleigh about her and Blake. Or about the baby.

"I've gotta get downstairs and open the shop, but I brought you some company. That's the other surprise."

Kayleigh stepped aside to reveal her sister and niece in the doorway.

"Auntie Vanna!"

"Harper!" Savannah stooped to hug and kiss her niece. Then she stood and wrapped her sister in a hug. "Laney! I can't believe you guys came all this way."

Savannah's eyes filled with tears. She'd desperately missed her sister's face, so similar to her own. Laney's hair was styled in an adorable pixie cut, top-heavy with shiny, dark curls.

After turning the television to a kids' channel for Harper and setting the little girl up with her favorite snacks, Laney slid onto the couch beside Savannah.

"You ready for this?" She indicated Harper, singing along with her favorite educational show.

"I will be." Savannah's hand drifted to her belly and tears stung her eyes.

"Aww, honey, don't cry." Laney squeezed her hand. "Everything's going to be all right."

"Everything is *not* all right. I really screwed up." Savannah shot to her feet and paced the floor. "I still don't have anything to support Gramps's claim. I'm apparently the worst burglar in the history of burglars. There is still the very real possibility the Abbotts could send me to jail. Then let's not forget that I'm unemployed and pregnant…by an Abbott."

She dropped onto the sofa again, cradling her face in her hands. Her heart squeezed in her chest as she remembered Blake's face. How hurt he'd been to learn the truth. The tears started again.

"And my baby's father hates me. He doesn't want anything to do with either of us." Savannah wiped away tears.

"Did Blake tell you that?"

"No. But I got the hint from his radio silence." Savannah sighed. "I honestly don't believe things can get any worse."

A soft smile played on Laney's lips. "Then they can only get better."

Savannah loved how her sister saw the good in people and had an optimistic view of the world. But in the midst of her personal hell, with the world crumbling around her, she had no desire to pretend everything would be okay.

"Laney, maybe you missed some of what I just said." Savannah swiped a sticky bun from the box, took a bite and murmured with pleasure. "So far, the only upside to this has been that I can eat whatever I want without an ounce of guilt."

Her sister's smile grew wider. She stood and extended a hand to her. "You've been cooped up in this apartment too long. You need some fresh air. Let's go for a ride."

"I'm not supposed to leave town, and believe me, Magnolia Lake is so small that by the time we start the car, we'll already be out of it."

"I made an appeal to the sheriff. Got permission to take you on a little field trip." Laney pulled Savannah off the couch and steered her toward the bedroom. "Now take a shower and put on something nice. We'll take a little ride and get something to eat. You'll feel better. I promise."

* * *

Savannah shoved her sunglasses on top of her head and returned her seat to the upright position as Laney pulled her rental car into the parking lot of a medical center in Knoxville.

"Why are we coming here?" Savannah turned to Laney. "Are you all right? Is Harper?"

"We're both fine." A wide grin spread across her sister's face. "As for why we're here...you'll see. C'mon."

Savannah and Harper waited in a sitting area while Laney spoke to the attendant at the front desk. Then they had their pictures taken for temporary badges and rode the elevator to the fourth floor.

Laney tapped on a partially open door.

"Yes?"

Savannah's heart nearly stopped when she heard the familiar voice. She turned to her sister.

Laney nodded and smiled, taking Harper from her arms. "You two need to talk. Harper and I will be in the cafeteria."

Savannah burst through the door. "Grandpa, what on earth are you doing in Knoxville? And why were you admitted here? Is everything okay?"

"You won't believe me when I tell you." He chuckled, raising his arms to her. "Come here and give me a hug."

Savannah gave him a bear hug, hesitant to let him go. Delaying what she needed to do next.

Come clean and tell him everything.

She sat beside his bed, gripping his hand. "I have so much to tell you."

"It'll have to wait." He sighed as he rubbed his

beard. "Because there are a few things I'd better tell you first."

"Like what?"

"Your sister told me why you came to Magnolia Lake, Vanna." He squeezed her hand, halting her objection. "Don't be mad at Laney. She did the right thing by telling me. If you should be upset with anyone, it's me."

"Why?"

"Because I left out an important piece of the story." His shoulders hunched and his chin dropped to his chest. "Joseph Abbott bought me out as a partner."

"You mean he already paid you?"

Her grandfather nodded. "A lump-sum payout to dissolve the partnership and secure full ownership of any recipes I helped develop."

"That changes everything, Grandpa. How could you not tell me that?" Savannah stood, her hand to her mouth. No wonder Blake thought they were crooks, trying to get one over on his family. "What happened to the money?"

His eyes didn't meet hers. "I had terrible drinking and gambling habits back then. Within a year, I'd gone through it all."

Savannah dropped into the seat again, too weak to stand. She'd risked everything based on a lie. A lie that led her to a man and a career she loved, but then had cruelly snatched them away.

"How could you let me believe all this time that you'd been cheated by the Abbotts?" Her body vibrated with anger.

"I may not have told you the entire truth, Vanna. But I did feel I'd been cheated. Joe didn't pay me my fair share. Then when he went on to make a fortune off formulas I helped create…" He sighed and shook his head.

Savannah was furious with her grandfather. And miserable over losing Blake.

"Do you have any idea what I've done to try and make things right for you? How much I've lost?"

"Laney told me." Her grandfather's eyes were shiny. He clutched her hand. "And I'm so sorry, dumplin'. To you and to the Abbotts. It was easier to blame them than to admit I'd chosen unwisely. That I'd only thought in the short term when I accepted that lump sum from Joe rather than being patient."

Savannah cradled her forehead in her palm, her lips pressed together to repress the scream building inside.

"I had no idea you'd take my words to heart, Savannah. That you'd act on them. You and your sister and little Harper… You mean everything to me. I couldn't protect your mama, but I've done everything I could to look after the two of you. I didn't want you to see me as a horrible failure. A man that never amounted to much of nothing."

"I never thought that, Grandpa. If it wasn't for you taking us in…who knows what might've become of Laney and me?"

"Still, what I done wasn't right, and I'm ashamed."

They were both silent for a moment. Savannah narrowed her gaze at her grandfather. "You still haven't explained what you're doing here in Knoxville."

"Joe Abbott."

"You talked to him?"

"He came to West Virginia to see me, a few days ago. Told me everything about you, about his grandson…and about the baby."

"You know about the baby?"

"I do. And I'm sorry about the split between you and the Abbott boy."

"Why? You always said not to trust an Abbott any farther than I can throw one." She folded her hands. "If Joe Abbott cheated you out of a fair price for your share of the partnership, that only proves you were right."

"We both made mistakes back then, but I've compounded them by misleading you." Martin ran his free hand over his head. "And maybe Joe wasn't fair then, but he's making it up to me...to all of us, Savannah."

"What do you mean?"

A slow smiled curved the edge of his mouth. "I mean you did it, honey. Joseph Abbott and his family are giving us a stake in King's Finest. Not half, of course. But he's giving me a five percent stake in the company and he wrote me a check outright."

"For what?" Savannah couldn't believe what she was hearing. Surely it was a dream.

Her grandfather dug a piece of paper out of his wallet and handed it to her. She unfolded it and read it twice. It was a check for $1.5 million.

"Is this real?"

"Yes." He smiled, tears in his eyes as he cradled either side of her face and kissed her forehead. "I can't believe the chance you took for me. Or Joe's generosity. He brought me here on his dime to see if I'd be a good candidate for the therapy program they're conducting."

"That's incredible, Grandpa. I'm really happy for you." Savannah handed him back the check. She forced a smile, but tears brimmed, spilling down her cheeks.

She'd gotten everything she wanted for her grandfather and lost everything she never knew she wanted for herself. Her job with the Abbotts, her relationship with Blake, a chance for them to be a family.

"I'm glad Joseph Abbott is a decent man after all." Savannah wiped away the tears.

"I don't think that's why he did this at all." He folded the check and returned it to his wallet.

"Then why?"

"He did it for your beau, Blake. And for you." A smile softened her grandfather's face.

"Me? We only met once. Why would he care about doing anything for me?"

"He was impressed with you. With what you were willing to do for me. And what you've already done for his company. Not to mention the fact that you're carrying the first Abbott great-grandchild." Her grandfather's smile widened. "And my second."

Savannah forced a smile in return, determined not to shed any more tears.

"Then they won't press charges against me?"

Something Blake hadn't bothered to tell her. Just as he hadn't bothered to return the message she'd left confirming her pregnancy. A clear indication he wanted nothing to do with her or their child. It was a reality she needed to accept.

"Don't worry about that anymore. As soon as I'm out of here, we can go back home to West Virginia, if that's what you want."

"Of course it is." Pain stabbed her chest. Memories of the nights spent in Blake's bed played in her head.

He nodded sadly. "All right then, Vanna. You go on home. Get some rest now that you know everything is okay. Come back and see me tomorrow, if you have time."

She had nothing but time.

"See you tomorrow, Granddad." She kissed the old man's whiskered cheek before making her way to the cafeteria to find her sister.

I honestly, truly did it.

So why was she more miserable than she'd ever been?

Because Blake wouldn't answer her calls or return her messages. But she wouldn't leave town without thanking him and Joseph Abbott for what they'd done.

Chapter 24

"Can I talk to you, son?" Iris Abbott stuck her head in Blake's office.

"Sure. Come in." He finished typing an email to a group of distributors before giving her his full attention. "What can I do for you, Mama?"

She fiddled with her scarf, her expression apologetic.

"Whatever it is, Mother, just spit it out." He sat on the edge of his desk.

She paced the floor. "It's about Savannah."

"What about her? Is something wrong with her or the baby?"

"No, it's nothing like that."

Blake was still furious with Savannah. She'd lied to him. Gotten involved with him under false pretenses. Hid her pregnancy. Yet he couldn't stop thinking of her. Wanting her.

"What is it, then?"

"Let's just say she did too good of a job around here." His mother sighed. "I'm plumb exhausted from trying to pick up where she left off."

"I see." Blake returned to his seat. "Ask Max to run the event manager ad again. Hopefully, we can find a replacement before you get too swamped. In the meantime, Zora and I will help however we can."

"I suppose that's one way to go."

Blake put down his pen and cocked his head. "You're not suggesting that we—"

"Who better to carry out these plans than the brilliant mind that devised them?" his mother interrupted. "Besides, the distributors liked working with her. I didn't dare tell them she wasn't here anymore. I said she was out for a few weeks on personal leave."

"How could you even suggest we bring Savannah back?"

"Because she did exactly what we hired her to do and more. Did you know she'd already booked several corporate events and weddings at the old barn?" Iris wagged a finger. "We'll need to hire permanent event staff out there just to keep up."

The storage room at the barn. That was the last time he'd been with Savannah. His body hummed with electricity at the erotic memory.

He tried to push the sights and sounds of that night from his brain.

"So we'll hire permanent staff for the space. But that doesn't justify bringing back someone we can't trust."

"But I do trust her, honey. You're right—she should've told us the truth. But she had free rein while she worked here. If she'd wanted to harm our company or sell our secrets, she could've. But she didn't, because that was never her intention."

"She's a liar with a heart of gold, is that it?"

"Something like that." His mother smiled sadly. "Did I ever tell you that when I was about ten years old a man came to town and swindled my daddy out of a good portion of his savings?"

"No." Blake had learned more about his family's financial past in the last week than he had in more than three decades.

"It nearly broke him, and to be honest, he was never quite the same after that. He felt he'd failed us. I guess in some ways he had, going for a get-rich-quick scheme like that."

"Must've been tough for Grandpa Gus."

"It was tough for all of us. Especially for my mom. She'd never trusted the man to begin with and she'd begged my daddy not to invest with him."

"Did Grandpa Gus ever get his money back?"

"No. And I used to dream about tracking down that man and making him pay for what he did to my father. And to us." She leaned back in her chair, her eyes steely. "I'd have done just about anything to bring him peace again."

"I can't believe you and Gramps admire what Savannah did, as if she's some modern-day Robin Hood. Don't forget that would make us the villains in this story."

"I do admire her. Look, honey, I know this isn't what you want to hear. She deceived us and she hurt you, even if she didn't intend to. But from what I hear, she's hurting, too. You know Grandpa Joe already gave Martin his money and his stake in the company. If that's all Savannah cared about, would she still be walking around looking miserable?"

"How do you know that?"

"It's Magnolia Lake, darlin'," his mother said matter-of-factly. "I know everything that goes on around here."

"Maybe she should've considered that before she put herself in this position. Before she put us all in a compromising position."

"Maybe so. But let me ask you a question. And I want you to be completely honest, if not with me, then at least with yourself."

"Shoot."

"If the shoe had been on the other foot, how far would you have gone to get justice for your grandpa Joe?"

Blake's attention snapped to hers. His mother knew how much he loved and admired his grandfather. He would've gone to hell and back to protect the old man, if he believed someone had wronged him.

Apparently, Savannah had the same level of love and affection for her grandfather. Unfortunately, he hadn't told her the whole truth. But then again, neither had his.

"What does Parker think about giving Savannah her job back?"

When their family had met to discuss the situation, they'd all been angry at first. But when his grandfather explained the history between him and Martin McDowell, most of them had softened their stance. Only Parker had objected to giving McDowell a stake in the company.

Surely, Parker would be Blake's one ally.

"Your brother says that if you can deal with Savannah coming back here, he can, too." A slow smile lit his mother's eyes. "Parker says that for him, it's about the bottom line. And she's certainly proven she's good for that."

"It would be awkward, us working together and having a child together, but not actually being together."

"It's important that you two get along. There's my grandchild to consider, after all. So perhaps this is a good way to force your hand." Her voice softened. "Of course, there is another option."

Blake raised an eyebrow. "Which is?"

"Things wouldn't be so awkward if you two were actually together."

"Mother…"

"I know you love her, son. You're just being stubborn, because your feelings and your pride were hurt."

"You make it sound as if I'm being unreasonable. Aren't you the one who always told us that honesty is the very least we should expect in a relationship?"

"True." She nodded gravely. "But then I also told you that we sometimes do the wrong thing for all the right reasons. Can't you see that's what Savannah has done?"

"I appreciate what you're doing, Mother, but it's not that simple." Blake tapped his thumb lightly on the desk. "Parker is right, though. This is about the bottom line. Savannah's impact in her short time with the company is undeniable. I'll consider it, I promise."

Blake loved Savannah. He honestly did. But he didn't know if he'd ever be able to trust her again.

He ruminated on the question for the rest of the day. It was still spinning in his head when he approached his driveway and found Savannah, parked there, waiting for him.

* * *

Savannah climbed out of her car as Blake pulled into the drive. She'd been parked there for an hour, determined not to leave until she'd said what she came to say.

"Hello, Blake." She was undeterred by his frown.

"Savannah." The iciness of his tone made her shudder. "Surprised you're still in town. After all, you got everything you came for."

His words sawed through her like a jagged blade.

"I needed to thank you and Mr. Abbott for everything you've done for my grandfather." Her mouth was dry and there was a fluttering in her belly. "You couldn't possibly know how much what you've done means to him and to our family."

"It means you won. Perhaps deservedly so," Blake acknowledged as he swiped the dogs' leashes from their hook on the wall. He opened the door and Sam and Benny raced toward her.

"Sam! Benny!"

The larger dog jumped on her, nearly knocking her backward. Blake was suddenly there with his arms around her, ensuring she didn't fall.

Her heart raced as her gaze met his.

Blake held her in his arms, his chest heaving. Sam poked her leg with his wet nose and Benny barked. Yet, in Blake's arms, it felt as if the world had stopped. It was only the two of them and the baby they'd made growing inside her.

"Thank you, Blake."

Blake released her without response. He grabbed the leashes he'd dropped, clamping one on Benny and the other on Sam.

"I missed you two." She showered the dogs with hugs and kisses. Their tales wagged and Benny licked her face. Savannah stood, meeting Blake's gaze. She swallowed the lump in her throat. "I've missed you, too, Blake."

Hurt and disappointment were etched between his furrowed brows. Yet there was a hint of affection in his dark eyes.

If she could peel away the layers of pain and distrust, maybe they could salvage the warmth and affection buried beneath. Grow it alongside the love she felt for him and for their child. Nurture it until it turned into something beautiful and lasting.

He didn't acknowledge her admission. Instead, he gestured toward the path by the lake. "I have to walk Benny and Sam."

"Blake, I... I love you." The words stumbled from her lips.

"I would've given anything to hear you say that a couple of weeks ago." He sighed. "Now, how can I trust that it's not just another ploy to manipulate me?"

"I never used what happened between us to manipulate you. Everything I said to you…everything we did… For me, it was real. All of it." She bit back the tears that stung her eyes. "I never intended to fall for you. But I couldn't help wanting to be with you."

Benny and Sam started to whine.

"Walk with us?"

She fell in step beside them.

"If you feel…the way you say you do…why didn't you tell me before?"

"I felt guilty because of the secrets I was keeping.

Making one confession without the other wouldn't have been fair to you."

"So what was the plan? To string me along until you found something?"

"There was no 'plan' where you were concerned." She wrapped her arms around herself as they stopped for the dogs.

"Then why did you get involved with me?" He studied her.

"It wasn't a choice." She couldn't help the involuntary smile or the tears that leaked from her eyes. "How could I not fall for you? You're the most amazing man I've ever known."

"But you couldn't trust me with the truth?"

"I was torn between what I felt for you and doing right by my family. After I lost my parents, I promised myself I'd never stand by and do nothing again. I was determined to protect my family at all costs. Even if that meant losing what I wanted most. You."

"So you used me to get what you wanted, and I played right into your hands." Blake turned on his heels and headed back toward the house.

"I wasn't trying to use you, Blake." She scrambled to keep up with his long strides. "You were just…this vortex that pulled me in. I couldn't resist, and after a while, I didn't want to because you were incredible. And you made me feel special in a way I never had before. You made me want things I never wanted before."

He stopped and turned to her. "Like a baby?"

"Yes." Her mouth curved in a soft smile. She wiped away tears. "I didn't plan this baby, but the instant I knew, there wasn't a question in my mind about what I should do. I was given the most amazing gift. A piece of you. *Our* baby."

His gaze dropped to her hand on her belly. He swallowed hard, neither of them saying anything for a moment.

Blake walked away without a word.

Savannah wanted to dissolve into tears, but she had no right to expect forgiveness. All she could do was hope that someday he'd want to be part of their child's life.

Blake took the dogs inside. Savannah's words pierced the hardened shell that had formed around his heart. Reminded him of the incredible moments they'd shared.

During the past week, he'd been forced to question every moment. Every kiss. Wondering if any of it was real.

Something deep inside him believed it had been, and that she truly did love him. He wanted to forgive her and to be excited about the child they were having.

But could he ever trust her again?

Blake stepped out into the garage again as Savannah opened her car door. The sight of her leaving triggered something in him. Maybe he didn't know for sure how things would end between them, but he knew he couldn't let her walk away.

"Where are you going?" He approached her.

"Back to my apartment, for now. Back to West Virginia once Grandpa is done with his treatments."

"Just like that...you're walking away?"

Savannah blinked, her brows scrunched in confusion. She shut the car door and walked toward him.

"You obviously don't want me here, and I don't want to make things worse. I just want you to know that you're welcome to be as involved in this child's life as you choose. I'd never stand in the way of that."

Blake took a few steps closer and swallowed the lump in his throat, unable to speak.

It was fear, plain and simple.

He wanted to be with Savannah. To raise their baby together. It would be difficult to get past this. To trust her implicitly. But it couldn't be worse than the torment that seized him as he watched her turn and walk toward her car again.

"Does that mean you don't want your job back?"

She turned toward him, eyes wide. "Your family would trust me to work for you again?"

Blake rubbed the back of his neck. "My mother, Max, Zora...even Parker... They all want you back. You're good for King's Finest. There's no disputing that."

"And what about you, Blake? What do you want?" She stepped closer and studied him. "As much as I love working with your family at King's Finest, I won't come back if it'll be too painful for you. I couldn't do that to you. I've already hurt you so much. I won't do it again."

Tightness gripped his chest as he stared into her lovely eyes, glistening with tears. His throat was raw with emotion.

Blake could see the love in her eyes. Hear it in her voice. He'd been right all along. Her feelings for him were real. Now that there were no more secrets between them, what remained was the love and friendship they'd been building. It ran deep, and it was as sweet and clear as the waters of King's Lake.

"What I want, Savannah, more than anything, is to be with you and our baby." He slipped his arms around her waist. "Because I love you, too."

He kissed her. Savored the taste of her sweet lips and salty tears. Then he took her inside, determined to make up for lost time. To make love to her and get reacquainted with every inch of her glowing skin.

Later, as they lay sleeping, he cradled Savannah in his arms, his hands perched protectively over her belly. His heart overflowed with the love he felt for her and for the child she carried.

Their child.

He pulled her closer, determined to never let them go.

Epilogue

Eleven months later

The old barn had become a popular wedding venue, and it had never looked more elegant than it did now.

Blake surveyed the crowd of people who'd assembled in their Sunday best to help him and Savannah celebrate their special day. Family, friends, employees and townsfolk. Most of whom he'd known his entire life.

Blake's hands were shaking. His breath was ragged and labored. A stone lodged in the pit of his stomach.

But he didn't have an ounce of doubt about marrying Savannah Carlisle. Aside from the day little Davis was born, it was the happiest day of his life.

So why was he so nervous?

Maybe he was afraid Savannah would come to her senses, turn tail and run. That she'd decide she didn't want to be part of this big, noisy, opinionated family.

Blake clenched his hands together in front of him and released a slow breath.

He was letting his nerves get the better of him.

Savannah loved him and their son. With a love he felt in every fiber of his soul.

He'd seen that love, true and deep, in Savannah's hazel eyes each morning. Felt its warmth as they played with their child.

Was rocked by its power when he made love to her. Felt it surround him as they fell asleep in each other's arms each night.

No, he didn't question the authenticity of her love for him.

And unlike the feelings he'd once had for Gavrilla, what he shared with Savannah wasn't contained within the small unit they formed. It encompassed both of their families.

"You ready for this?" Max, his best man, stood beside him.

"Never been more ready for anything in my life." Blake smiled at Davis, who waved his arms at him as his great-grandfather bounced him on his knee.

As the ceremony began, Blake's pulse raced. He watched their family and friends march down the aisle. His mother. Daisy, arm in arm with his cousin Benji. His brother Cole and his cousin Delia. Dallas Hamilton and Zora. Kayleigh Jemison and Parker—who had managed to be civil to each other through most of the proceedings. Then Savannah's sister, Laney.

His grandfather carried little Davis—the honorary ring bearer—down the aisle.

Laney's three-year-old daughter, Harper, scattered rose petals onto the white, custom aisle runner printed with his and Savannah's names and the words *Always and Forever.*

When the music changed and everyone stood, his heart felt as if it would burst. Savannah stood at the head of the aisle on her grandfather's arm.

The love of his life was an incredible vision to behold in an off-shoulder, antique white lace wedding gown. The mermaid silhouette hugged the curves that had mesmerized him the moment he laid eyes on them.

Savannah's hair was pulled into a tousled, messy bun low over one shoulder. A spray of flowers was intertwined in her hair.

She floated down the aisle toward him. All eyes were on her, but her gaze was locked with his. As if only the two of them were there in that old barn.

Savannah turned and kissed her grandfather's cheek, and Blake shook the old man's hand. Mr. McDowell was grateful he'd lived to see his granddaughter get married, and that he had the health and strength to walk her down the aisle.

Blake extended his palm and Savannah placed her delicate hand in his.

"You ready for this, baby?" he whispered as they turned and stepped onto the stage.

Savannah grinned, her eyes glistening with tears. "Blake Abbott, I can't wait to become your wife."

They stood before the magistrate in a room filled to capacity with the people they loved most, and she did just that.

* * * * *